Ruth

The Monster Behemoth

with warmest wishes

S. L. Russell

Visit us online at www.authorsonline.co.uk

A Bright Pen Book

Copyright © S.L. Russell

All rights reserved. No part of this publication may be reproduced, stored in a retrieval system, or transmitted in any form or by any means, electronic, mechanical, photocopy, recording or otherwise, without prior written permission of the copyright owner. Nor can it be circulated in any form of binding or cover other than that in which it is published and without similar condition including this condition being imposed on a subsequent purchaser.

Scriptures and additional materials quoted are from the Good News Bible ©1994 published by the Bible Societies/Harper Collins Publishers Ltd UK, Good News Bible ©American Bible Society 1966, 1971, 1976, 1992. Used with permission. www.biblesociety.org.uk; and from the Revised Standard Version of the Bible copyright ©1946, 1952 and 1971 by the Division of Christian Education of the National Council of Churches in the USA. Used by permission. All rights reserved. Extracts from the Book of Common Prayer, the rights in which are vested in the Crown, are reproduced by permission of the Crown's Patentee, Cambridge University Press.

ISBN 978-07552-1272-9

Authors OnLine Ltd
19 The Cinques
Gamlingay, Sandy
Bedfordshire SG19 3NU
England

This book is also available in e-book format, details of which are available at www.authorsonline.co.uk

*Dedicated to the memory of my father,
Peter J. Reynolds, 1920-2009*

A M D G

Many people have contributed to this book, and I am grateful to them all, but I owe special thanks to the following for the generous sharing of their time and expertise: Mandy Elmes, Donna Fleisher, Nikki McVeagh, Paul McVeagh, Rosemary Plumb, Derek Russell, Philip Sutton and Roger Sykes.

Look at the monster Behemoth;
I created him and I created you...
The most amazing of all my creatures!
Only his Creator can defeat him.

Job 40: 15,19

Thursday 31 October 1996

'You'll get piles, sitting on that damp bench. It rained here yesterday, you know.' The old lady paused for a moment, leaning on her stick, looking down at Eileen, her head tilted.

'You're probably right,' Eileen said. 'But I won't be here much longer.'

'Ah. Well, that's all right then.' The woman moved slowly on, crisp brown leaves whirling round her unsteady feet. Eileen smiled to herself, remembering similar advice from her mother forty years ago against sitting on damp door sills. She looked at her watch.

Ten minutes. Ten minutes, and then I'll go in.

Two small children came hurtling past her, through the mounds of leaves swept up earlier by the park gardener. A girl of about eight years, wearing a flapping black shiny cloak, a tall pointed black hat, and a hideously warty and misshapen plastic nose, raced ahead of her younger brother, from whose fair curls sprouted two crimson horns. A matching cape hung from his shoulders, and his pudgy fingers gripped a red plastic trident. A few yards behind came their mother, a young woman pushing a buggy with a well-wrapped sleeping baby in it. As she passed Eileen she gave her a smile of faintly guilty indulgence.

Hallowe'en seemed an ironic date for an inquest. Natasha had obviously thought so too.

'Someone's got a funny sense of humour, Mum,' she had said as they sat in her tiny, bright kitchen, sipping coffee, a few days after Eileen had received the letter inviting her to attend.

'Probably completely accidental,' Eileen said. 'The cogs of the legal process grinding blindly away, etcetera.'

'Are you going?' Natasha asked. 'To the inquest? You don't actually have to, do you?'

'No. But maybe I will. I'll see how things are.' She glanced up at the kitchen clock, which was in the shape of a bright yellow sunflower. 'I'll have to be going, Tash. I have things to do in my flat. I've still got loads of boxes lying around.' She got to her feet and took her empty cup to the sink. 'Anyway, I'm not too bothered about Hallowe'en. The next day is All Souls, which kind of makes up for it.'

'What's that about, then?'

'I think it's when saints and martyrs are celebrated. Talking of saints, did I tell you about the girl on the floor below me? She's a funny kid, perhaps not a hundred per cent all there. She has a bit of an obsession about ecclesiastical things, even named her baby after the parish church.'

'Which is?'

'St. Augustine's. The baby's called Gus. He's a charmer, all chubby toes and toothless smiles.'

'Is that the church you're thinking of going to?'

'Yes, probably. It's a nasty Victorian pile, but it's the nearest.' She put on her coat. 'See you soon, Tash. Give my love to Sean.'

Natasha followed her to the door. 'I can't see me and Sean naming any of our kids after a saint. It's like tempting fate.'

'Oh, I don't know,' Eileen said, smiling. 'What about Polycarp, for instance?'

'You've got to be joking, Mum! Sounds like a cross between a fish and a parrot!'

Eileen was still grinning as she slammed the car door shut and drove slowly down the road, waving as she went.

She looked at her watch again. Time to go in. She stood up stiffly, brushed a leaf from her coat, and threw the remains of her lunch in the bin.

The Council offices in Lambury were reached by broad, imposing steps. Eileen climbed them slowly, feeling her reluctance increase. What was she doing here? She didn't have to be here. But she carried on, through the swing doors, across the deep-pile purple carpet, to a small sign with an arrow pointing to the right. 'Coroner's Court, Waiting Room.'

It was a large room, and the small number of people in it seemed lost. They stood or sat, singly, in pairs, in small tight-knit groups, murmuring to each other, but avoiding the eyes of others waiting. Eileen positioned herself as far away as possible from the nearest group and tried to look inconspicuous.

After a few minutes a door opened at the far end of the room and a tall, grey-haired man in a sober suit ushered in an elderly couple. The woman, weeping, clutching a large white handkerchief, leaned on the arm of a red-cheeked man who looked out of place in his tight suit, his feet in great black boots, his meaty hands seeming too big for his body.

The grey-haired man accompanied them across the room to the exit. Eileen heard him say softly, 'Will you be all right, Mrs. Edwards? There's a vending machine in the foyer if a cup of tea would help.' The woman nodded dumbly, mopping her face. Then they were gone, and the grey-haired man crossed the room again and disappeared through the inner door. Eileen shivered, thinking of the human misery, the waste and tragedy, recorded within these walls on the first and third Thursday of every month.

The grey-haired man reappeared and coughed. 'Would all those attending the Arrowsmith inquest please come in now.'

Hearing Christopher's name gave Eileen an unexpected jolt. She stood, waiting for others to go first. The coroner's clerk smiled at her as she passed. She felt awkward, alien, but somehow driven. *I don't want to be here. I'd like to run. But I have to be here. No use trying to explain. I don't understand it myself.*

The room was arranged in broad semicircles of chairs and desks, facing a long bench with an ornate chair, presently empty, behind it. Eileen found herself a place at what she hoped was a discreet distance. A few rows ahead, with their backs to her, sat Brian and Geraldine Arrowsmith, huddled in winter coats, silent, but every so often turning to one another with a painful smile. On the far side sat a young woman, thin, sharp-featured, her wrists clanking with bangles, her pen poised over a jotter. Eileen assumed she was a journalist. In the centre, facing the coroner's empty chair, sat a policeman in uniform, a thick-set, pleasant-faced thirtyish man with cropped hair and prominent pink-tinged ears. Immediately behind, and leaning forward to speak quietly to him, was a tall young man in dark-rimmed spectacles and smart striped suit, complete with buttonhole. Behind him, towards the back of the room, a group of five sat together: three men, one middle-aged, two young, and two women. All were smartly dressed, and all looked nervous.

There was no sign of the coroner. The clerk, sitting immediately in front of the bench, looked at his watch, stood up, and left the room by a small dark door at the far side to Eileen's right.

In the silence, broken only by occasional whispers, Eileen let her thoughts range back to the day, three weeks before, when she knew she had to be here, at Christopher's inquest. She had just had a convivial lunch with Marie and Philip at their house in the Close, a meal awash with wine and punctuated by the Abbey bells marking the quarter hours, and she had left feeling benign, very slightly drunk and more than a little envious. On her way home she had decided to call in at a hardware store for a tin of emulsion and had to her surprise met Charley, her former foster-son Michael's social worker, on a similar errand.

'Eileen! How nice to see you,' Charley said. 'Are you OK? I heard you were ill.'

'I'm fine, thanks, Charley. Quite recovered. How about you?'

'Well, you probably haven't heard all the scandal, as you've been out of circulation,' Charley said. 'I'm on my way out, as it happens. Got a new job. I'm going to Wales in a few weeks, going to run a children's home with my boyfriend, Al. Might even get married, who knows?'

'Oh. Was this a sudden decision, Charley? You'll be missed at Caxford.'

'I've been getting itchy feet for a while now. Thought I'd try something different. But all the trouble at Social Services has sped up the process.'

'What trouble?'

'You really have been out of it, haven't you? It's been in the local press.'

'I've been busy, too,' Eileen said. 'Starting a new life, really. I sold my house in Holton. I live at Allerton now.'

'Are you in a hurry? Time for a cup of tea and a chat maybe?'

'Fine, why not, Charley? If you're decamping to Wales it may be the last chance for a while.'

Over tea Charley leaned forward confidentially. 'Things have really gone crazy at Social Services. It's all to do with that poor lad who topped himself in your woods, the one you found. There's an internal inquiry going on right now, and the social worker is in the frame. I know him slightly: chap called Mick Cohen. I'd be surprised if he even met your tramp guy more than a few times. Don't suppose he was much of a priority with the caseload Mick's got. None of it's anything to do with me, I know: I've never been on the mental health team, but mud sticks, and I aim to be well out of the way before any of it gets thrown.' She frowned.

'Guilt by association, you mean,' Eileen said.

'Something like that. It's a health issue really, of course, and I imagine something very similar is happening in the NHS. That's where the psychiatrist is based, and the CPN, and probably the care support worker as well. Heads may be about to roll.'

'Why, exactly?'

'I don't know how it all started. Maybe the fellow's family kicked up. Bottom line is, Eileen, what's a young guy supposedly in the joint care of the NHS and Social Services doing holed up in the woods – and dead into the bargain? Seems like nobody knew. It does make you think there was some neglect, doesn't it?'

Eileen shook her head and said nothing.

'But there's more,' Charley said. 'One of the other residents of that house has vanished, and nobody knows where he is. The house has been closed and all the residents sent elsewhere. The Press have been snooping round, but everyone else has been trying to keep the lid on it. It's been a real mess.'

'Will anything come of it?' Eileen asked.

Charley shrugged. 'Who knows? I'm out of it, anyway. I feel sorry for Mick, though. OK, so he didn't do what he should've, but I guess he's got fifty or sixty clients to deal with, and some of them very time-consuming. Anyway, Eileen,' she said, brightening, 'enough of all this doom. What about you?'

'Oh, not much,' Eileen said. 'I've got a nice little flat, and I'm job-hunting.'

'Anything in mind?'

'Not really. Just anything to pay the rent till I find something I'd like to do.'

'All change, then.'

'So it would seem.'

They fell silent for a few moments, and then started talking together.

'Got to go, I'm afraid.' 'Lovely to see you.' 'All the best. Hope it goes well.' 'Good luck with the job-hunting.'

Then she was alone again, the silence washing in like waves onto a deserted beach. Walking back to the car, she realised with a pang that she had forgotten to ask Charley about Michael. She asked herself guiltily how she could have forgotten a boy who had been her almost-son for three years. Charley might have had news; certainly no one else would. It was too late now.

'Rise, please.'

The clerk had reappeared unnoticed. People shuffled to their feet as the coroner, a tall, slim man with receding hair and half-glasses, came in and took his seat.

'Coroner's Court taking place at Lambury in the county of Essex, 31st October 1996, Mr. Richard Somerville presiding,' said the clerk. 'Please be seated.'

The coroner moved papers, then looked up and around the assembled company. 'This is the reopening of the inquest, first opened and adjourned on 24th June 1996, into the death of Christopher James

Arrowsmith, born in London on 8th January 1973, a single man, the son of the Reverend Canon Brian Arrowsmith and Mrs. Geraldine Arrowsmith of Barnwell in this county. At the time of his death the deceased was resident at 16, Denbigh Street, Caxford, also in this county.' He paused for a moment and turned over a page. 'The body of Mr. Arrowsmith was identified in Lambury mortuary on 18th June 1996 by his father.' Somerville turned to the Arrowsmiths, nodded, and said to them courteously, 'Canon and Mrs. Arrowsmith, I have your statement here and other depositions, but should you wish to share any other information with this court you are at liberty to do so. You also have the right to question witnesses, should you think it necessary and appropriate.'

Eileen thought she saw Brian Arrowsmith move convulsively. Perhaps she imagined it. His wife laid a hand on his arm, and he subsided.

The coroner gazed around the court, leaning back slightly in his chair. 'Mr. Arrowsmith left notes to his family and to the designated authorities, notes which leave little doubt that he died by his own hand and fully intending to take his own life. However, the content of these notes makes this case more complex than it might at first appear. I feel it is incumbent upon me to inquire further into the circumstances leading up to this young man's tragic death. The peculiarities of Mr. Arrowsmith's situation may have a bearing on other, related, matters, as will become clear. In addition, I have received from Canon Brian Arrowsmith, the deceased's father, a letter drawing my attention to certain issues which, in my view, merit the attention of this court.

'I must make it clear at this juncture that the purpose of this court is not to apportion blame. There is no question of any individual or group being under interrogation. Our purpose is to arrive, as far as we can, at a true understanding of the circumstances of Mr. Arrowsmith's death. However, all those called to witness are obliged under oath to tell truthfully what they know and to conceal nothing that could be helpful.' Again he looked around the room, as if assuring himself that everyone present had heard and understood the seriousness of the matters in hand.

'Very well. Let us proceed to the witnesses. Sergeant Weston, please.'

The clerk rose and swore in the policeman, who coughed and referred to his notes. 'Sergeant Gary Weston of Caxford Police, sir. At 1pm on 17th June this year I was alerted by a passer-by by telephone to the presence of the body of a young male in Holton Woods. I called paramedics who attended, as did the Police Surgeon, Mr. Harris, who confirmed death, giving the time of death as approximately 7am that morning. The body was undisturbed except for the effects of a resuscitation attempt. An empty medicine container, an empty vodka bottle, and two notes were found at the scene.'

'Thank you, Sergeant Weston.' The coroner addressed the court. 'Mrs. Harding, who found Mr. Arrowsmith's body, has given a statement which I will paraphrase. Mrs. Harding, a local resident, was taking a stroll in the woods near her home, as she often did, when she came upon Mr. Arrowsmith's body. Although she thought it likely that he was dead she tried to resuscitate him. She observed the bottles of alcohol and tablets but left everything undisturbed and called the police. Mrs. Harding confirmed that she had seen Mr. Arrowsmith around the woods once or twice in the preceding weeks. At the time of this incident she was resident at 5, Church Cottages, Holton, but now lives at Allerton in Hertfordshire. Is this correct?' He glanced at Eileen. 'Thank you. Could we now call Dr. Manser, please?'

The tall young man with the buttonhole was sworn in. 'Dr. Joseph Manser, Hospital Pathologist. I carried out a post-mortem on Christopher James Arrowsmith, a Caucasian male twenty-three years old, 1 metre 75 in height and weighing 70 kilos. There were no signs of illness or injury to the body except for a small scar on the left thigh. The toxicology report on the pill residue in the stomach was inconclusive. There was alcohol in the blood but no real chemical indicators of the cause of death.'

The coroner interrupted. 'Dr. Manser, are you aware of the substances that the deceased claimed he had taken?'

'I am, sir. I believe he was on a regime of chlorpromazine and a tricyclic antidepressant, to which he added vodka, and seconal, a barbiturate.'

'In your opinion would this cocktail have been sufficient to cause his death?'

'Yes, sir, it would.'

'What, then, would you say was the probable cause of death, Dr. Manser?'

'Acute heart failure, stemming from alcohol and drug overdose, sir.'
'Thank you, Dr. Manser.'

The pathologist resumed his seat. The coroner wrote a note or two. His pen sounded scratchy in the silence. Then he looked up, laid down his pen, and cleared his throat.

'I have no intention of reading Mr. Arrowsmith's notes to the court. As to the one addressed to his family, that is a private matter. However, the other was addressed "to the authorities," so I feel it is in order for me to refer to its contents. I am concerned about Mr. Arrowsmith's access to seconal, a barbiturate which nowadays is rarely prescribed, and clearly was at no time prescribed for him. I am also concerned about the stockpiling of antidepressants which he should have been taking regularly, and which, in conjunction with the chlorpromazine present in his system, and alcohol, would have been sufficient to cause his death, as Dr. Manser has told us. It is clear also from Mr. Arrowsmith's notes that he himself was quite aware of the probable result of this mixture that he had taken. In view of the questions arising from the issue of medication I feel it is my duty to call the professionals involved in Mr. Arrowsmith's care to give the court a clearer understanding of his situation at the time of his death. Dr. Partridge, please.'

The clerk swore in a man in his fifties, sporting a yellow bow tie.

'You are Dr. John Partridge, a Psychiatric Consultant based at Osewick Hospital?'

'I am.'

'I believe you had the general responsibility of Mr. Arrowsmith's medical care. Could you please tell the court how this was managed?'

Dr. Partridge seemed to stutter a little. The coroner waited, smiling slightly.

'Hm, yes, I had the overview of Mr. Arrowsmith's case, for about five years.'

'How often did you yourself see him?'

'Only twice a year now.'

'And when was the last time?'

'On 10th June.'

'I see. Just a week before his death. How did he seem to you?'

John Partridge looked at the ceiling, his lips pursed. 'I thought he seemed anxious and restless. There was also a tendency to be withdrawn. I mentioned to him the possibility of involvement in a self-help group, but this was not well received.'

'Tell me, if you will, Dr. Partridge, about Mr. Arrowsmith's medication.'

'Chlorpromazine was administered by injection monthly, by a member of my team.'

'Did Mr. Arrowsmith attend regularly for this injection?'

'Yes.'

'Was he taking anything else?'

The psychiatrist shuffled his feet. 'He was on an antidepressant originally prescribed by the hospital. He was registered with a local GP in Caxford, Dr. Lowe, who provided repeats. This drug regime was administered by the Community Psychiatric Nurse. I myself was not aware that the prescribed drug was patchy in its effects. Mr. Arrowsmith never mentioned it.'

The coroner wrote a note on his pad, then glanced up again. 'Could you tell us, please, something of Mr. Arrowsmith's medical history?'

'Certainly. Mr. Arrowsmith suffered from a form of schizoaffective disorder following a catastrophic breakdown at the age of eighteen. I came to the conclusion that, after some considerable time of treatment and supervision, he was sufficiently stable as to be able to live semi-independently. In my opinion, there was nothing to indicate that he was suicidal.'

'Thank you, Dr. Partridge. You may stand down, but I may consult you again if the need arises.'

Dr. Partridge went back to his place, sat down heavily and wiped his handkerchief over his face. The silence in the room was almost audible.

'Mrs. Leach, please.'

The older of the women of the group of five, sitting next to Dr. Partridge, a short, slight woman with dark eyes and heavy features, took the stand.

'You are Mrs. Sandra Leach, a Community Psychiatric Nurse of the Lambury District Health Authority?'

'Yes.' Her voice was very quiet, and the coroner looked up from his notes.

'Christopher Arrowsmith was your client?' he said.

'Yes.'

'Could you tell the court about how you managed his medication: in this case, the antidepressant prescribed by the hospital?'

Sandra Leach cleared her throat. 'There was a case conference, right at the beginning, months ago, when Christopher – Mr. Arrowsmith – first went to Denbigh Street. It was agreed by everyone that he could manage his own medication on a daily basis. He was very sensible.'

'I see. How exactly was this done?'

'Well, if he needed more tablets he told his care worker. She would organize it and pick up the prescription. He kept his pills in a locked box in his room, and he knew he had to keep the key with him at all times, to keep the other residents safe. He was careful and reliable.'

'How often did you yourself see Mr. Arrowsmith?'

The CPN looked down. 'I was supposed to see him every month.'

'Supposed? When was the last time you saw him?'

'In March.'

A muted buzz greeted this statement. Mr. Somerville raised his eyebrows. 'That's three months before the date of his death, Mrs. Leach. Why the gap?'

Sandra Leach leaned on the table, as if for support. 'I didn't regard Mr. Arrowsmith as a problem, to be honest. I had, and still have, a caseload of almost sixty patients. Some of them have obsessive/compulsive disorders and ring me constantly. That's in addition to meetings and paperwork. Patients like Mr. Arrowsmith, who gave no trouble, just don't get seen as often as I would like. There aren't enough hours in the day. I have been off work this year with a stress-related illness, and when I returned to work the backlog was enormous. I tend to rely on care support workers to let me know if anything is amiss. Miss Gibson saw Mr. Arrowsmith frequently. She would have told me if there was a problem.'

'Thank you, Mrs. Leach. One more thing: there had been, I believe, a change in Mr. Arrowsmith's prescription.'

'Yes. He was on clomipramine at first. It helps people with phobias and obsessive states. Mr. Arrowsmith had nightmares at one time. Then, when he settled down a bit, he was switched to doxepin. He was anxious and uptight, and doxepin has tranquillizing effects.'

'Did Mr. Arrowsmith comment on this tablet at all?'

Sandra Leach shook her head. 'Not to me. Miss Gibson did, I believe, once mention that it made him feel woolly-headed, kind of out of touch.'

'Thank you, Mrs. Leach. Stand down now, if you will. I may have to ask you more questions later. Miss Gibson, please.'

A fair-haired young woman with a placid expression was sworn in.

'You are Miss Jacqueline Gibson, a Care Support Worker?'

'That's right, sir.'

'And Mr. Arrowsmith was one of your clients?'

'Yes.'

'Were any of the other residents of Denbigh Street your responsibility?'

'Yes. David Rimmer and Sylvia Courtney.'

'How often did you see Mr. Arrowsmith?'

Jackie Gibson seemed to think for a few moments. 'Well, mostly my job was to take him to his appointments. If he was at home I sometimes saw him when I was helping one of the others. He was very independent, though, and no trouble. He hardly ever asked for anything, and he was always neat and clean and punctual.' She sniffed and brushed a tear from her cheek.

The coroner paused for a moment. 'Can you tell me about his medication, Miss Gibson?'

'Yes. He kept it locked in a box. He always kept the key on him, even in the bathroom. He was very good about his medication.'

'Can you recall when you last saw him?'

'On 10th June. I took him to see Dr. Partridge.'

'How did he seem to you on that day?'

'On the way there he was quiet as usual. After the appointment he seemed a bit agitated.'

'Were you aware of any particular friendship between Mr. Arrowsmith and the other residents of Denbigh Street?'

Jackie Gibson frowned. 'He was friendly with everyone, but there was no one special friend. Until Maurice came, that is. Mr. Bentley, I mean. They seemed to strike up quite a friendship for a while. But then I had the impression it tailed off.'

'Thank you, Miss Gibson. You may stand down.'

For a long moment the whole room was silent. Mr. Somerville wrote at some length. Then he took off his glasses and laid them down. 'Miss Gibson has mentioned Mr. Maurice Bentley, and I would like to pursue this line of inquiry further.'

There seemed to be a general stiffening round the courtroom. Eileen leaned forward. She had begun to think that nothing would come out regarding Maurice Bentley, but now her hopes began to rise.

The coroner continued. 'A relationship of some kind has been noted as having existed between Mr. Arrowsmith and Mr. Bentley. I am able to tell this court that, by his own admission, Mr. Arrowsmith had, over a period of several weeks, been purloining barbiturate tablets belonging to Mr. Bentley, who had himself stored them from a previous prescription.'

A buzz followed this announcement. Mr. Somerville waited patiently for it to subside. Eileen felt the hammering of her heart. *This man knows what he is doing.*

'Mrs. Leach,' the coroner said, 'would you please resume the stand, bearing in mind that you are still under oath?' As she stood Sandra Leach was visibly trembling.

'Mrs. Leach, may I inquire if you are also responsible for Mr. Bentley?'

'Yes.' Her voice was barely above a whisper.

'Thank you. Am I right in saying that Mr. Bentley is the subject of a supervision order, and that he is currently in breach of that order?'

'Yes, that's right.'

'Are Mr. Bentley's whereabouts known?'

'Not to me.'

'I see.' Somerville looked steadily at Sandra Leach, whose face was moon-pale. 'To your knowledge, is he being sought?'

'Yes, I believe so.'

'Can you give me the date of his disappearance?'

'He was last seen around Denbigh Street on 29th June.'

'So he has been missing for four months?'

'Yes.'

'Please stay where you are, Mrs. Leach, while I address the court. Let me remind everyone that we are not here to inquire into the background of another person, except insofar as it might impinge on the life and death of Christopher Arrowsmith. Mr. Bentley's medical details are, of course, confidential, and as far as this court is concerned, will remain so.' He turned again to Sandra Leach and smiled kindly, noting, as did everyone else, her pallor and her laboured breathing. 'Mrs. Leach, were you aware of Mr. Bentley's medical history?'

'Some of it, yes.'

'Were you aware of the reasons for the supervision order?'

'Up to a point.'

'Were you aware of any particular friendship between Mr. Arrowsmith and Mr. Bentley?'

'They seemed to strike up a bit of a rapport when Mr. Bentley first came to Denbigh Street. I didn't think there was anything in it. Mr. Bentley was much older.'

'Did you at any time regard Mr. Bentley as a threat?'

'Not at all.' Sandra Leach's voice rose, sounding suddenly defensive. 'He was only at Denbigh Street as a temporary measure. In fact he should have moved on earlier. The circumstances of his original breakdown were quite different and long ago. Mr. Arrowsmith always seemed level-headed, well able to take care of himself.'

'Thank you, Mrs. Leach. That will be all for now. Before we go on I would like to call as witness another professional involved with the deceased's care. Mr. Michael Cohen, please.'

Eileen looked closely. This was the young man Charley had mentioned. As he took the oath he was clearly terrified.

'Mr. Cohen,' said the coroner, 'you are, I believe, a social worker employed by Lambury Council in the Caxford district, where you are a member of the mental health team.'

'Yes, sir, I am.'

'Can you tell the court what your responsibilities were towards Mr. Arrowsmith?'

Mick Cohen took a deep breath. 'I had to arrange case conferences to decide how to go on. I was responsible for day-to-day things, like accommodation, managing money, relationships with the family. I had planned a meeting between Mr. Arrowsmith and his family, but he never seemed keen on the idea.'

'Did Mr. Arrowsmith tell you what his own wishes were?'

Cohen shrugged. 'He said he wanted his own flat. I was looking into it.'

'I see. Did you regard Mr. Arrowsmith as a high-priority client?'

'Not really. He seemed OK at Denbigh Street, and he never made a fuss. I have a huge number of clients, and some of them are very demanding.'

'Yes, I am sure they are. Were you aware, Mr. Cohen, at any time, of trouble between Mr. Arrowsmith and Mr. Bentley?'

'No. Mr. Arrowsmith was not very forthcoming.'

'Thank you, Mr. Cohen. You may stand down.'

Again there was a brief pause while the coroner made a note, hesitated, then wrote again. He put his pen down, adjusted his glasses and straightened himself in the high-backed chair, lacing his long fingers together. 'So, ladies and gentlemen, we are arriving at a picture of a seriously disturbed young man, disturbed enough in the end, it would appear, to take his own life, and yet the professionals responsible for his care think he "seemed OK", was "not suicidal," and was "well able to take care of himself"; someone who, it seemed, never made a fuss. I do not doubt that Christopher Arrowsmith, despite his illness, was an intelligent person capable of giving to other people an impression of greater stability than he truly enjoyed. Nor do I discount the considerable demands made on the attention of these same professionals. However, we must still ask ourselves certain questions: what was Mr. Arrowsmith doing in Holton Woods? How long had he been living there? And perhaps most importantly, why? What drove him away from Denbigh Street? I refer again to his note, which I take to be addressed to myself. In essence, he says that, while he does not want to get anyone into trouble, in his view Maurice Bentley is a very ill and potentially predatory individual about whom more should be known by the professionals involved.'

The coroner looked towards the group of five at the back of the room, and everyone else's eyes followed. Sandra Leach looked stricken, her face paler than ever. The coroner inclined his head towards her and said, 'Mrs. Leach, you have given your opinion, supported by Dr. Partridge, that one of the former residents of Denbigh Street is capable of giving his evidence to this court, and that to do so will not be to his mental detriment.'

Sandra Leach gulped and nodded, clearly unable to speak.

The coroner looked up. 'Will Mr. David Rimmer take the stand, please.'

Eileen leaned forward, remembering how, under the rustling summer trees, Christopher had described to her his fellow-residents. This was Dave, the man with the infallible lottery system, now taking the oath, dressed in shirt, tie and jacket, his light hair neatly combed.

'You are David Arthur Rimmer, formerly of 16, Denbigh Street, Caxford, currently residing at 45, Moulton Street, Lambury?' Somerville said.

'Yes, sir.'

'How long did you live at Denbigh Street, Mr. Rimmer?'

'About eighteen months, I'd say.'

'So you saw both Mr. Arrowsmith and Mr. Bentley arrive?'

'That's right.'

'How well would you say you knew them?'

'I knew all of the residents. We looked out for each other.'

'What, in your opinion, was the relationship between Mr. Arrowsmith and Mr. Bentley?'

Dave Rimmer glanced around, seemingly aware of everyone's eyes on him. He blushed a little and grinned, a sly grin which he tried at once to suppress. 'Well, sir, Chris, Mr. Arrowsmith, was already there when Mr. Bentley came. I think Chris was going through a bit of a bad patch. He had some new pills he didn't like much. Maurice was only supposed to be there a few weeks, till they found him somewhere else. That's what he said, anyway. He reckoned he shouldn't even have been in our area. Anyway he was that much older than most of us. He seemed a real nice chap, bit of a cut above, if you get me. Turned into a kind of father figure almost. After a while him and Chris seemed to get quite matey.'

'Please go on, Mr. Rimmer.'

'It all happened over a fair period, months maybe, but in the end we all knew what was going on. Sometimes we'd see Chris in all his gear.'

'Gear, Mr. Rimmer? Please explain.'

'Maurice made out Chris was a girl, sir. He called him Tess. Don't know why he picked that name. He made Chris dress in girls' clothes as well – not just ordinary girls' clothes, but really frilly stuff, lots of pink, you know. Chris's hair got ever so long too. He never looked like a proper girl, of course. Blokes don't, do they? But I guess it served Maurice's purpose.'

'What was his purpose, in your opinion?'
'Well, he had Chris as a kind of sex-slave, I'd say, sir.'
From somewhere in the courtroom came a muted groan.
'Do you have any concrete evidence for this opinion, Mr. Rimmer?'
'Depends what you call evidence, sir. All I know is, Chris was always in Maurice's room. If they ever came down to join the rest of us, Maurice behaved like Chris was his girlfriend, always got his arm round him, stroked his hair, called him "my poppet", "Tess darling", all that kind of stuff.'
'How did Mr. Arrowsmith respond to this?'
'Chris seemed out of it most of the time. I think it was those new pills. He didn't talk a lot, just hung around, staring at nothing. But we didn't see him all that much anyway. They were mostly upstairs, together.'
'How long did this go on?'
'I don't know. Quite a while. Then Chris seemed to snap.'
'Could you tell the court about that?'
'His mum rang him up. He answered the phone in his full gear – jewellery, makeup, the lot. He knew we thought it was funny. He went mad at his mum, yelled and screamed, then slammed the phone down and ran upstairs. Maurice wasn't there at the time; I can't remember where he'd gone. Next thing we knew, Chris came haring down the stairs waving a pair of scissors around. We were in the lounge, a few of us, watching TV. We were a bit scared at first, but Chris wasn't violent, not ever. He just wanted someone to cut his hair. Sylvie did it in the end. About half an hour later I heard the front door slam and I saw him go out. He was running, just like someone was after him. But he was looking quite normal. I mean, he was wearing men's clothes, and he'd got rid of the makeup. After that I didn't see him again, except once or twice, and then not really to speak to.'
'Were you aware of his absences?'
'Yes, we all were.'
'Did you not think you should have told someone?'
Dave Rimmer shrugged. 'We thought it was his business.'
'I see. And what about Mr. Bentley? Did he remain at Denbigh Street?'
'Yes, but I didn't see a lot of him. He used to go out most of the time.'
'When you did see him, how did he seem?'
'Same as usual. If anything, more kind of confident than ever.'
'Did he mention Mr. Arrowsmith's absences?'

'Not to me, no, sir.'

'How did you learn of Mr. Arrowsmith's death, Mr. Rimmer?'

'Sandra told us all. Mrs. Leach, that is.'

'Was Mr. Bentley present?'

'Yes.'

'How did he respond?'

Dave shook his head. 'It was weird. He changed completely. He went pale and never said a word. I didn't think about it at the time, because we were all really shocked, but Maurice was like he'd had the stuffing knocked out of him. Then, a week or so later, he vanished.'

'What happened after you were told of Mr. Arrowsmith's death?'

'What, at Denbigh Street? Everything seemed to go nuts. Poor old Chuck had to be taken back into hospital. Then the rest of us were moved, to separate houses. Jackie and Sandra were in a terrible state. We're all right now, though.'

'Thank you, Mr. Rimmer. You may stand down.'

Eileen saw Dave take his place and exchange a few whispered words with Sandra Leach. There was a general fidgeting in the courtroom, as if people were easing stiff limbs. The coroner bent over his paperwork for some minutes, wrote briefly, then paused, tapping his pen gently on the documents before him. Finally he looked up. 'Ladies and gentlemen, I understand that at the present moment internal inquiries are under way at Social Services and within the Health Service to determine to what extent these bodies failed to protect Christopher Arrowsmith and contributed to the state of mind which led to his death. As I made clear earlier, it is not the work of this court to apportion blame, but in view of what we have heard today interested parties, in particular the deceased's family, may see fit to take legal advice, which is, of course, their right.

'To sum up, then: we have been given a factual cause of death as acute heart failure, brought on by an overdose of drugs and alcohol. Given all the circumstances, there is no doubt in my mind that Christopher James Arrowsmith committed suicide, knowing that his chosen cocktail of drugs and alcohol would kill him. There is also no doubt, in my view, that the reason for his state of mind was, to whatever extent, and allowing for other effects of his illness, his inability to cope with the relationship with Mr. Bentley – one which was, in Mr. Arrowsmith's own words, "predatory". The fact that his medication was, in the case of the chlorpromazine, uneven in effect, and in the case of the antidepressant, not being taken at all, would no doubt have added to his confusion and anxiety. It only remains for me, while recording a verdict of suicide, to express my hope that the inquiries I mentioned earlier may arrive at conclusions and result in actions which will protect those most vulnerable in our society; and to offer, on behalf of this court, my sincerest condolences to Canon and Mrs. Arrowsmith on the loss of their son.

'This inquest is now closed.'

The coroner pushed his chair back. The clerk, getting to his feet, said, 'All rise!' Everyone stood up, and the coroner walked briskly to the side door and was gone. There was a moment of hesitation, almost of suspension; then the clerk began to usher people out, back into the waiting room, where another small group of people sat tensely by the wall. Eileen slipped out as unobtrusively as she could, into the foyer, through the swing doors, down the steps, into the fresh air.

The sun had come out, a weak autumnal sun with little heat in it, and in the park small children were playing and dogs were chasing scents, and the bench where Eileen had been sitting was now occupied by two young mothers, each with a pram. Eileen looked at her watch. There was still plenty of time before her train went. She had come by train partly because her ancient car needed attention and was unreliable over anything but short distances, partly to give herself time to think. She walked slowly through the busy streets of Lambury, seeing little. She bought a cup of coffee at a small, rather pretentious café, and sat by the steamed-up window, staring into her cup.

Where was Maurice Bentley now? He had been missing for several months. Was someone sheltering him? Was he still dangerous, still compulsively trapped in his own obsessions, or was he broken by the tragic chain of circumstance in which he had been so instrumental? And who was Tess? Eileen felt sure that she was a real person, real and important to Maurice Bentley. As she drank her cooling coffee she wondered about the fallout for the Health Service and Social Services. She had seen the young journalist leave the Court, brisk and determined. What, if anything, would be in the papers? Would Brian Arrowsmith find some comfort in blaming those who should have cared for his son, perhaps to the point of taking legal action?

She sighed, finished her coffee and got up. She walked to the station and sat on a seat on the draughty platform, waiting for her train. The sun had disappeared behind a wall of grey, and the day was chilly. As her thoughts circled and settled she felt some satisfaction, however small and bleak, that, finally, Christopher's last weeks were better understood and that something of his life was known to others beside herself. For good or ill, Maurice Bentley had been unmasked. Someone had poked the nest with a stick, and the wasps were angrily buzzing. But whatever happened now was nothing at all to do with her. She got to her feet, watching the Allerton train thunder into the station, and feeling somehow far from certain that Christopher's benign shade, for herself and for others, was yet completely laid to rest.

Sitting in the speeding train through the darkening afternoon, Eileen watched the countryside flash past. As the evening closed in and the shadows lengthened, swallowing everything in their path, the suburbs crept forward, becoming higher and denser and dirtier as the train slowed on its way to rest in the dark heart of the city. A thin grey rain streaked the windows, blurring the view. Eileen felt herself torn forcibly away from the past, thrust unwillingly into the realities of the present. For a moment she clung on, feeling Christopher's reality slipping away into death's mysterious kingdom. Fading images of him appeared briefly before her mental view: sitting on the tree stump, devouring the food she had brought; in her house, asleep on the carpet in a patch of sunlight; appalled and shaking as he told her, in fits and starts, the story of his descent into hell; and, finally, Christopher under the grey blanket, snuffed out.

Then the present and practical reasserted itself, as it must. With no great enthusiasm she thought about the weekend ahead: finishing the decorating in her first-floor flat, part of a tall Edwardian house in a dusty unremarkable street; then Sunday at her new church, St. Augustine's, where she thought the vicar might prove interesting, but where she knew almost no one, except Penny, the girl from the flat downstairs, and someone to whom Penny had introduced her, a woman called Maureen Parry, who seemed friendly. It was not a big congregation. She thought, with a small shudder, of Monday, when she had an interview at a shop selling women's clothing. *Decidedly not me. But I have to pay the rent.* As the train slowed to a stop she prayed. *Thank you, Lord, for the inquest, and the fairness of the coroner. Whatever happens as a result, let it be just. Please, may the right things happen for everyone's good, including Maurice Bentley. Be with the Arrowsmiths in their continuing pain. Be with me, and guide me, and teach me, hour by hour, to depend on you and not on myself.*

Buttoning her coat, she made for the door, and climbed down from the train. She sighed deeply. It was, she supposed, an ending. Of a sort.

Mothering Sunday: 22 March 1998

Eileen was late, and had to walk briskly down the churchyard path from the road, where she had parked hastily and at an angle from the kerb. It was a bright spring day, blown about with a gusty wind that chased ribbons of cloud across the sky. She squeezed into the pew between Maureen Parry and Penny Schofield.

'Morning,' she whispered. 'I see the congregation has tripled.'

Maureen nodded and smiled, and passed Eileen a hymn book open at the right page.

Eileen glanced around. The usual congregation of about a dozen, most of them elderly, was swelled by the occasion. The Sunday School, such as it was, were all present, from cherubic four-year-olds up to sullen adolescents, these last soon, no doubt, to rebel and be seen no more. Then there were the parents and the grandparents, in church to receive their tiny bouquets of truncated daffodils. For St. Augustine's, usually so quiet, it was almost festive.

The Reverend Louis Belmartin emerged from the vestry. He caught Eileen's eye as he strode to his place, and smiled. Somehow Louis' smiles were never simple. There was often, it seemed to Eileen, more than a hint of conspiracy. But the service produced no surprises. Louis' sermon was, for him, quite anodyne and unchallenging, the presentation of flowers went off without mishap, none of the little ones cried, and it was all over in forty-five minutes. Eileen had come to know Louis well enough over the past eighteen months to be prepared for caustic remarks about sentimentality; but after the service, as he stood at the door saying goodbye to everyone, being quite charming with no hint of hypocrisy, he laid a hand on her arm and said, 'Don't rush off just yet, Eileen. I need to talk to you for a moment.'

Fifteen minutes later, in the vestry, Eileen said, 'So what is it, Louis?'

'Disaster,' Louis said with some drama, folding his arms across his chest. 'Muriel has defected.'

'What? You make her sound like a Russian spy.'

Louis was not to be put off. 'Just like that, Eileen. "Sorry, Reverend," she says – how I wish she wouldn't call me that! – "sorry, but I'm going to New Zealand."'

'New Zealand? Why?' Muriel Thompson was the organist at St. Augustine's, and known to go absolutely nowhere.

'Apparently Muriel is a twin. Did you know that? No, neither did I. She has a twin sister, one Sylvia Campbell. Twenty years ago or more they had a falling-out and swore never to speak or visit again. But, it turns out, just recently Sylvia's granddaughter came over here on a visit and called on great-aunt Muriel. Sylvia, she tells Muriel, is ill, possibly terminally so. The upshot is, Muriel has decided to go and see her sister before it's too late. Guess where Sylvia lives.'

'New Zealand?'

'Exactly so. Muriel who, as you know, never goes anywhere, has a fair old stash in the bank. "I've bought my ticket, Reverend," she says. "Blood is thicker than water, you know."'

'Oh, dear. Well, there is a plus, Louis. At least there'll be no more bitching between her and the dragon, at least not for a while.'

'It's not much of a plus,' said Louis moodily. 'I am now minus an organist for Easter.'

'What about Muriel's grandson? He's deputized once in a while, hasn't he? What's his name? Jamie somebody.'

'Not available. He's diving in Thailand all through the vacation.'

'Oh. I thought students were always broke.' She looked at Louis for a moment. 'I have a feeling you're going to ask me to play, aren't you?'

Louis spread his arms in another theatrical gesture. 'What else can I do?'

'Louis, I'm as rusty as a crypt hinge, and that's not false modesty.'

'Please, Eileen. Tide me over till the old bat comes back.'

'Which is when?'

'Six weeks, she said.'

Eileen sighed. 'I'm not at all keen. And I'll have to fit in with work. But of course I'll do it. Just don't expect anything fancy, that's all.'

'I won't, Eileen. Just hymns will do. And thank you.'

'I'll need to practise here. Can you let me have a key?'

'No problem. And when you come to practise, be sure to call in at the vicarage for a reviving cup of tea.'

Eileen smiled despite herself. 'With an offer like that, resurrecting my moribund musical skills won't be quite such a chore.'

'Perhaps you'd like a cup now, just to get things rolling.'

Eileen looked at her watch. 'I'd love to, Louis, but I must dash. I'm going to Natasha and Sean's for lunch. Mother's Day, you know.'

Louis' chuckle died and his face closed up again. 'Of course. Off you go, and have a lovely time.'

Driving home, Eileen thought about Louis. He was a strange man, very clever, inclined to changeable moods, sometimes sullen, sometimes flamboyant, but rarely dull. He and Eileen had had tentative talks of a mildly theological nature once in a while, usually after some particularly stimulating sermon, and with a congregation such as his Eileen guessed that any reasonably well-informed comment would be unlooked-for and welcome. She would have said, had anyone asked, that he was a friend, but she knew, really, very little about him. She wondered if he was ever lonely, rattling around in his draughty Victorian vicarage. She had spoken of him once to Natasha, and Natasha had said bluntly, 'Well, you know, Mum, he's probably gay.'

'How can you know that? You've never met him.'

'I know, but it's from what you say. How old do you reckon he is?'

'I don't know: early forties?'

'A bachelor, yes?'

'Well, yes, but that doesn't necessarily mean anything. Maybe he's never met anyone he liked enough.'

'Any sign of a girlfriend? Any mention?'

'Not to me. Or of a boyfriend, come to that.'

'Well,' Natasha said, 'I don't suppose he would, would he? From what you've said, Mum, I reckon he's gay, or at least not that comfortable with women.'

'I can't say I've really thought about it. It seems a big leap to make on so little information.'

Natasha nodded wisely. 'I bet I'm right, though.'

Eileen stopped at her flat to pick up a plant she had bought for Sean and Natasha's tiny garden and to drop off her music. She let herself in and said hello to her cat, a long-legged, glossy tabby, stretched out elegantly on the sofa. 'Hello, beautiful boy.' She scratched behind his ears. He rewarded her with a wide yawn and a loud purr, then went back to sleep in a way that conclusively shut her out.

As she was gathering her things the phone rang.

'Mum,' came Natasha's guarded voice, 'it's me.'

Eileen experienced a moment of alarm, wondering why Natasha had called when they were about to see each other. 'You all right, Tash?'

'I'm fine, so's Sean, and we're looking forward to seeing you, Mum,' Natasha said. 'But I thought I'd better warn you. Maybe it's not going to be the nice relaxed Mother's Day lunch we were expecting. Christina's here, and she's in a state.'

'Christina? But she wasn't coming home this vac. She was going to stay and revise.'

'I know. But something's happened. You're needed over here.'

'What's wrong?' Eileen asked, alarm now taking hold. 'She's not ill, is she?'

'No. Look, Mum, I can't say much on the phone, and I'm only talking to you now because she's in the loo, but she arrived on our doorstep late last night and all I've managed to get out of her is something about some bloke dumping her, and she seems to have gone completely to bits over it. She knows you're coming, of course, but she doesn't know I'm ringing you now. I just thought you'd better be prepared.'

'Right, Tash. Thanks, love. I'm on my way.'

Eileen took the country route from Allerton to Lambury. A journey of twenty miles, crossing the county boundary, it took her longer to reach the outskirts of the city than to cover the rest of the distance. A brisk tail-wind bowled her along the country roads, empty on a Sunday lunchtime, and she felt a momentary pang for her old life and the fields and woods of Holton; but remembering them brought back a darker and unwelcome memory, of a dead boy among the sodden ferns and mosses, and with it a sensation that everything in her was being pinched and squeezed. She fought it down grimly and concentrated on driving.

To her surprise, when she entered the road on the small housing estate where Natasha and Sean lived, she saw Christina leaning over their front gate. As Eileen got out of the car Christina brandished a bunch of daffodils and said, 'Happy Mother's Day, Ma. Sorry – these were all the local petrol station had left.'

'At least you didn't steal them from the cemetery,' Eileen said. 'Thank you, dear. How are you doing?'

Christina opened the gate and let her mother through. Still clutching the daffodils – just like the four-year-olds in church this morning, Eileen thought fleetingly – she put her arms round her mother's neck and hugged her. As she did so her whole skinny body convulsed with sobs and she broke into rivers of tears.

'Sorry, sorry,' she mumbled. 'I am totally pathetic at the moment.'

Eileen guided her gently towards the front door. 'Come on, Christie, let's go inside. Sean and Tash are bound to have something alcoholic we can guzzle. It may be temporary, but it's effective.'

'OK. But then I'm going to bed for a few hours, Mum. Tash and Sean can fill you in. We were up till the small hours, and I slept badly, so I'm really knackered.'

They went inside. Christina patted her mother's arm. 'I think I'll decline the alcohol. See you later.' She disappeared up the stairs.

Natasha emerged from the kitchen, wiping her hands on a towel. 'Hi, Mum. Some Mother's Day. But we didn't get up till late, what with staying up till two o'clock with Christie, and I haven't really got started with the cooking.'

'Not to worry. We'll do it now, all of us together. You can tell me what's going on while we peel spuds or whatever.'

Natasha organized her husband and her mother with the tactical skills of a seasoned general. Before long they were dutifully peeling and chopping while she herself dealt with the Sunday joint.

'I had an idea something was up ages ago,' Natasha said. 'But then I didn't hear anything, and Christie didn't say much out of the ordinary, so I put it to the back of my mind.'

'When you say "ages ago" how long do you mean, Tash?' Eileen asked.

'It was at Dad and Margaret's wedding. Last September. You noticed it too, didn't you, Sean?'

Sean nodded. 'She wasn't herself somehow. All through the reception she was getting and sending texts, quite discreetly, but a lot more than you'd expect. Then I went to the gents and bumped into her in the corridor. She was on her mobile, laughing in a peculiar high-pitched way. She seemed a bit manic. You'd have thought she was drunk, but it wasn't quite the same.'

'Anyway,' Natasha said, 'I know for sure she hardly drank – or ate – anything. She just wasn't normal, that's all. Then afterwards, when Dad and Margaret had left, a few of us were going for a curry, and we thought Christie was coming with us, but she made some excuse about getting back, and disappeared off to the station.'

'You mean she went from Aberdeen back to Exeter that same night?' Eileen said, dismayed.

'Yes. Then we didn't hear much from her, just the odd routine phone call,' Natasha said.

'Me, too,' Eileen said. 'She seemed all right, said she was working hard and so on. Then she said she'd been invited up to Scotland for Christmas, and did I mind? Of course I minded not seeing her, but I was pleased she was seeing more of your dad and maybe getting to know Margaret better.'

'That's what we thought. But I found out later, from something Dad said, just by chance, that she only spent a few days there.'

'Oh. So where did she go for the rest of the time, then?'

'Well, back to Exeter. And now we know why. Mum, you aren't going to like this one bit. For the past year or more Christie's been having an affair with a married lecturer down there.'

For a split second Eileen surprised herself by a small rush of relief. She had envisaged debt, depression, drug addiction, some mortal danger. The reality was bad enough, but it felt more like something she could assimilate and understand.

She sighed. 'And now, you say, the boyfriend's given her the elbow?'

Natasha nodded. 'He's decided to end it because it's unfair on his wife.'

'Does the poor woman know?' Eileen asked.

'No, Christie is sure she doesn't. There are two sons as well, teenagers taking important exams. The thing is, Mum, Christie is obviously completely nuts about this guy, and she's totally shattered.'

Eileen was silent for a moment. 'I wonder how she thought it was going to end.'

'I don't know,' said Natasha. 'Maybe she didn't think that far ahead.'

'That's not like Christie,' said Eileen, frowning. 'She's always seemed a rational sort of girl.'

'Sometimes it's the sensible ones as fall the hardest, Mum,' Natasha said, giving her mother a meaningful sideways look.

'Maybe. These potatoes are ready for the oven now, Tash.'

They finally sat down to lunch at half past three.

'What do you think, Sean?' Eileen asked as she finished off the last of her roast potatoes. 'Has she said much about this man of hers?'

'Only that he's one of her lecturers,' Sean said. 'I know, Eileen, you're probably thinking he's a cheating bastard taking advantage of his position. That's what I thought at first. When Christie turned up here in such a bad way I wanted to go down there and sort him out. But according to her it's not like that: he's a decent bloke who's got himself into a mess and now he's feeling guilty about his wife and family. Whatever he's really like, Christie won't hear a bad word about him.'

'Do you want some pudding, Mum?' Natasha said, getting up to clear the plates. 'Sean made it.'

Eileen smiled. 'In that case, I can't possibly refuse.'

'My cookery skills aren't the greatest,' Sean said modestly. 'But I'm practising.'

'Yeah. On us,' Natasha said as she went into the kitchen, emerging a few minutes later laden with dessert.

Eileen frowned. 'What are we going to do about Christie? She's got her finals in a couple of months. I don't want her throwing away three years' work because of a badly-timed broken heart.'

'She doesn't want to go back yet,' Natasha said, passing the cream jug to her mother. 'She can stay here. Sean doesn't mind.'

'She can come and stay with me if you need a break,' Eileen said. 'I can clear the lumber out of my spare room. It's about time I did it. I haven't sorted out those boxes since I moved.' She laid a hand on Natasha's arm. 'Between us, we have to put her back together again, Tash.'

'If she'll let us.'

For a few minutes they ate in silence. Then Natasha said, 'I was saving this day, you know, Mum.'

'I know, love. It's been a lovely meal anyway. And the pudding is delicious.' She looked up at Sean and grinned.

'No, there was something I was saving to tell you, it being Mother's Day, though, as usual, my darling sister has kind of got in the way. At one time she even thought she might be pregnant. Don't worry, Mum, she isn't. But I am.'

'What? Oh, Tash, that's brilliant news! How long?'

'Nine weeks.'

'Congratulations, the pair of you! I'm really delighted.'

Sean, beaming, got up from his chair. 'Time for a toast, I think.'

He returned a few moments later with a bottle of champagne and three glasses.

'Not much for you, ma-to-be,' he said to Natasha, half filling her glass and charging his own and Eileen's to overflowing.

'Whoa, Sean! I've got to drive home later.'

Sean raised his glass. 'To our son or daughter.'

'To parenthood,' Eileen responded.

'To grandparenthood,' Sean said slyly.

'Oh, dear. Shall I have to take up knitting?'

'Don't bother, Mum,' Natasha said. 'You knitting would be painful to watch. I'll just get everything from that shop in the Arcade. Expensive, but nice.'

'So, save me the sums, then: when's this baby due?'

'October 14th.'

Eileen leaned back in her chair and took a long gulp of champagne. 'Well, call me drunk if you like, and I know grandmothers are supposed to be incorrigibly biased, but this is likely to be a very beautiful, intelligent and kindly baby. And a lucky one.'

'Steady on, Mum,' Natasha said. 'We'll all be crying in a minute. And we've had a gutful of that with poor old Christie.'

'I must go and see her before I go home,' Eileen said. 'Do you think she'll be awake?'

'It's almost five. It won't hurt to wake her now,' Natasha said.

'Then I must get back. Poor Fletcher will be hungry.'

'Queer name for a cat, I always thought.'

'I named him after a friend.'

Eileen climbed the stairs and knocked gently on the spare bedroom door. An inarticulate sound came from within, and she opened the door and went inside.

'Hi, Mum.' Christina stretched out a thin arm and switched on the bedside light. Her hair was sticking up and her face was pale. She looked very young and vulnerable.

'How are you doing, love?' Eileen said, perching on the bed and taking her hand.

'Oh, well, still more or less alive. Have Sean and Tash told you my tale of woe?'

Eileen nodded. 'Some of it.'

Christina sat up, shivering. Eileen handed her a jumper that was draped over the chair.

'I expect your first thought was to be angry, wasn't it?' Christina said. 'I know Sean's was. He's such a lovely brother-in-law. It's a pity there aren't two of him.'

'I don't know what to think, Christie.'

'Well, it takes two, Mum, whatever you say. And John is a good person, not a seducing, manipulative monster.'

'Tell me about him.'

Christina sighed. 'His name is John Simmonds. He is forty-four, and has been married to a nice lady called Helen for twenty years. He has two sons: James is eighteen, and about to take his A levels, and Richard is sixteen and studying for his GCSEs. John is one of my English lecturers, one of the better ones, and that's not just me being partial. He's not exactly handsome and dashing; in fact, he's not particularly tall and not at all athletic. He has curly hair and wears glasses. He is kind, clever and funny, and at the moment he is in a worse state than I am.'

'How did it all get to this, Christie?'

Christina looked at her mother, her blue eyes full of sadness. 'We were stupid, of course. It's both our faults, Mum, mine as much as his.

I'm not a child. It just got out of hand. But he says we have to end it, and he's right. Helen hasn't done anything wrong. She and the boys don't deserve to have the family torn apart. He loves them too.' Her eyes welled with tears. 'Here I go again. Hand me that box of tissues, can you, Mum?' She blew her nose. 'Sean and Tash have been angelic.'

'Did you know Tash is pregnant?'

Christina was startled. 'She never said. Oh, Mum, I am a selfish bitch, taking over her life like this, stealing her thunder. What a rotten sister I am.'

Eileen leaned over and put her arms round Christina's thin shoulders. 'We've got to help you straighten yourself out, Christie. I don't want you wasting all the work you've done by falling apart just before your finals.'

'Don't worry, Mum,' Christina said, smiling bleakly. 'I know what I've got to do. I'll write to the university and tell them I'm ill and won't be back till the end of April. Term's almost over anyway. If you or Tash and Sean will have me, I'll stay home and lick my wounds. Maybe I'll even get some revision done. You guys will have to help me, though. You see, Mum: I'm human after all.'

'Of course you are, love. And this kind of grief is part of being human.'

'You know the hardest thing?' Christina said, tears running down her face unchecked. 'It's thinking about John being as carved up and helpless as I feel right now. It's stupid, but I want to comfort him for the pain we've inflicted on ourselves. And then I think, how am I going to face seeing him when I go back?'

Eileen hugged her. 'Worry about that when you come to it.'

'I won't feel like this forever, will I, Mum? Because right now it feels like my life is over. Oh dear, how melodramatic that sounds.'

'It will be hard, of course it will. But you'll get through it. And we'll be here to prop you up, me and Tash and Sean.'

Christina nodded, speechless.

'I must go, Christie. I've left my poor starving cat long enough. And I have to be at work by seven-fifteen tomorrow: early shift.'

'Of course, Mum. See you soon. I hope you're not too ashamed of me.'

'Don't be ridiculous. That will never happen. Goodbye, love. Remember, I'm only on the other end of the phone.'

Eileen left the room, blowing Christina a kiss from the doorway.

Downstairs, Sean and Natasha were stacking the dishwasher and looked up enquiringly as she entered.

'Is she OK?' Natasha asked.

'She will be, I hope. We just have to keep an eye on her and keep in touch.' She crossed the room and hugged them both. 'I'm very proud of you two.'

'What for?' Natasha said suspiciously.

'For being such a good sister and brother-in-law,' Eileen said. 'Maybe it's easier for Sean, but I know you and Christie have always had a bit of rivalry going, haven't you, Tash? And I guess you've often felt she's had the best of the bargain.'

'Yeah. Well, maybe not any more, Mum. Poor old Christie's got her life in a shambles right now, and I've got Sean and little Horatio. I can afford to be nice.'

'Even so. Your graciousness revives my faith in human nature.'

'Blimey.'

'I must go before I get too over the top. Thank you for a lovely lunch, my dears. I'll call soon. And when we've got Christie back on her feet, we'll go out shopping for baby stuff – OK?'

Natasha grinned. 'Sean will be relieved. It's a date, Mum.'

Eileen drove home in the gathering dusk. The clocks were not due to go forward for another week, and the evening was chilly, as if to remind her that winter was not yet quite gone. She headed for the main road home to cut down the journey time. Fletcher would, no doubt, by now be roaming round the flat howling piteously for his supper.

I should have got Penny to feed him. I never thought I'd be so long.

Penny Schofield, with her little son Gus, lived in the flat below. Penny would feed Fletcher, and Eileen sometimes looked after Gus on the rare occasions when Penny had to go somewhere without him. Eileen thought about her own children, how little, after all, she knew them. All their lives, more than twenty years, she had been their protector and provider; now they were grown up and full of surprises.

Lord, watch over my little family: Natasha, Sean, the tiny new life even now growing out of sight, but very much in our minds. Watch over Christie especially. Give her fortitude, wrap your loving arms around her, protect her from folly. Thank you for all of them.

She sighed. Christie was safe with Sean and Natasha. They would let her know if they needed her for anything. She had to let them get on with it.

Then the lights of the city were all around her. A gusty rain began to fall, and she switched on her windscreen wipers. Weary now, she parked at the roadside and ran up the steps to the front door of the flats, groping in her bag for her key as a thin trickle of rain ran coldly down her neck.

Home. Curtains drawn against the darkness. And in the morning, work. Patients, colleagues, friends. Problems and solutions – or not, for some. The daily round went on; and she must think about Easter.

Eileen woke in the middle of the night with a heart-stopping jolt. Her whole body was running with sweat. She threw off the covers, disturbing a sleeping Fletcher, who removed himself from her feet, stalked disdainfully to the fire-escape door and demanded to be let out. Eileen opened the door for him, letting in a chill breeze which made her shudder in her thin nightdress. She closed the door quickly, put on her dressing-gown and went to the kitchen to make a cup of tea. It was two-fifteen by the kitchen clock.

Blasted menopause. It's a bit of a laugh when Maureen and I are comparing notes but it's no joke at this dead hour when I've got to be at work at seven. She sighed, washed her cup and went back to bed.

Two hours later she was awakened again by a pitiful mewing and scratching at the fire-escape door.

You forgot to unlock the cat flap, idiot. She staggered out of bed to let in her damp cat, who immediately leapt onto her clean quilt with dirty paws and purred loudly enough to wake the street. Eileen took two painkillers for a threatening headache and went back to bed.

At five thirty the alarm sounded, wakening her from a horrible dream in which she was obliged to carry her cat everywhere for fear he would escape, except he was not only a cat but also a grinning, wriggling, milk-drinking, nappy-wearing baby. The dream involved climbing down a perilous cliff from which, if she fell, she would dash herself to pieces on the rocks below. She knew the cat/baby needed supplies which were kept in a locked car; but Philip and Marie had the key, and as she looked from the cliff-top she saw them, tiny but distinct, disappearing into a distant forest. At this point the precarious sandy ledge on which her foot rested crumbled away, and she felt herself helplessly falling, arms and legs flailing, mouth open in a dream-silent scream.

She awoke, legs kicking, to the shrilling of the alarm. She switched it off, groaning, and stumbled to the shower feeling as if she had spent the night in a boxing ring with the world heavyweight champion. Revived a little by the hot water, she dressed, dried her hair and made some toast. Fletcher, refreshed and debonair, circled round the table until she put food into his bowl.

She tried as she ate her breakfast to think about the day ahead. She had not been at work since Friday, and anything might have happened over the weekend. She thought of the patients, twenty-six of them at the moment: the unit was very full. More than usual, she felt unequal to the task of caring for such sick and troubled souls.

The job she had had when she first moved to Allerton, selling lingerie in a women's clothing store, had lasted only three weeks before she had given it up in despair. Then, fortuitously, her acquaintance at church, Maureen, had suggested she apply for a nursing assistant's job at the Psychiatric Unit at Allerton Hospital, where Maureen herself worked.

'I know there's been an ad. in the paper, Eileen. I think they've interviewed a few people. It's not a job for everyone, but I think you could do it.'

'Wouldn't I need special qualifications?'

'I haven't got any. Common sense, I suppose. Why not go for it and see what happens?'

Eileen applied. Within a week she had an interview with Christine the Ward Manager and Josh the Charge Nurse, and before another week had passed she got the job. Maureen was right. Despite the drag of shift-work and the often harrowing state of the patients, Eileen found the work suited something in her: the need to try to put things right, perhaps. And it kept something of Christopher alive. It was as if she worked as a silent tribute to him.

Fletcher finished his breakfast and sat washing his paws. Then he strolled over to the door. Eileen got up and unlocked the cat flap. 'Go carefully, puss. See you later.'

She put her plate on the draining board, went to the bathroom to clean her teeth, gathered up her bag and keys and went to work.

Palm Sunday: 5 April 1998

'Louis, you beat all. Where in heaven's name did you manage to find a donkey?'

Eileen came into the vestry, her arms full of books. Louis was pulling his surplice over his head, which made his hair stick up at the back. Eileen suppressed an urge to flatten it down. A hint of a smile lurked at the corners of Louis' mouth and flashed from behind his glasses.

'A man I know owed me a favour,' he said enigmatically.

'But a donkey, Louis! You kept that quiet. So where does one keep a donkey in the heart of Allerton?'

'You'd be surprised. This fellow has two in his back garden. He loaned me the one less likely to nip the children. Anyway, I thought the procession went off rather well, didn't you? It made the Sunday-market shoppers stop and take notice.'

'It was wonderful. Especially with our youngsters handing out palm crosses. How did you persuade them?'

'A little bribery. And I charmed the Sunday school dragon.'

'Ssh! She might still be around.'

Louis was unperturbed. He hung up his robes and put on his jacket. 'Time for a coffee, madam organist?'

'All right, but not for long. We need to talk about Easter. It's only a week away, and I'm panicking.'

'You are doing very well.'

'You would say that, since there's no one else.'

'Not at all. I am a paragon of truthfulness, as you know.'

'Hm.'

Louis locked the church door and they walked across the graveyard to the vicarage. Eileen sidestepped a splatter of donkey dung on the path. 'That might have been handy for the roses in your garden, if you had any.'

'I am a thinking man, not a gardener.'

'A garden is a great place to think.'

Louis pushed open the back door and stood aside to let Eileen enter. A vision of kitchen chaos greeted her.

'So, can you have great thoughts while tending a window box?' Louis swept a pile of letters aside from the worktop and took the kettle to the sink.

'No, and donkey manure would be far too powerful for my modest plants.'

'You could do the vicarage garden if you're feeling deprived.'

'What? Organist, gardener, what next? You'll be getting me to clean up your kitchen, I shouldn't wonder.'

Louis looked around, frowning. 'What's wrong with it?'

'Forget it, Louis. The words "pig" and "sty" spring to mind, that's all.'

'How very impolite. Anyway, since you think I'm such a slob, perhaps you'd better wash up these coffee cups. At least then they might meet your exacting standards.'

'Gladly. But I don't have exacting standards. Just vaguely normal ones of health and hygiene.'

Completely unruffled by her criticism, Louis sat on a kitchen chair and put his feet on the table. His shoes needed mending. Eileen said nothing. She made the coffee, set the steaming cups on a more or less uncluttered square of table, and sat down opposite him.

Louis took a sip. 'How's your daughter doing?'

'Which one?'

'The troubled one.'

'Ah. Well, all right-ish. Between us we're trying to put her back together again. Her finals are coming up; she can't afford to be an emotional wreck.'

'She's like you, I think.'

'How do you mean?'

'A bit secretive. Likes to think she's in control, perhaps. Doesn't want to need help.'

'However did you come to that conclusion?'

'I'm not blind.'

Eileen drank her coffee, uncertain how to continue. Louis sat looking at her across the table, his chair tilted perilously.

'She'll be OK, I think,' Eileen said finally. 'But it was a bad blow, obviously. A shock to her as well as to the rest of us, the way it knocked her off her feet.'

'Have you ever been knocked off your feet, Eileen?'

'Of course. Haven't we all? The way you're fooling around with that chair you're likely to be in a heap on the floor yourself. Anyway, hadn't we better talk about the music for Easter?'

Louis smiled: a smile that filled his whole face with light and banished for a moment the habitual closed-in, brooding look which his face had in repose. He shook his head and stared at the ceiling, his chair still poised on two spindly legs.

'Classic avoidance,' he said, as if to no one in particular. 'What a shame. But you're right, of course. Easter music.'

Easter Day: 12 April 1998

They met Louis striding across the graveyard, his surplice billowing. A fine misty drizzle was making everything insidiously wet: there were raindrops in Louis' hair and the new leaves on the churchyard trees were slick and shiny.

'Good morning, ladies. A happy Easter to you.'

'And to you, Louis. This is my daughter, Christina. She's staying with me at the moment.'

Louis shook hands with Christina. 'Good to meet you. And to have you with us. You will swell our little congregation in no small measure.'

Christina smiled. 'I had to come. Mum tells me this is the best day of the year.'

'So it is.' Louis smiled back. 'Let's get in out of this damp, shall we? All set, Eileen?'

'As near as I ever am,' Eileen said. 'I've been working on an Easter voluntary. Joyful, but simple. It has to be simple.'

'You are far too modest.'

Louis ascended the pulpit steps. Eileen slid off the organ seat and slipped into the empty choir stall, where there was a cushion. She looked down into the congregation, and saw Christina, sitting two rows back with Maureen, Penny and Gus. There was a sharp spring smell of daffodils coming from the flower arrangement on the altar.

Louis looked over his little flock and smiled slightly. 'The Lord is risen!'

'He is risen indeed: Alleluya!' came the ragged response.

Louis opened his Bible. 'Today,' he said, 'all over the world, in great cathedrals or in churches much like this one, in St. Peter's Square or in thronged churches in Africa with mud floors, in vast crowds or in tiny, persecuted groups, Christian people, like us, gather to praise One who conquered death and lives for ever. What does that mean for you, my brothers and sisters, and for me, today, here in Allerton, in England? Let me paraphrase the words of that great Christian writer of our century,

C.S.Lewis: Jesus has smashed down the door which has been locked since the death of Adam. From now on everything – *everything* – is different. Today, the day of his rising, is the beginning of God's new creation. And we, my friends, you and I, and all people, can be part of it.

'Let's look back at how all this came to pass, and why it had to happen. In Corinthians 15 verse 2 we read: "For just as all people die because of their union with Adam, in the same way all will be raised to life because of their union with Christ." Further on, in verse 49, St. Paul writes: "Just as we wear the likeness of the man made of earth, so we will wear the likeness of the Man from heaven."

'But how is this possible? Every one of us knows that he or she is a sinner. Our very nature is sinful. We sin each moment; our sinful actions are the logical outworking of our flawed natures. If you think I am exaggerating, try being perfect for ten minutes, or even behaving well for a day! We can't help it: our union with Adam is inherited and involuntary, and we can't escape its implications. The best of us have felt this conflict: you will remember St. Paul himself agonizing over the gulf between his heartfelt desire to do good and his failure to achieve it. This is our involvement in the Fall: to be human is to be sinful. Our union with Christ, on the other hand, must be willed by us. It is an offer, an invitation, to be accepted or refused. What shall we say? Is it to be yes, or no? Because on this hangs the eternal destiny of each one of us.'

He paused for a moment and turned over a page of his notes. Then he cleared his throat and looked up again. 'Further on in St. Paul's letter to Corinth the apostle sets forth the consequences of Christ's resurrection. First comes the raising of Christ himself, the greatest miracle of all, the very hinge and pivot of our faith. Then, at the end of time, when he returns, there comes the raising of all those who have said "yes" to his invitation, who have lived as his followers, who belong to him. Then, we are told, comes the final defeat of all God's enemies, and the handing over to God of all spiritual powers and authorities; and, finally, the conquest of death itself. So Christ's resurrection paves the way for our own raising and the defeat of evil; but it also paves the way for the restoration of fallen creation and for God to take his rightful place as creator and king, ruling over all.

'This, then, is the great cosmic destiny to which we are called. It's a mind-blowing thought, isn't it? What will it be like, you might wonder, for us, there at the end of time? Well, of course, we don't know. There is a kind of veil over our earthly eyes, and it is vain – if tempting – to speculate. However, the Bible does give us some powerful clues. Listen to these words from Isaiah 60: "Arise, Jerusalem, and shine like the sun;

the glory of the Lord is shining on you! Other nations will be covered by darkness, but on you the light of the Lord will shine; the brightness of his presence will be with you. Nations will be drawn to your light, and kings to the dawning of your new day." Later in the same chapter we read: "No longer will the sun be your light by day or the moon be your light by night; I, the Lord, will be your eternal light; the light of my glory will shine on you. I, the Lord, will be your eternal light, more lasting than the sun and moon."

'What does this mean for us? Let's go to St. John's Gospel and look at his opening verses, verses which we hear read to us at Christmas every year, verses which are surely familiar to us all: "The Word was the source of life, and this life brought light to humanity. The light shines in the darkness, and the darkness has never put it out. God sent his messenger, a man named John, who came to tell people about the light, so that all should hear the message and believe. He himself was not the light; he came to tell about the light. This was the real light – the light that comes into the world and shines on everyone."

'At this point we might just feel like throwing up our hands in despair and giving up. We might with some justice ask: "How can we, terrestrial and mortal as we are, even in our freest flights of imagination, ever begin to comprehend that great effulgence of light that surrounds the throne of God? Is it not too much, the very idea of it, for us who are so limited and weak?" And of course you would be right, and I feel that weakness too. But we must try to keep in our minds two related things. The first is this vision of light shining on all of us who will accept it, and by accepting it be part of the renewal of all creation; this is our eternal destiny if we keep faith with him who came to call us and is calling us still. The second thing is this very idea of "keeping faith." Let me return for a moment to St. Paul and his famous verses in chapter 15 of 1 Corinthians. Paul becomes almost ecstatic when he writes of death's destruction: we read of the trumpet sounding and the dead rising, and then comes Paul's challenge to death itself, "Where, Death, is your victory?" But, at the end of this passage, in verse 58, Paul writes: "So then, my dear brothers and sisters, stand firm and steady. Keep busy always in your work for the Lord, since you know that nothing you do in the Lord's service is ever useless." As in other places in his letters, Paul concludes with the ordinary, the pragmatic, the day-to-day. He rises to the heights in contemplation, but he always returns to the valleys to be alongside his fellow-travellers. A message to us all on this Easter Day: yes, today we are full of joy. Now we must take that joy into the every day of service.'

Louis paused again, but he had not finished with them yet. He leaned slightly forward, his hands resting on the edge of the pulpit. Someone coughed at the back of the church. 'We all know,' Louis continued, his voice quiet, almost confidential, 'that to be a faithful servant of Christ in our day is not easy. It never has been easy; for some it is painful in the extreme, and we have been warned that we will face trouble, even persecution. But in John's Gospel we find a word of encouragement. You remember when Jesus, after his resurrection, appears to his disciples and especially to Thomas. Thomas, finally convinced, falls on his knees and says, "My Lord and my God!" and Jesus answers him, "Do you believe because you see me? How blessed are those who believe without seeing me!"

'This, my friends, is us. We have not seen; we were not there, like the women at the tomb or the disciples behind locked doors. Yet we believe. Why is this? I suggest to you that, leaving aside for the moment any special personal revelation we might have been given, it is because we have read, and so in our own way seen and therefore believe, with the help of the Holy Spirit, through the promises of Scripture. Jesus himself, you remember, opened the eyes of his disciples, on the road to Emmaus after his resurrection, by explaining to them the Law, the Psalms and the Prophets. This very Law, these Prophets and these Psalms, in other words the Bible Jesus knew and we have today, is our faith's foundation.

'This should be a profound encouragement to us all, and a strength to take with us into that daily and often difficult life of service. I would say to you that this belief and faith of ours, in the face of all the deceptions and disappointments of this fallen world, and the temptations to which we are all subject, brings a special glory to God as well as a special blessing to us. We have not seen; and yet, with Scripture as our rock, we place our whole selves, our destinies, trustingly into his hands. St. Peter wrote to the scattered Christians of Asia Minor in his first letter: "You love him, although you have not seen him, and you believe in him, although you do not now see him. So you rejoice with a great and glorious joy which words cannot express, because you are receiving the salvation of your souls, which is the purpose of your faith in him."

Louis paused again briefly, giving them time to take in his words. When he resumed, his voice was ringing, almost urgent. 'When Christ returns in glory, when faith gives way to sight, that life of faith which we have now will be over. So I say to you today, on this great day of all days, when Christ has defeated death for us, when the light from heaven pours down on us, let us go from here to live that life of faith to which each of us has been called, in Christ's strength alone, and bearing in our hearts that special blessedness of those who have not seen, but yet have believed.'

The silence was broken only by Gus Schofield running his toy car up and down the book-rest. Then Louis said, 'Let us pray.'

There was a shuffling of feet, more coughing, and a kind of collective sigh.

'Risen Lord Jesus: May your glorious light be a reminder to us of our eternal destiny. Grant that today we may truly rejoice with your saints, because every corner of this universe has been illuminated by your light and all darkness banished. May that light be also a lamp to our feet and guidance on the road, so that, seeing you with the eyes of faith, we may not stumble on our journey. In your name we ask, Amen.'

Louis looked up, his gaze sweeping over all their upturned faces, and he smiled.

'The Lord is risen!' he said, and they responded, 'He is risen indeed: Alleluya!'

Christina came into the vestry as Eileen was hanging up her robe. 'That was some sermon. Bit high-flown for some, I'd guess. And "effulgence"? What's all that about?'

Louis came through the door. Christina started guiltily and blushed.

'It's true, I have been accused of breakfasting on the dictionary,' he said affably, 'sometimes by your mother. But what do you make of the message, Christina?'

'I hardly know,' Christina said, frowning. 'It seems to me you were talking about the big picture, the whole purpose of human life. I can't comment on that. I just don't know enough.'

'Eileen will tell you what that purpose is, I am sure,' Louis said, hastily divesting himself of cassock and surplice. 'I must dash: I have been honoured by a lunch invitation from my sister in London. Nice to have met you, Christina.'

'So what is it, then, Mum? The purpose of human life?' Christina asked as they walked to the car. The drizzle had stopped, but the air was damp and clinging.

'Well, according to Louis, it's "to glorify God and enjoy him for ever."'

'Did he make that up?'

'No. It comes from the first article of the Westminster Shorter Catechism.'

'Never heard of it. So, is that what you think too, Ma? You exist to glorify God?'

Eileen opened the car door and grinned at her daughter. 'Got any better ideas?'

An hour later, finally ready, Eileen paused at the door of the flat and looked at Christina, who was curled up on the sofa with a book and a sheaf of lecture notes. 'You could still come with me, you know. I'm sure Marie and Philip would be happy to see you.'

Christina looked up and smiled. 'It's OK, Ma. I'd rather be here, on my own. Things are getting better, thanks to all of you, but I still feel a bit feeble. Not up to jolly socializing, really. And there's the question of work.' She waved the book in her mother's direction.

'You'll be all right?' Eileen said.

'Of course I will. I'm sure I can find my way to the fridge. Go on, Ma, it's time you went.'

'I won't be late back.'

'For goodness' sake! Go, and have a lovely time.'

In the car, part of the steady stream of Sunday traffic eastwards to Osewick, Eileen thought about her younger daughter. Christina seemed to have regained her usual calm and control, but Eileen felt sure it was a thin film over a cauldron of turmoil.

She had arrived at Eileen's at the beginning of the previous week, with her rucksack and books. 'Time to give Tash and Sean a rest, I think. Share out the ailing relative.'

She was an amiable flat mate, good-humoured and thoughtful as ever. There had been, so far as Eileen knew, no long, tearful phone calls, and John had not been mentioned. Christina went out for brisk walks, revised, cooked meals; she smiled and chatted. But there was none of the girl who hummed and sang around the place, and Eileen felt a palpable sense of something tense and desperate which worried her.

As she left the main road and drove towards the city centre, with the Abbey now in sight over the rooftops, she thought of Louis, and remembered another sermon in which he had quoted that same definition of life's purpose, saying (rather grimly, Eileen thought), 'Perhaps all of us need to let that sink deeply into our consciousness: the purpose of our existence, given to us by God, is to glorify him – not ourselves – and enjoy him – not ourselves – for ever. I know, and I am sure you know, how difficult this is.' At the time Eileen had not given much thought to what he had said. Now, negotiating the last roundabout and turning into the peace of the Close, it came to her with a small shock that perhaps that was what she had been doing in all those meetings with Christopher: glorifying herself. It was an uncomfortable and unwelcome thought, coming when she had managed to dismiss Christopher from her conscious mind for some weeks. Thinking of Louis and of Christopher at the same time, wondering if Christopher's ghost would ever cease to inhabit the borders of her mind, she thought again that, one day, if she could, if the right moment arose, she would tell Louis about him and ask the questions which came at her unheralded from unexpected quarters to stir up her conscience and destroy her peace: If I had not interfered, would he still be alive? Did I do wrong? Am I to blame?

Marie opened the door before Eileen had time to knock. A waft of cooking smells blew out with her, and her cheeks were flushed from the kitchen heat.

'Eileen, dear, how lovely to see you. Come along in.'

Eileen accepted a glass of sherry and stood in the spacious drawing room, looking out onto the walled garden bright with deep-green spring grass and bordered with daffodils. Marie called from the kitchen among the clashing of saucepans.

'How's Christina? Is she still with you?'

'Yes. She seems all right, but you know, there's something I'm not sure about. There's so much I feel I don't know.'

Marie came into the room, wiping her hands on her apron. 'It must be a worry for you.'

'Mm. I know she's got to sort herself out, and she won't be asking me for help. But she seems kind of fragile. Not like the old Christie.'

'She'll be all right, Eileen.'

'Of course. Well, I hope so. Philip not back yet?'

'Oh, he stayed behind after Eucharist, some meeting or other with the choir parents, not sure exactly what about. He'll be over in a moment. That's why I'm in a bit of a tizz. He never has a lot of time on a Sunday, of course, and today being Easter makes it busier still. Lunch has to be slotted in just so.'

Eileen smiled. 'But you're not expected back for Evensong?'

'No. Not today, anyway. Plenty of time to chat later.' The front door banged shut. 'There's Philip now.'

Philip came down the hall, carrying folders of music precariously under one arm. He greeted Eileen with a smile, and slid his free arm round Marie's waist, his sun-browned hand resting on her hip.

'Lunch is ready,' Marie said. 'Go and get rid of that music now and let me drain these vegetables.'

Lunch was relaxed. Philip produced a bottle of Beaune and filled their glasses liberally. 'Present from an old chorister.'

'Nice present,' Eileen said, sipping appreciatively.

'Very, especially as there are eleven more of these.' Philip smiled.

'Philip, tell Eileen about the concert,' Marie said as she stacked the plates.

'Which one? Oh, you mean "Elijah." Marie wants you to come and sing with us, Eileen.'

'Us?'

Philip rolled his eyes. 'Osewick Choral Society. It's part of my contract to be their musical director. Nice people, not all of them competent.'

'Miaow.' Marie made a face. 'I dare say I'm one of the less competent myself. But we can always do with a few more altos. And it might be fun, Eileen, who knows?'

'It's certainly a good sing, "Elijah"', Eileen said.

'Perhaps not Mendelssohn's greatest work,' Philip said. 'But yes, why don't you come along?'

'Would I need an audition?'

'Hardly. I know what you can do.'

'It's on a Tuesday evening, Eileen, at the Conference Rooms on Ward Street,' Marie said.

'I know it.'

'Seven-thirty to nine-thirty, the rehearsals start on 21st of this month and the concert is in the Abbey on July 18th. Do say you will. It means I shall get to see you more often. I know it's a bit of a drive for you.'

'I wouldn't be able to make every rehearsal, not with working shifts. Wouldn't that be a problem?'

'I don't think so,' Philip said. 'Why don't you come and see what you think?'

'All right, why not?' Eileen said. 'It'd be like old times. Well, almost.'

'Better than old times, from my point of view.' Philip pushed his chair back. 'I must go, I'm afraid. Rehearsal for Evensong's at two. See you later, Eileen. Sorry to leave you with the washing up.'

Marie followed him to the front door, and Eileen, taking a tray of dirty crockery into the kitchen, caught a glimpse of them there. Philip had drawn Marie close with one arm, and he brushed a stray tendril of hair from her forehead with gentle fingers. Marie looked up at him, smiling. Then the front door banged again and he was gone.

'Philip looks happy, Marie,' Eileen said.

'He is. He is back where he belongs, doing the job he loves.'

'And he has you.'

'Yes. He has me.' She giggled. 'What a lucky fellow. Now, Eileen, let's get these dishes away and you can fill me in on your exciting life.'

'What? Work, errant offspring, playing the organ on Sundays? What's exciting about that?'

'I'm sure there's lots you never let on about. What about this vicar of yours?'

'Louis? Louis is a friend. Natasha thinks he's probably gay.' She felt a pang of disloyalty and fought it down crossly.

'Oh. Pity. What about your boss at work?'

'Which one?' Eileen said, amused. 'Surely you can't mean Dr. Caton, the shrink?'

'No, not him. He's married, isn't he?'

'He is. To the ever-elegant Andrea.'

'No, the chap in charge of your unit: what's his name? I forget.'

'Oh, you mean Josh. Don't be daft, Marie, we're just colleagues.'

'Says you.'

'Yes, says me, you dreadful old matchmaker. Just because you're in clover with Philip.'

Marie sighed. 'I would like to see you happy, Eileen.'

'I am quite happy enough, thank you, dear. And what's to say some man might not just ruin my happiness?'

'Cynic. At the very least I seem to remember you actually admitted to envying me once.'

'Just the sex, Marie.'

'So?'

'I don't think I'm quite up for that, not really, flinging myself into some affair. Even if it was on offer, which it isn't. Have you got another tea towel? This one's wet.'

'That's it, change the subject.'

'Thanks, I will. How's Stephanie?'

Marie's blue eyes brightened. 'She's doing really well. It seems a queer thing to say about your child in jail, but I'm quite proud of her.'

'Good. Next time you are visiting, be sure to include me in your itinerary. Just ring first in case I'm working.'

'Thank you, dear. I'll do that.'

Marie made a pot of coffee and they drifted back into the drawing room and settled in comfortable chairs.

'So, all well with Natasha and Sean?' Marie asked.

'Fine, as far as I know.'

'Fancy you about to be a grandma.'

'Don't. It makes me feel even more ancient.'

'Talking of age, it occurs to me you have a significant birthday coming up, Eileen.'

'That's a long way off yet. Six whole months. I am still in my forties. Just.'

'How are you going to celebrate?'

'No idea. Maybe I won't. Maybe I'll drive off into the country somewhere and try to forget.'

'What a spoilsport. The rest of us might like a party.'

'Don't you dare.'

Marie laughed. 'All right, I'm only teasing. Oh, Eileen, I almost forgot. I was in Lambury last week, and I saw Michael.'

Eileen sat up, her scalp prickling. 'Did you? Did you speak to him?'

'No, he was on the other side of the road with his mother. I don't think he saw me.'

'How did he seem?'

'He's so tall, Eileen. As tall as his mum. He looked fine. They were laughing about something.'

'Just the two of them, then?'

'Yes.'

'I remember when he first came to live with us,' Eileen said softly. 'Five years old, he was.'

'I remember too. Face of an angel, but not a happy child. How he changed.'

'He's nearly eleven now. It doesn't seem possible. But I'm glad if he's OK.'

'If he is, it's largely down to you, Eileen.'

'Maybe.'

'Do you miss him?'

'Yes, I do. But all our lives are different now – you, me, David, Tash, Michael, Christie.'

'True. Do you think Christina will stick it out? With this chap of hers? Or will she go back to him?'

'Do you know, I've no idea. Sometimes I don't think I know her very well at all. There's so much she keeps to herself.'

'Just like her mother. You're another one that likes to keep her cards close to her chest, aren't you? Another one that hates to admit being vulnerable.'

'So you say. But in my case there's nothing to tell.'

'Well, I reserve judgment on that one.'

They fell silent for a moment. Eileen wondered if her friend was right. Was she, Eileen, secretive? If she was, why was she? Knowledge was power, of course; someone knowing about you gives them power over you. But why should she worry? Marie was her good friend. She hardly knew why, but keeping things quiet had become a habit. She had never told Marie about Christopher. She had never told anyone. Now, she didn't know if she could. But was Christie the same? She didn't want her to be.

'What shift are you on tomorrow, Eileen?' Marie broke her train of thought.

'Early. I have to be at the hospital by seven-fifteen.'

Marie shuddered. 'I don't think I could do that kind of work. Don't you find it depressing?'

'No. Disturbing, sometimes. Harrowing. Anyway, you worked with the old people for years, and some of them were completely out of it, weren't they?'

'That was different, somehow. They weren't mad exactly. More pathetic.'

'So are some of our patients. Seeing them makes me realize how fortunate I am: to be myself, to have the life I've had, however imperfect, to have the family and friends I have, to be so normal. Well, except for you, of course.'

'Very funny.'

'It's sad, sure; some of those poor souls are quite pitiful. But it's interesting, hearing their stories, trying to help them.'

'Can you help?'

'Sometimes. Sometimes, I grant you, it does seem a bit hopeless. Trying to help people in depression can be a real slog. But worth it, if you can make some headway. It's the young ones I find hardest. We've got a young patient, just a teenager, with an eating disorder. It's tearing her family apart.'

'I imagine it would.'

'Just helping them to cope is a challenge, quite apart from their actual illnesses. But it's like what you said about Philip: it's odd, but I do feel I belong there, at least for now. And the people I work with are a good bunch, on the whole.'

Eileen stayed long enough to have a cup of tea with Philip and Marie after Evensong. Then they stood in the doorway and waved to her as she drove down the Close. Thinking about them, Eileen smiled. She thought about their old life in Holton, and how it had turned out. *God bless them. I'm glad they're happy.*

As she filtered onto the main road her thoughts turned homeward, and Marie's observations about Christina came back to her.

'Don't let her be like me,' she muttered, vaguely addressing God as if he were in the car with her. 'Let her have more sense. Marie's right: I do keep things to myself, and it's a bad habit. I thought I'd learned my lesson, but here I am, at it again, trying to go it alone. Help me to defeat myself.'

She thought again of telling someone about Christopher. The thought terrified her, and yet at the same time she was lured by it. She had thought of telling Marie, but somehow the old Marie was gone from her, at least for now, and she was not sure that Marie would want to understand. She had thought of telling Christina, as a sort of cautionary tale; but would Christina think her mother's experience relevant? Probably not. She had thought of telling Josh, but she was afraid he would, as a professional, think less of her. No, if it were anyone, it would have to be Louis. It was, after all, more than anything now, a spiritual matter, a question of conscience. Louis would understand, of that Eileen had no doubt; but she feared his disapproval. She shivered. Sometimes she felt her self-control as the thinnest of skins round a living, growing, swelling something that threatened to burst out and flood her whole ordered existence with chaos. Sometimes it felt as if sanity itself hung by a thread, and that the severing knife was hovering, ready to reduce her to gibbering panic. Then, usually, something banal happened, and the terror receded, and life, with its reassuring platitudinous mendacity, reasserted itself. But the reassurance was fragile and untrustworthy, and the need to speak was growing. In the days when she had believed in herself, however tentatively, Eileen had never been as afraid as this.

Dusk was falling as she arrived in Allerton and negotiated the busy roads back to her own relatively quiet street. As she parked the car her neighbour Penny arrived at the gate, pushing Gus in his buggy.

'Hold on, Penny. I'll give you a hand up the steps.'

'Thanks, Eileen. Just been for a walk, haven't we, Gus?'

Eileen unlocked the front door and let Penny in. She ruffled Gus's dark head and he waved his favourite toy monkey at her. Penny paused by her own front door. She looked ever so slightly furtive. 'Your Christina's got a visitor. A man. Never seen him before.'

'Oh, has she? I'd better go up and see. Bye then, Penny. Bye, Gus.'

Frowning, she let herself into the flat. Fletcher appeared from nowhere and wound himself round her ankles. In the lounge, sitting on the sofa, not close, were Christina and a man, who got to his feet as Eileen came in. She saw someone of middle height, with curly brown hair and glasses, an anxious expression in his mild brown eyes.

'Hello, Mum,' Christina said. 'This is John.'

Eileen shook hands in a daze, mumbling some conventional greeting. Christina got up. 'I'll walk you to the station, John.'

Within moments they had put on coats, said farewells and left. Eileen stood, rooted for the moment, until Fletcher's indignant miaow brought her back to herself with a jolt.

Twenty minutes later Christina came back, letting herself in quietly. She looked at her mother in silence as she unwound her scarf from her neck. 'I'll make some tea,' she said finally.

When she came back with the cups she said, 'You know, Mum, I had no idea he was coming. This wasn't planned. I'm not that underhand.' She sipped her tea. 'After you left he phoned. He's been in London, and he asked if he could come down. There were things he wanted to talk about.'

'I thought it was over, Christie.'

'It is, Mum. He wanted to sort out how we were going to handle it when I go back. That's all, I promise.'

'I just don't want you to go to the dogs. Throw everything over. That's what worries me.'

'It won't happen. I promise it won't. When I get back I will hardly ever see him. He isn't my tutor this year anyway. Finals are in five weeks. I'll be in my room, or in the library, working. I won't blow it.' She sat down on the sofa next to Eileen and took her mother's hand. 'Trust me. It hasn't been easy, but I'm steady now. You guys have been a huge help. It would be an insult to you to mess up after all you've done.'

'I'm thinking of your life, Christie.'

'I know, Mum. So am I. And to prove it I'm going to do some revision right now. Please, don't worry.'

'All right, Christie. I'll try not to. I have to accept what you say; what can I do anyway? You'll do what you do.'

Christina nodded. 'It's nearly time I went back, I think. Get out of your hair. I'll go at the end of the week. But I'll keep in touch, with you and with Tash and Sean.' She leaned forward and kissed Eileen's cheek. 'Thanks for everything, Mum. And don't fret.'

A little after nine o'clock Christina emerged, blinking, from the box room which Eileen had set up for her as a temporary refuge. The rickety garden table which served as a desk was spread with books and papers in a pool of lamplight. On the end of Christina's bed, curled up in a nest of rumpled quilt, an oblivious Fletcher lay asleep.

Christina yawned. 'I think I've just about had enough for one day. I'm going to make some tea. Do you want some, Mum?'

'Yes, that would be nice, thanks.'

'What are you reading?' Christina asked from the kitchen.

'Oh, just my Bible reading for today. And this pamphlet Louis lent me. I'm looking up all the references I can find to freedom.'

'Hm. Now there's an interesting concept. Caused a few wars, that one.'

'It's not political freedom this is about, though. As far as I can work out, it's about freedom from self.'

'Wow. Is that even possible?'

'Well, I suppose. But I'll have to let you know when I find out myself. I think I've got a fair way to go yet.'

Christina came in and put a mug of tea on the low table next to Eileen's chair. 'I shall be interested to hear your conclusions. It's good to see you are still thinking in your old age.'

'Funnily enough, I seem to do quite a lot of it.'

'I think you always have.'

'Maybe.'

'I'm going to turn in, Mum, and amuse myself with a trashy magazine. Does this idle cat need turfing out?'

'Yes, but he won't like it. I think it's started to rain. Come on, Fletcher, time for a last stroll.' Eileen got up, picked up the warm, sleek cat from the bed and tucked him under her arm.

'Goodnight, Christie. Sleep well.'

'Yeah. Goodnight, Mum.'

Eileen opened the door onto the fire escape and put Fletcher out. He shuddered in the cool breeze, growled a little in protest, then was off down the steps with a disdainful flick of his tail.

Eileen sat down again, took a sip of her tea, and reopened the booklet that Louis had lent her. *Why does he think I am interested in this? How does he know I have a problem with practical obedience? Is it that obvious, or is it just that Louis has particular insight?*

She went back to her reading.

'"Freedom is what we have – Christ has set us free!" it says in Galatians 5 verse 1. "Stand, then, as free people, and do not allow yourselves to become slaves again." What are we free from? What have we been slaves to? The answer, of course, is sin. And what is sin, at rock-bottom? It is the worship of self, rather than the worship of God. In Romans 6 verse 22 it says, "But now you have been set free from sin and are the slaves of God." The death of self, it seems, is a prerequisite of the Christian life. Galatians again, chapter 2, verse 20: "I have been put to death with Christ on his cross, so that it is no longer I who live, but it is Christ who lives in me."'

Eileen looked up from the page, her brow creased in concentration. *It's not to do with us, is it? It's all to do with him, who he is, what he has done.*

She looked down at the page again, and in the next paragraph her thought was eerily echoed: "'So then," says Romans 5 verse 18, "as the one sin condemned all the people, in the same way the one righteous act sets all people free and gives them life." Again, in Acts 13 verse 38, we read "...everyone who believes in him is set free from all the sins from which the Law of Moses could not set you free."'

The commentary went on: 'But this freedom, while a once-for-all act of grace, true for all time, nevertheless has to be worked out each day by every individual believer in his or her own special circumstances. Our addiction to self runs deep; it is fed by the Enemy in many ways, and all the conventional teachings of our age serve to reinforce it with their emphasis on rights, self-assertion and ambition. The sinfulness and inutility of dependence on anything else but God, whether it be oneself or others or anything this world has to offer, is clear from the pages of Scripture; but it runs counter to everything we have been taught to take for granted. The old Adversary has been, it seems, at his well-prepared and ever-so-subtle work, massaging our pride, our greed, our overweening selfhood. But if, in serving ourselves, we give our allegiance to him, what is his reward for our discipleship? In a word, it is misery: loss, damnation, loneliness, extinction. And this, of course, is what he wants. Sometimes we may experience something of these things in this life, and for some of us this may act as a wake-up call, which we can recognize as an example of God's mercy, however painful it may feel. As Isaiah says in chapter 42 verse 7, "You will open the eyes of the blind and set free those who sit in dark prisons." Look at the last chapter of John's gospel: here the risen Christ appears to his disciples as they try to go back to the life they knew before they met with him, trying for a catch of fish, but utterly failing by their own efforts. When Jesus tells them where to cast their nets, then their haul is so huge they have to call their friends to help them. So it is with us. If we listen to him, if we obey his teaching, then we shall be truly free. In Ephesians 1 verse 14 we read:

"The Spirit is the guarantee that we shall receive what God has promised his people, and this assures us that God will give complete freedom to those that are his."

'What does it mean, to be his? What does God really want from us? Back in the days of the Old Testament we can learn much from the story of King Saul. Chosen by God to lead Israel, he was too inclined to go his own way, which almost certainly applies to all of us as well. The prophet Samuel said: "Which does the Lord prefer: obedience or offerings and sacrifices? It is better to obey him than to sacrifice the best sheep to him. Rebellion against him is as bad as witchcraft, and arrogance is as sinful as idolatry."

'Strong words, we may think. But to be driven by the desire to please ourselves *is* a form of idolatry. There are only two alternatives available to us: to serve God, or to serve self. And the only way to cut ourselves free from self-serving is consciously and daily to put ourselves at the disposal of his will. In this alone lies our true freedom. For in the final analysis Christian freedom is freedom from self, from the circularity and pointlessness of having oneself at the centre of the universe. It is freedom *for* something too: for the glorification of God in the imitation of Christ!'

Eileen closed the booklet and smiled to herself. No wonder Louis liked this stuff. It was just what he had been saying in many a sermon. Maybe he even wrote it. She looked at the title page; but the author was someone else.

She drank her cooling tea, still thinking. Had she done wrong, in all those weeks with Christopher? She had done what she thought was right, what she thought God would have wanted her to do under the general instruction of "Love thy neighbour." But, it seemed, she must be careful not to give too much weight to what she thought.

Enough for now. It's getting late. I must call my cat in and get ready for my early start.

She got up, stretched and yawned, then opened the fire escape door and peered into the darkness.

'Fletcher? Are you there?' But the cat was punishing her by absence and silence; he would come in on his own terms.

The telephone rang, breaking shrilly into the peace of the flat. She closed the fire escape door and picked up the receiver.

'Eileen? Hello, it's Maureen.'

'Oh, hello, Maureen. Just back from work? How was it?'

'All right, but I thought I'd better tell you —'

'Hold on a minute, I can hear Fletcher scratching.'

She put the phone down and opened the fire escape door again. A damp and haughty cat stalked in, immediately leapt up onto the warm chair which Eileen had vacated, turned his back on her and proceeded to wash.

Eileen picked up the phone again. 'Sorry, Maureen. I am a slave to that cat. What were you saying?'

'I thought you'd want to know, Eileen, as you're coming on shift in the morning. Karen Colley is back, and she's slashed her wrists.'

Sunday 26 April 1998

Her mind full of other things, Eileen did not at first notice that nothing happened when she turned the key in the ignition. The deadness of her car brought her back to reality with unwelcome speed. The dashboard was in darkness. Sighing, she got out of the car and lifted the bonnet: a symbolic gesture, because although she looked with concentration and even poked a few things, the intricacies of a car engine were for her an unmapped wasteland.

She looked up and down the road. Predictably, it was deserted. She closed the car and crossed the churchyard again, weaving her way between the gravestones to the vicarage. Louis saw her coming and opened the door, his eyebrows raised enquiringly. 'Did you think of some knotty theological point? Or perhaps a pressing pastoral concern?'

'Neither,' Eileen said. 'Do you know anything about cars? Because my little treasure won't start, and I have to be at work at one-thirty.'

'Sorry, no. Such expertise as I have is largely confined to the Ivory Tower. I can drive you if you like.'

'Yes, please, Louis. I'm sorry if I am messing up what remains of your Sunday.'

Louis picked up his jacket. 'What are you going to do about the car?'

'Ring the breakdown people when I get home, I suppose.'

'Why don't you give me the keys and tell them to pick them up from me?'

'You're a saint.'

'Not yet, but I'm working on it.'

He opened his car and Eileen got in.

'Your place, then?' Louis said.

'Yes, please.'

'What about getting to work?'

'That's OK. There's a bus.'

'Are you sure?'

'Absolutely.'

'And getting home?'

'Another bus. I will be fine.'
Louis turned onto the main road and joined the roaring traffic. 'No Maureen this morning. Is she at work?'
Eileen frowned. 'No. She's on shift with me this afternoon.'
'How do you find the shifts?'
'I'm used to it.'
There was silence for a few minutes.
'How was your Easter lunch with your sister?' Eileen asked.
'Quite stimulating, as it turned out,' Louis said. 'She'd invited some of her colleagues, which was entertaining.'
'I didn't know you had a sister.'
'Strictly speaking Frances is my half-sister,' Louis said. 'She's the product of my father's second marriage, to the worthy Rosemary. I was thirteen when Frances was born, and I took a very dim view of it at the time. We get on surprisingly well now, though. I don't see her that often: she's a busy metropolitan woman.'
'What does she do?'
'She organizes events, concerts, that sort of thing, so she knows a lot of musicians and suchlike.'
'A far cry from preaching in Allerton.'
'Indeed. Though preaching has its theatrical aspects.'
'I'd noticed.'
'How is Christina?' Louis asked.
'As far as we know, all right. Holding on to sanity, working hard.'
'And you? Holding on to sanity too?'
Eileen looked at him sideways. 'More or less. Do you realize that next Sunday will be my last as organist? Muriel, I seem to remember, is due back on 5th May.'
'Somehow I had managed to bury that fact. I shall be sorry. What about you?'
'Hm. Kind of.'
Louis looked at her, smiled his amused smile, and said nothing. He pulled up at some traffic lights. 'So, anything thrilling going on in your life?'
'Well, if you call it thrilling, I started rehearsals for a performance of "Elijah" last Tuesday.'
'Oh? Where?'
'Osewick. I think I told you, I know the organist at the Abbey, Philip Elsdon. His wife's an old friend. Looking through my copy reminded me of some things I want to discuss with you.'
'Such as?'

'I can't remember chapter and verse, but it's the bits about wrath and judgment. And how, or so it would seem, God is particularly unfair and hard on his most faithful servants.'

'Ah. Well, I shall look forward to hearing your thoughts.' There was a hooting from the car behind.

'The lights are green, Louis.'

'So they are.'

Eileen looked out of the window. 'Look, there's Penny and Gus. They've come a long way.'

'A fast walker is our Penny. It's no use offering her a lift.'

'I know. She believes in exercise for herself and fresh air for Gus.' Eileen waved, and Penny, catching sight of her, grinned widely and waved back. As they passed, Eileen saw her bend down to her little son and point. Gus looked up and waved both arms.

'What a great little boy he is,' Eileen said. 'I don't think I've ever seen him cranky.'

'That could all change soon, couldn't it?' Louis said. 'I'm no expert, but he is coming up for two, isn't he? Isn't that when small children turn into monsters?'

'Could be. You know Penny pretty well, don't you, Louis? How long have you known her?'

'Ever since she came to St. Augustine's, very pregnant. Did you know I'm Gus's godfather?'

'No, I didn't. But it doesn't surprise me. Penny thinks the world of you.'

'Hm. She doesn't have that many supporters.'

'I know.'

'But you are one, I think.'

'I hope so.'

'Do you know much about her background?'

'Well, she told me once, after she'd had a glass of wine in my flat, in a sort of confiding fit, that Gus's father was a mate of her dad's. Apparently he gives her money for Gus once in a while, when he's flush, but she makes him post it. She doesn't want to see him. She doesn't seem to like him at all.'

'That's true. She also blames her father for not looking after her and leaving her vulnerable to the wiles of seducing middle-aged men. Penny was only eighteen at the time, and nothing like as street-wise as the average eighteen-year-old.'

'Of course she wasn't. She still isn't. What happened to her mum?'

'Died of cancer when Penny was eleven.'

'Poor kid.' Eileen was silent for a moment, then she said, 'Penny's a funny girl. She had a social worker come to see her the other day. She was terrified. She asked me to go down to be with her when the woman came. It was all routine enough, as far as I could tell, but Penny is always scared that they're going to take Gus away. Why would they do that? Penny may not be the brightest, but she is a lovely mum and Gus is a happy, healthy child.'

Louis nodded. 'Who knows, with Penny? Her thoughts are opaque to me. I've never known anyone name her baby after the parish church, for a start.'

Eileen smiled. 'True. She is keen on churchy things. But it suits him. Gus, I mean.'

Louis drew up at the kerb. 'Your palatial residence, madame.'

'Thank you, Louis. You have saved the day.'

'I thought your original plan was to move.'

'It was. This flat was supposed to be a stopgap till I found somewhere to buy. Renting seems such a waste of money.'

'So what happened?'

'I don't know. I like it here, it's handy for the shops, I like the neighbours, and it's reasonably quiet.'

'Might you move, though?'

Eileen got out of the car, shut the door and leaned in at the window. 'Maybe. Who can say? But Fletcher likes it here, and cats don't care for upheaval.'

Louis started the engine again. 'Penny's thoughts aren't the only ones that are opaque to me, I see. Fancy organizing your life round a cat.'

'I must fly. See you soon, Louis.'

By the time the bus wheezed to a halt outside the hospital it was ten to two and spitting with rain. Eileen half-ran along the covered walkway and into the main door, barely avoiding a porter pushing a wheelchair as she made for the lift. The corridors seemed endless, the people in them slow and aimless. As she tapped in the code on the C Block outer door she was panting and felt a stitch forming in her side. She pushed the door open and hurried down the ward. A solid figure in a white tunic came out of the doctor's room and held her at arm's length to avoid a collision. Distracted though she was she noticed the warmth and rough skin of his hands.

'Steady, love,' he said. 'Hell's army after you, is it?'

'Sorry, Josh.' Eileen gulped. 'My car wouldn't start, I had to take the bus, and it got stuck in all those road works by the flyover.'

'Go and get your coat off and cool down,' said Josh. 'You haven't missed much.'

'Anything I need to know?'

'Things are quiet, but we're short-handed.'

'No change there, then.'

'Maureen's rung in sick, so I've got Carol to fill in, but she can't get here for another hour. Ollie said he'd cover, but only till Carol gets here. Do you know what's up with Maureen?'

Eileen shook her head. 'No idea, I'm afraid. How's Karen?'

'Worrying about visitors.'

Eileen sighed. 'If they don't come she frets, if they do come they stress her out.'

'Soon as you're ready, go and chat to her. She's had her medication.'

'Will do. Thanks, Josh.'

'For what?'

'For not bawling me out for being late.'

'It's Sunday, Eileen. I try not to be nasty at weekends. It's bad for my heart. You should get a motorbike. I never have trouble with traffic jams.'

'I'd probably last about ten minutes on a motorbike in this town.'

Eileen crossed the ward and went into the nurses' room. She took off her coat, hung it up and put on her uniform. She put her bag into her locker and pocketed the key. As she passed the mirror she paused to smooth down her wind-blown hair. She wore it shorter these days, and people said it made her look younger. She smiled at her reflection. Any help she could get in that direction was welcome. She had never regained all the weight she had lost during her illness, and her reflection showed a tall, big-framed woman with fair hair, and bright eyes under brows that were several shades darker. She knew herself to be a different person from the one she had been two years ago. She even looked different. But the changes went much deeper, even if they were invisible. She supposed she was the same, at some level, similar enough to be recognizable; but she felt different, as if Christopher had set off something, jolted her out of her cautious, defensive rut, opened her up to new things. Or maybe she was just being fanciful.

She knocked on the door of the side room opposite the doctors' room.

'Come in.'

Karen Colley was sitting by her bed in an armchair. Beside her, perched on the edge of the bed, in her pyjamas, was Alice Walters.

Karen looked up wearily. Her arms, resting on the arms of the chair, were still heavily bandaged.

'Hello, you two,' Eileen said. 'I'll come back later as you're busy.'

Alice stretched and yawned. 'Hi, Eileen. I'll be off soon anyway. Josh keeps on at me to get dressed, so I suppose I'd better.'

Karen looked up at her and smiled faintly. Her face was yellow-pale and her eyes shadowed and sunken. A small, pretty, dark-haired woman, she looked older than her thirty-two years. 'You'd better make yourself presentable for when your visitors come, Alice,' she said. 'Have a shower, freshen up. You know what your mum's like.'

'You saying I smell or something?' Alice said, giving Karen a gentle shove.

'You teenagers are such slobs,' Karen said. 'Still in your PJs at two in the afternoon. It's not as if you've had a wild night, so you can't use that excuse.'

'All right, grandma. I'll go in a minute.'

Eileen closed the door. The fragile friendships that sometimes grew up on the ward were, she thought, often of more help to the patients than all the medical interventions. Karen and Alice would probably never have met, let alone been friends, anywhere but here, and Eileen felt mildly encouraged by the company and support they offered each other. She had seen Karen sobbing in Alice's thin arms. She had also heard her scold the girl for refusing food.

She walked further down the ward into the communal area. The tables had been put away, but the smell of lunch lingered. The TV was on, showing the repeat of a soap episode, and slouched round it, their backs to her, were the Unholy Trio, as she and Maureen privately called them: Marion Darlow, in her late forties, a wiry woman with a lined, thin-lipped face and scraggy hair tied back tightly in a pony tail, sat watching the screen with an expression of absorbed disapproval on her face. Beside her, curled up in her chair, sat Cathy Lloyd, younger, a chubby, busty blonde with pink cheeks, her short-sighted eyes behind thick lenses. These two formed a society of two who bolstered each other's opinions and echoed each other's frequent complaints. Recently they had added Jodie Parkes to their group, though she seemed an unlikely friend. Jodie was a thin nineteen-year-old with blonde hair showing dark roots. It was not clear whether she was suffering from schizophrenia or whether her escalating drug habit was giving her similar symptoms. She had referred herself after a frightening episode and was currently under observation. The other two were there suffering from depression, but after a stay of several weeks were now sufficiently stable to be considered for discharge.

'Afternoon, ladies. How are you?' Eileen said.

'We're cheesed off, if you must know, Eileen. Turn that garbage off, Cathy, can you,' Marion snapped.

Jodie protested, 'Hey, I wanted to see what happened!'

'This is more important, Jodie. You were moaning just as much as us,' Marion said.

Jodie subsided sulkily.

'So what's the problem?' Eileen said patiently, knowing that the problem was likely to be the same as it had been on her last shift, and the one before. Marion and Cathy were now well enough to be actively critical and self-righteous.

'It's having to share this place with so many weirdos,' said Marion. 'At least the old biddy's gone now, and not before time. I mean, how's anyone supposed to get any sleep with her yelling half the night?'

'Poor old Dorothy was very distressed, I know,' said Eileen. 'But she couldn't help how she was, and she's moved on now. There wasn't anywhere else for her to go at first. It wasn't ideal for anyone.'

'Where did they take her, anyway?' Jodie said.

'To a geriatric ward. It's difficult to know what to do with her. She's got nobody, and she can't look after herself. We might all come to that one day.'

'I'd top myself first,' Marion said. 'Anyway, we've still got the other two. And I can tell you, Cathy's dead worried. My kids are all grown up, and they don't live round here, but she's got youngsters thirteen, eleven and nine, and they come visiting us here in a place with two paedos.'

'If you're talking about Tony, we don't know that he's any such thing,' Eileen said.

'He was hanging around a school when they fetched him in, wasn't he? Wasn't it the police brought him in?'

'Yes. But he wasn't doing anything he shouldn't. Looking at Tony, I'd guess he didn't know where he was. He's lived on the road so long, away from other people, that nobody knew how ill he was. I think he's harmless. Maybe you ladies should be a bit more charitable.'

'I'm thinking of my kids,' said Cathy. 'My Eloise is at a dodgy age, you know, easily led astray.'

'You said you were concerned about someone else,' Eileen said.

The two older women leaned forward. Jodie hung back, her pale face blank.

'It's Carl,' Cathy said in a low voice. 'We think he might be one as well.'

'But you know as well as I do that Carl is here for a completely different reason,' Eileen said.

Cathy nodded. 'Yes, I know. He told us, when he first come in, he was having – what was it, Marion?'

'A psychotic episode,' Marion said, her lip curling. 'That's what he called it, anyway. At least he doesn't take drugs, not like some I know.' Jodie shifted uncomfortably in her chair. 'It's no good looking like that, Jodie. You know what I think about druggies.'

'So why is he suddenly a paedophile?' said Eileen.

'It's something he said to Jodie,' whispered Cathy. 'Isn't that right, Jodie?'

'I don't want to talk about it no more,' Jodie said, flushing. 'I'm fed up with talking about it. Maybe he's a paedo, maybe he isn't. But he's going out soon, so who cares?'

'What about all them kids he might be preying on out there? Don't you think of that?' Cathy said indignantly.

'Like I said, I'm sick of thinking about it. If you two don't want to watch TV, I'm going for a fag. You coming, Marion?'

'Yeah, might as well.' Marion got up. 'See you in a minute, Cath.'

'So why have you three got it in for Carl all of a sudden?' Eileen said when they had gone. 'I thought you liked Carl.'

'We did, at first,' Cathy said. 'He's a nice-looking bloke, nice to talk to. It was what Jodie said. But I think you'd better talk to her about it. Marion and I will be out of here soon, with any luck. I mean, how's being here, with all these weird sickos, supposed to help with depression?'

Eileen shook her head. She had tried on several occasions to make the women see things differently. 'Well, as you say, Cathy, with any luck you'll be going home soon. And I'm sure you can keep an eye on your kids and keep them safe. It's a dangerous world, and we all have to live in it.'

'You can say that again,' Cathy said.

They were interrupted by loud laughter coming from the open door of the kitchen. A round-faced black man in a tight-fitting uniform appeared, grinning widely. 'Hello, ladies! You look like you need a bit of cheering up.'

'Make us a cup of tea, Ollie,' Cathy said. 'I expect Marion and Jodie could do with one too. That might make us feel more normal.'

'Certainly, my love,' chuckled Ollie. 'Anything for you beautiful women. You know I only come to work to see you, don't you?'

'I believe anything of you, you African pervert,' Cathy said, sounding exactly like Marion. 'But you do make a nice brew, I'll say that.'

'All right, and then I must tear myself away from you and go off duty. I shall sit in my lonely flat and dream of you lovely creatures.'

'Very funny. So who's coming in?'

'Carol. Maureen's not well, apparently,' Eileen said.

'Carol's all right, but she's not as daft as you, Ollie,' said Cathy.

'It's my admiration for you that has turned my head, darling,' Ollie said, crowing with laughter as he went back to the kitchen to put the kettle on.

'I'll leave you to your tea, Cathy. See you later. Are your family coming in?'

'Supposed to be,' said Cathy, kicking her slippered toe against the chair leg. 'Though I don't know why they bother. Vince is always moaning about the kids, especially Eloise, and they're always moaning about him.'

'I expect they miss you at home,' Eileen said. 'It can't be easy for Vince coping with things all by himself.'

Cathy grunted. From what she had said in the past, Eileen suspected that her eagerness to leave the hospital was mixed with apprehension: her home life had clearly contributed to the sudden downturn in her illness.

'Here's Marion and Jodie back,' Eileen said. 'I'll leave you to it.'

Eileen walked down to the end of the ward. On the way she knocked on the door of the third side ward, where Tony Tully lived. There was no answer. She went to knock again, then paused. A loud snoring came from inside. She smiled and went on. Tony had been brought in by the police a few weeks ago; a head teacher had alerted them after he had been seen hanging around a school playground. Some of the children, and even more some of the parents, had become alarmed. Tony had been living rough all his adult life and had travelled the length and breadth of the country despite having only one leg. When he had been brought in he was very agitated and obviously delusional. Now a regime of rest and care and regular meals was having some good effect.

Further on down the ward Eileen put her head round the partition of the end bay. Carl Ryland was sitting alone, reading. He looked up as he noticed Eileen, smiled a little sadly and waved.

'You OK, Carl?' Eileen said.

He nodded.

'I'll come down for a chat later,' Eileen said. 'I just want to talk to Karen before visiting time.'

Carl nodded again. He never had visitors.

Eileen retraced her steps. As she turned into the short end of the Lshaped ward she heard laughter from the communal area. Ollie was being his usual exuberant self and making the unhappy women laugh.

Eileen knocked on Karen's door, opened it a crack and put her head round.

'Come in, Eileen. Alice has gone for a shower.'

'It's good to see you two are taking care of each other.'

Eileen pulled up a hard chair and took Karen's hands in her own. 'I haven't seen you in a while, Karen. How've you been?'

'You know I went home for the day, don't you? Just to see how it went.'

'Yes. How was it?'

'Not too bad. Chopper is a love, fussing round me all the time. I think he feels guilty. It was that row with him that made it all go wrong. You remember. But it's not really his fault. He can't change the situation, can he? That's always going to be there.'

'No, he can't change the past,' Eileen said. 'But it must help to have someone around who obviously loves you.'

'I know I'm lucky,' Karen said. 'I've put Chopper through a lot.'

This poor woman thinks she is lucky. She remembered coming in to work a fortnight before, the day after Karen had been admitted. Karen had been lying on her bed in the side ward, kept apart from the other patients because she was deemed actively suicidal, thin and pale against the white sheets, sedated and bandaged. Eileen had sat with her for an hour, holding her hand, listening to her, and although she knew Karen's story and was used to the horror of it, this new, flat, hopeless Karen made her ache with pity.

Dean and Karen Colley had been an unremarkable couple. Their son Bobby had just started at school, and their daughter Nicky was happily established at pre-school. Their modest house was decorated; the garden, complete with new decking, was neat and full of flowers. Dean was happy in his work, driving a breakdown lorry, and Karen had found a part-time job in a solicitor's office. When she became pregnant, the family rejoiced. Privately Karen had been broody for some time, but it had taken her a while to persuade Dean. After nine months with no special problems a healthy son was born to them, and they called him Simon. Karen went home from hospital with her baby and settled back into contented motherhood.

Then, when the baby was two weeks old, he disappeared. Karen had arranged to meet a friend, also with a young child, for a shopping expedition. The two women, with the babies' prams close by, had been looking at racks of clothes in a large, crowded shop. Their attention had been elsewhere for only a matter of minutes. When they went to reclaim their sleeping infants, Simon was gone.

Karen and Dean, and the rest of their family, were utterly distraught. Despite an intensive police investigation, no trace of their baby was ever found. No one reported hearing a baby cry in a house where there should have been no baby; no tiny body was ever discovered. Now, almost two years later, the investigation, while still officially active, had cooled, superseded by other, more pressing, cases. But for Karen it was the end of all her innocent happiness. Tortured by guilt and uncertainty, she fell prey to bouts of deep depression. Her marriage was an early casualty: Dean dealt with the loss in his own way, and was now living elsewhere. His girlfriend, Mel, a sweet-natured, gum-chewing blonde with long legs, had become a second, sunny mother to the two older children, who began to spend time shared between their parents. From time to time Karen, helped by her own mother and sister, picked herself up and tried to put her life back together. She found a new man, Duncan, always called Chopper because of a time when, working on an offshore oil-rig, he had almost lost his life to a helicopter. Chopper was an uncomplicated, sometimes foul-mouthed, but kindly man, and he adored Karen. But Karen's agony recurred.

'If Simon was dead,' she had said to Eileen, 'I could bury him and grieve and move on. But nobody knows what's happened to him. I dream about him all the time, and it freaks me out. Sometimes I think I'm going mad. Dean won't let the kids come round when I'm that bad. He says I scare them – my own kids! And now even Chopper's getting fed up. He's the best bloke in the world: he puts up with endless rubbish from me. Most of the time I can't be bothered with anything: the house is a mess, there's no food in the fridge, and I haven't even washed by the time he gets in from work. He's a patient man but everyone's got their limits, haven't they? I mean, sex is out of the window. We had a row, he threatened to leave, he told me I'd lose him and the kids, then he went to the pub to cool off. I knew he'd be back. I know he really loves me. I'm lucky to have him. But when he'd gone, I thought, Why bother? If I top myself it'll all be over. I'll never have to think about my Simon again. If he's dead, I'll be with him. If he's not, I won't care. So I found a razor-blade and got into the bath. But Chopper came back. And here I am.'

Now, two weeks on, Karen was no longer in that darkest pit of her personal hell from which self-destruction had seemed the only escape. Instead, she appeared resigned, terminally sad, a sadness broken only by anxiety. Could she convince her family that she was able to resume her life? Would they accept that she was "normal" enough to see and care for Bobby and Nicky? Sometimes she herself doubted her own ability to contribute to the care of her children, and it was this, more than anything, that had her teetering again on the lip of that terrible darkness.

Knowing that Karen felt useless and inadequate, that she needed to feel that someone relied on her and needed her attention, Eileen asked, 'How do you think Alice is doing? You probably know more than anyone about how she is, how she feels.'

'She's still way too thin. But I think that therapy she has, whatever it's called, is helping. You know she dreads visitors, don't you? Like I do, but for different reasons.'

Eileen nodded. 'Her family aren't the most understanding, it's true. Her dad seems to be totally out of his depth. But at least they keep on coming. That says something.'

'Alice is plain terrified of her mum,' Karen said. 'It made me feel awful when she said she wished I was her mum. Not that I'm old enough. Her mum means well, but she's a bit overpowering. And as for the little sister, call me old-fashioned but she needs a kick up the backside.'

Eileen smiled. 'I've never heard one of those being prescribed. But I know what you mean. And it's true, the people that love you the most can be the worst for you.' She got to her feet. 'I'm going to have a chat with Alice before visiting time. I'll pop in again later.'

Eileen found Alice sitting cross-legged on her bed, a towel wound round her head. She was looking at a small, battered photograph in a frame: a picture of herself in healthier, happier days, taken at the beach with half a dozen friends.

'That's him,' she said, pointing to one of the boys in the picture. 'That's Zak. I told you about him, didn't I? That's when I started having all those nightmares, after he died.'

'You nearly died yourself, your mum said.'

Alice nodded. 'I was in the back with Zak. I think he would have asked me out that day. There were six of us in the car; Jess was in the front with Nick, and Sam and Jamie were in the back with us. It was a tight squeeze and none of us had seat belts on. Yeah, I know it was stupid. Nick had only passed his test the week before. He'd been taking something earlier on, I don't know what. Anyway, you know what happened. I came round lying in the road. When they put me on the stretcher in the ambulance I saw a body covered with a sheet. It was only later I realized it was Zak. For ages I saw that every time I closed my eyes.'

'Do you think the accident, Zak dying, was what made you ill in the first place?'

Alice shrugged. 'People ask me that. I've asked it myself. I don't know. Things weren't great before. Mum got the idea at some parents' evening at school that I was clever, and she was forever going on at me to do loads of school work. She wanted me to do better than her, she said. She never had a job she liked. I don't think she liked being at home with me and Louise either. Not that I blame her. Louise was a little cow even then. I don't know how two sisters can be so different. She still behaves like a slag now, Louise does. You've seen what she dresses like. She's got some man hanging around that's twenty-nine. She's only fourteen but Mum and Dad have given up trying to make her change. She's got a filthy temper. Maybe they're scared of her. I think we must be what they call a dysfunctional family.'

'What about your dad?'

'Dad? He's OK, I guess, but no match for Mum, let alone Louise.'

'What did you have for lunch, Alice?'

Alice picked up an empty glass. 'This milkshake, and a piece of toast.'

'How much of the shake went down the sink?'

'None, I promise. I wouldn't lie to you. Anyway, it isn't worth the hassle. Mum will be in later. She'll be quizzing me about every calorie.'

'She wants to see you well.'

Alice sighed. 'You know what, the idea of going home isn't that great.'

'What's the alternative, though? There must be something other than wasting away.'

'I'm eating, OK? Nagging I don't need.'

'All right, Alice, I'm sorry. No more nagging. How do you think Karen is getting on?'

'She's not crying any more. She's just kind of dull. I told her about Zak. She was really kind. Do you think it might help if she had another baby? She's got a boyfriend, hasn't she? That bloke she calls Chopper?'

Eileen shook her head. 'She's very fragile. I don't know if she could cope.'

Alice nodded thoughtfully.

'I'd better go,' Eileen said. 'Come and see me later if you want. I'm here till nine-thirty.'

'OK. Maybe I will.'

Eileen heard Ollie shouting goodbye. In the staff washroom she found Carol Macnamara doing something to her makeup in front of the mirror.

'Hello, love,' she said to Eileen. 'This is a fine bloody Sunday, isn't it? I had to get my John to drive me in, and it's a good job we weren't stopped. He'd been in the pub at lunchtime, and I had to wake him up when Josh called me. I just hope he got home all right. He weren't best pleased at being dragged out, I can tell you.'

'Maureen seemed all right on Friday,' Eileen said. 'Maybe it's the flu.'

'Well, it might be, but I doubt it.'

Something about Carol's tone made Eileen look up. 'How do you mean?'

'She's a mate of yours, isn't she?' Carol said. 'Ever met her husband?'

'What, Des? Yes, once. I took her home one time and she invited me in. He seemed a nice enough bloke.'

'Oh, he's all right to talk to.'

'What are you getting at, Carol?'

Carol paused in the doorway. 'I wouldn't want to speak out of turn. Maybe she don't want to say anything to you. But I don't reckon things are as they should be in her house. You must have noticed how many so-called accidents she has.'

'What? Are you saying he's violent?'

'I don't know as I'd say that exactly. But I wouldn't be surprised to find he's not above fetching her one once in a while.'

'Why would he do that?'

Carol shrugged. 'You tell me, love. I wouldn't put up with it, that's for sure. And maybe I've got it all wrong. But I don't think so. You won't tell her I said anything, will you? I don't want to make no trouble.'

Eileen shook her head. 'No, of course I won't. I'll keep my eye on her, though.'

'You do that. She could do with a good mate, if I'm not mistaken.'

'Have you seen Josh anywhere?' Eileen said.

Carol, going past with an armful of clean sheets, shook her head. 'No, love. Not for a while. Have the visitors gone?'

'Just.'

'Some of the patients will need their feathers smoothing down, then.'

'Probably.'

'There's Josh, in the corridor. See you in the kitchen later.'

'Right.'

Josh came back into the ward, looking slightly furtive.

'What are you doing out there?' Eileen asked.

'I was just taking a look at the secure unit.'

'What for? There's nobody in it.'

'I know that. Come into the office a moment, Eileen.'

He shut the door behind them.

'You're being very mysterious, Josh.'

'At the risk of seeming unprofessional, I was actually hiding from Dawn Walters.'

Eileen laughed aloud.

'Ssh!' Josh said. 'Don't tell the entire world.'

'So why were you hiding from Dawn Walters?' Eileen said, grinning broadly.

'You know as well as I do. She'll pin me up in a corner and interrogate me down to Alice's last calorie. You can't get away from her. It's worse on Sunday. They've all got more time.'

'Well, don't worry. I fielded Dawn's questions for you.'

Josh sighed with relief. 'Thanks. I am in your debt.'

'Be sure I will call it in. Anyway, I just referred her to Dr. Caton's chart, and told her what Alice had eaten in the last twenty-four hours. She seemed content with that.'

'You are a genius. Nobody else can quite satisfy Dawn.'

'Maybe she can see that Alice is making progress and so she isn't quite so anxious. So, are we expecting anyone in the secure unit?'

'Not that I know of. There's been nobody there for over a year.'

'Longer, I think. Certainly not in my time. Who was the last one? I don't even know why someone would have to be in there.'

'The last one was that fellow who was up for murder. What was his name? Chapman, Eddie Chapman. Don't you remember? It was in the papers.'

'Yes, vaguely.'

'He was here for a few weeks for some kind of mental health appraisal. I wasn't a party to it. He's in jail now, of course.'

'Hm. So what sort of patient might be in there? Apart from criminals.'

Josh shrugged. 'People who can't be put with other patients in an open ward, whether for their own sake or the other patients'. Someone who might be violent or likely to do a runner. Anyone requiring tight security, special protection, or whatever. There are a number of different criteria.'

Eileen nodded thoughtfully. 'I'd better go and start thinking about the patients' suppers.'

'And I,' sighed Josh, sitting down at his desk, 'have some paperwork to do.'

'Nothing new there. Oh, Josh, I almost forgot. Did you know that the Unholy Trio are gunning for Carl?'

Josh looked up. 'In what way exactly?'

'They're calling him a paedophile. You know they think the same of poor old Tony, don't you? Well, now their righteous obsession has spread to Carl.'

'I wonder why.'

'I don't know, but I might find out from Jodie if I get the chance.'

'Jodie. There's a very vulnerable young woman. Well, since you seem to be the person everybody speaks to, I'll rely on you to keep me posted.'

'OK. Do you ever regret being promoted, Josh? With all this paper-chasing you aren't as close to the action as you must have been once.'

'True enough.'

'How long is it you've been in this job?'

'Mm, nine years. Before that I did twenty-two years in the Army.'

'Twenty-two years! So what was that like?'

'I realized it wasn't for me after a very short time. But I couldn't afford to get out, so I served the minimum. I saw a lot of action and a lot of tragedy. That's why I'm in this game now.'

'I'd like to hear about that some time.'

'Over a pint, perhaps?'

'What's this, a date?'

Josh grinned and pulled a sheaf of documents towards him. 'I wouldn't get too excited if I were you.'

'I'll try not to. Meanwhile I'll keep my ear to the ground as requested. See you, Josh.'

The shift ended, and handover was brief. Eileen put on her coat and looked out into an evening darkened by a misty drizzle. She trudged to the bus stop at the corner of the car park. By the time the bus arrived, ten minutes late, the rain was coming down steadily. Eileen climbed aboard, shivering, her shoes uncomfortably wet. The only other passenger was an elderly man in a long greasy raincoat. He slumped in his seat, asleep.

The bus ground on towards the city centre. Though it was brightly lit there were few people about. They hurried past, collars turned up against the weather, and the pubs were full as usual, their windows fogged. Eileen thought about the shopping trip she had had with Natasha the week before, looking for baby clothes and supplies. The shops had been quiet because the children were back at school, and it had been a pleasant morning, ambling from shop to shop with two stops for refreshment.

'Have you heard from Christie?' Eileen asked as she put her coffee cup down.

'Yes. Haven't you?'

'Not since the weekend. Anyway, I think she tells you more of what's really happening.'

'I'm not sure she tells me anything much. She says she's OK, bearing up, working hard.' Natasha shrugged. 'If it's all going wrong I wouldn't know. I can only take what she tells me. You know Christie.'

Eileen sighed. 'Kids. What a worry.'

'Hey,' Natasha protested. 'Not me, I hope.'

'Not now, but you've had your moments. I'm telling you, Tash, parenthood is no bed of roses.'

'That's OK. If little Horatio is a pain I'll hand him over to Sean.'

'Somehow I knew you'd have an answer.'

'Talking of babies, I've been thinking over what you were telling me about your neighbour Penny.'

'Oh? Why's that?'

'I don't know. She seems to have a bit of a murky past.'

'You watch too much TV. Penny's a bit of a victim, really, doing the best she can in the circumstances.'

'What if your vicar was really her little boy's dad?'

Eileen laughed. 'I thought Louis was gay, according to you.'

'It happens, Mum.'

'I dare say, in the pages of trashy magazines. But if it were true Louis would acknowledge Gus.'

'It would wreck his career, though, wouldn't it? And Penny does seem to like him rather a lot.'

'Penny is very fond of Louis. He's kind to her. He's Gus's godfather. And that, my speculating gossip-monger, is it.'

'Well, don't be too shocked if you find it's a different story.'

'I would be shocked. At the deceit involved. No, sorry to disappoint you, Tash, but I know Louis better than that. Gus's father is a man called Dave, a friend of Penny's dad from way back. I've seen her with him. He's in his forties, he has skinny legs and wears his hair in a pony tail. He's a builder of sorts. Penny keeps him at arm's length. She doesn't think much of him at all. In fact, she tries to keep well away from her dad and his circle, as if she wants to distance herself from her past.'

'She must have liked Dave at one time.'

'Who knows? Penny's very young and innocent in some ways. And she didn't have your advantage of a wise mother while she was growing up.'

'Yeah, yeah, Mum. Whatever.'
'Anyway, love, what about you? Horatio behaving as he should?'
'Yes, everything seems to be fine.'
'Sean OK?'
Natasha rolled her eyes. 'Sean is the most excited dad in the world. He's painting the spare room for the baby, whistling away, and he talks about him/her all the time. He's such a softie.'
Eileen smiled. 'So, everything going as planned.'
'I worry sometimes, though, Mum.'
'What about exactly?'
'Oh, you know, is this baby going to be OK, will I cope, what sort of life will he have.'
'The unknowability of the future. It comes to us all some time or other. It does concentrate the mind when you're going to have a baby, though.'
'I suppose. I'll just keep on eating well, read the right books and hope for the best. But you're right about the future. It's kind of spooky when you think about it.'

The bus trundled on into the suburbs, leaving the city centre glare behind. A few people got on, huddling silently in their damp clothes, staring out of the steamy windows into the night. Eileen thought about the city that was her home. The darkness hid some of the ugliness and chaos of construction and road works, and sometimes she was surprised by the unexpected beauty of the urban landscape, as now, seeing street lights in ranks, shining down on the black roadway wet from the rain, their chemical radiance fractured by the moisture in the air.

She remembered suddenly a print on Louis' study wall, of a painting by Brueghel the Elder called The Tower of Babel, a complex ziggurat of walls and rooms and buttresses, part-demolished or perhaps unfinished, and it made her think of this city with its milling thousands, this hub of human activity, ingenuity, anonymity and crime. Here she felt comfortably hidden and yet also alienated; she thought with a pang of nostalgia of the woods and fields of Holton, and of the tainting of Caxford, Georgina, Stephanie and Christopher by the seeping poison from London. Here in Allerton it was the same, if on a smaller scale: here was Louis' empty church, one among many; here were the huddled groups of children in playgrounds and shop doorways and on street corners, dealing in drugs; here were the patients that Eileen saw every day of her working life, their dislocated minds and skewed imaginations a symbol of the society from which they sprang. Here was the teeming hive, vital and restless, full of shifting tides of population and passing fashion, creating both order and havoc, building, destroying, breaking down and throwing together.

She was reminded of something Louis had said about the city as an image. The prophet Micah blamed Israel's rebellion on its capital, Samaria, and Judah's idolatry on Jerusalem, and yet, a few pages later, this same prophet spoke of the Lord's teaching coming from Jerusalem: "...from Zion he speaks to his people." She shook her head. Nothing was ever simple. The more she thought about it the more mysterious it seemed. Of all man-made things a great city was the place where the myth of autonomy could most easily be fostered, perhaps because those who lived there were at many removes from the sources of their sustenance. If you could go into an all-night supermarket and buy a pint of milk, why think about the dairy farmer and the cow? And maybe the historical closeness to nature of the country-dweller was more likely to breed a sense of littleness and dependency. At Babel human beings set out to usurp the proper place of God; in the modern city – and not only there – the same arrogance was everywhere. Now the supremacy of humanity was broadly regarded as self-evident. *And yet what can any of us really do? At the end of it all is death, which defeats all our posturing. I must talk to Louis about these things. No doubt he will have been there already; he's always ahead of me.*

Thinking about Louis made her realize that the bus was approaching her stop. She got up from her seat and went to the front. The bus groaned to a halt.

'Goodnight, love,' said the driver, a small woman with ginger hair and a coat several sizes too big. 'Mind how you go.'

'Yes, thanks. Goodnight.'

The breeze was freshening. As the tail lights of the bus disappeared under the railway bridge Eileen zipped up her jacket and walked briskly in the direction of home. It was only a few hundred yards, but at this time of night she knew better than to be lost in her thoughts, even in her quiet neighbourhood. She kept every sense alert till she reached her front door; but the street was empty.

She let herself in and slowly climbed the stairs, feeling suddenly tired.

Tea. Pyjamas. The late news. A comfortable bed, a warm cat for company. No more thinking for today.

Thursday 7 May 1998

'I'm sorry to be so late, Eileen.' Marie came in flustered, smelling of fresh air and perfume. 'I can't believe how difficult it is to get around this town on a bus.'

'I know, only too well,' Eileen said. 'The few days my car was off the road were grim. Not to worry – you're here now.'

'I hope you haven't cooked anything that's spoiled.'

'Not at all.' Eileen smiled as she hugged her friend. 'It's hard to wreck soup and sandwiches.'

Marie shed her coat. 'So is your car all right now?'

'Ssh. Don't give it any ideas. It's very old, and the man at the garage says it's hanging by a thread. But I can't afford a new one. Sit yourself down and I'll go and warm up the soup. Shall we open a bottle and drown our sorrows?'

'Why not?' Marie said. 'It might just send me off to sleep on that dreadful bus home.'

'Philip couldn't drive you today, then?'

Marie sighed, taking a glass of wine from Eileen. 'No. He's had to go to some dreary meeting. They're forever having meetings at the Abbey. What about I hardly know.'

'Let's hope Philip is better informed.'

'Well, do you know, I don't think he is half the time. I think he sleeps through most of them.'

'The soup's ready. Come and have it while it's hot.'

Marie pulled up a chair.

Eileen said, 'So, tell me, how's Stephanie?'

'Astonishing,' Marie said. 'Full of quiet determination and good humour.'

'Well, well. How long do you think she's got in there now, Marie?'

'If she doesn't mess up, she could be out in a year.'

'And then?'

'She has plans, but I can't keep up with her. Somehow, once they let her out, I get the feeling we won't see her for dust.'

'Well, she's stuck it out this long without cracking. It looks hopeful, doesn't it?'

'I hope so, dear. I do hope so. Wretched child.'

They were silent for a moment or two, drinking their soup. Eileen refilled their glasses and passed Marie the plate of sandwiches.

'Marie, there's something I want to pick your brains about,' she said. 'But it's a bit sensitive, so feel free to tell me to shut up.'

'Pick my brains? I wouldn't have thought there'd be much to pick.'

'That's nonsense.'

'Well, go on – what is it?'

'There's someone I know at work, and at church, a friend – I've mentioned her to you: Maureen Parry. She was off sick a while back when she should have been on shift with me, and the woman who came in to cover for her, someone who's known her for longer than I have, was dropping some dark hints that she might be getting knocked about at home. I've seen her since, and she's not bruised from head to foot or anything like that, and she seems normal enough. She's a quiet, shy person anyway. I just wondered, with your experience, if you could shed any light on this whole domestic violence thing.'

'Well.' Marie frowned. 'I wouldn't call myself an expert, and I don't think my experience was typical at all – if there is such a thing, which I doubt. Ray, as you know, was fine at first. But I think he was a bit of a psycho, to be honest with you. Have you met Maureen's husband?'

'Des? Yes, once. He seemed all right. Certainly not a hulking, broken-nosed, drunken monster.'

'Does she talk about him much?'

'Not really. She's not a gushing woman anyway – more the guarded sort.'

'Not like me, then.'

'No.'

'Do you know anything about their circumstances?' Marie asked.

Eileen thought for a moment. 'I don't think things are especially easy. Des was made redundant about six months ago, quite suddenly. He worked for a small engineering firm and it had to make swingeing cuts or go bust. He'd been there years, so I think he was quite bitter. And he seems to be one of those men whose life is work. He doesn't seem to have any interests much.'

'Family? Pets?'

Eileen shook her head. 'One son, living in Canada with a wife and baby. Maureen would love to visit, but they're living on her pay now. Actually, I think they've got savings from what she's said, but Des is one of those careful, old-fashioned types who'd rather go without than spend.'

'Mm. The way you're telling it, it seems not impossible.'

'But what do I do? Should I say anything? She's a very private soul.'

Marie shook her head. 'I suppose you could ask her if everything was OK, as she's been looking a bit out of sorts. Let her know you're around if she needs you. After that it's up to her.'

'Yes. Perhaps I'll do that. I don't want to poke my nose in, but I wouldn't want her to think I didn't care.'

'She's probably ashamed to say anything.'

'It's hardly her fault, is it?'

'No, but it seems a kind of failure when you're in it.'

'Do you want some pudding?'

'No thank you, dear. I'm absolutely stuffed. I'm getting a bit too rounded as it is.'

'I'll make some coffee, shall I?'

'That would be nice.'

Eileen took plates and bowls to the kitchen, and Marie kicked off her shoes and stretched out on the sofa.

Then the phone rang, its shrill jangle breaking the peace. Eileen came back, drying her hands, and picked up the receiver.

'Eileen?' It was Louis. 'I'm sorry to disturb you, but I need to talk to you. Today, if possible.'

'What's up, Louis? You sound quite agitated.'

'I'd rather not go into it on the phone. Could you come over?'

'Yes, but later. I've got a friend here for lunch at the moment.'

'I'm so sorry, breaking into your day off.'

'Don't worry. I'll see you later on this afternoon.'

'Thank you. See you then.'

Eileen put the phone down, pulling a mystified face. 'My vicar,' she said to Marie. 'Sounds in a bit of a state.'

'I gather he can be something of a drama queen,' Marie said.

Eileen smiled. 'I wouldn't quite say that. He does get a bit intense at times. But most of the time he's a lovely man, very clever, too good for this little backwater. I'll drop by later and see what's getting him steamed up.'

'I can't stay long anyway,' Marie said. 'I'll have to disappear soon. With the bus service as it is I probably won't get back to Osewick before tomorrow.'

Eileen laughed. 'I hope it's not quite that much of an expedition. But it's been great seeing you – twice in one week! – and I'm glad Stephanie's doing OK.'

Louis let Eileen in. His lips were shut tight, as if to keep in unwelcome words, and his face radiated anger. Eileen had never seen him like this.

'I think we'll go through to the study,' he said, and led the way without further ceremony down the dark hallway. Eileen noticed the threadbare carpet and the walls in need of paint, and she wondered if the gloom of this nineteenth-century vicarage ever settled on his spirits like a damp blanket. But then, Louis' moods came from within, and outer circumstances had little power over him. Even so, it might be time some money was spent on his neglected place. No doubt had Louis been a family man his wife and children might long since have protested against the dreariness of the house.

'Do come in, Eileen,' Louis said. Eileen noticed a sigh of resignation in his voice and a lightening of his tone, and she realized with some relief that if he was angry she was not the cause. She sat down on the ancient bulging sofa and looked at him enquiringly. He perched on the edge of his cluttered desk and folded his arms.

'If I had known you had a guest I wouldn't have called,' he said. 'I'm beginning to think I have rather over-reacted. In fact I feel badly at dragging you over here.'

'My friend had to leave anyway,' Eileen said. 'She has to go all the way to Osewick on the bus. Are you going to tell me what the problem is or keep me in suspense?'

'Yet again,' said Louis, with a bitterness that was almost comic, 'Muriel has let us down.'

'Oh, she's back, then.'

'Yes, and she lost very little time in marching over here and announcing her intentions.' He began speaking like Muriel with unnerving accuracy. '"No sense in starting what I don't mean to carry on, Vicar. I'm not as young as I was. And you can't say as I haven't given good service. Anyhow, you've got someone else, I hear."'

Eileen smiled despite herself. 'I gather Muriel has decided to resign as organist, then.'

'Well, it seems that she has been thoroughly reconciled with her sister Sylvia and all the New Zealand branch of the family, to the extent that she plans to sell up here and go over there to live out her remaining days. Just like that, and as soon as possible. I pointed out to her that you had taken over merely as a stopgap to cover her holiday. Frankly, she has shown herself in her true colours as a high-handed, self-centred old bat.'

'I won't tell anyone you said that.'

'No, please don't. As I said, I expect I am over-reacting. But I am dismayed, to say the least, on your account as much as my own. Not that I don't want you to carry on: I'd much rather have you than Muriel. At least you don't insist on calling me "Vicar" and "Reverend" in that very untruthful way.'

'I'll try to remember not to use those terms of respect.'

'And now,' Louis growled, 'I shall no doubt be expected to thank her for her faithless defection. I shall feel a complete hypocrite.'

Eileen said mildly, 'But Louis, you won't be thanking her for her defection, as you put it. You'll be thanking her for what she has done over the years, not for ceasing to do it. And, you know, she has the right to resign, even if we think her method's a bit unfortunate and puts us about.'

'You are quite right, of course. I shall be gracious when it comes to it, even if through gritted teeth. But what am I going to do?'

'Ask me to stay on.'

'Would you?' He looked suddenly pleading.

'Yes, of course I will. Anything to defuse this fury. It can't be good for you. Anyway,' she added, 'it's not so bad. As long as you understand that I can't always play if I'm on shift, I'll battle on. Think of the unequalled opportunities it will give me to quiz you on matters of faith and theology. You might come to regret asking me.'

'I suppose one good turn deserves another,' he said, a gleam of merriment lighting his dark eyes. 'Didn't you say you had something to chew over with me?'

'Yes,' she said. 'Elijah. What a man. But it struck me that he was a good example of the way God apparently ill-treats his most faithful servants.'

'Ah,' said Louis. 'And as a natural corollary, he lets the wicked prosper – or so it seems to our limited sight. Well, you're in good company. Quite a few psalms are on that very theme.'

'The bit that makes me sad is when Elijah says, "O Lord, I have laboured in vain, yea, I have spent my strength for naught." Somehow I imagine you might feel like that sometimes, Louis. Not that I think you are spending your strength in vain. But there are so few of us here, and I can never tell who's awake.'

'Miaow. No, if that thought comes to me, I try valiantly to banish it. I like to think that God hasn't quite finished with me yet. And there are lots of places in the Bible where this problem is addressed.'

'Go on, if you have the time.'

'It's the least I can do after dragging you out on your day off to listen to my sorry rants.'

He went to his desk and sat down, picking up his Bible which lay open there and leafing through it. 'Here we are: Job 5 verse 17. Now there was an innocent man, a good man, you might justly think, whose suffering was apparently permitted by God. It says, "Happy is the person whom God corrects! Do not resent it when he rebukes you. God bandages the wounds he makes; his hand hurts you, and his hand heals."'

'It's an uncomfortable thought, God hurting you.'

'It is, but I don't think it means gratuitously. Listen to this. Hebrews 12, 7-11: "Endure what you suffer as being a father's punishment; your suffering shows that God is treating you as his children. Was there ever a child who was not punished by his father? If you are not punished, as all children are, it means you are not real children, but bastards. In the case of our human fathers, they punished us and we respected them. How much more, then, should we submit to our spiritual Father and live! Our human fathers punished us for a short time, as it seemed right to them; but God does it for our own good, so that we may share his holiness. When we are punished, it seems to us at the time something to make us sad, not glad. Later, however, those who have been disciplined by such punishment reap the peaceful reward of a righteous life." The inescapable conclusion is, I am afraid, that God wants us to be holy rather than happy. And people being what they are that means discipline, protracted and painful.'

'Probably not a good idea to tell that to the tentative looker-in at the church door.'

'If there were such a creature, I would be as gentle as a lamb. But if he or she were looking, it would probably mean they had begun to suspect that there is more to life that pleasing yourself for eighty years and diving into oblivion at the end of it.'

'Sometimes I ask myself if I am hardy enough for this tough trek.'

'Well, you know the answer to that, I imagine. You aren't. No one is. But he has promised to walk with us, and he will pick us up when we fall down. And if we chafe at how hard it is, if we start to think he is nastier to us than anyone else, remember he did it to his own son too. "Christ himself carried our sins in his body to the cross, so that we might die to sin and live for righteousness. It is by his wounds that you have been healed." 1 Peter 2. And there's that prophetic passage in Isaiah 53, where he speaks of the Servant being "pierced for our transgressions and crushed for our iniquities."'

Eileen sighed. 'If only it wasn't all so mysterious.'

'You can hardly expect it to be anything else,' Louis said, smiling.

'But everything I have ever read, thought, suffered and prayed about, till now, tells me that, however it seems on the surface, I can be sure that God has got it covered.'

'That's some faith.'

'Well, if you read a bit more about Elijah, though he despaired of being able to bring the Israelites back to God, he was one of the few who were actually seen to be particularly honoured. He was whisked away to heaven in the fiery chariot and missed out on death altogether. Which is more than you can say for poor old Isaiah.'

'Why, what happened to him?'

'Tradition has it he was martyred by being sawn in two.'

'That's vile.'

'That's us humans for you. We're a very nasty bunch.'

'Well, I know when you look at history you see a lot of examples of cruelty, and it's still going on, of course. But the fact is that you and I meet people who seem to be pretty nice on the whole, not brutal or sadistic.'

Louis nodded. 'But sometimes that can lead to a general blanket of self-satisfaction which blinds you to the realities of the situation. Perhaps if you are an obvious and extreme sinner you are more likely to see it and repent. I'm working on a sermon at the moment, as it happens, on the theme of rebellion and repentance. Not sure when I'll preach it yet, but you're going to be obliged to be around most Sundays now, so I guess you won't miss it.' He grinned, his eyes crinkling. 'Lucky you.'

Eileen was silent for a moment, deep in thought. 'Louis, that bit about your father punishing you, the whole idea of God as your father, don't you think that might be a real barrier to some people, especially if their own father didn't match up? Did your father punish you? Did you respect him as a result? Did it do you good, do you think? I'm thinking about my dad now; he was a quiet, peaceful sort of man and I can't remember being punished exactly.'

'I think it can be a problem, the whole thing about your attitude to fatherhood and your own experience. But even good fathers aren't perfect, and we have to see God as being the perfect ideal of fatherhood, which we can all relate to in some way, I imagine.'

'Did you get hauled over the coals as a boy?'

'Constantly. My father was a teacher at a small public school for boys, so he knew their evil ways intimately.'

'Did you go to his school?'

'Yes, until I was thirteen. Then, fortunately, I was sent to boarding school.'

'Did you like it there?'

'It was good in parts. But I was away from home a lot, which suited me fine.'

'How come, if you don't mind me asking?'

'It isn't very exciting, or anything out of the ordinary. My father was a good enough father and he didn't beat me, if that's what you were thinking. No, nothing like that. Just before I went to boarding school he remarried. Nice enough woman, Rosemary, but we never got on. She didn't like me much, I'm afraid. I expect I was troublesome. Then the following year my sister was born and I was only too pleased to be out of the way. I was not at all impressed with babies and regarded my father's marriage as treachery. No doubt I was very hard on him.'

'What happened to your mother?' Eileen asked.

'She died of cancer in 1965.'

'How old were you?'

'Nine.'

'Poor Louis.'

'Yes. I was very devoted to my mother and Rosemary was no substitute. Once Frances came along my father didn't have much time for me, so I buried myself in books. Which was no hardship at all.'

'Quite a lonely childhood.'

'Perhaps, but I wasn't a rough-and-tumble outgoing sort of boy anyway. I was a weedy bespectacled bookworm. Still am.'

Eileen laughed. 'What a description. So what then?'

'Do you really want to hear my entire biography?' he said, his eyebrows raised.

'Why not?'

'In that case I shall go and put the kettle on. Come down to the kitchen. It's friendlier than this gloomy hole, if still the predictable pigsty.'

Eileen followed him down the stairs. In the kitchen he pushed aside some of the unwashed pans and dishes and filled the kettle.

'I want to know how you came to be here, a parish priest,' Eileen said.

'Ah. Yes, well, I was, as I said, a bookish lad and I got a scholarship to Jesus College, Cambridge to read history. It was a symbolic choice, in the light of what was to come.'

'So what happened?'

'I was converted in my final year. But I think that will have to be another story. I went to a theological college, also in Cambridge. At my ordination selection conference I was told I should seek a little more knowledge of the outside world – quite rightly, you may say. I endured two not particularly successful years of teaching. Then I was ordained, aged twenty-six, still wet behind the ears, but full of piercing insights, or so I believed. After that I spent three years as a curate, six in a rural parish, and came here, as you know, seven years ago.'

He handed her a mug of tea. 'I'll just see if I've got any milk.'

'Don't worry, Louis. I'll have it black.'

She sipped her tea, which was very strong and very hot. 'Have you had a communication from Penny?'

Louis looked up. 'A communication? What do you mean?'

'Nothing to worry about – it's just that you will be receiving an invitation shortly to Gus's birthday party.'

'Nothing to worry about, she says. I dare say you are expecting one as well.'

'Mine has arrived. Penny made them herself. Nothing but the best for Gus.'

'But his birthday isn't until next month, if I've remembered it right.'

Eileen nodded. 'June 11th. But you know Penny. She likes to be well prepared. I babysat for her yesterday while she went round the shops looking for presents for him.'

'Do I really have to go?' Louis groaned. 'I'm not one for children's parties. I have to visit the Sunday School one, of course, but that's a once-a-year painful duty that I'm resigned to.'

'Penny would be terribly disappointed if you didn't.'

Louis sighed. 'I suppose there'll be scores of tempestuous toddlers and loud young mothers there.'

'I don't think Penny knows that many people. I reckon it will be a select little gathering.'

'Oh well, if you are going I dare say I can bear it.'

'Thanks.'

'Sorry, that did sound a bit damning-with-faint-praise.'

'You know, Louis, I do think there's something strange about Penny. Have you been in her flat recently?'

'No.'

'It's spotless. There isn't any junk, and she never keeps things. Obviously Gus has clothes and lots of toys, but as soon as he's grown out of them they are dispatched to the charity shops. Penny takes a sack regularly when she goes out. She hangs them from the handles of Gus's buggy. I wonder if she feels she has to be a sort of super-parent. Maybe it's connected to her fear that Social Services will swoop down one day and whisk Gus away for ever. Or maybe she's trying to compensate for the rather chaotic life she had with her dad.'

'I can't say that I have any insight into the workings of Penny's mind. She is a dear girl and a muddle.'

'You probably think I am being fanciful, but I do sometimes think there is more to Penny than she's letting on. I told you she gets rid of everything the moment it's surplus to requirements. Yesterday while I was looking after Gus we were having a game of hide-and-seek and Gus hid himself in Penny's wardrobe. I knew where he was because he hasn't quite mastered the art of hiding quietly yet. When I found him – after lots of walking around saying loudly, "Oh dear, wherever could Gus be? I can't find him anywhere. He must have run away to sea," etcetera – I flung open the wardrobe doors with exclamations of amazement, and out tumbled Gus, giggling fit to burst. But I also saw, stuffed at the back, a sack. Perhaps I shouldn't have looked in it, but I did, and it had baby clothes in it, tiny things, suitable for a very young baby, and a quilt and a blanket and a few soft toys. I didn't really think anything of it; I thought perhaps these were the only things Penny was sentimental about and couldn't bear to part with, for some reason meaningful to her. But when she came home I offered to take the sack to the charity shop as I was going myself soon, and her reaction baffled me. She blushed and stuttered as if she had some guilty secret.'

'Nothing is completely straightforward with Penny. You know that. It probably doesn't mean anything. What could it mean?'

Eileen shook her head. 'I don't know.'

'You, on the other hand,' said Louis, looking at her unnervingly, 'I feel sure you have plenty of skeletons in the closet.'

'Why do you say that?'

'It's the way you head off any personal enquiries with bland generalities,' Louis said. 'And if you feel someone is getting too close you remember a pressing engagement.'

Eileen laughed. 'You might be right,' she said, putting down her mug. 'As it happens, I do have to go to the supermarket.'

'Ha! You see what I mean?'

'My cupboard is bare. My cat is hungry. And as to "bland generalities," perhaps that's because my life has been generally bland and devoid of interest.'

'That I don't believe.'

Eileen pushed her trolley slowly up and down the supermarket aisles. The schools were out, and the place was full of mothers with small, tired children. Eileen was distracted and annoyed with herself. Louis was right: she did shrink from any personal revelation. Had she always been like that? Or was it something she had learned to do since Christopher, always wary and covering her tracks? And yet such a short time ago she was contemplating telling Louis about Christopher. Sometimes it was so strong, that feeling that she must, she should, tell someone, that it would lift a huge weight from her; but she was afraid, that was the long and short of it. And would it give her another, different load to bear? Was her friendship with Louis strong enough for this? How well did she really know him? And how was it that he so often seemed to know what she hadn't ever mentioned? She shivered. He was a strange man.

She shook herself mentally and brought herself back to the present. *I must concentrate, or I shall go home with nothing that I need.* Mechanically, avoiding buggies, smiling at five-year-olds, she put things in her trolley and lined up at the checkout.

But there as she stood in the queue, feeling suddenly weary, another worrying thought came to peck at her like some insistent bird. When Louis had asked her, giving her that slightly-frowning look of his, what meaning Penny's bag of baby clothes could have, she had answered, hastily, fearfully, that she didn't know. And that was the truth, as far as it went: she didn't know. But that pecking bird would not let her rest. Try as she might to thrust the thought away, the image of Karen Colley, pale and grieving, rose up in her mind.

For heaven's sake! What is the matter with you? Haven't you got enough to think about that you have to see coincidences as conspiracies? Forget it. Your imagination's running out of control.

She drove home. Thinking about Penny and Gus's birthday she remembered another invitation that she had received by post a day or two earlier. Here was someone else who was alarmingly well-organized: Andrea Caton, wife of the psychiatrist responsible for many of the C Block patients. Every year in mid-June the Catons held a barbecue for the C Block staff in their large, tree-lined, immaculate garden, or, if the weather was unkind, in the vast tiled sun room at the back of their spacious and beautifully-appointed house in a leafy suburb to the north of the city. Eileen cast her mind back to last year's party. She had been new to the unit then, feeling her way, knowing very few people and none of them well, and going to work on every shift feeling apprehensive and unequal to the patients' problems. Maureen had not gone to the barbecue, and Eileen found herself alone, nursing a glass of some kind of fruit punch, wishing someone she knew would arrive. Then Josh came, and she knew him, if not very well, and she was relieved. He spoke briefly to his hosts and took a drink, then came over the neatly-mown grass to where she stood under a cherry tree. They had chatted for a while, then Josh had said in a low voice, 'I don't know about you, but I'm not a great one for these gatherings. I come to show willing, but there's something that annoys me about the Catons' dos. It's all a bit too like distributing largesse to the peasants.'

'Nice garden, though,' Eileen said. 'I miss my old garden, living in a flat. Window boxes aren't quite the same.'

Josh nodded. 'I'm not much of a gardener myself, so I don't mind not having one. But sometimes I do miss the countryside. I remember being a boy in Yorkshire and walking the hills with our old mongrel. Smelly, hairy old thing he was, but tough as nails.'

'Whereabouts was that?'

'I grew up in a village not too far from Wakefield. My family are all still up there.'

'Do you ever go back?'

'Once in a long while.'

'So what brought you down south? I thought most Yorkshiremen were snooty about the Home Counties.'

Josh grinned. 'They can be. I came down here for work. And, I suppose, to escape my past.'

'You make it sound intriguing. What did you leave behind? A life of crime?'

Josh shook his head. 'Just a washed-up marriage.'

'Sorry,' Eileen said. 'It's none of my business. I shouldn't be so nosy.'

'Water under the bridge, love,' said Josh. 'Distant past.'

He had left not long after that, exchanging civilities with different people as he passed. Eileen felt a little bereft and made her own excuses soon after. Now she wondered if he would go to this year's party. She hoped he would. Josh was a good boss and a friendly man, but reserved. Eileen knew little enough about him, except that he lived in a flat in a run-down area of the city and rode a huge black motorbike which he kept in perfect condition. On the days when they left the hospital at the same time she had seen him roaring away, free of the clogging traffic, with the deep-throated sound that such big machines make, and wondered what he did when he was not at work. Did he spend hours maintaining the bike, read philosophy, go fishing or to evening classes? Was there a girlfriend, perhaps, that visited, filled his off-duty hours? Nobody seemed to know.

She dragged herself back to the present. For once there was a parking space right outside her flats and she pulled into it. She saw Penny's curtains twitch and a moment later Penny herself appeared on the top step.

'Hello, Eileen,' Penny said breathlessly. 'Been to the shops?'

'Just the supermarket,' Eileen said, opening the boot of her car. 'Nothing fascinating.'

'I got some great things yesterday for Gus's birthday.'

'Yes, you said.'

'I couldn't show you them straight away because he was still up. Do you want to come down later on, when he's asleep, and see what I got him? You're not going out, are you?'

'No, I'm not going out. Unless some dashing bloke rolls up in a sports car and insists on taking me out to dinner.'

Penny giggled. 'Wouldn't that be nice!'

Eileen carried her bags inside. 'I don't know if I could cope, not after a day at work,' she said with a smile. 'I'd have to send him down to you. Give me an hour or two to put my shopping away and feed Fletcher and make myself something to eat, then I'll pop down and see what you've bought.'

Eileen went downstairs in her slippers at eight o'clock and tapped gently on Penny's door. Penny let her in, putting her finger to her lips as if Eileen had been stamping and shouting. 'He took ages to go off tonight,' she whispered. 'I had to tell him four stories before he'd let me go. Come in, Eileen. Do you want a cup of tea or anything?'

'No thanks, Penny.'

She glanced around the flat. Considering that Penny had only just got her not-quite-two-year-old to sleep it was very tidy.

'I don't know how you do it, Penny,' she said. 'You're a lot neater than me, and I've only got myself to blame for the mess. Fletcher doesn't really count.'

'Ah, well, you see, Eileen,' Penny said, nodding wisely, 'I always get rid of stuff straight away. That's the secret.' She blushed suddenly, the blood rising vividly in her already rosy cheeks. 'I must have just forgotten that old bag of Gus's baby stuff in the wardrobe – silly, aren't I!' She laughed in an odd, high-pitched way. 'Anyway, I've done it now. Taken the whole lot to that charity shop on Market Street.'

'That's a long way for you, isn't it? There must be a nearer one.'

'Yes, but the lady in that one is much nicer. She talks to me and Gus and doesn't start frowning and giving us dirty looks if the buggy's in the way or we've been there too long.'

'Oh, I see.'

'Anyway, Eileen, come through to the kitchen. I'm going to have a cup of tea even if you won't.'

Eileen spent the next half hour admiring Penny's purchases and chatting about nothing much. Then she got up with a yawn.

'I must go, my dear. Gus will love his presents, I'm sure. He's a lucky lad.'

Penny followed Eileen to the door. 'I'll just look in on him,' she whispered. 'Make sure he's covered up. Sometimes he kicks his quilt off.'

Gingerly she opened the door to the tiny box room where Gus slept. In the dim light from the hallway Eileen caught sight of him, flat out, his spiky hair dark against the pale blue pillow, his arm around a one-eared toy dog.

'He looks very peaceful,' she said as Penny closed the door. 'Goodnight, Penny. Be seeing you.'

Unusually for her, that night Eileen lay awake. It was a clear night, the moon sailing high in a dark blue sky with only the odd wispy cloud. For a while she sat at the window, looking out into the darkness. The deep glow of the city centre lights never went out, but here on the edge the street lights were further apart, and the roofs of the houses on the other side of the road were black against the blue. There was little traffic now, just the occasional whoosh of tyres on the tarmac and tail lights disappearing into the distance.

She sighed. Her thoughts would not be silent. She thought about her conversation with Louis, and wondered what he was going to put in his sermon on rebellion and repentance. *Have I truly repented? I don't know. How do you tell? I don't know that either. Sometimes I think I know almost nothing. Maybe that's the truth of it.* Why was she worried about Penny now, after all this time? It had to be because of Karen Colley. But why would she ever think that Penny could steal someone's baby? Just because Gus was the right age. So were many hundreds of little boys in the city. And maybe Simon Colley wasn't in Allerton any more. Maybe he wasn't even in England. Maybe, God forbid, he was dead. Something was nagging at her, but it wasn't anything factual. It had to be just her imagination, which didn't put her in a very good light at all. How had she become so suspicious? Neurotic, even? Even if Penny had been capable of such a terrible thing, how was it possible that she had never been found out? It was all nonsense, anyway. Louis had said he had first got to know Penny when she came to live in the flats here and first went to St. Augustine's, obviously pregnant. He had known Gus since his birth. He had baptized him. But why would Louis think anything was wrong? He didn't know Karen, and Eileen couldn't tell him. The only other person who knew both Karen and Penny was Maureen, and she didn't seem to have these mad thoughts. *It's just me. What is the matter with me?*

She went to the sideboard and poured herself a small brandy, shuddering as it burned her throat going down. The sleeping face of Gus came to her unbidden, and her heart seemed to constrict as she thought, against her own wish, that maybe, just maybe, the little boy she knew as Penny's was, in fact, Simon Colley. *Stupid, stupid.* Penny wasn't the brightest star in the firmament. How could she ever have pulled it off? It was all nonsense. *Lord, I must be going crazy. Please, save me from myself.*

Chilled, she went back to bed. Fletcher growled quietly, annoyed at being disturbed. The brandy began to take effect, and finally she slept.

She found herself standing, in her dressing-gown, at night, on a level grassy field, in front of a great building. She took it to be a temple, although it was built of dark red bricks and had square battlements, a half-raised portcullis and a drawbridge over a dry moat, like a castle. Along the high wall, in a white dress, gliding like a ghost, came a woman resembling a younger, slimmer, taller version of Maureen Parry, who, reaching the spot above the portcullis, stopped and turned, facing outwards. Her head was flung back, her eyes closed, and in her outstretched arms she held a baby, also clothed in flowing white. She held it out over the plunging drop as if she meant to throw it down. Eileen, fearful, started forward towards the dry green moat. But then Sean, her son-in-law, appeared, tugging urgently at her sleeve, and the castle/temple disappeared, and she was in a tiny, overstuffed room where all the dark, heavy furniture was covered in thick dust. A wild-eyed Sean was still with her, now clutching a black Bakelite telephone. He was telling her that Natasha had been kidnapped. Eileen started to leave the room, but he stopped her. 'Don't go there,' he said. 'They're in there.' Eileen knew, with unease and foreboding, that Sean was right. She couldn't go there, because it was not permitted. She did not belong. 'In there' were shadowy figures, and one of them was Louis. She did not know who the others were, and she did not know what they were doing. She turned to Sean in protest, but at that moment a huge crack opened in the ceiling of the dusty room, and plaster began to fall.

And then she woke with a heart-stopping jolt, and found herself staring into the wide green eyes of Fletcher, who had landed on her chest, purring loudly.

'Wretched cat,' she groaned. 'You scared me half to death. Settle down or go out, for goodness' sake.'

Fletcher jumped off the bed, and a few moments later she heard the clack of the cat flap. She turned over, and darkness took her, and the gremlins were silent.

Pentecost Sunday: 31 May 1998

The singing was ragged, and Eileen stumbled over her own fingers in the penultimate verse. But then she pulled out some more stops for the last verse and they all managed to bring the worn old hymn to a resounding finish. Louis pronounced the blessing, and Eileen rattled through a mercifully simple snippet by one of the Bachs. By the time she was done the church was empty.

'Another one over, then,' she said in the vestry, where Louis was filling in the service record.

Louis raised his eyebrows. 'Is that how you think of the services, Eileen?'

'Well, yes, if I am brutally honest. Certainly on days when I have to be on shift at one-thirty, like today. Your sermon was good, though, as usual.'

'Thank you. How are things with you?'

'All right, I guess. Nothing thrilling.'

'You always say that.'

'Probably because it's true.'

'Hm. How are your daughters these days?'

'Christina's about to take her finals. She seems focused, if not exactly happy. I'd like to think things are a bit more stable in her life, but how do I know what's really going on? Natasha's very upbeat, though. She had her eighteen-week scan a few days ago, so she knows everything is going well. They gave her a grainy print of the baby which she showed me very proudly.'

'Any indication as to gender?'

Eileen smiled. 'No. It was adopting a very modest pose.'

Louis laid down his pen and swivelled round in his chair.

'What about "Elijah"? Is that progressing well?'

'Not bad. What's this, Louis? Interrogation?'

'Just taking an interest,' Louis said. 'In the life of a member of my ever-dwindling flock.'

'Oh. I see. Well, thanks.'

'And since you mention it, how is work? Busy?'
'Always that. Up and down, I suppose. It has its moments of satisfaction, but it's hard going.'
'That sounds familiar.'
Eileen stowed her music on the shelf and took her coat down from the peg.
'Got to go,' she said. 'Be seeing you, Louis. When we get a minute, I'd quite like to quiz you about the gifts of the Spirit.'
'Name a time. I am always at your service.'
'That's nice to know.'

Driving to work, with only a part of her brain focused on the task in hand, Eileen thought about the patients. Relations between Marion, Cathy, Jodie and Carl were simmering, creating a background of tension which affected the other patients. Even those who were normally calm were sounding strained and querulous. The only person apparently oblivious was Tony Tully, who was delighted to be in a caring environment, his worries sorted out by other people. Tony was sunny to the point of idiocy, but he provided a welcome antidote to the snapping and snarling of the Unholy Trio. Then there was young Alice, who seemed to take a step forward only to creep back again. Her recovery, if such it was, was grindingly slow. Karen Colley had gone home for a while, no longer suicidal, but worried about Chopper and the children. Eileen sighed. She was sure that Karen would be back. And there was a new patient, an older mother suffering from severe post-natal depression. Much as she tried to maintain a professional attitude, Eileen found herself wrung out with pity for this suffering woman.

Things other than the patients were weighing on Eileen's spirit. Her concerns about Penny and Maureen hovered uncomfortably at the back of her mind, and the shadow of Christopher was never far away. Should she say anything to Louis? That question stalked her, like an insistent ghost that refused to be appeased. She shrunk from the thought. Her friendship with Louis was warm, relaxed and undemanding, at least as it stood. She was reluctant to disturb it with other people's troubles. Perhaps that was selfish; but she had come to know her own weakness. She shivered suddenly, though the day was mild.

Threading her way through the Sunday traffic onto the main thoroughfare, her thoughts tracked back to Louis' Pentecost sermon. He had begun by referring to Jesus' promise in John 14, the promise of "another Helper, who will stay with you forever." The congregation had already heard read the account in Acts 2, and Louis retraced that extraordinary day when the uncertain apostles had been gloriously transformed. Filled with the Holy Spirit, visible as tongues of fire, they had begun to speak languages they could not possibly have known. Louis made a point of emphasizing that these were the languages of the various elements in the crowd, not gobbledygook. The apostles were gifted in order to communicate with everyone, not to confuse, nor to glorify themselves; and Peter explained this amazing happening with a reference to another prophecy, where God, speaking through Joel, says "I will pour out my Spirit on everyone."

'This gift at Pentecost,' Louis said, 'brought something quite new into being, something with which we are familiar now, the notion of the Body of Christ. That's you and me, of course, and all believers. Any number of sermons have been preached on the subject, and no doubt you have heard a few of them in your time. It's just one way of expressing the truth that we are all interrelated and interdependent. Each of us has something to contribute, each of us is supposed to work in harmony with the rest for the glory of God and the benefit of the other members. But of course there are other ways of describing this in Scripture. As St. Paul tells us in Romans 8, "Those who are led by God's Spirit are God's children." In Galatians 4 he says "...when the right time finally came, God sent his own son...so that we might become God's sons and daughters." And he tells the believers at Ephesus "...you are now fellow-citizens with God's people and members of the family of God." So there we have the idea that we are part of the family, the household of God. Another idea is that of God's temple, where each of us is a building block. Again writing to the Ephesians, Paul says "In union with him you too are being built together with all the others into a place where God lives through his Spirit." And in 1 Peter we are invited to "Come as living stones, and let yourselves be used in building the spiritual Temple..."

'Within this new community, the Holy Spirit has continued to operate down the centuries, and he is still active today. He gives his gifts, as he chooses, to each Christian believer, man, woman or child, to you, to me, to everyone. Some of you may not know what your special spiritual gifts are. You can find out, and on another occasion I will tell you how. But some of you may think you have no gifts. To you I must say, with every deference, you are mistaken. Your spiritual gifts are not the same as your natural talents; spiritual gifts are given only to believers. But sometimes your natural inclinations, desires or aspirations can give a clue to what your spiritual gifts may be. These gifts have been given to each of us, in different numbers and combinations, but in ways which are perfectly suited to our temperament and circumstances. If you doubt me, I assure you it is because you have not yet discovered them.' Louis paused, smiling, looking out over the pulpit at the small group of people in the pews, well aware that most of them, certainly the elderly, thought they were past worrying about their spiritual gifts. For them, physical realities, the frustrations and pains of advancing age, were all too present. For them, survival day-to-day had become the priority of their narrowing lives. But Louis knew his duty, and was not to be deflected.

'Our gifts are unique to each of us. Whatever they are, whether they propel us to prominence in the public eye, or whether they are more modest, makes no difference to God. What he requires of us is faithful stewardship and service. By the proper exercise of our gifts, within God's grace, the rest of the Body is built up and encouraged. By the same token, because our gifts are unique to us, their neglect or abuse can bring harm to our Christian brothers and sisters. We can be sure that the outworking of our spiritual gifts in this life, to the help of others and the glory of God, has eternal value. Paul writes to the Corinthians "…if the one who plays the bugle does not sound a clear call, who will prepare for battle?" Neither you nor I may be called to be buglers, but I am sure you get the point.

'The fulfilment of a believer's gifts, his or her special function within the Body of Christ, builds up the Church in both quality and quantity. This is why meeting together for worship, mutual teaching, encouragement and support, as we are doing this morning, is so vital. I have sometimes been asked, and perhaps you have too, "Do I have to go to church to be a Christian? Can't I try to live a good life by myself?" Well, you have heard me say before that, sinners as we are, we can't be good by ourselves, let alone achieve the perfection which God intends to work in us. Perhaps that thought needs another sermon. But as to being a private Christian, that is not an option that is open to us. In Hebrews 10 we are told quite clearly not to give up meeting with one another. Isolation leads to atrophy, a withering, even if a gradual one, of faith and service.

'Perhaps you are asking yourselves, "What gifts do I have? I am not an especially spiritual or even talented person." Well, as I mentioned before, there are ways to discover your gifts, if you have not already done so. We will go into that another time. But I suspect that most of you here are exercising your spiritual gifts all the time in your daily lives. Perhaps some of you don't even realize it. Often we can't see ourselves as others do, and certainly not as God does. So be encouraged. Within the body, the household, the living temple, we have the means to enrich and sustain the lives of our bothers and sisters, through the working of the Holy Spirit, just as those first apostles did. Let us pray for a fresh outpouring of God's Spirit today, so that we may each sound our bugles, loud and clear.'

Eileen grinned to herself at the thought of Louis and his bugle. Then a loud blaring of car horns brought her back to the present with a heart-shrinking shock. She jammed on her brakes just in time to avoid shooting a red light and ramming a pair of ambling teenagers on a pedestrian crossing.

'Wake up, woman,' she muttered angrily to herself. 'You are a danger on the road.'

Eileen expected the usual Sunday afternoon post-lunch sleepiness when she opened the inner swing doors onto C block. But immediately she was aware of some disturbance, some buzz in the atmosphere. There seemed to be more people moving about in the ward, and there were voices raised above the normal level. As she headed for the nurses' room to take off her coat, Carol Macnamara came round the corner, looking uncharacteristically agitated.

'Thank goodness you're here, Eileen,' she said, sounding out of breath. 'Where's Josh got to?'

'He's not late, is he?' Eileen said. 'What's up, Carol? You look hot and bothered.'

'Come in here and close the door,' Carol said, ushering Eileen into the nurses' room.

'This is all very mysterious,' Eileen said.

Carol turned to face her. 'It's been like all hell let loose the last hour. Jodie and Carl have barricaded themselves in one of the empty side wards, and Marion and Cathy are having a fit of the vapours. You can imagine.'

'I certainly can,' Eileen said. 'How long did you say they'd been in there?'

'Well, I don't exactly know. We just discovered they were missing when we came to dish up the patients' lunches.'

'So the Unholy Trio has become a duo,' Eileen said. 'What's got them going?'

Carol shook her head. 'They seem to think Jodie is in danger. Which is unlikely, considering that when Cathy shrieked through the door, "Jodie! Are you all right?" I distinctly heard Jodie say, "Get lost, moron." The thing is, Marion and Cathy have got quite a few of the other patients agitated as well. You know what it's like in here. It doesn't take much to get them flapping about like headless chickens.'

Eileen suppressed a chuckle. 'I know exactly what you mean. And presumably you're due to go off duty, and would quite like to be on your way home.'

'I certainly would. The way those two are squeaking you'd think we'd had a murder. Why have they got it in for Carl all of a sudden?'

Eileen hung up her coat and put on her uniform. 'It's been going on for weeks. They seem to think Carl is a paedophile.'

'Oh, for goodness' sake.'

'Look, Carol, you get off home. Josh will be here any minute. I can cope till he gets here, and if it all gets out of control I can shout. Where's Christine, anyway?'

'Called in sick. You sure you don't mind? Only the buses aren't that frequent on Sundays.'

'It's fine. You've done your bit. Go home and have a stiff drink.'

'I think I will.'

Eileen left the nurses' room as Josh came through the doors, still in his biking gear and carrying his helmet.

'Hello, Josh,' Eileen said. 'Looks like we're in for one of those shifts.' She told him what Carol had said.

'Come into my office a minute, Eileen,' Josh said. 'I'll just get out of this kit and we'll see what we can do. You been down the ward at all?'

'No, I only just arrived myself.'

Five minutes later Josh strode down to the side ward where Jodie and Carl were supposed to be locked in. A cluster of patients, with Cathy and Marion in the forefront, were hovering round the door.

'All right, then, everybody,' Josh said, his voice mild and reasonable, but with a hint of steel. 'What's all the fuss about?'

'It's Jodie,' said Cathy. 'Carl's got her in there. It's been hours, and there's no sound. She could be dead!'

One of the patients let out a little shriek.

'Don't be daft,' Josh said. 'If you don't know what they're up to in there, I'm surprised at you. Let's all go back to whatever we were doing and let them get it out of their systems. They'll come out by themselves sooner or later.'

Marion pushed herself forward, glowering. 'Jodie's just a kid. She might come to harm. Don't you care what happens to her?'

Josh shook his head. 'Jodie's an adult. She went in there of her own accord. Carl's harmless, whatever anyone may have been saying about the poor blighter. Perhaps this is their way of telling us what they think of us. Sticking two fingers up, maybe. So let's stop enjoying the little drama and break up the meeting, shall we? It'll all get sorted, I assure you.'

He turned to the other patients, who were milling around uncertainly. 'Come on, everybody. Get back to your games and your magazines and your TV, or whatever you were doing. I'll get Eileen to make us some tea. Don't get upset. We'll see everything's OK.'

'I'll put the kettle on, Josh,' Eileen said. 'Do you want some?'

'Please. I'll be in my office. Got some paperwork to do.'

Ten minutes later Eileen wheeled the creaking tea trolley round the ward. She spoke to each of the patients, trying to find out who was genuinely upset and who was simply enjoying the frisson of a little scandal. To her surprise, she found Cathy Lloyd sitting alone by her bed, her back turned.

'Cathy? You OK?' Eileen heard a stifled sob. 'Hey, come on, it can't be that bad.' She sat down on the edge of the bed and patted Cathy's shoulder. 'Jodie's fine, I'm sure.'

Cathy turned a red, teary face towards her. 'Jodie, that little bitch. She called me a moron. Supposed to be a friend. And now Marion's not talking to me either.' She sniffed.

'It'll all blow over, Cathy. It just isn't worth you getting all upset about. Here, have a cup of tea, good old British remedy for everything.'

Cathy managed a weak smile. 'Thanks, Eileen. I'm stupid, I know. It's being in here that does it. Everything gets out of proportion. I'm even quite looking forward to seeing Vince and the kids later, just for a bit of normality.'

'Well, you'll be going home very soon. I think you're right. You'll be more in control of your life away from here, and you'll manage fine.'

'Do you really think so?' Cathy's voice shook.

'Yes, I do. You're stronger than you realize.' She got up. 'I'll pop down later, Cathy.'

Eileen finished up at Alice's bed. 'Do you want some tea, Alice?'

The girl pulled a face. 'No, thanks. Horrible stuff.'

'How are you doing?'

'OK, I guess. What about Jodie and Carl, then? I knew something was going on, but I didn't think they'd advertise it like this.'

'Really? I hadn't noticed anything.'

Alice smiled knowingly. 'You're not here all the time, are you? I've seen her sneak off round to Carl's when the others are all glued to some soap on TV. He's a bit old for her, I'd have thought. Nice-looking, though. Perhaps they couldn't stand it any longer.'

'What?'

'Well, there's only so much hand-holding and snogging and

whispering in corners you can do, isn't there, before you're kind of looking for the main event. And there's not exactly much privacy in here.'

Eileen laughed. 'You're probably right. I'd better get this tea to Josh before it gets cold.'

She wheeled the trolley back into the kitchen, poured a mug of tea and took it into the office. Josh was sitting at the desk, forms and files spread out in front of him, a look of patient gloom on his face.

Eileen put the mug down on the desk. 'You're the last in the queue, I'm afraid, so it might not be too hot.'

Josh took a sip. 'It's fine, thanks. How are things on the front line?'

'Quiet now. Cathy was weepy, though. I think she felt a bit deserted, by Jodie and Marion.'

'She'll be a lot better off away from Marion altogether. Somehow that's not been the best of friendships for Cathy.'

'Surely it must be close to discharge time for her.'

'Yes. There's a meeting due this week. Shouldn't be long.' He stretched out his legs under the desk and sighed.

'You handled the whole episode well, I thought, Josh. But then, you always do.'

Josh looked up, his eyebrows raised. 'Compliments! And I was thinking it was going to be a bad day.'

'No, I mean it. Sensible and calm, that's what you need around here. But I guess you've come across many situations like today's.'

Josh shrugged. 'No two days are the same, no two patients either. But you get a nose for when to panic, and I didn't think today warranted it. Apart from anything else, Jodie will have to come out soon. There's no toilet in that side ward, and women always need to pee after sex.'

Eileen laughed aloud. 'Do they, indeed? You're an expert, of course.'

Josh grinned. 'Of course.'

'I'd better let you get on,' Eileen said. 'Otherwise this conversation will get out of hand, and your paperwork will never get done.'

A knock came on the door, and before Josh had a chance to answer, the door opened. Jodie stood in the doorway, a lighted cigarette conspicuous between her fingers.

'Need to talk to you,' she said, ignoring Eileen and fixing Josh with a challenging stare.

'Yes, you do,' Josh said quietly. 'You and Carl both. But not smoking. Finish your smoke in the proper place, then come to see me.'

Jodie stared silently for a few moments more. Then she turned on her heel and marched back down the ward.

'Best of luck, Josh,' Eileen murmured, turning to go.

'I'd like you to be here, Eileen,' Josh said. 'When they come back. Best if there's two staff members present. I've got a feeling those two plan to discharge themselves.'

Eileen was startled. 'Can they do that?'

'Oh, yes. Both of them are informal patients. Referred themselves. Sure, they've got care-plans like anybody else, but it's more open-ended in their case. They can go when they like.'

'But will they be all right?'

Josh shrugged. 'Lap of the gods, really, like a lot of things round here.'

'Right. I'll keep my eyes open.'

An hour later Eileen saw Jodie and Carl outside Josh's office. Glancing back down the ward she noticed a bulging bag beside Jodie's bed. Josh was right: Jodie was packed and ready to go. As soon as Eileen saw the office door close behind them she went over and knocked.

'Come in, Eileen.'

Carl and Jodie were sitting in chairs opposite Josh's desk. Josh waved Eileen to another chair to one side.

'Right, you two,' Josh said pleasantly. 'What's going on?'

Jodie glanced at Carl and he gave the briefest of nods.

'Well, me and Carl, we're together.'

'I think I'd gathered that,' Josh said. 'Bit obvious, wasn't it, shutting yourselves up like that in the side ward? Not too considerate to the other patients, was it? At least one of them thought you were in danger, Jodie.'

Jodie's fists clenched on the arms of the chair. 'Yeah, well, that's because some ignorant people in this hospital think Carl's some kind of pervert. Which he ain't.'

'I know that, and so do most people here,' Josh said. 'It's just one or two get a stupid idea in their heads, nobody knows where from, and they won't let go. You don't want to let it bother you.'

'I ain't bothered for me. I don't like them saying stuff about Carl, that's all. Stuff that ain't true, dirty stuff.'

'Fair enough. So why today?'

Jodie shrugged. 'I dunno. We just wanted to be like normal people, I reckon. There's nowhere private in here. It's like bleedin' prison. If you must know, I felt like it. It's been months.'

'All right, Jodie. That's your part of it. What about you, Carl?'

Carl leaned forward, smiling slightly, a pink flush colouring his cheeks. 'Same, really, Josh. Sorry if we upset people. Fact is, I'm feeling a lot better. Thought it was time to make a move. Jodie's decided to come with me. Maybe we can make a better job of it together. Life, I mean. Back each other up.'

Josh looked at them silently for a few moments. 'So what have you decided? You both going to live in Carl's flat?'

'Yeah, that's the idea,' Jodie said.

'You going to remember to take all your medication?'

Carl nodded. 'Definitely. No question. We plan to keep out of here, don't we, Jodie?'

Jodie seemed to relax. A hint of a smile appeared in her blue eyes. 'That's the deal. And Carl says he'll kick me out if I do drugs again. But I'm off them for good. I told him.'

'All right, then, there's just a form here I have to fill out and you sign,' Josh said. 'Then you're free to go. And for your own sakes, I hope I don't see either of you again. Except maybe down the shops, or in the pub.'

He pulled two sheets of paper towards him and wrote. Then he handed a sheet to Carl and another to Jodie. 'Read it first before you sign.'

There was silence for a few minutes, and then it was done. Carl got up, took Jodie's hand and pulled her out of her chair. 'Just want to say thanks for all you've done, all of you,' he said. He stretched out his hand over the desk, and Josh shook it.

'Best of luck, mate. Don't let her ruin your life.'

'Cheek!' said Jodie, unable to suppress a grin.

'Just one thing,' Josh said as they went to the door. 'Your choice, but it would be a nice idea to make it up with Cathy. She might be muddle-headed, but she was only looking out for you, Jodie. And in this bad old world you need friends more than you need enemies.'

Jodie looked at the floor. 'Yeah. OK. Cathy's all right, when she's not being Marion's little monkey.'

Eileen left the office with them. Carl collected his bag, and said goodbye to one or two people on his way back. Jodie went to find Cathy, and Eileen saw them talk, and then hug each other.

Carl said, 'I really am going to keep her off the drugs. She'll be all right.'

Eileen nodded. 'I hope so, Carl.'

Jodie rejoined them, her bag over her shoulder. They went to the lift, all three together.

'Look, you two,' Eileen said, 'if things go pear-shaped, I hope you won't be too proud to come back. It's no shame to need help from time to time.'

'We're going to be OK,' Jodie said as the lift doors opened. 'Right, Carl?'

Polite to the last, Carl offered his hand. 'Bye, Eileen. Thanks for everything.'

Eileen let herself back into Josh's office. 'How many floors up are we?'

Josh frowned. 'Two. You know that as well as I do. Why?'

'Well, the lift doors were barely shut before those two were on each other as if they'd been shut up in separate prisons for twenty years. But two floors doesn't give them too much time.'

'Just as well,' Josh said. 'We'll have visitors here any minute.'

'That would give Dawn Walters a shock, wouldn't it?' Eileen said.

Josh held up his hands, warding off the thought. 'Don't. I have enough trouble with Mrs. Walters without her finding two of our ex-patients having it off in the lift.'

Visiting-time was unusually animated, with the day's gossip livening up the patients and giving them something to talk about with their families and friends. By the time the visitors had gone Eileen was beginning to feel a bit worn, and she noticed that several of the patients had fallen asleep in their chairs, or on their beds. Sunlight streamed in at the wide windows, and a sweetly-scented breath of spring ruffled the curtains. It would have been good to be outside. But there were still a few hours to go before her shift ended, and one or two patients seemed still to want to chew over the Jodie-and-Carl scenario. Cathy, Eileen noticed, seemed calm, and was chatting to the most recent arrival, the woman suffering from past-natal depression. Cathy was perched on the woman's bed, holding her hand. Marion, however, was sitting in front of the television, glowering. Eileen sighed and went to wash up the tea-cups. Her mind flitted back to this morning – was it only this morning? – and Louis' sermon. What were her spiritual gifts? Was she using them well, or at all, today on C Block?

At nine-fifteen Ollie made his usual flamboyant entrance. As soon as he appeared on the ward a number of patients greeted him loudly, and were soon regaling him with the day's big event. A few minutes later Maureen arrived for the night shift. She came quietly into the nurses' room where Eileen was getting ready to go home.

'Hello, stranger,' Eileen said. 'You all right?'

Maureen smiled. She was pale, and her eyes looked dull and sunken. 'Fine, thanks.'

'You don't look fine,' Eileen said. 'You look as though you might be sickening for something.'

'No, I'm OK,' Maureen said, with an obvious effort. 'Looking forward to a night shift with Ollie. What's all this about Jodie and Carl?'

'Oh, you've heard, have you?'

'That young kid from D Block was in the lift. She said something about them having sex in a side ward. You know how gossip flies about in this place.'

'Mm. Some of it wildly inaccurate,' Eileen said. 'But gossip wouldn't be gossip if it was dry and factual, I suppose.' She told Maureen what had happened that afternoon. 'Cathy seems to have got over it. But you might have a spot of bother with Marion. She looks full of self-righteous disgust. I don't envy you the task of talking her down if she gets a bit shrill.'

'Marion, I think, is a very lonely lady,' said Maureen. 'Worse now, I guess. If the other patients are OK I'll go and have a chat with her. Did she have any visitors today?'

'Not that I saw.'

'I wonder where her husband was. I'll see what I can find out. Maybe it's not just the break-up of the Unholy Trio that's got under her skin.'

'I'm off, then, Maureen. I hope it's quiet for you. I'll give you a ring in the next day or two.'

'OK. Goodnight, Eileen.'

Eileen zipped up her coat and slung her bag over her shoulder. Josh was still in his uniform as she passed the open office door. 'You got a minute, Eileen?'

Eileen paused in the doorway.

'I wondered if you fancied a quick drink,' Josh said.

'What, now?'

'Yes. Just give me a couple of minutes.'

'Oh. All right. Why not?'

Josh put on his leather biking-jacket but stowed the trousers and his helmet in the bike's panniers. 'What about the Feathers? That's the nearest that isn't too spit-and-sawdust.'

'Fine by me.'

They walked together round the corner of the street and into the small, brightly-lit pub. Josh got the drinks and brought them to the rickety round table by the window. There were no curtains, and Eileen looked out onto the quiet side street, lit up now by street lamps.

'So what's the idea, then, Josh? I thought you'd be only too pleased to get home after a day like today.'

Josh stretched and took a swig of his pint. 'I needed to unwind. Not got a lot to dash home for, anyway. You?'

'Just my cat.'

'Kids?'

'Not at home. My older daughter's married to a lovely man called Sean, and they're going to be parents in October. My younger daughter's in her final year at university. She starts her exams next week, so she's working. Well, I hope she is.'

'What's her subject?'

'English.'

'Clever, is she?'

'Yes, I rather think she is. What about you?'

Josh shifted in his chair, leaning back. 'I have a son, Martin. He's thirty-one, which makes me feel rather old. He lives in Yorkshire, near his mum, with his young lady, Paula. She's a nice girl. My ex would very much like them to have kids, but so far she's out of luck.'

'I'm not at all sure how I feel about the idea of being a grandmother,' Eileen said. 'As you say, it has a ring of old age about it. But I'm sure I'll be as doting as most grannies when he or she arrives.'

'I don't see you as either old, or ever doting,' Josh said.

'Thanks. But the grim reality is, however hard I try to run away from it, I have a big birthday coming up in November.'

Josh grinned. 'You could always hide under the bedclothes and pretend it wasn't happening.'

'That would probably be my way of dealing with it,' Eileen said. 'Or a long walk somewhere lonely. But I have a feeling my family and friends won't let it slide by unnoticed.'

They were silent for a few moments, then Eileen said, 'So, do you see your son much?'

'Not that much,' Josh said. 'I don't go up to Yorkshire above two or three times a year. I'll see Martin and Paula then. I go to see my old mum as well when I'm there. She still lives in the same village. Eighty-four, she is now. Dad died in 1982. He was a Methodist local preacher – did I tell you that?'

'No, you didn't. Hence your Biblical name.'

'Ah, but that's not all. I'm the third of four brothers, and the others are Adam, Seth and Samuel.'

'So where are they these days?'

'All in Yorkshire still. I'm the only stray lamb.'

'Any regrets?'

'Plenty, but I don't regret coming down here. I much prefer the work I do now to being a soldier.'

'I have to say I can't imagine what it must be like, to be in the Army for – what did you tell me? – twenty-two years. There were a few grim situations in that era, if I remember right.'

Josh nodded. 'I joined up in 1963. Managed to avoid National Service. I was in Aden in '67, Ireland in '69, seconded to Oman in '71, back to Ireland in '72. There were a lot of bombs that year.' He shuddered. 'Germany again, Ireland again. Then the Falklands. Retired in 1985. Huge sigh of relief.'

'Did you come down south straight away?'

Josh nodded. 'Decided to retrain, specialized in psychiatric nursing, and never looked back. And, best of all, when I came here I discovered my trusty bike. I first saw one in Ireland, and had a hankering for one ever since. Know anything about motorbikes?'

'Nothing at all,' Eileen said.

'Well, it's a Norton Dominator 650, built in 1962. So it's older than my son. And in beautiful nick.'

'It certainly looks well cared-for.'

'So there you have it,' Josh said. 'My not very spectacular life. What about you?'

'Not spectacular at all. Grew up, parents died, sister emigrated, went to work, got married, raised the kids, got divorced, came here.'

'What went wrong with the marriage? D'you mind me asking?' Josh said.

'No, I don't mind. A bit of drifting apart, a helping of pig-headedness, a dash of misunderstanding, a lot of foolishness. That about sums it up. I'm sure I could have handled it better if I hadn't been so stiff-necked. In a sense I feel a bit of a failure. But the girls still see their father, he has remarried and seems happy, and I am not miserable either, so it could be worse. What happened to you?'

Josh sighed and leaned his elbows on the table. 'Kath and I got married very young. We had Martin a year after. Kath wanted more kids. But I'd been in the Army a few years by then. I knew just how easy it would have been to get killed or injured. Seeing the things I saw didn't encourage me to bring more kids into this nasty world. I pr~ ʰably wouldn't see it quite so black-and-white now. But I refused to   ny more babies. That was the start of it. And I was away so ɴ made the best of it since. She's with Gordon now, been ꞌ time. He seems a solid sort of bloke. Pity of it is, sʰ kids. Something went wrong, and she had to ʰ Perhaps that's why she's itching to be a grandrʳ Kath is. She's a hairdresser these days, got ͱ

99

think I was much of a husband, though I tried to be a reasonable dad, when I was around. Like you, I feel a bit of a wash-out.'

'Not a lot to recommend either of us, then, is there?' Eileen said. 'What about your dad? Was he a fiery preacher? I imagine that had an impact on you as a boy.'

'It did. I learned a great deal about the Good Book. Still remember most of it. But a lot of that went, that childish faith, during my soldiering days. I saw so much horror. So much bloody waste.' He fell silent, his eyes blank, as if remembering some distant tragedy. Eileen said nothing, watching him. She noticed the crinkles round his eyes, the freckles on his cheekbones, his wiry red-brown hair. He blinked, noticed her watching him, and smiled. 'Sorry. Miles away. I was remembering my chum Billy Painter. Lost him in Ireland, 1972. I visited him in the hospital. He'd had his legs shot away. Poor devil went crazy before he died. He was only twenty-four. He was the reason, him and the others, why I changed my life right around, soon as I could, when I left the Army. I'd spent my career killing people and seeing people killed. Made me want to put them back together again. So here I am, trying to help people put their heads back together. Not always successfully. Do you want another drink?'

'No, thanks, Josh. I'd better be getting home. Thanks for telling me your story, even if it was such a sad one.'

'Hope I haven't bored you too much.'

'No, you haven't at all.' Eileen stood up and put on her coat. 'One thing, though, that bothers me. You know I got this job through Maureen, don't you? And I like to think she's a friend. But I am concerned about her. She doesn't look well, and I've heard things said by other people which worry me. Do you know much about her?'

Josh held the door open, and they stepped out into the mild May night. 'I've known Maureen a few years, and I know a bit about her life. But she's a very private lady, Maureen is. I wouldn't want to break any confidences.'

Eileen paused under a street light. The weak glow made even Josh's ruddy face ghostly. 'Of course not,' she said. 'And I'm not trying to snoop. I just want her to know I'd help if she needed it.'

They walked slowly back through the quiet streets to the hospital car park and paused by Eileen's car. There was hardly anyone about.

'I don't know,' Josh said. 'It's a tough one. Just tell her, I guess. Tell her you're concerned, and you are there if she needs you. What more can a mate do?'

Eileen nodded. 'I will. I'll ring her in a day or two. I'd better go, or I'll ⁓ off at the wheel.'

'Thanks for your company tonight, Eileen,' Josh said. 'Maybe we could do it again some time.'

'Sure, why not?' Eileen got into the car and looked up at him as she fastened her seat belt. 'Goodnight, Josh. See you at work.'

Driving home through brightly-lit main roads and dark side streets, Eileen thought about Josh and what he had told her. She was mildly surprised at his candour, and suspected that he didn't have many people to talk to. It struck her also that in this assumption she was only guessing, because although he had told her something of his past, he had said next to nothing about the present. Perhaps he had a girlfriend who happened, tonight, to be out on the town. Or at a conference. Or visiting her mother. And she, Eileen, was just a colleague to have a friendly drink with at the end of a tiring day. Perhaps.

Trinity Sunday: 7 June 1998

Louis ascended the pulpit steps and opened his Bible.

'First, the good news,' he said. 'It's Trinity Sunday, but I am not going to preach another dry sermon on the theology of the Trinity so that you all go home glassy-eyed, fit for nothing but lying down in a darkened room.' He smiled, and there was an answering ripple of laughter from the pews. 'Nor am I going to attempt to concoct yet another analogy for how one God can be Three Persons. It has always seemed to me that the more ingenious such analogies are, the less satisfactory they are in deepening our understanding of what is, and must be, a great Mystery, certainly on this side of death. No, if anyone here has a desperate need to read about the Trinity, I can guide him or her to books written by people more knowledgeable than I. But here's the bad news, or so it may appear to some of you. I am going to talk about rebellion and repentance, and first I am going to tell you about some very long-ago monarchs.

'In the Book of Kings we read about the glorious reign of Solomon, David's son, including how he built the Temple in Jerusalem, and his great knowledge and wisdom. We also read how he became disloyal to God, led astray by his foreign, pagan wives. Being a bachelor myself, I am in no position to have any opinions about the influence of wives in general, so I shall remain silent.' The corners of his mouth twitched, then he became serious again. 'Towards the end of Solomon's reign things began to fall apart, and under his son Rehoboam the kingdom was divided into two parts, Israel in the north, and the southern kingdom of Judah. 1 and 2 Kings is the record of the doings of these monarchs from God's point of view. All of Israel's kings failed the test, while the record of Judah is a mixed one.

'Among the kings of Judah there were some very bad men, but there were also some who stood out above the rest in loyalty and dedication to the God who had brought the nation out of Egypt and stuck with them through thick and thin. One such was Hezekiah. In the parallel books of Chronicles, in Book 2 chapters 29 and 30, we read of the cleansing and rededication of the Temple, followed by a spectacular Passover. In chapter 30 verse 27 we read, "The priests and the Levites asked the Lord's blessing on the people. In his home in heaven God heard their prayers and accepted them." So far, so good.

'About eighty years later we find another good king, Josiah, Hezekiah's great-grandson. Josiah was a radical reformer. Let me read you a few verses from 2 Kings 23, just to give you an idea of how Josiah swept away the evidences of pagan worship. "He removed from the Temple the symbol of the goddess Asherah, took it out of the city to the valley of the Kidron, burnt it, pounded its ashes to dust, and scattered it over the public burial ground." I think we can safely say that Josiah was a man of great zeal. The account goes on to describe how he cleansed the Temple by destroying the living quarters of the Temple prostitutes, how he desecrated the heathen altars, tore down the altars to the goat-demons, and destroyed Topheth, where children were sacrificed to Molech. Wherever he found altars dedicated to anyone but God – whether to the worship of the sun, or Astarte, or Chemosh – he pulverized them, and all the pagan priests were put to the sword.

'What had started Josiah off on this all-out campaign? Well, earlier in his reign the Book of the Law had been rediscovered, and Josiah realized how far astray his nation had gone from God. Again, this purification of the Temple, this purging of worship and the renewal of the covenant between God and his people, was followed by an extraordinary Passover. 2 Chronicles 35 tells us that 30,000 sheep were sacrificed, 3,000 bulls, 2,600 lambs and young goats, and that was by no means all. It goes on, "For seven days all the people of Israel who were present celebrated the Passover and the Festival of Unleavened Bread. Since the days of the prophet Samuel, the Passover had never been celebrated like this. None of the former kings had ever celebrated a Passover like this one celebrated by King Josiah, the priests, the Levites and the people of Judah, Israel and Jerusalem in the eighteenth year of Josiah's reign."

'So, why am I telling you all this? Because I believe that we, too, have a need for repentance, not just once in our life, but a daily, hourly turning around, an ongoing commitment to that revolution in our thinking and actions, just like the cleansing of the Temple. We, too, have to get rid of our equivalents to pagan altars, whatever they may be, before we can look forward to that great Passover at the end of time. But we have no need to sacrifice vast quantities of hapless cattle and sheep. God immolated himself in the person of his Son; one sacrifice was, and is, sufficient to bear the whole weight of human sin down the ages. I am, of course, talking about Christ's death on the cross.

'Let me backtrack a little. What do we really mean by sin? Well, we all know what wrongdoing is. Moses brought the tablets of the Law down from the mountain, and we do well to abide by the Ten Commandments as a rule for our lives. But we, knowing of Christ's atoning sacrifice, have a greater responsibility than those far-off Israelites in the desert. In Hebrews 10 we are told that sin is worse when committed by people who should know better, who know Christ and profess to belong to him – in other words, us. It has been said, and with some justice, that the unsatisfactory lives of professing Christians, including the shameful disunity of the Body of Christ, is the greatest single factor keeping people out of the Church. Ours is the privilege of knowing Jesus; ours too is the responsibility of living well in his name. It is not just that we are spoiled and sub-standard. Each one of us, in his or her heart, and I include myself too, is a rebel. In each of us lurks that tendency to pride, the self-loving arrogance so deep-seated in the human psyche, that says we can do very well without God. This is the theme of so much of the Old Testament, and we can see it actively at work in today's Israel, the Church.

'So what is to be done? Hebrews again gives us some clues. It tells us to persevere under ill-treatment, to keep up our courage, to take care not to drift, to keep our hope in sight at all times, and to hold fast to our loyalty to God. The victory comes to those who renounce their sinful lives, depend on God's grace alone, keep striving and hold on to the end.

'And although the words of Hebrews remind us of judgment, we must remember that our High Priest Jesus has gone into the very presence of God, and he, in his humanity, can feel sympathy for our weakness. We are told to keep our eyes firmly fixed on Jesus, who has run the race before us. I will leave those who are so minded to read that wonderful passage in Hebrews 12.

'Is that the end of the story? That we are arrogant rebels who must lay down their arms? That we must all cleanse our own particular Temple? Not quite. Because we know Jesus, sin is not only proud rebellion. It is also a wounding of the heart of love. God's mercy is always directed at the undeserving: you and me included. And all we are asked to do is accept that mercy in a spirit of humility and gratitude, to turn away from our natural tendency to serve ourselves, and to walk the path of obedience, even as Jesus himself did, to the bitter end. For, surely, what's good enough for the Master is good enough for his disciples.'

Eileen lay in bed, wide awake. Her stomach was churning, and she had the beginnings of a headache. She closed her eyes, but it only made her more conscious of her ills. Something in Louis' words that morning was rankling in her mind, demanding attention that she was unwilling to give. She had a sense of something within her that was imperfectly sealed, from which some toxic fluid was leaking, scalding where it touched.

Since starting work at the hospital she had used almost none of her holiday entitlement, and was now obliged to take a few days off work in order not to lose it. She had planned to give the flat an overdue spring-clean. But with no work till Friday, and only a rehearsal for "Elijah" and Gus's birthday party to break up the week, she felt as if she had somehow lost her anchor and was floating, alone and adrift, in an uncharted ocean. It was an uncomfortable feeling.

She got out of bed, taking care not to disturb Fletcher, who was curled in a tight ball by her feet, his nose under his tail. She put on a dressing-gown and padded to the kitchen. The sudden bright light made her blink and the headache began to grip. She made a cup of tea and found some pain-killers in the bathroom cabinet. Then she went back to the bedroom, twitched the curtain aside, and sat by the open window. She washed the pain-killers down with a sip of tea. A cool, sweet breath of early summer wafted in, bringing a scent of distant parks. This high up, the chemical smells of the city were less obtrusive than they were on the ground.

She knew, beyond doubt, that the time had come to deal with the past. But she was deeply reluctant. For a long time she had avoided anything but the briefest prayer, and now it was like the opening of a long-neglected door in a derelict house, a door with rusty hinges, and rank grass growing up around its base. It would need a hacking of the undergrowth, a painful yank on the handle, and to reveal what? Foul-smelling darkness, the odours of concealment? *Now you are getting fanciful.*

She looked out of the window. The blue of the sky was not yet at its darkest, and there were neither moon nor stars visible. The unceasing susurration of distant traffic and the sucking of the breeze against the curtains were the only sounds.

Lord, I don't know where I'm going. I feel lost, and I'm beginning to panic. I need a sense of direction, no, more than that, I need some clarity, some urgent guidance. Lord, I need the will to be obedient. I'm afraid I'm going adrift again. That mustn't happen. After everything that's gone on, I should know better. But Lord, I don't. I'm like a prisoner inside myself. Help me, please. I'm going astray. In my need to keep a lid on the past I am whirling away out of my orbit around you, my Sun. Please stop me. Bring me back again, whatever it costs. Bring me back as you did before, and forgive me for having closed my ears to your calling. It's not too late, is it? No, I know you are merciful. Show me what I must do to break free from myself and my besetting weaknesses. At some level I have begun to abandon you. But I don't want to. It's like a sort of poisonous habit. Lord, I am searching for you. Come and find me, please.

She came back to herself like a swimmer surfacing from the cold, dark depths of the sea into the sunlight, and was surprised to find that tears were running down her face.

She closed the curtains and climbed back into bed. The cat growled quietly in protest. Sleep took her.

She was sitting on a beach of fine, white sand. She could feel its grittiness under her hands. There were other people there, moving about with no apparent purpose. Some of them were familiar: Marie was there, and Christina, and Stephanie. There were others that Eileen didn't know, but they were all women, oddly. They were laughing and shoving each other playfully, and two or three were bouncing a ball. Then they all started to strip, and in a moment ran into the sea, an inviting sea with tiny rippling waves. They shrieked and jumped and plunged in with enthusiasm, the water running off their bodies and soaking their hair. Several of them turned back, and called to Eileen to join them, and she wanted to, but she was fully clothed, and when she tried to take her clothes off, her fingers were awkward and stiff. At last she managed it, but by this time the others were far out to sea, swimming and waving and splashing. Eileen was left wearing a pair of heavy boots, tightly-laced. She tried to take them off, but failed. Frustrated and angry, she tugged at them fiercely, but succeeded only in making her feet bleed. She laid her head on her knees and wept, as the voices of the free women grew ever more distant.

She woke to a grey dawn and the sound of small birds foraging in the guttering of the flats. A shivering moment of clarity came to her mind, and was gone. *I have to shed my spiritual hobnails if I am ever to dance in the surf.*

She woke again to full day, and the insistent nudging of a hungry cat. The details of her dream were becoming hazy, but she felt as if a door had opened somewhere in the cluttered depths of her mind, and when she got out of bed she felt lighter, as if those tight laces were beginning to loosen. For a moment, standing in the kitchen in the sunshine, she felt faint and had to hold on to the back of a chair.

I must not lose this. I must not let it go. I will talk to Louis on Thursday, after little Gus's party. Dear Christopher, you are going to come out of the closet where I have locked you for almost two years. For the last time, perhaps, you are going to walk in the world.

Thursday 11 June 1998

A few minutes before three o'clock Eileen decided it was time to face the inevitable. She washed and put on some half-decent clothes, brushed her hair and wafted some perfume around. Then, with a sigh, she gathered up Gus's birthday present, wrapped in jolly paper with red and yellow clowns on it, closed the door of her flat behind her, and descended the stairs.

The door to Penny's flat was open, and already from inside came adult laughter and childish shrieks. Eileen knocked and went in. 'It's me, Penny.'

Penny appeared in the hallway, flushed and frowning. Doing her best for Gus was not always an unalloyed pleasure. 'Eileen, hello. I'm glad you're here. I was trying to get the children to play some games, but they're all running around and knocking each other over and bouncing on the sofa.'

'Two's probably a bit young for proper party games,' Eileen said gently. 'Have you got any music we could put on?'

Penny nodded. 'There's a tape in the machine.'

'You don't happen to have a whistle, do you?'

'I'm sure Gus has got one somewhere,' Penny said. 'I'll go and find it.'

'And a few prizes, please.'

Penny scurried off, beaming.

Eileen spent the next half hour persuading a dozen very young children to dance to music and throw themselves on the carpet whenever she blew the whistle. At some point Louis arrived and put his head round the door. He shook his head in disbelieving horror and vanished.

Eileen was rescued by Penny who came in carrying trays of party food. Some of the other mothers were finally helping her, seating their own children, tying on bibs, wiping hot faces and hands. Eileen escaped to the kitchen, where she found a couple of mothers drinking tea and chatting, obviously only too pleased to be free of their responsibilities for a while. Louis was sitting at the table with them, a mug of tea in front of him. He looked faintly guilty when Eileen came in.

'You a mate of Penny's, then?' one of the mothers asked Louis.

Louis smiled. 'I'm Gus's godfather.' He was dressed casually, and had left off his dog-collar for the occasion.

'Nice you could get the time off to come to his party,' the mother pursued.

'Ah. Well, some people would say I only work on Sundays.'

'Eh?' The young woman looked suspicious.

'I'm a clergyman,' Louis said.

'Oh. Right. Yeah, I think I heard Penny talk about you once.' She turned abruptly to her friend. 'I'm going in the other room, make sure my Megan's behaving. You coming?'

Within moments they were gone.

Eileen leaned against the door frame, grinning. 'What an effect you have on people.'

Louis raised his shoulders in a theatrical shrug. 'It was ever thus. Even when I come in disguise.'

'Well, if you can't help out with the children, at least you can do the washing up.' Eileen handed him a tea towel and he got to his feet with a groan. 'Poor old Penny,' Eileen said. 'She does her utmost to be mum of the year, but I think she'll be just as glad when it's over as you and I are.'

'Is it likely to last much longer?' Louis whispered.

'I shouldn't think so. Toddlers have a short attention span. And one or two are bound to eat too much and be sick, or get over-excited and cry.'

'I thought the idea was to have fun,' Louis said gloomily, putting a stack of dirty dishes on the draining board.

'Somehow we all feel obliged to go through these rituals,' Eileen said. 'You've escaped very lightly. But I'd guess once the little ones have had their tea and been cleaned up, there'll be a time for Gus to open his presents, and then before long they'll be off home. I hope you remembered a present for Gus?'

'I am a rotten godfather, but not that rotten. Can we slip away after that?'

'I should think so.' Eileen wiped the table free of crumbs. 'But there's something I need to talk to you about, if you have any free time.'

Louis glanced at his watch. 'I'm expecting a phone call from my boss early this evening. I am referring to the Bishop, not God,' he added, catching Eileen's look. 'Apart from that, I'm at your disposal.'

In the end it all passed off without drama. Mothers gathered up children clutching bags of sweets in their sticky hands, while Gus sat in the middle of the carpet surrounded by wrapping-paper and toys, his face smeared with food and beaming happily. Eileen offered to help Penny tidy up but Penny preferred to do things her own way.

Eileen and Louis shut the flat door and grinned at each other like conspirators.

'Where would you like to hold this whatever it is?' Louis said. 'And is it as a friend you want to speak to me, or as a pastor?'

Eileen felt a frisson of apprehension. 'Actually, I think it is probably a spiritual matter more than anything.'

Louis observed her change of mood and was instantly sober. 'In that case, perhaps the Vicarage would be the appropriate place. Then I won't be twitchy about missing my phone call.'

'My flat's in total uproar anyway,' Eileen said. 'I'm giving it a bit of a blitz. Long overdue. Is this a serious communication from the Bishop? I hope you haven't been misbehaving.'

'The ways of the Bishop are inscrutable,' he said. 'Shall we go?'

Louis had walked from his place to Penny's, so Eileen drove him back. They strolled across the churchyard in the sunshine. Louis ushered Eileen into a dusty sitting-room which looked as if it was rarely used.

'I'll make some tea,' he said.

'Do you mind if I open the French windows?' Eileen said.

'Go ahead. They're probably very stiff. They haven't been opened since the year dot.'

Louis was right. The doors eventually yielded with a reluctant squeal. Warm air flowed in from the neglected garden.

Louis came in with a tray of tea and put it down on a low table. He handed Eileen a mug. 'So, lamb of my little flock, how can I help you?'

Eileen stirred her tea. A distant memory of Monday's faintness echoed in her mind. She took a deep breath. 'It was your sermon on Sunday. It made me think. And remember, and worry. All that stuff about cleansing one's own Temple.' She looked up. 'Though I liked the bit about the Passover at the end of time.'

Louis smiled. 'I wanted to end on a positive note. But after that, you know, it all went to pot again. Are you familiar with the story?' Eileen shook her head. 'God couldn't forget the wickedness of King Manasseh, Josiah's grandfather. And Josiah's son, Joahaz, returned to the bad old ways after his father's death. Why am I not surprised? Joahaz ended his days as a prisoner of conquering Egypt. His successor Jehoiakim ruled over a tributary nation under the thumb of Babylon. Then along came Nebuchadnezzar, who raided the Temple and deported the people. The puppet King Zedekiah rebelled, the rebellion was crushed, and Zedekiah himself was blinded.'

'Grim.'

'Yes, but oddly, Zedekiah was finally released. They let him live peacefully in Babylon till he died. I suppose a blind old man was no threat. He'd been in prison for thirty-seven years.'

'Good heavens.'

'I'm sorry, I don't know why I told you all that when it's you who are trying to tell me something. Do go on. Tell me to shut up if I interrupt.'

'It's fine, really. But you know how you are always saying you think I have something to hide? Well, I suppose I have.' She shot a look at Louis, who was looking slightly smug, one eyebrow raised. 'There's something I've been trying to relegate to the past. But it still has power over me. The long and short of it is, I am worried in case I have done wrong. I've come to the conclusion that I must share it with someone.'

'Thank you for trusting me that much,' Louis said.

'You may not thank me when you hear what I have to say,' Eileen said. Then, hesitantly at first but with growing fluency, she told Louis about Christopher, from the meetings in the woods and the sharing of Scripture to the revelation of corruption and the horror of the end. Louis said nothing, and hardly moved. He sat opposite her, chin in hand, his dark eyes intent.

When she stopped speaking, he said, 'Does anybody else know about this, Eileen?'

She shook her head. 'Only Michael. It was because of him that I started helping Christopher in the first place. I was very dubious about it. But then there came a point when I promised I wouldn't tell anyone he was there. It was either that or lose him altogether. That's how I saw it at the time. I know it's right to help people, but I think my own selfish motivations were mixed in somewhere. I wanted to find out more about him. To be honest, there wasn't much in my life then. After I had made that promise, I think I began to lose control of even my own part in the situation. I was bound to Christopher. And all sorts of things got in the way of sizing it up rationally. That sounds like an excuse, I know.'

'What is it that troubles you exactly?' Louis asked.

Eileen felt her hands shake and gripped them together in her lap. 'It's the thought that if I had done something differently, I don't know what, Christopher might still be alive.'

Louis was silent. He leaned back in his chair and stared out of the window. Then he said, 'Eileen, did you feel that you were doing God's work?'

'I hoped I was. I was frightened that I'd got into something I couldn't handle. But I cared about Christopher. I still do, even though he's dead.'

'If you were doing God's work, did you ask for God's guidance?'

Eileen looked at the floor. 'Not enough, I guess. I did study my Bible during that time. But I don't suppose I prayed enough. Not nearly enough. And I still don't. Perhaps it's because I am afraid of the answer I might get.'

'You are a very independent person, I think.'

'Is that a bad thing?'

'In worldly terms, of course not,' Louis said. 'But we are not speaking in worldly terms, are we? As a Christian, you must be aware that it is useless to depend on anyone or anything other than God. Including yourself. Not only useless, but ultimately sinful. Because it denies God's rightful place in your life.'

'You think I did wrong, then.'

Louis shook his head. 'I can't tell you that. Only your own conscience can witness to the details of the situation and your own motivation. I know only what you have told me. Knowing you, I believe you were sincere in your desire to help. But we all have mixed motives, and few of us are blessed, or otherwise, with much self-knowledge. I can't possibly say what might have happened to that poor young man if you had acted differently. And clearly there were many factors affecting his stability which had nothing to do with you. But all that is past. We cannot help Christopher now. My concern is with you, because you are obviously troubled.'

Eileen sighed deeply. 'My mother died when I was eighteen,' she said. 'My father didn't last long without her. My mother taught me to be independent, and life has confirmed that for me. I know I have held on to this thing too long. That's why I decided to talk to you about it. I did pray, during those weeks I was seeing Christopher. But only when it seemed that things were getting desperate. I suppose I thought God had given me certain abilities and trusted me to get on with what I had to do and not bother him unless I found I couldn't cope. Is that wrong?'

Louis smiled, and there was reassurance and warm friendship in his face which brought tears to Eileen's eyes. She blinked them away. But there was a painful knot in her chest.

Louis said, 'Do you remember the story in Luke 5, when Jesus tells Simon to drop his nets over the side after he'd been out all night and caught nothing? And when he did, he had a huge catch? I believe it's like that with us, Eileen. It's not that we can do things a bit better with

God's help. It's that without it we can do nothing at all. Your idea of going for help when you are not coping is a delusion. Because none of us can cope without him. Your independent spirit, admirable as it is in other ways, may have been the door through which the Enemy crept. Coming to God every day in prayer keeps us from straying too far. Sometimes the alternative is a shock, something that knocks us off our feet. Isn't that what happened to you?'

'I suppose so. I didn't think it was quite so black and white.'

'I am not so brave as you. I don't trust myself to contemplate the possible shades of grey. Perhaps it's because I am aware how easily I fall prey to certain temptations. Your temptation, I guess, is the desire to go it alone. Am I right?'

'Of course you are. Just look where it got me.'

'But you have learned a great lesson.'

'Have I?'

'Your own weakness.'

'It's something I would rather not have known.'

'What, and be forever cut off from your only sustenance by pride?'

'Is that what I am? Proud?'

'We all are. Every one. But listen, Eileen. The moment you realize that you are blind, living in a world of darkness, that's the moment when you can come to God for enlightenment. When you throw away the delusion of independence, which is a lie that comes from the Deceiver, then you are free to become the person you really are. The Gospel is full of such paradoxes. To lose yourself, in the end, is to find yourself. To die is to live. When you come to the end of your resources, then God can begin to work in you. And prayer is the constant companion of daily dependence on God. We are told it rises like the smell of incense to God's throne. It's the Christian's hidden weapon that no oppression can destroy.'

For a long moment there was silence in the room. Then Eileen said, 'What about you, Louis? Is prayer your constant companion?'

'Most certainly,' Louis said. 'How do you suppose I have survived seven years here without the support of leaning on God hour by hour?'

'Survived? Has it been so bad?'

'Perhaps that was a bit over-dramatic. But it hasn't been easy. And it's getting harder, seeing the congregation aging and falling away year by year. We may be about to lose another of our fellowship. Dear old Henry Hutton is in hospital.'

Eileen shook her head. 'I didn't know.'

'Well, he's eighty-seven and has a weak heart,' Louis said. He sighed.

'I just remember coming here with all sorts of plans and full of optimism, and I've seen that eroded till I sometimes feel I'm slogging on out of duty alone. It's still a duty that springs from love, but the rewards are getting smaller all the time. If I neglected prayer, I would utterly fail.'

'It's true, a man of your talents is wasted here, Louis.'

'Maybe. I must be where I am sent. But enough about me. Tell me what happened after Christopher died.'

Eileen wrapped her arms around herself and stared at the floor. 'I fell apart,' she said. 'I hardly got out of bed for five or six weeks. It's given me a tiny bit of an insight into what some of our patients have to go through.'

'How did you recover?'

'Well, you would probably say it was a bad thing, but I got better because I knew I had to keep the secret. That I had got to know Christopher so well. When I look back it doesn't seem rational. But if I had told someone then, if I had let all the anger and grief out, if Christopher had become public knowledge, I think I would have stayed in that deranged state for a lot longer, maybe permanently. Does that make sense?'

'Within the framework of you struggling along in your own strength, yes, it does. But don't you think it's time you changed all that?'

Eileen closed her eyes for a long moment, and when she opened them again the room was swimming out of focus. 'I do think so. Maybe today is day one of that process. Maybe that's why I am telling you all these painful and discomfiting things. Doing it is going to be the hard part.'

Louis leaned forward. 'It will be hard. It will be like an undoing of all your habits. But God is on your side. And I will help if I can.'

'You have helped, and I am very grateful. But I should go and leave you in peace.'

'What happened to the other man — what was his name? Maurice?'

'Maurice Bentley. I don't know, Louis. He disappeared.'

Louis' eyebrows shot up. 'What?'

'He decamped. Very soon after Christopher's death. Maybe he has been found by now. I have no way of finding out. But he was still missing at the time of the inquest the following October.'

'Have you forgiven him?'

Eileen sighed. 'Sometimes I wish you were less perceptive,' she said. 'I didn't want to talk about Maurice. It's not for me to forgive him, I know that. He has not offended me, or if he has, he could hardly have intended it. But you are right. I am very angry with him. I hope I don't actually hate him. He is ill, too, I realize. But no, I guess I haven't forgiven him.'

Louis said nothing, and Eileen realized that he had no need to comment. She had said it all herself. She got to her feet. 'I really must go.' She made for the door, and Louis followed.

'It's funny,' Eileen said. 'Down there in the woods it was Christopher who was the pupil and I the stumbling and ignorant teacher. The blind leading the blind. Now I am the learner and you are teaching me.'

Louis opened the door. 'It's still the blind leading the blind.'

They walked down the passage to the front door. Louis opened it for her and the sunlight streamed in, showing up the dust and neglect. Eileen paused in the doorway. 'Christopher was convinced he was being pursued,' she said hesitantly. 'By a deafening, accusing voice he took to be God's, and by huge angelic figures. Who or what do you suppose they were?'

'You say he was brought up in the church?'

'Yes. His father's a clergyman. Brian Arrowsmith.'

Louis thought for a moment. 'I think I might have met him. At a conference. No matter. I expect Christopher's visions were products of his illness, clothed in images he'd unconsciously remembered. But maybe he was sensitive to the spiritual realm.'

'Are you, Louis? Are you aware of things that you can't actually see?'

'Not in the general way, no,' Louis said. 'But I can see the effects. Hold on a moment. I've got another of those helpful little booklets. I'll get it for you.'

He disappeared back into the house, and returned a few minutes later wiping the dust from the cover of a slim volume. 'You might find this interesting,' he said with a smile.

'Thank you, Louis. I'm going home to think.'

'And pray.'

'Yes. And pray.'

Eileen sat among the disorder of her sitting room, for the moment oblivious to boxes piled on the table, to furniture out of place, to cleaning materials scattered about. It was too late for such work; she would finish it tomorrow. The book that Louis had lent her lay open in her lap. Her eyes were closed, but she was not asleep.

"God created the Universe, and ultimately everything is his," she had read. "But since the Fall this world has been a rebel territory, under the sway of the Prince of Darkness. He it was who tempted Jesus in the desert, offering him authority over all the kingdoms of the world, if only he would bow down and worship. He it is who blinds and deceives, and keeps people from believing. 2 Corinthians 4 v 4: 'They do not believe, because their minds have been kept in the dark by the evil god of this world.' Then, addressing those who have become believers, we read in Galatians 4 v 3 : '...we too were slaves of the ruling spirits of the universe before we reached spiritual maturity.' And again, in Ephesians 2 v 2: 'At that time you followed the world's evil way; you obeyed the ruler of the spiritual powers in space, the spirit who now controls the people who disobey God.'

"Jesus himself acknowledged the presence of this evil being. In Luke 22 v 53, addressing the chief priests and the Temple guard who had come to arrest him, he said, 'But this is your hour to act, when the power of darkness rules.' For a moment, it seems, the Evil One was allowed to operate. But Jesus knew that through his death on the cross the power of darkness would be ended. In John 12 v 31, speaking of his imminent death, he said, 'Now is the time for this world to be judged; now the ruler of this world will be overthrown.' Through the cross, by his obedience as a man to the will of God, Jesus had mortally wounded the heart of evil. The chains which weighed down the sons of Adam were broken.

"We, as believers, still have our part to play. In Ephesians 6 v 12 we are told, 'For we are not fighting against human beings but against the wicked spiritual forces in the heavenly world, the rulers, authorities, and cosmic powers of this dark age.' And in John's first letter, chapter 5 v 19, we read, 'We know that we belong to God even though the whole world is under the rule of the Evil One.' Spiritual dangers are still very much a part of our lives: 'The Wicked One will come with the power of Satan and perform all kinds of false miracles and wonders, and use every kind of wicked deceit on those who will perish.' 2 Thessalonians 2 v 9.

"But we are not alone, and Scripture rings with reassurances for the believer. In 2 Kings 6, Elisha's servant went to his master in fear when he saw the house surrounded by the army of Syria. '"Don't be afraid,' Elisha answered. "We have more on our side than they have on theirs." Then he prayed, "O Lord, open his eyes and let him see!" The Lord answered his prayer, and Elisha's servant looked up and saw the hillside covered with horses and chariots of fire all round Elisha.' Hebrews 12, in a famous passage, remarks on the great 'cloud of witnesses' with which we are surrounded. And in Romans 8 v 38 St. Paul made a claim that has the fragrance of heaven, as if all the bells of new Jerusalem are ringing: 'For I am certain that nothing can separate us from his love: neither death nor life, neither angels nor other heavenly powers, neither the present nor the future, neither the world above or the world below – there is nothing in all creation that will ever be able to separate us from the love of God which is ours through Christ Jesus our Lord.'"

Eileen opened her eyes and looked around. For a moment she did not recognize her own room. The feeling of having been somewhere very far away remained with her as she did a few last chores. Then once again she sat by her window and looked out into the night. It was late, and the streets were quiet.

Here I am, Lord. I have been in this very place before: grateful for deliverance, determined not to stray. But I have failed. I know why; I just have to translate knowing into doing. Thank you for all the help I have received from you today. And for Louis, for taking the time. Be with him, too, Lord, in all that you are calling him to do.

As for me, I come to you again: for forgiveness, for guidance, for strength. If my resolve falters, encourage me. If I am wrong, teach me. If I seem to forget you, remind me. My human wisdom is in tatters, revealed as futile. Help me at all times to depend on you, and only on you.

I have read a lot today, thought, listened, learned. I have talked about Christopher. That was a great step. Now I am weary and must go to bed. But I will be back.

Sunday 14 June 1998

Louis caught up with Eileen at the church door.
'You seem out of breath,' Eileen said.
'I am not used to having to run,' Louis said. 'Ambling is more my line. And it is rather warm, sultry even.'
'The weather forecast on the radio said we might have storms later. What were you running for, anyway? Not for exercise, I imagine.'
Louis opened the door and they went into the cool church. Two elderly sidesladies looked up from arranging hymnbooks and wished them good morning.
'I wanted to tell you,' Louis said quietly, 'that dear old Henry Hutton died the day before yesterday.'
'Oh. I'm sorry to hear it. I liked Henry.'
'He was a popular man. But not a well one, I'm afraid. Could you play for his funeral? It's on the 24th at twelve.'
'I'll have to check my shifts and let you know. But of course I will if I can.'
'Thank you.'

After the service Louis seemed inclined to chat. Louis in a sunny mood made Eileen faintly uncomfortable, though she could not have explained why; and somehow, since she had told him about Christopher, Eileen felt a need to withdraw, as if she had taken a step too far. For the last few days she had felt an unaccountable sense of disappointment, as if Louis had let her down. *What did I expect? Sympathy? Vindication? Absolution?* It seemed to her that Louis had already dismissed Christopher from his mind, while for Eileen he was even more painfully present since she had brought him out into the light. How could Louis have been expected to respond? He, after all, had never known Christopher. She had asked for his counsel as a pastor, rather than as a friend, and that was what he had tried to give her. She shook her head. Inexplicably she was annoyed with Louis, and with herself; and the problem that was Christopher, far from being eased, had been dumped squarely back in the lap of her conscience.

Louis said as he hung up his cassock, 'No Maureen today again. Have you seen her recently?'

'No, our shifts haven't coincided much,' Eileen said. 'I should see her this afternoon, though. It's the annual work party.'

'Oh?'

'Our consultant psychiatrist gives a barbecue every summer for the workers.' Eileen paused with her hand on the vestry door handle. 'He and his elegant wife have a large, beautifully-appointed house and immaculate garden in Shawbury. Maureen didn't say she wouldn't be going.'

Louis sat down at the table and uncapped his pen. 'She's missed quite a few Sundays lately.'

'I know. I have a niggling worry about Maureen that won't go away. Do you know her husband?'

'Des? Yes, I've met him on occasions. Seems a nice enough chap. Why?'

'I don't know, Louis. Not enough to put into words. But I sense that something is wrong.'

Louis smiled. 'Maybe you worry too much.'

Eileen sighed. 'Maybe. Anyway, I hope to see her later. Perhaps we'll get a chance to catch up.'

Andrea Caton greeted Eileen by the garden gate.

'How nice to see you,' she said. 'Do forgive me, but I have forgotten your name.'

'Eileen Harding. I'm a nursing assistant in C Block.'

'Of course. Do come in.' She ushered Eileen through to the garden, a third of an acre of perfect lawn, shady mature trees, weedless borders and radiant roses. Andrea was a tall, slim woman, improbably well-groomed, and wearing an understated dress that spoke of equally understated wealth. Eileen felt tousled by comparison.

'I brought you this,' Eileen said. 'I know you are a great gardener.'

Andrea took the tiny patio rose. 'How charming. Thank you, my dear. And you? Are you a gardener?'

Eileen shook her head. 'Just window boxes these days.'

'Ah. Well, there are drinks in the gazebo, so please do help yourself, won't you? Ralph and Oliver are starting the cooking now. I hope we'll have a chance to chat later. Meanwhile I'm sure there are some people here you know.'

Eileen helped herself to a glass of chilled punch and strolled back out onto the lawn. She saw Carol Macnamara sitting at a white wicker table with her husband, a heavy-set man who looked as if he might break the spindly chair at any moment.

'Hello, Carol, hello, John. Can I sit with you?'

'Course you can, Eileen. Lovely day for it.'

'The sun always shines for the Catons. Probably in more ways than one.'

'True enough,' Carol said. 'Seen any familiar faces?'

Eileen gazed around. 'Mm, there's that young nurse from D Block, can't remember her name, and isn't that Ollie? Otherwise, no. Is Maureen coming, do you know?'

Carol shook her head. 'She never said either way. But I doubt it. I haven't seen her out anywhere lately. You know she lives near me, don't you?'

'In the same street, isn't it?'

'No, next street down. But I haven't seen her in the corner shop. And she seems very quiet these days, even at work. Did you ever say anything to her?'

'I never got the chance,' Eileen said. 'I was hoping to talk to her today.'

'If she comes, she'll come with Des. So it might not be so easy.'

'I used to work with Des Parry,' John Macnamara said. 'Funny bloke. Ever since he lost his job you never see him in the pub.'

'Maybe he can't afford to drink,' Carol said. 'You was one of the lucky ones, love. You weren't out of work long. Des never really bounced back.'

John grunted his agreement and took a long swig of his beer.

Carol lit a cigarette and waved it in the direction of the gazebo. 'There's Josh.'

Eileen felt a wash of relief, a loosening of the tight ties of her anxiety. Josh knew Maureen. Perhaps he would have some words of wisdom and comfort.

Josh pulled up a chair and squeezed himself in between Eileen and John, putting his glass down on the tiny table. 'Bit of a squash, this,' he said. 'You all right, John?'

'These chairs are dodgy,' John Macnamara said. 'The wicker's cutting into my backside and the legs are wobbling all over the place.'

'Don't eat too much, then, love,' Carol said. 'We don't want you in a heap on the floor. I wouldn't hear the last of it at work.'

Eileen turned to Josh. 'Is Maureen coming, do you know?' she said. 'I wanted to have a word with her.' A look flashed between Josh and Carol, instantly suppressed.

'Somehow I doubt it,' Josh said gently. 'Maureen hasn't been herself lately.' He smiled. 'Aren't any of you lot hungry? Looks like Ralph's getting busy over there – I see smoke. I'm going to see if there's anything ready. You coming, Eileen?'

'OK.'

They joined a small crowd round the barbecue. Josh greeted a handful of people on the way. Ralph Caton, a striped apron tight around his paunch, his normally neat grey hair flopping over his forehead, his face ruddy from the heat, greeted them cordially. Beside him in a matching apron, a dark haired, sullen-looking young man tore open packs of meat.

'Hello, there,' Ralph said. 'Good to see you. Have you met my son Oliver? Just come down from Cambridge. Last one to fly the nest. Eh, Ollie?' Oliver gave his father an inscrutable look and favoured Josh and Eileen with a barely-perceptible smile. 'So what'll you have?' Ralph said.

Josh and Eileen chose their meat and went to the gazebo for bread and salad; then they made their way back to the table. Carol and John had gone. Eileen saw Carol wave to her from the other side of the garden. 'They've seen someone they know, I think,' she said.

She sat down and sipped her drink. 'Josh, you and Carol are being very mysterious. I know you know something about Maureen. All this saying nothing is making me more and more anxious. Aren't I Maureen's friend as well?'

Josh sighed. 'It's not that. It's just Maureen made us promise. You know what gossip's like in a place like ours.'

Eileen ate a few mouthfuls, then put down her fork and looked up at Josh. 'He hits her, doesn't he?'

'Please, don't let's talk about it here,' Josh said, looking swiftly around. 'There are too many ears, ears that love to hear the latest. No, I know you're not one of them. Look, let's get out of here as soon as we can. We'll have to stay for an hour or two or it looks bad. You can think of some good excuse. Then I'll tell you what I know.'

For the rest of the afternoon they ate and drank and mingled and chatted. The garden filled with well-dressed people, and the air bubbled with loud voices and alcohol-fuelled laughter. The heat and humidity began to build. Crisp cotton began to look limp, and smart hairstyles to sag with sweat.

Eileen had done the rounds of the people she knew and exchanged politenesses with her hosts. She found Josh refilling his glass in the gazebo. 'I need to get some air,' she said. 'It's stifling.'

'All right,' Josh said. 'Just let me finish this.' He sank about half his beer in one swallow. 'Do you know Brumpton Park? It's about half a mile from here. Might be a bit cooler.'

'Did you come on your bike?' Eileen asked.

'No, I walked. My place isn't far.'

Eileen pretended surprise. 'I didn't realize you lived in a posh suburb.'

'Don't be daft,' Josh said. 'On my pay? You can see my block of flats from the end of this road. Even posh suburbs have to end somewhere. You got your car?' Eileen nodded. 'Good. You can drive me to the park. But we have to leave separately.'

Eileen's eyebrows shot up. 'What? That's a bit paranoid, isn't it?'

'Believe me,' Josh said. 'Allerton Hospital is a snakes' nest of scandal.'

'We're only going for a walk in the park, Josh.'

'I know that, and you know that. But they'll make something of it.'

'Who are these people?'

'Don't ask. Thought of a good excuse?'

'My cat needs his dinner.'

'You'll have to do better than that, love.'

'I'm expecting a phone call from my daughter.'

'Which one?'

'Take your pick. One's waiting for the results of her exams and the other's expecting a baby.'

'That'll have to do.' Josh finished his beer and put the glass down on the table.

'Mind you,' Eileen said, 'the results aren't out for another week or two, and the baby isn't due till October.' She began to thread her way through the guests towards the garden gate.

'You don't have to be too specific,' Josh said.

'So how come it was all right for us to go for a drink the other night?' Eileen said, her breath short from climbing in the sweltering heat. Brumpton Park rested on top of a hill, and she and Josh were aiming for the top. 'You didn't seem paranoid then.'

'I checked there was nobody in the car park.' Josh wheezed as he toiled up behind her.

'Are you kidding?'

'Nope. Well, not much. Save your breath for climbing. I'm worn out already.'

Ten minutes later they collapsed on a convenient bench beside an overflowing bin.

'Josh, I can't stay here. The wasps will drive me mad.'

'OK. Just let me get my breath back.'

'Over there looks better. Under the tree.'

The tree was a spreading oak, and the tent of its foliage dropped coolness onto the dry earth. Eileen flopped down with a groan. 'It seems to have got hotter than ever.'

Josh creaked down beside her, muttering about his joints. 'If we get that storm they promised, we will probably be struck by lightning. They'll find us in the morning, two crisp black corpses identifiable only by their teeth.'

Eileen laughed. 'Do try not to be so cheerful.'

'Then the gossips will talk about us even though we're dead.'

'But we won't care. I have to say I don't actually care anyway.'

Josh shook his head. 'Reckless woman.'

Eileen sat up and wrapped her arms round her knees. 'Josh, you were going to tell me about Maureen.'

'Let me get comfortable. This ground's hard.' Josh propped himself up with his back against the oak. 'Well, of course, you've guessed what's going on. Maureen does have a tough time at home. If we believe everything she says, it's just an occasional thing. I'm not saying Maureen is untruthful. She's a lady of great integrity. But she doesn't want to admit it to herself, let alone to anyone else. She's ashamed, poor soul. It all started when Des lost his job. No fault of his, but he hasn't made much effort, as far as I can see, to find anything else, not even hobbies or voluntary work. He's drifting, he's angry and frustrated, and he takes it out on someone who loves him. Stupid, aren't we? People. Self-destructive.'

'But I get the impression things are getting worse,' Eileen said. 'Even in the time I've known Maureen I'm sure she's been going downhill, especially lately.'

'Mm. I think you're right. But what are her mates to do? She warned us not to interfere. She says she can cope. Says it's not his fault. That he's really sorry. Maybe he is, but it's not good enough. Not in my book.'

'Nor in mine,' Eileen said soberly. 'Couldn't Maureen go to her son in Canada?'

'Of course she could. He's asked her more than once. Says maybe his dad can look for work there. Maureen reckons her son doesn't know what's going on. Said she'd do anything to keep it from him. But I wonder. He's not stupid, young Neil. Trouble is, though, Des won't go. And Maureen won't go without him.'

Eileen sighed. 'She's very loyal. I don't think I could live with anyone who thumped me.'

Josh scowled. 'I can't stand the idea of any bloke hitting his wife. Whatever the reason. Cowardly, that's what it is. I've tried to talk to her, more than once. But her line is she married him for better or worse, and she's not going to desert him when things are tough.'

'I must say I admire her guts, even if I think she's a fool. For goodness' sake, what's she thinking of? He could do her serious harm.'

Josh shrugged. 'I know. But what can we do? You got any ideas?'

'I'll think about it.' Eileen bit her lip. 'Compared to Maureen I feel I let my marriage fall apart for far flimsier reasons.'

'Such as?' Josh pulled up a blade of dry grass and wove it between his fingers.

'Oh, I don't know. David made me angry and resentful once too often, I suppose. I just let that coldness and sense of distance grow and grow till there was no going back. I guess I am just as stiff-necked as Maureen, but in a more selfish way.'

'Maybe you're a bit hard on yourself,' Josh said.

'Well, maybe. I'm going to talk to Maureen, first chance I get. If she gets annoyed with me, so be it. I can't just do nothing.'

'What can you say, though?' Josh said, looking at her from under his brows. 'That hasn't been said before?'

'I shall tell her that if it all gets too much she can come and stay with me. She'll probably turn me down, but you never know. Perhaps one day she might need somewhere to go.' She looked at Josh, feeling a wave of uncertainty, needing some assurance. But she could see he felt just as helpless.

Josh looked out from the shelter of the tree. 'I think we'd better get back to the car,' he said. 'There are some menacing-looking clouds coming our way.' He got to his feet and stretched out his hand. She took it, feeling his warmth, and pulled herself up. It seemed to her he took his time letting go.

Black clouds were rolling in, and the wind was getting up, making the bushes and trees creak and sway. Josh and Eileen walked quickly back down the path, but not quickly enough. By the time they were in sight of the car, parked on a small square of tarmac at the bottom of the hill, they could hear the growl of thunder behind them like some huge pursuing beast, and then there came the first fat splashes of warm rain, sending up a smell from the parched earth that brought back to Eileen's mind a sharp memory of forgotten summers. She started to run. 'Come on, Josh! We're going to get soaked.'

They ran and slid down to the car as the rain fell in gusty sheets, soaking their hair and thinly-clad shoulders in seconds. Eileen fumbled in her bag as she ran, finding her car keys. She flung open the door and fell into the driver's seat, laughing. Her shoes were wet through and her cotton dress was stuck inelegantly to her legs. She leaned over and opened the passenger door. Josh got in and slammed it behind him. Within seconds the windows were steamed up and the outside world vanished behind the windswept curtains of the rain.

Eileen looked at Josh and grinned. 'That was sudden,' she said. 'You are dripping all over the place.'

'So are you. Do you want to come to my place and dry off?'

Eileen started the engine. 'That sounds suspiciously like a proposition.'

'Please yourself. I can offer towels and a hot cup of tea.'

'Irresistible.'

Josh's flat was on the sixth floor of an eight-floor block. The lift was broken, so they ran up the stairs until their breath gave out, then groaned and struggled the rest of the way. By the time Josh put his key in the lock their clothes were half-dry.

Josh closed the door behind them. 'Make yourself at home. I'll get a towel for your hair.' He opened a door for her into a sitting room and disappeared down the passage.

Eileen made for the other side of the room where French windows opened onto a railed balcony. Hugging herself for warmth in her damp dress she looked out over the city roofs. The sky was still chaotic, with rags of grey, drizzling cloud being whipped away to the horizon.

Josh came back and tossed her a towel. 'I'll put the kettle on,' he said. 'Do you want to change out of your wet clothes? Or is that too much like a proposition?'

Eileen smiled. 'No, thanks, I'll be fine. A cup of tea would be great, but then I'll get home. My cat really will need feeding.'

'Right.'

The flat was spacious, moderately tidy, but rather dark. The furniture seemed haphazard. There were books on shelves, but nothing ornamental, and only one photograph, in a frame on the mantelpiece, of a young boy in football kit. Eileen rubbed her hair with the towel.

Josh came in with two mugs of tea. 'I don't suppose you take sugar, do you?'

'No. Thanks, Josh.' She waved a hand towards the photograph. 'Your son?'

'Yes, that's Martin, aged about twelve. It's the only one Kath let me take. Lad looks a bit different now. Sit down if you like.'

Eileen sat on a cracked brown leather sofa. 'I was looking at your view.'

Josh grunted. 'It's one of the few advantages of this place.'

'So where's the bike?'

'I rent a garage round the corner.'

Eileen sipped her tea. 'Have you lived here ever since you came down south?'

'Yep. It's a bit of a dump, but I could never think of any reason to move.'

A silence fell, and Eileen felt slightly uncomfortable. Josh seemed to be watching her, as if he was waiting for a signal. She had the sense that what she said next would define something: what, she couldn't say. She said nothing; but the pressure in her own mind mounted.

She finished her tea and put the mug on a low table next to a pile of biking magazines. 'I'd better be going.'

Josh did not move. 'When are you back at work?' he said.

'Tomorrow morning.'

'Ah. I'm in for the late shift, so I'll see you at handover. Did you know Karen Colley's back? Came in at the weekend.'

'No, I didn't. Oh, dear. Poor Karen. I was hoping she might be managing a bit better this time.'

Josh stood up and thrust his hands into his pockets. He was still in his damp clothes. 'I can't see how there's any real way forward for Karen,' he said. 'Not all the while there's no news about her baby. Whatever we try in the way of finding coping strategies seems to fall apart.'

'But Karen isn't what I would call mentally ill at all,' Eileen said. 'She's just a nice, normal woman who's had something terrible happen.'

'Maybe. But it's affected her mental health. Sometimes I look at her and I wonder if there's anything at all we can do for her. It's almost like she's bound to top herself one day, just from the sheer day-by-day agony of bearing that loss.'

Eileen shuddered. 'I hope you're wrong, Josh. What a terrible waste that would be. But people do find strength from somewhere, even in the worst of circumstances. And she cares about her other kids.'

Josh shook his head. 'I've seen it before, people convincing themselves that their family would be better off without them. That grim logic which seems so wrong to us on the outside. But maybe I'm being too pessimistic.' He started to walk aimlessly around the room, frowning, flattening the rucked-up rug with one socked toe.

'You found that strength, though, didn't you?' Eileen said quietly. 'When you were in the army. How did you keep on going all those years, with all the horrible things that were happening, and knowing it was the wrong life for you?'

Josh stopped in front of her, staring over her head and out of the window. 'I don't know. I was a lot younger, and didn't think about things as much as I do now. I guess I just concentrated on keeping alive.' He looked down at her. 'What about you? You always seem calm. What gives you strength?'

'I think you probably know that,' Eileen said. 'My life rests on my faith in God. How I lived before I knew him I don't know. How other people can bear this life without him I can't imagine. What keeps them from that pit of despair? What kept me? I can't remember. Perhaps then I put my faith in myself, and valued other things. I suppose that's what people do. But you've only got to think of how death puts paid to all our endeavours, and you just feel swamped by the futility of it all.'

Josh took a deep breath and blew it out again. 'I wish I could believe all that. I did once.'

'Well, who knows? Maybe you can get it back, if you really want to.' Eileen stood up, and Josh backed away. 'I really must go, Josh. Thanks for the tea.'

He followed her to the door. 'You know,' he said, pausing in the doorway, 'you are good to talk to. You make sense.'

Eileen shook her head. 'Sometimes I do. Sometimes I talk rubbish. But thanks for the vote of confidence.'

Josh looked at the floor. 'Would you like to go somewhere, next time we have some time off?'

She hid her surprise. 'What did you have in mind?'

'I hadn't really got that far. What do you like doing?'

Eileen thought. 'What I would really like is to get out of the city for a while. I'm not a natural urban-dweller really. There must be some hills and forests somewhere.'

'Of course there are.'

'All right, then.' She turned to him and smiled. 'I'll check my shifts.'

He smiled back, his eyes crinkling at the corners. 'And pray for good weather.'

At the front door of the flat Eileen paused. 'Just suppose, for one wild moment, that Karen's little boy was found,' she said. 'Do you think that would put everything right? After all she's been through?'

Josh looked startled. 'I don't know. I guess it would go a long way towards her healing. She would have to do some painful adjusting. There would be a lot of conflicting emotions. But that's just speculation. It couldn't happen, could it? Not after all this time.'

'No, I don't suppose it could.'

Leaning idly on the draining board, Eileen looked out of her kitchen window. She had nothing compared to Josh's aerial view. All she could see was the blank wall of the house next door, a muddy alley and the corner of the street. The rain had slowed to a miserable trickle and the wind was fitful. Because of the weather the darkness was closing in early. Eileen sighed and drew the curtains, shutting out the gloom. She turned on some lights, trying to dispel the heaviness of her spirit. She prowled restlessly around the flat, without purpose, trying to think. But her brain seemed to be in slow mode.

Fletcher appeared from nowhere, his coat damp and smelling of fresh air. He rubbed himself round her ankles and looked up at her enquiringly with his bright yellow-green eyes. She put food into his bowl and he demolished it with graceful speed. Then he gave his paws a thorough wash, ambled through to the sitting room and sprang into an armchair. Eileen scooped him up and sat down herself, putting him onto her lap, where he stretched out to his full length and purred loudly. She stroked his sleek fur. 'Puss, you are a tyrant, but easily pleased.'

The thought of Karen Colley pressed on her mind with painful urgency. Yet what was she to do? Her worries were nothing but baseless suspicions, phantasms of her own making. For the first time she dreaded going into work. There was no course of action open to her, and yet she felt that some obscure responsibility lay on her conscience. Trying to put Karen aside, she thought about Maureen and Des and the whole messy business of marriage. Had she let her own go without a fight? Was she a quitter, as Maureen so clearly, and perhaps perilously, was not? Thinking of David she imagined him as he must be now, happy, she hoped, with Margaret, a pretty woman with a soft Scottish accent and a wry humour. She looked around her quiet room, and felt a cold wave of loneliness. She fought it down fiercely, gripping the arms of the chair. *You got what you wanted, didn't you? Now you have to live with it. There's no room for self-pity. If your life is a bit empty you've got only yourself to blame.*

Eileen picked up the cat and put him gently down on the warm chair. He turned his back on her, curled his tail around his body and shut his eyes. She went into the kitchen, made a sandwich, and ate it while flicking through a free paper that was delivered through the door. Here were so many people all busy with their interests, so many societies and things going on, so many places she would never visit and people she would never meet. She thought of Josh. Did he ever feel lonely? What did she know about him anyway? Next to nothing. Was his invitation just a friendly one, or was there something else on his mind? She didn't know, and thought perhaps that neither did he. She welcomed his easy friendship; whether she would welcome anything else she shrank from contemplating.

Impatient with herself she pulled her Bible towards her, along with the commentary she was using, and turned to the song of the exiled Israelites in Psalm 137:

"How can we sing a song to the Lord in a foreign land?

May I never be able to play the harp again if I forget you, Jerusalem!

May I never be able to sing again if I do not remember you, if I do not think of you as my greatest joy!"

Eileen imagined the weeping exiles by the rivers of Babylon, mourning their lost Temple, strangers in a foreign land, wilful children who had squandered their heritage. Then she turned to Nehemiah 9:

"You warned them to obey your teachings, but in pride they rejected your laws, although keeping your Law is the way to life.

Obstinate and stubborn, they refused to obey.

Year after year you patiently warned them.

You inspired your prophets to speak, but your people were deaf, so you let them be conquered by other nations.

And yet, because your mercy is great, you did not forsake or destroy them.

You are a gracious and merciful God!"

Then the commentary: "The exile should not be seen only or principally as a mark of God's disfavour, but as evidence of his love. What mattered was that the people recognized and acknowledged their failure, and also the grace of God, who, then as now, does not hesitate to use harsh measures if they are what is required to bring his people back to obedience."

Eileen closed the book. She rested her head in her hands and tried to clear her mind. *Thank you for speaking to me so clearly tonight. It doesn't often happen; or if it does, I am rarely receptive. Help me, Lord, to sort out for myself everything that has happened, everything I have been told, today. Please take care of your hurting children, especially Maureen and Karen. Please, Lord, bring an end to their suffering, and help me to find the right ways to help them.*

Like the rain clouds chased into rags and tatters by the wind, fragments of a dream slithered in and out of conscious view. Ralph Caton, fat and oily like an oversized slug, wrapped in his striped apron, stood in the doorway of an old-fashioned butcher's shop with a bloody cleaver in his hand, slowly metamorphosing into someone bearing a passing resemblance to Christopher, who, with wild eyes, raised the cleaver and smashed all the shop windows.

Then Eileen was running barefoot through a forest, carrying a swaddled, crying baby under one arm. The baby's wrappings started to unravel and trail, and she stumbled and began to fall, but she never hit the ground. She found herself lying in a field full of yellow and white cartoon daisies, and a strong sun beat on her closed eyelids, and the flowers were singing. She knew the words were important, that they carried a message she needed to know, but she could not understand what they were saying.

Darkness fell, and there was a loud roaring, like a hundred waterfalls. The noise shut off suddenly, and then there was only silence.

Wednesday 17 June 1998

Eileen woke to a dull morning of heavy cloud and intermittent rain. Fletcher was irked by the weather and fidgeted in and out of the cat flap, onto the fire escape and back again, giving Eileen accusing looks as if she was responsible for the curtailment of his mysterious feline pleasures. Eileen herself felt restless, and anxiety clouded her thoughts. She sat at the kitchen table, staring blindly at a cooling cup of coffee, thinking of her Monday morning shift at work, two days ago. An uncharacteristically sombre Ollie had met her in the nurses' room.

'Karen's back,' he said.

Eileen nodded. 'Yes, I know. How is she?'

Ollie shook his head. 'Poor lady. She is bad. Been sobbing all night. Christine gave her a sedative in the end. She's sleeping now. I told my wife about Karen. She thought about losing one of our little ones, and she cried. I don't see my wife cry much. She's a strong woman.'

Eileen patted his shoulder as she left the room. 'I think Karen makes us all want to cry, Ollie. I'll look in on her when she wakes up.' Later that morning Eileen had spent an hour sitting with Karen, holding her hand as she alternately wept or sat in a dazed silence, and knew there was nothing she could say.

Now, with a free day before a night shift, she tried to put work and patients to one side, but she was unsuccessful, even though she knew that dwelling on their troubles was unproductive. Josh, too, was on her mind, and Maureen, and she felt pulled along in the slipstream of other people's lives, in directions she had not chosen.

Bother, bother, bother. She got up suddenly. *I will do something positive and not waste this day in pointless brooding.* She tipped the remainder of her coffee into the sink, picked up the phone and dialled Louis' number.

'Louis? Hi, it's Eileen. I was thinking of coming over and doing a bit of practice for Henry's funeral. Could I have a church key?'

'Of course,' Louis said. 'When were you thinking of coming? I have a meeting with the Bishop later this morning. But I could leave the key under the flower-pot.'

'That would be fine, thanks. Another run-in with the Bishop? Whatever have you been up to?'

'Just the usual subversive stuff. Nothing to worry about.'

'Well, I hope so. I'll put the key through your letter box if you're not back.'

'OK. Bye, Eileen.'

An hour in the quiet church calmed her, laying a bridge of music over the turbulent river of her thoughts, a bridge on which she could stand and look down and take stock. The challenge of Bach and Buxtehude and Pachelbel absorbed the turmoil of her spirit for a while, and when she emerged from the church into the grey, wet day she felt an unaccustomed peace. *Thank you for that small oasis, Lord. Stay with me.*

She locked the church door and picked her way across the churchyard to the vicarage. She did not take the path, but cut across the sodden grass, making her way to the gate in the high red-brick wall that gave onto the front drive. As she approached the gate she had an unusual view of the back of the church, a neglected area of old, abandoned graves which now had no one left living to keep things tidy. The height of Louis' wall made this part of the churchyard invisible from the ground floor of the vicarage, and on the other side of the church a line of dark firs shielded it from the neighbouring houses. Frank, who had the responsibility of keeping the grass down, seemed to attend to the back of the church less often, because nobody ever went there. So when Eileen caught sight of a brief flash of light her eyes were drawn to a group of leaning, mossy gravestones. She was astonished to see a child's buggy parked there. The light must have been the sun, appearing briefly from among the clouds, glancing off the buggy's rain-soaked plastic cover. The child within was obscured, but Eileen recognized the buggy immediately as Gus's. Whatever was Gus doing in the graveyard in the rain, with no sign of Penny? It was unthinkable.

She hesitated for a moment, unsure what to do. Clearly she could not leave Gus alone in a deserted graveyard. Had something happened to Penny? Putting the church key in her pocket, she started back over the wet, tussocky grass. Then she stopped. Penny appeared from behind the group of gravestones, wiping her hands down the side of her coat. As Eileen watched her, puzzled, Penny took hold of the handles of Gus's buggy, turned it roughly round, and began to push it over the lumpy ground towards the path. The rain had started again, and her head was down. She had not seen Eileen.

Eileen made her way slowly along the edge of the wall to where it met the gateway that led out into the street. As she approached, Penny looked up, and Gus waved his chubby hands. Penny hesitated when she saw Eileen, then pushed on with redoubled vigour. Her face was flushed.

'Hi, Penny. You OK?'

'Oh, hello, Eileen. Yes, fine, thanks.' Penny's voice sounded odd, as if she was being choked. Her face was wet. Rain? Tears? Her eyes were red and puffy.

Eileen frowned. 'You sure you're OK? Can I help?'

'No, no, everything's fine. I must dash. You know, things to do. See you, Eileen.' She strode on determinedly, pushing the buggy hard so that the lying rain sprayed up from its wheels. Eileen stared at her retreating back in perplexity, watching her as she rounded the corner onto the main road and disappeared. *How odd. What a strange girl Penny is.*

Something was making itself felt in the recesses of Eileen's mind, something that made her shiver with a nameless dread. She stepped gingerly onto the soggy grass and waded across to the back of the church. Victorian gravestones were grouped here, abandoned and overgrown. On some of them stone angels presided, one staring, blank-eyed, at a book, one holding a sheaf of lilies to its cold breast, another with a sword pointing heavenward. Eileen went on, ignoring her soaked legs. As she came round the back wall of the church she noticed that on one of the graves a small square of stone had been roughly cleared of grass and moss. On this square stood a jam-jar of water, in which someone had lovingly arranged a handful of flowers: a rose or two, a cluster of large daisies, and some greenery. Eileen shook her head. Was this Penny's work? What was going on?

Deep in thought Eileen recrossed the graveyard and let herself through the gate. Louis' car was parked by the door. She rang the bell, and after a few moments Louis came to the door. He looked strangely cheerful.

'Hello, Eileen. How was your practice?'

'Fine, thanks. Louis, whose grave is that, at the back of the church? The one with the mournful angel and the lilies?'

'What, those old Victorian ones? I think that one belonged to a family called Chandler. They used to be prominent citizens, way back. Made a modest fortune in the tea trade, or something. I looked them all up once, but I've forgotten the details. There's no one left of the family now, of course, at least not living here any more. They all get scattered or die out. Why do you ask?'

'I saw Penny round by those graves, and Gus in his buggy, in the rain. What on earth would she be doing there?'

Louis laughed. 'Well, we know Penny. There's no accounting for her whims. Maybe she feels a certain affinity with one of the long-departed Chandlers. I've no idea, Eileen.' He looked at her. 'You're soaked. Do you want to come in?'

'No, thanks, Louis. I must get back. How was your meeting with the Bishop?'

'Oh, you know, quite routine. I'll be seeing you, Eileen. On Sunday, no doubt.'

'Yes, Sunday,' she echoed. As Louis climbed the steps to his front door, Eileen noticed he was humming.

She turned away, and started down the drive towards the road and her car. Then Louis called her. 'Eileen! Sorry, there's something I forgot.' She turned back, and he caught up with her. 'I was wondering if you could get me a ticket to "Elijah." Would that be possible?'

'What, our concert next month? I suppose so. I didn't know you were into oratorio.'

'I don't know if I am.' He grinned. 'I thought I should find out.'

'Oh. Well, yes, I'm sure I can get you a ticket. I'll see if they're ready yet. The next time I'm at rehearsal.'

'Thanks.' Then he was gone again, bounding lightly up the steps and disappearing behind his front door. Eileen shook her head. First Penny, now Louis. How odd people were. Perhaps she was odd herself.

On the way home she called in at a small supermarket and stocked up on some necessary supplies. Back at the flat she contemplated doing some laundry, but put it off for another day because of the weather. She tried to rest in the afternoon, thinking of the night-shift ahead, almost eleven hours that might be without incident, but could just as easily be stressful and exhausting. Stretched out on the sofa, she flicked through a novel she had taken out of the public library, but it failed to keep her attention, and her eyes grew heavy. At six o'clock she was awakened by Fletcher landing on her stomach. She heaved herself up with a groan and went to the shower.

After feeding the cat and making a meal for herself, she left for work. The rain clouds had blown away and the evening was mild. Sleeping in the day always made her feel blank, hollow, as if in suspension. As the shadows lengthened she drove through the city, and found herself humming music from "Elijah": 'Behold! God the Lord passed by! And a mighty wind rent the mountains around...' She wondered idly what had prompted Louis to ask for a ticket. She shrugged. Who could say? Louis, like Penny, was a law unto himself.

She let herself into the nurses' room a little before nine o'clock. As she shed her jacket she heard a sound from the adjacent toilet, and stopped. It was the sound of muffled sobbing. For a moment she stood unmoving, holding her breath. She knew without any doubt that it was Maureen. She crept to the toilet door and tapped.

'Maureen? Is that you? It's Eileen. Can I help?' An intake of breath from the other side of the door, then silence. 'Maureen, please. I know it's you. Please come out and talk to me.'

Silence. Then, Maureen's low voice. 'Leave me alone, please, Eileen. There's nothing you can do.'

'Maybe not. But I am still your friend. If you're in trouble, let me share it. Don't freeze me out.'

After a few uncomfortable moments Eileen heard the bolt slide back, and the door opened. Maureen came out, smoothing her hair down with both hands. Her eyes were swollen.

'Maureen, what on earth's going on?'

'If you must know, I'll show you,' Maureen said dully. 'You know anyway, I dare say. Everyone knows. Nobody can keep their mouth shut for long in this place.' She came out into the light, and pulled down the neck of her jumper. Down the side of her neck were red weals, and there was an ugly black bruise on her shoulder. 'Satisfied? I've got a few more like that,' she said bitterly, covering herself up. 'Now you know. And no, I didn't fall down the front steps.'

'Maureen, my dear, I'm not a tattler, you know that. Surely you do,' Eileen said in anguish. 'For heaven's sake, I want to help you. If I can. And so do your friends, Carol, Josh. We don't go around talking about you.'

Fresh tears rolled down Maureen's face unchecked. Expecting to be pushed away, Eileen put her arms round her and hugged her. But Maureen stood still and wept. Eileen led her gently to the wash basin. She ran some cool water, soaked a paper towel and dabbed her friend's face, still with one arm round her shoulders. Little by little Maureen's sobs subsided. Eileen looked at her. 'Tell me what I can do,' she said. 'Anything at all.'

Maureen shook her head. 'You can't do anything,' she said. 'Nobody can. I know you aren't like the others, Eileen. Or Josh, or Carol. I'm sorry if it sounded like that. But you can't help. It's down to me. I could leave him, but I don't want to. That would just seem like worse failure. I've got to keep going. I have to keep trying to persuade him to get help. He always says he will. But he's afraid, Eileen. I truly believe that he would go to pieces if I wasn't there. Please say you understand.'

Eileen sighed. 'Kind of. But I'm afraid too. For you. I don't want this to keep on happening.'

Maureen gripped Eileen's hand. 'I have to handle it myself. You see that, don't you? I must go home now. After what happened this morning he'll be frantic, searching the streets if I'm late.'

'All right. But promise me something, please. On a stack of Bibles, or your grandson's life, or whatever you hold most dear. If you get to a point where it's more than you can cope with, get in a taxi and come over to my place. I don't care if it's the middle of the night. OK?'

Maureen nodded. 'All right. Thank you, Eileen. Now I must go.' She put on her jacket, wincing at the pain in her shoulder. She picked up her bag, smiled tremulously, patted Eileen's arm, and went quickly out into the corridor, her head down. Eileen watched her go, feeling utterly wretched and helpless. She sighed, put on her uniform, and went out into the ward.

It turned out to be one of those nights when, if nothing went spectacularly wrong, nothing much went right either. Some of the patients were fractious, sleepless, demanding. Staff levels were low, with some people taking advantage of cheaper holidays before the schools broke up. At two in the morning Eileen made a pot of tea for herself and Carol Macnamara, and sat in Josh's empty office with her feet propped on another chair.

'Is it worth it, Carol? To have a few days off? A night like this. It seems endless.'

'It's worth it to me, love. A day asleep, then two free ones. To do what you like. Anyway, whether we like it or not, nights have to be covered.' Carol took a gulp of her tea. 'That's more like it. I might revive by about seven o'clock.'

Eileen closed her eyes, feeling frayed and stretched. 'Have you been to see Karen?'

Carol shook her head. 'She's been asleep since I came in.'

'Right. I'd better look in on her. Poor soul. She's in a worse state than I've ever seen her. Just defeated. Is there any hope for her, do you think?'

'I don't know, love. There's no answer to her problem, is there?'

Eileen turned her head to look at Carol. 'What do you think happened to that baby, then?'

'He must be dead, I reckon,' Carol said soberly. 'Poor little blighter. Some nutter took him – a woman, it's got to be, someone desperate for a kid – then they panicked and did him in.'

Eileen frowned. 'But there was no body found, was there?'

'No. But it's not like trying to get rid of an adult, is it? The poor mite was tiny, just a fortnight old.'

'I suppose so.' Eileen finished her tea and swung her legs to the ground. 'Oh, well. I'll go and look in on Karen. If she's awake she might need some company. You OK to keep an eye on the others?'

Carol grunted her agreement. 'Sometimes I wish we had some stuff we could spray around the ward. Knock them all out, especially when they're all over the place like tonight.'

Eileen laughed. 'Don't let Christine hear you say that.'

She left the room, closing the door quietly. From somewhere down the ward she could hear a patient moaning, and someone else hissing, 'Shut up, can't you? People are trying to sleep!'

She knocked softly on the door of the side ward and put her head round the door. Karen was awake, sitting up in bed, her bedside lamp on. She turned her head sluggishly towards Eileen as the door opened. Her eyes were dull, her skin yellow in the lamplight, and her hair was tied in a stringy pony tail. 'Hello, Eileen,' she whispered.

'Need some company, Karen?'

Karen nodded. 'Sit down. Tell me what you've been up to.'

Eileen sat in the chair beside the bed. 'How are you doing?' she asked.

'Pretty bad. I'm not supposed to say it, but I'm thinking more and more about how it would be not to feel like this ever again, you know? And there's only one way out that I can think of.'

'Oh, Karen.' Eileen took her hand. 'What about Bobby and Nicky?'

At the mention of her other children Karen's eyes welled with tears. 'Even them, Eileen. They seem, I don't know, not quite real. Or maybe it's me that's not real. And Chopper could find someone else and have a normal life.'

'I've met Chopper. He'd rather have a life with you.'

Karen shook her head. 'It's weird, Eileen, but you know what? I reckon I wasn't really mad to start with, just shocked and grieving, but coming in here so many times, thinking of myself as a mental case, that and all the drugs I've had pumped into me, now I'm actually crazy. I can't live like this. Not any more. It's not living, is it? More like slow death by torture. I'm not strong enough.'

'Nobody I know is stronger than you, Karen,' Eileen said, feeling herself choke. 'If I'd had to go through what you have, I don't think I could have lasted five minutes. Is there anything you want? Anything I can do for you? A drink?'

'No, thanks. Just something so I never wake up. But I wouldn't want you to go to jail, not on my account.' She managed a feeble smile.

Eileen stood up. 'We have to find a way, Karen,' she said. 'We have to get through this somehow. I can't just watch you fade away.'

'Fade away,' Karen echoed. 'How lovely that sounds. Don't you worry about me, Eileen. Just forget all about me. You've got better things to think about.'

'I pray for you every day, you know.'

'Do you?' Karen smiled sadly. 'Doesn't seem like God's listening, then, does it?'

Karen's words echoed round Eileen's mind all the rest of that long night, and followed her as she drove home, battling with the early commuter traffic. Her eyes prickled and every bone ached with weariness. She thought with longing of a hot bath and sleep. But she knew that Karen was beyond the benefit of such simple things. She drew up outside the flats and sat quietly in her car for a few minutes, listening to the cooling engine tick.

Lord God, only you can help Karen now, in the state she's in. Whatever she says, I know you look on her with a grieving heart, a heart full of compassion. I know too that you often call us to be the answer to our own prayers. But I have no idea what to do. Please help me. Help me to do good and not harm. Defend Karen with your strong arms, and be beside her in her agony. Show me the way forward, please. Or if it's not me you want to help her, raise up someone. Lord, she needs you. As do we all.

Eileen awoke at noon to the sun streaming through the thin curtains of her bedroom. She felt such an extraordinary clarity of mind that it made her light-headed. She knew she had dreamed, though she could remember no part of it, and the dream had contained some message, whether from outside or from somewhere deep within her own mind she did not know. But she had a sure sense that not only something must be done, but that there was something she herself could do. What it was she had no clue, not yet. *I must not rush in with flashing lights and ringing bells. I must think.*

There was no sleep left in her. She swung her legs out of the bed and stretched. *Thank you, Lord. You are very merciful. Now be with me, every step. I mustn't foul up. Keep me listening. Keep me ready. But thank you. You are astonishing.*

Wednesday 24 June 1998

Eileen played the last few bars of 'O rest in the Lord' and switched off the organ; the noise from the bellows tended to drown out speech. She swivelled on the seat and looked down into the body of the church. There was a shuffling and muted talking as people took their places in the pews. Summer sunlight streamed through the high arched windows onto the handful of mourners in unseasonal black. Eileen recognized three elderly ladies from the regular congregation, in a huddle at the back, and in the front pew Henry's brother Ned, whom she had met once, and a middle-aged couple, probably Ned's son and daughter-in-law. Then the church doors creaked open, letting in a flood of light, and Eileen heard Louis' solemn voice.

"'I am the Resurrection and the Life, saith the Lord. He who believeth in me shall not perish, but have everlasting life.'"

Eileen shivered. The words reminded her inevitably of Christopher's funeral.

Louis led the procession: first Henry's coffin, carried on the shoulders of four burly bearers from the undertaker's, then Henry's daughter, red-eyed, leaning on the arm of her husband, and their two weeping daughters, and finally Henry's son, silver-haired himself, following with his wife. With a swift glance at their relatives they took their places as Louis faced the congregation and the bearers heaved the coffin onto the waiting trestle, bowed, and left. Louis spoke a few words of welcome and condolence, and the service proceeded.

Eileen did her part, and Louis handled the sad situation as well as he always did, taking the opportunity to remind people that Henry's fate was a universal one, and that we should all look to our own destiny. He celebrated Henry's life of charity and service, and said, truthfully, that he would be much missed. He emphasized the faithfulness of God, taking as his example the wilderness journey of the Israelites after the flight from Egypt, and quoted Exodus: "'I will send an angel ahead of you to protect you as you travel and to bring you to the place which I have prepared.'" He smiled and leaned forward in the pulpit. 'The end of the Israelites' journey was the Promised Land of Canaan, flowing with milk and honey. The end of ours, if we will put our trust in God, is God's own house, which we may be sure is a glorious place of beauty, joy and worship.'

A solemn hymn followed, prayers, and a final blessing from Louis, now quoting from Romans 15: "'May God, the source of hope, fill you with all joy and peace by means of your faith in him, so that your hope will continue to grow by the power of the Holy Spirit.'" Then it was over. The bearers, at a nod from Louis, returned and took back their burden; the mourners followed, one by one washed with light as they passed through the doors, out into the churchyard for the burial. Eileen played quietly until they had all gone. Then she gathered up her music and went out.

To her right, at the side of the church facing the main road, in the newer part of the graveyard, she saw the funeral party in their sombre clothes gathered at the graveside, and Louis in his robes reading aloud, with bright wreaths of flowers round their feet. But her eyes were caught and held by someone at the gate directly ahead of her at the end of the path, a short, plump figure in a summer dress, with a child in a pushchair. As soon as she caught sight of Eileen she turned and hurried away, disappearing round the angle of the wall.

Eileen frowned and shook her head. Now what was Penny up to? She had known Henry, and perhaps she had wanted to be present but had not come into the church in case Gus made a noise. But why rush away? Normally Penny would always chat to Eileen, and she welcomed any opportunity to spend time with Louis.

Somewhere beneath Eileen's heart the weight of suspicion grew, like something unseen and lethal, a cancer, an incubus. Instinctively she shied away from turning that suspicion into knowledge. But then the image of Karen rose up before her eyes, Karen at the end of her endurance, and while Eileen's anger had died down her pity remained, and with it her silent promise, to herself, and to Karen.

She unlocked her car and opened the door, and a wave of stuffy heat hit her. She threw her music onto the passenger seat and drove into town. It was a long way home, but she would pass a row of shops where she could park in the street. One of the row was a small charity shop which she sometimes used on the rare occasions when she cleared out her wardrobe. She parked and went in. Ten minutes later she was on her way home again, with a small stack of picture books for Gus. She felt guiltily devious, but she fought it down. If there was nothing to it, then she would silently beg Penny's forgiveness and thank God that the problem was not hers to solve. But she had to know.

She parked the car outside the flats, and let herself in. After the warmth of the street, the hallway was pleasantly cool and shady. With the books under her arm she took a deep breath and knocked on Penny's door.

After a minute or two Penny opened it and peered out. 'Hello, Eileen.' She spoke guardedly, and again Eileen felt a surge of apprehension. But she answered as blithely as she could. 'Hi, Penny. I was in town just now, in that little shop in Dent's Row, you know the one. I thought Gus might like these.' She showed Penny the books.

'Oh. Well, thanks, Eileen. That was kind of you.' She opened the door a little wider.

'Is Gus asleep?' Eileen said.

'No, he's right here,' Penny said. 'He's getting a bit of a pain when it comes to sleeping in the day. But then he's worn out and grumpy by teatime.' Gus appeared behind her.

'Hello, Gus,' Eileen said. Gus answered her in his own way; he was no great talker, even though he made a lot of noise.

Penny seemed to relax. 'I was just going to have a cup of tea,' she said. 'Would you like one? Gus can look at his new books. Then I'll see if he'll have a sleep.'

'Thanks, that would be nice,' Eileen said, following Penny down the passage. 'I'll sit with Gus for a while, if you like. We can look at the books together.'

'See what Eileen's brought you, Gus?' Penny said. 'You are a lucky little boy.'

Penny made tea and handed Eileen a mug. They sat on the rug and Gus turned over the pages of his books carefully, as Penny had taught him. Again a pang of guilt gripped Eileen. *Please let this not be true, this horrible fear I have. Penny is a lovely mum, and Gus is a happy child. Help! I am getting way out of my depth here.*

She sipped her tea. 'I see you came to pay your respects to Henry,' she said lightly.

Penny nodded. 'He was a really nice man. Always polite to me, and kind to Gus. He never looked snooty when Gus made a noise in church. I'm sad he's dead.'

'Yes, we'll miss him. Our little congregation is getting smaller and smaller. It's a shame.' She got to her feet with a groan. 'I'm getting too old to sit on the floor.' She wandered idly round the room. 'Is this a new photo of Gus?' She pointed to a framed picture on the shelf.

'Yes,' Penny said with pride. 'It's nice, isn't it? I had it done for his birthday.'

141

'It's lovely, Penny. He has such a bright smile. He's not much like you to look at, is he? Does he take after his dad?'

'Huh! I hope not!' Penny said. 'He's no oil-painting.'

Eileen laughed. 'You must have thought so once, I imagine.'

Penny shook her head fiercely. 'You've seen him. He's old, and he doesn't look after his teeth. Yuck!'

'So how come you were with him at all, then, Penny? If you don't like him, and you don't even think he's attractive?'

Penny looked gloomy. 'Don't ask me. I must have been crazy. I was younger then, wasn't I? I think I was a bit lonely. My mum was gone, and my dad was always at the pub. And Dave kept coming over. He brought me presents sometimes. He used to come round and watch TV with me. He told me I was pretty. Me!'

'Well, you are, Penny,' Eileen said.

'Don't be daft. He was nice to me, friendly, you know. I suppose he got a bit too friendly. I didn't have a mum to tell me things, and dad was never there, and I was dead innocent then. Louis said Dave took advantage.'

'It certainly sounds like that. But one good thing came out of it, didn't it? You have Gus. You're really lucky to have such a sweet little son.'

'I know I am.' Penny grinned. 'Even if he is being a bit of a monster at the moment.'

'Well, he is two now. Children can be monsters at that age. Mine were a headache at times.' Eileen sighed.

'What's up?' said Penny. 'Do you miss your girls now they don't live with you any more?'

'No, it's not that. I was thinking about one of our patients. A very sad lady.'

'What, one of your mad people?'

'This lady's not really mad at all. Just very, very unhappy. Someone stole her baby.'

Penny gasped. She grabbed hold of Gus, who was sitting between her knees, quietly looking at the pictures in his book, and squeezed him so hard to her chest that he squealed in protest. She looked up at Eileen, her eyes round behind her glasses, her mouth open. 'Oh, Eileen, what do you mean, someone stole her baby?'

'Just that. She was out shopping with a friend, and when she looked around the pram was empty.'

The tension in the room made the hairs on Eileen's arms prickle. Penny was gaping at her in horror, still tightly holding a wriggling

Gus. 'Was it a little girl?' Penny said, her voice barely above a whisper.

'No, a baby boy, and it happened a couple of years ago, so he'd be Gus's age,' Eileen said. 'Nobody ever found him, and nobody knows what happened to him. Poor Karen. She is desperate. It never goes away for her.'

Penny was silent for several minutes. 'You've got to keep your eye on them,' she said. 'You can't be too careful.' It was as if she was reciting a lesson.

'Yes, that's true,' Eileen said. 'I had better go, Penny. I need some lunch. It's getting late. And you'll be wanting Gus to have a nap.'

Penny got up, and Gus clung to the hem of her skirt as she followed Eileen down the passage to the door. As she opened it to let Eileen out she said, her voice small and hesitant, 'I hope that baby is all right. Maybe someone nice looked after him.'

'I hope so too, Penny. But it doesn't help poor Karen. Not knowing what happened to her baby. It's nearly driven her mad. She has to come into the hospital quite often. She has two other children, but she tried to kill herself a little while ago, just to escape from the pain. And sadly there's not a lot anyone can do to help her.' Feeling utterly horrible, she patted Penny's plump arm. 'Thanks for the tea. I'll be seeing you.'

In her own flat Eileen made a sandwich and sat by the open window, chewing mechanically. The street below was quiet in the afternoon sun, with just the occasional passer-by: a man holding a small child by the hand, a lad sheltered from the world by his headphones, two women in tracksuits, jogging along the pavement, laughing. The sound of their voices floated up to Eileen, and was gone.

What have I done? She felt squeezed, in an agony of doubt. *What have I said, what set in motion? Please don't let anyone come to harm through me.* But harm had already been done, incalculable harm. She reasoned with herself: if Gus was, indeed, simply Augustine Frederick Schofield, son of Penny and Dave, then what harm could come from mentioning Karen to Penny, even though Eileen had, knowingly, breached patient confidentiality? And if Gus was not Gus but Simon, then how could this situation continue? Gus, in his innocence, was happy; but Penny must know what she had done was wrong, and as for Karen, she was, it seemed, through no fault of her own, on a straight road to imminent disaster. *Lord, what else could I do? Maybe I am imagining it all. But if I am not, to say nothing would surely be collusion. I am scared, Lord, scared witless. How will it all end?*

She got up, took her plate to the sink and washed it. She felt an urgent need to get away from the flats, away from Penny and her own worries. *I'll go and see Tash. I haven't been over there for a while. There's nothing else to do here. I've done enough, maybe too much.* She crossed the room and picked up the phone.

Monday 29 June 1998

Eileen opened her bedroom curtains. A mist hung, motionless in the still morning, around the roofs of the houses opposite. It was early, but there was already movement below: car doors slamming, people hurrying along the street to work. Eileen stretched and smiled to herself. She had the day off, and today was the day that she and Josh had arranged to spend together. There was no night shift for either of them to recover from, and no night shift tonight. It had taken this long to find a day when they were both so free.

She showered, ate some breakfast and fed Fletcher, who then vanished away to his own pursuits. Eileen scratched around in the back of her wardrobe and found her old walking-boots. The last time she had worn them was years ago, when she had taken Tillie on a long hike, in the days when Tillie had been younger and fitter. Eileen sighed, thinking of her old dog. The boots were beaten up and dusty, but they would do for today.

She drove through the city as it was coming fully awake. By the time she arrived at Josh's the traffic was heavy and the pavements thronged. The mist had been burnt away by the sun, already warm and promising a day of cloudless heat. At eight o'clock she rang Josh's bell. His gruff voice answered. 'On my way down.'

A minute or two later he appeared, dressed like Eileen in a cotton shirt, well worn trousers and comfortable shoes. He carried a small rucksack, which he threw onto the back seat as he got into the car.

'Well, where are we off to?' Eileen said as she restarted the engine.

Josh opened his map and folded it on his knees. 'I've thought of the ideal place,' he said, turning to her with a smile. 'I've been there before once or twice, though not lately. It'll mean getting uncomfortably close to London, and we'll have to cross the M1. So it's a fair drive. But it'll be worth it, especially on a day like today. It's a great estate, hundreds of acres of chalk ridge and beech forest, right on the northern tip of the Chilterns. There's no hurry, is there? We've got all day.'

'OK, then, I'll just follow your directions.'

Getting out of the city on a busy Monday morning was enough to take all their attention, but once on the main road heading west the traffic flowed more freely.

'This is the road I would use if I ever went back to my old stamping-grounds,' Eileen said. 'Only in the opposite direction.'

'Ever been back?' Josh asked.

'No. Not since I moved here. Except once.'

'What was it like?'

'Very different. I lived in a little village, on a hill overlooking an estuary. That's one thing I miss, being close to the sea.'

'Mm. We're landlocked here, and where we're going today is even further inland. It's got lakes and rivers, though.'

'It sounds lovely.'

'It's all right. Nothing like Yorkshire, of course. But not bad for the south.' He grinned. 'Do you miss your old place? Ever want to go back?'

'Maybe one day. Not yet.'

'Bad memories, then?'

Eileen shook her head. 'Well, you know. I was there twenty-five years. There was good and bad. Just at the end, though, yes, things were difficult.'

Josh was silent for a moment as Eileen negotiated a busy intersection. Then he said, 'Feel like telling me about it?'

Eileen glanced at him. He was looking at her steadily under his bushy red-brown eyebrows, as if he was studying her. She thought about what he had said for several minutes. 'I probably will, yes. If you're really that interested. But not today. Let today be for exercise and peace and beautiful country and good company, not for worries and troubles and soul-baring. We have few enough days like that, don't we?'

Josh chuckled. 'True enough. OK, it's a deal. But I'll hold you to it. One day.'

'And while we're on the subject, let's not talk shop either.'

'What?' Josh protested. 'Whatever else is there? You'll reduce me to silence.'

'You can save your breath for walking, then. Or are you terribly fit?'

'Average, I suppose. Play a bit of badminton occasionally. Getting a bit long in the tooth, muscle turning to flab, but not completely washed-up yet. How about you?'

'Probably about the same. I used to walk more in the days when I had a dog. It'll seem strange to be out without one.'

'Is your dog part of the story you don't want to tell me about?' Josh asked delicately.

Eileen laughed. 'I had a darling old dog called Tillie. Lost her to old age and infirmity two years ago.' She sighed and fell silent for a moment, thinking. 'So much happened that spring and summer. My dog dying was just one of them.'

Josh said nothing, but there was a quality in his silence that told her he was listening intently; and oddly, she felt no threat.

They arrived at a major junction. 'Which way? Concentrate, Josh.'

'Sorry.'

In the end the traffic was kinder than they had a right to expect and they arrived before ten o'clock. The sun was high and hot as they parked and got out of the car. Eileen stretched and felt her shirt part company with her trousers. For a moment before she tucked it in she felt the sun's warmth on her bare skin. She sat on the tailgate and put on her boots, then went back into the car for a pair of binoculars which she hung around her neck.

Josh raised his eyebrows. 'You look like you mean business with those.'

'Not really. My ex runs a nature reserve in Scotland. His interest rubbed off on me, I suppose. Taking binoculars everywhere's just an old habit. It's not a great time of year for birds, though.'

'Well, if you see a golden eagle, let me know.'

Eileen laughed. 'Not too likely, I'm afraid. But David's seen them, I believe. Are we ready?'

'Well, I am. Let's go.'

They covered about eight miles, striding out briskly at first, then as the sun rose and grew hotter, ambling, admiring the views, and once or twice flopping in the long grass to rest. There were few other people about. The school holidays were still more than three weeks away, and most people were at work. They passed a couple of elderly ramblers and wished them good morning; otherwise they had the place to themselves. There was little wind, and the heat silenced even the birds.

They emerged from a long, rutted ride through a forest of tall, handsome beeches, and found themselves on top of a ridge, which fell away down steep grassy slopes, giving them an unimpeded view of patchwork fields that shimmered in the heat.

Eileen sat down in the grass with a groan. 'My calves are aching. Have you got any water in that rucksack, by any chance?'

Josh triumphantly produced a plastic bottle. 'It's probably a bit lukewarm.'

Eileen unscrewed the cap and took a long swallow. 'Nectar.' She handed the bottle back to Josh and lay flat. The tall plumes of the grass tickled her face. She shut her eyes, and felt the sun beating down on her eyelids. 'Do you know where we are?' she said lazily.

'More or less.' She heard Josh take the map out of his back pocket and spread it on the ground. 'I thought we'd go round in a big circle and make our way back to the car via the lake and the house,' he said. 'Then we can go and find a pub for some lunch.'

'Wonderful,' Eileen said, opening her eyes. 'It wouldn't happen to be all downhill from here, would it?'

Josh swatted her with the map and got to his feet. 'I've no idea. We'd better get going, or you'll be asleep by the looks of things. Come on.'

He stretched out a hand to help her up, and she took it.

'You've got grass all over you,' Josh said. 'I'd better not offer to brush it off, or I might be accused of exceeding the bounds of propriety.'

Eileen laughed. 'That would never do.'

A mile or so from the estate boundary, they came to a village complete with cricket green and duck pond and two pubs. They chose the less crowded one, ordered food at the bar and took their drinks to a table in the shade of a bowering oak.

Josh took a long pull of his beer.

'Do I still have grass in my hair?' Eileen said. 'Only you have foam in your moustache.'

'That's the best bit.'

Eileen looked around. 'You'd never think this place existed, would you? It looks like a postcard of ye olde England. How far are we from the smoke? Not that far, I'd guess.'

'I don't know. I'm just thankful that there's no sign of it. Except,' Josh nodded his head in the direction of a tableful of noisy people, 'in some of the clientele, maybe.'

'How do you know they're not locals?'

Josh shook his head. 'Just listen to them.'

'Mm. On this occasion, I admit your prejudice is well founded.'

A woman in a very short skirt and high-heeled sandals swayed over the garden from the pub, smiled automatically, and put their plates down in front of them.

'Enjoy your meals,' she said, her eyes scanning over their heads.

Eileen grinned to herself when the woman had gone.

'What?' Josh said.

'Nothing. I was just indulging in a little prejudice myself.'

Josh shook his head and applied himself to his food. After a few minutes he looked up. 'You've caught the sun,' he said.

'What, a blistered nose?'

'No, just a blush of pink across your cheekbones.'

'That's rather poetic from a hardened Yorkshireman,' Eileen said. 'You've caught the sun as well, come to that. In the form of another twenty freckles.'

'I should have brought a hat. My mother was a flaming red-head in her youth, and I have her fair skin. It goes with the poetic tendencies.' He smirked and took another bite.

'I suspected you had hidden depths all along,' Eileen said. 'But somehow I didn't expect poetry. So what *do* you do when you're not at work, other than looking after your motorbike?'

'I make models of cathedrals out of matchsticks.'

'What?'

Josh's lips twitched and his eyes crinkled. 'No, I am lying,' he said. 'But I know someone who does. An old boy from the pub round the corner from my block of flats, where I sometimes hang out. Ernie Pierce. He's seventy-five and his hands shake like leaves in a gale, but he makes these models. They are extraordinary. I haven't the heart to ask him why.'

'So, apart from hanging out at the pub?'

'I read a fair bit, anything that takes my fancy. They know me well at the library. Then I shamble down to the Crown for the odd game of pool and a chat with Ernie and the lads.'

'Anything else?' Eileen said sternly, knowing he was sending himself up.

Josh shrugged. 'Once in a while I get a phone call from a local charity that collects and stores unwanted furniture for needy folks. I drive a truck for them when I can. There you have it: the thrilling life of J.W. Randall.'

'What does the W stand for?'

'Winifred.'

'I asked for that.'

'I rather think you did.' Josh put down his cutlery. 'So, now the interrogation's over, what about you?'

Eileen leaned back in her chair. 'I go to work, I see my family and friends, I look after my cat. Other than that, I sing with Osewick Choral Society, and at the moment we are rehearsing for a performance of "Elijah." A very good friend of mine is married to the organist at

Osewick Abbey, and he also conducts the choir, a little reluctantly, I think. I am also an organist, of a very much lower order, at St. Augustine's. Not much else, really.'

Josh raised his eyebrows. 'Sounds quite enough to me. How long have you been playing the organ?'

'I played the piano as a child, and got nobbled for organ-playing now and then at the church in Holton. But this job I've only been doing for a few months.' She told Josh the story of Muriel's defection and Louis' heartfelt plea.

'So this vicar of yours, he's a mate, is he?' Josh said.

'I'd like to think so. He helps me out sometimes if I have problems. Of a theological nature, of course.'

Josh's eyes narrowed. 'Does he indeed?'

Eileen grinned. 'Anyone would think you disapproved of my having a clergyman for a friend. I'd have thought they'd be the best sort.'

'Hm. I'll have to think about that one.'

The afternoon vanished in lazy banter that masked, but only just, a sharp-eyed quest for knowledge. Josh proved easy, undemanding company, relaxed and good-humoured. Eileen began to notice that people were leaving their tables and driving away, and she looked at her watch.

'I don't believe it can be almost four o'clock! We've been sitting here for over two hours. I'm surprised the mutton-and-lamb waitress hasn't asked us to leave.'

'If she hears your uncomplimentary description she probably will,' Josh said. 'But I guess you're right: we'd better go. As it is we're likely to get caught in the rush-hour traffic. You fit?'

Eileen got up. 'I've been sitting so long I'm bent double,' she said. 'I'll just go and visit the ladies and then I'll be ready.'

As she washed her hands she caught sight of herself on the washroom mirror. *What a sight.* Her hair was unkempt and still had bits of grass in it, and her face was flushed from the sun. She tried, and failed, to smooth down her hair, and grinned at her reflection. *It really doesn't matter.*

After the expected struggle with the early evening traffic, Eileen dropped Josh off outside his flat at ten to six. 'My cat will cut me dead for being so late,' she said as he opened the door. 'Thank you, Josh. Today has been one of the happiest days I've had in a long time.'

'You worry a lot, I think.'

'Where did that come from? I think a lot, certainly.' She caught his look and sighed. 'OK, yes, and worry too.'

Josh smiled and patted her hand as if he were her elderly uncle. 'I shall hold you to what you said, that you'll tell me your story, one day.'

'If I must.'

'And we should think of something to do, next time we have time off. Which could be months, the way some fool organizes our work patterns.'

'We could always swap shifts.'

'Good thinking. Maybe I might even cook you a meal.'

'What? You can cook as well?'

Josh got out of the car, shut the door and leaned in at the open window. 'Of course I can cook. I wasn't in the army for twenty-two years for nothing. I can also sew, though I draw the line at knitting.' Eileen laughed, and he frowned. 'Some say I am quite a good cook. Far be it from me to boast, of course.'

'I look forward to it, Josh. Whatever it is. I must go. I'll see you at work.'

She started the car. At the corner of the street she looked in her rear-view mirror to wave goodbye, but he had gone.

Eileen drove home, tired, hot and dusty. She wondered belatedly if she should have said something to Josh about her fears of a connection between Karen and Penny. She dismissed the thought; after all, such evidence as she had was flimsy in the extreme. Then she thought about what Josh had said, and a pang of apprehension struck her. What would he think, as a professional, if she told him about Christopher and what had happened that summer two years ago? Would he be critical of her? She shook her head. *I didn't know then what I know now. And what I know now isn't much, if I'm honest.* But would Josh understand?

She parked outside her house, let herself in and ran up the stairs. An irate Fletcher met her noisily as she opened the door to her flat.

'All right, all right, stop complaining, I'm back. I'll give you your dinner, and then I really must have a shower. I feel like a scorched scarecrow.'

She woke in the dark to the sound of the telephone ringing. She must have fallen asleep in the chair. She was still in her bathrobe and her hair was damp. She dragged herself up and switched the light on as she went to the phone. It was nine-thirty by the kitchen clock.

'Mum? It's Christie. Where've you been? I've been trying to reach you since yesterday. Don't you ever pick up your messages?'

'Sorry, sweetheart. I've been out all day. Must have forgotten to check the machine. Are you OK?'

'I am fine. And, Mother, I have my results. I got a 2:1.'

'Oh, Christie, that's brilliant news! Congratulations!'

'Thanks. I'm pretty chuffed myself. So now you have to come to my graduation ceremony and preen with all the other parents.'

'Try and stop me. When is it?'

'On 11th July. It's a Saturday, at two o'clock. Some people get dressed up. I've even heard hats mentioned.'

'I'll see what I can do. Will you be coming home with me afterwards?'

'I don't think so, Mum. I've got a bit of tidying up to do here. Got to clear things out, all the debris of three years. Then I'm going to Italy, with my friend Jenny.'

'Not Isabel?'

'No, she's getting married.'

'So soon!'

'Anyway, Mum, I'll be in touch, and we can fill the details in when you come down.'

'All right, love. And I'm delighted by your news. Well done!'

'Thanks. You OK?'

'Fine. We'll catch up.'

'Course we will, Mum. Bye for now.'

Tuesday 7 July 1998

Eileen parked the car opposite Marie and Philip's house in the Close. The exhaust had been making sinister noises all the way from Allerton. She sighed. *More expense.* She would have to face it sooner or later: the car was old, and only minimally maintained. It was on the way out. Then what would she do?

Eileen leaned into the back seat and retrieved her handbag and her music. When she emerged to lock the car there was Marie, looking fresh in a floral cotton dress.

'I saw you arrive. Or heard you, rather,' she said as she gave Eileen a hug.

'I'm afraid the exhaust's on its last legs,' Eileen said. 'You look nice. You make me feel hot and unkempt.'

'Nonsense,' Marie said. 'Anyway, you are a hard-working woman, and I am a lady of leisure. Nothing to do all day but make myself look presentable. And a little light shopping.'

Eileen laughed. 'When you can summon up the energy.'

'It's a fact, idleness can be wearing. Are you ready?'

They walked unhurried along the flagged pavement. It was warm and windless, and there were still plenty of people about, locals and tourists, smiling at each other benignly in the low evening sun. Eileen could not help noting the contrast with Allerton.

'This is my last rehearsal,' Eileen said. 'I'm working on the next one. I have to buy a ticket for Louis.'

'Really?' Marie turned to Eileen, her eyebrows raised.

'I can't imagine why he wants to come all of a sudden,' Eileen said. 'I didn't think this would be his kind of thing. Though, come to think of it, I don't know what his kind of thing is.'

'I should have thought it was obvious why he wants to come,' Marie said.

Eileen shook her head. 'Do give over, Marie. Louis' motives are fathomless, but I'm sure they don't include a fascination for my company. Which he won't have anyway, with him in the audience and me in the choir.'

'I'm quite sure you're wrong,' Marie said firmly. 'Anyway, I should very much like to meet Louis. Why don't you invite him to come over early for a drink and a bite before the performance? You could travel together. Then you wouldn't have to worry about your car,' she said with an air of triumph, as if she had just discovered some incontrovertible truth.

'Well, that's kind of you, Marie, but I'm afraid you are giving in to matchmaking again.'

'So?'

'Please, don't. I promise you it would be very inappropriate and embarrassing. Please swear you won't, or I shan't invite him.'

'I thought you liked Louis.'

'So I do, very much. I am actually quite fond of him. But anything else...no, sorry, Marie, it just won't do.'

Marie sighed. 'All right. I'll behave. But come over anyway, about five.'

'Thank you. I'm not entirely convinced you'll do as you say, but I'll ask him. Look, there's Philip. He's in a hurry.'

Philip was striding across the green towards them, a bundle of music under his arm as usual. He took his other hand out of his trouser pocket and waved.

'Hello, you two,' he said, smiling, as he joined them. 'How are you, Eileen?'

'I'm fine, thanks, Philip.' Philip took Marie's hand and they walked along together. 'I can't say that "Elijah" is really taking shape for me yet, though.'

Philip turned to her and frowned. 'Will you be at the Saturday morning rehearsal?'

'I'm afraid not. I'll be working. I won't finish till one-thirty.'

'That's a pity. "Elijah" with an orchestra in the Abbey is a very different thing from singing to a piano in the practice room. And the soloists have some of the best moments.'

'I'll just have to wait for Saturday night, then, won't I?'

'It'll all come together, you'll see,' said Philip. 'The atmosphere of the Abbey will help. Sometimes it's better not to be over-rehearsed.'

'Unlikely, in my case,' Eileen said.

Philip looked at his watch and nearly dropped his pile of music. 'I'd better go ahead,' he said. 'I'll see you inside.' He strode on and disappeared round the corner of Ward Street. Eileen and Marie followed at a more leisurely speed.

'Any news?' Marie asked.

'Heavens, yes, how could I forget?' Eileen exclaimed. 'Christie got her results, a 2:1. And I'm to go to a grand degree ceremony the week before our concert.'

'Well now,' said Marie, clapping her hands, 'that's splendid! It must be a relief that she didn't let that little trouble of hers get in the way.'

'I think it was more than a "little trouble" to her,' Eileen said.

'Yes, I'm sure.' Marie looked up at her, her eyes bright as a bird's. 'Is it really all over, Eileen?'

Eileen shrugged. 'As far as I'm aware. She says she's going to Italy with her friend Jenny for the summer. What do I know, Marie? She's not mentioned John for months, not in my hearing. I can't keep quizzing her. She'll think I don't trust her. And anyway, it's her business, isn't it?'

'Yes, of course. But it still affects you.' She patted Eileen's arm. 'We'll just have to hope. And Natasha and Sean? All well with your grandchild? Do we know if it's a boy or a girl?'

'No, we don't. But as far as I know everything's fine.'

'How exciting!'

'Yes, it is.'

'You don't sound very excited.'

'Well, I am. How is Stephanie? Have you seen her recently?'

'A fortnight ago. And she's doing well.'

'I am very glad to hear it. Here we are. We'd better not dawdle any more. You can fill me in later.'

It was still light when Eileen parted from Marie outside her house soon after nine-thirty.

'See you on 18th,' Eileen said.

'Five o'clock. And bring Louis.'

'Well, I'll try. But I'll let you know, of course. I suppose I'll have to come in my concert gear.'

'You could change here, if you wanted.'

'Hm. Maybe that would be better. Be seeing you, Marie. Look after yourself.'

'You too. Don't work too hard.'

Eileen started the engine and watched her friend's retreating back in the rearview mirror until the front door closed and hid her from view. Then she pulled out and drove off, the noisy exhaust shattering the repose of the Close. She pulled a face. *I shall have to get that fixed.*

It had been a rather tense rehearsal, with things going wrong that Philip had thought conquered. People were tired; some had come straight from a long, hot day at work, some were elderly, and none had

Philip's inexhaustible supply of energy for music, something it was clearly hard for him to understand. But he was more patient these days, more human, less Olympian. Eileen wondered if the reinvented Philip, calm and constructive, had found his way to the Abbey choir as well. Eileen hoped so. Some of those boys were very young.

She took the slip road onto the main highway westwards and accelerated away. The noise of the exhaust was lost in the roar of the traffic, heavy even at this time of night. Eileen's thoughts slipped from Philip to Marie, and she thought again with wonder of the change in her friend. She shook her head and smiled at the transparency of Marie's plotting, and wondered what Marie would make of Louis. He, of course, would be charming, clever, self-deprecating, funny. But Marie was no fool. Would she understand why it simply wouldn't do? Eileen thought back to Natasha's confident, if wholly ignorant, assumption that Louis was gay. Was he? She didn't know. Perhaps he didn't either. Beneath the surface she suspected he was a maze of confusion in this, and perhaps also in other ways. With a conscious effort she put Louis' preferences, assuming he had any, out of her mind. The whole subject had danger signs all over it.

And then, why did he want to come to "Elijah"? Just to hear the music? Eileen thought not. So what was going on in his mind?

She asked herself too why she felt disappointed, let down, by Louis' response to her telling him about Christopher. She had asked his advice as a pastor, and he had given it. But it seemed to her that he had failed to make some vital connection, had not seen the effect that Christopher had, and continued to have, on her. And yet Louis was a man of exceptional intelligence and insight. Could it be that his blindness was wilful? Eileen could understand it if he had felt the need to keep some distance from a subject that would inevitably draw them closer. But ever since they had spoken of Christopher, Louis had been particularly friendly, as if they had arrived at some mutual understanding. Eileen was puzzled and a little anxious. What did Louis want? Was he pursuing some devious agenda of his own?

She pulled off the road at her exit, and fought down a yawn. Weariness was creeping up on her. She drove home carefully through the darkening suburbs, the lights of the city centre a dull glow in the distance. She had finally told someone about that summer two years ago, shared the secret that for her was so significant a burden; and yet it was as if she had never spoken. As far as Christopher was concerned, she was still as alone as she had ever been.

Saturday 18 July 1998

Louis called for Eileen at four o'clock. There had been little time to do anything since she arrived home from the hospital. The car exhaust had finally given up and was awaiting replacement, and for the last few days Eileen had been obliged to take buses to and from work, which meant long delays, especially at weekends. She found time to take a shower and put her long black skirt and white shirt in a bag with some suitable shoes. On the way down the stairs she knocked on Penny's door and asked her to feed Fletcher. Penny agreed, but she seemed anxious to shut the door, and spoke in monosyllables, avoiding Eileen's eyes.

She slid into the passenger seat of Louis' car feeling hot and irritable. Louis seemed to pick up her mood in some subliminal way and said little. He hummed to himself as he drove.

'I didn't know you were a fan of Mendelssohn,' Eileen said as they sped eastwards along the main road.

'It's not so much that,' Louis said mildly. 'I haven't been to any musical event for a long time, nor have I been to Osewick recently. It seemed like a good opportunity.' He glanced at her and smiled. 'You don't mind, do you?'

'Of course not.' She heard her own bluntness and relented. 'It's kind of you to give me a lift. I don't know how I would have got there with my car in dock.'

'When is it likely to be back on the road?' Louis asked.

'They're fixing a new exhaust on Monday.'

'Ah. So, tell me about your friends. It was nice of them to invite me.'

'Philip and Marie? What can I tell you? Philip is organist at the Abbey, a great musician as you might well expect, but really in a class of his own. A very modest man in private though, even a little awkward. Marie has that quirky humour some Irish people have. She's hospitable and sociable and full of fun.'

'Do they have children?'

'No. They've been married less than two years. Philip was the Abbey organist some while back, then had a break, which is how we met him. He was organist at the little church in the village where I used to live. His leaving the Abbey was an unedifying story of church politics, I'm afraid. Philip was the victim of some unpleasant goings-on. I don't know the details, but it involved the previous Dean.'

'How intriguing,' Louis said.

'Mm. An apt choice of words. But it's all back to how it was for Philip, except that he's acquired a wife on the way, and he's very happy to be where he belongs.'

'And Marie?'

'Marie's life has been completely turned around,' Eileen said with a wry smile. 'From being a divorcee with a teenage daughter, renting a cottage and working in old people's homes, she is now living a leisured and privileged life in a beautiful eighteenth century house in sight of a medieval abbey, and married to a younger man who adores her.'

'Sounds like a fairy-story.'

'Doesn't it just.'

'You're not envious, are you?' Louis turned to Eileen in feigned shock.

'I think I probably am. It might be nice not to have to work, not to have to worry about fixing a clapped-out car, not to be thinking about bills quite so much.' She grinned. 'No, I don't really envy Marie. I'm very pleased for her, actually. Anyway, you'll see for yourself.'

'So I will,' Louis said as he took the Osewick exit. 'You say Marie has a daughter?'

'Yes. Stephanie. She's twenty. She's been in Allerton jail for the last two years.'

'Good grief! What on earth for?'

'Drug-dealing. And she stabbed a young man in the arm.'

Louis shook his head. 'You're not making all this up, are you, Eileen? Just to enliven my dull clerical life, perhaps?'

'Of course not. It's all part of that story I was telling you a few weeks ago. It was a turbulent time for a number of people, not just me.'

'So I see. Well, I'm glad you told me these things. I know what subjects to avoid now. It seems extraordinary that so much drama could happen in what you describe as a rural backwater.'

'Well, maybe I'll tell you about it one day,' Eileen said. 'But not now. We'll be there in a few minutes. I can see the Abbey spire.'

If Eileen felt a little less frazzled when she climbed out of Louis' car in the Close, her mood was to change again. When they arrived Marie was loading her dining room table with platefuls of food, and Philip had uncorked a variety of wines.

'Heavens, I shall be too drunk to sing!' Eileen said.

'You could always be restrained,' Marie pointed out.

'There's a thought.' She introduced Louis, and he, as she had rather sourly anticipated, was charming and witty. They sat in the garden with plates and glasses, enjoying the early evening sun. Philip had to leave early, but before he went he and Louis discovered a number of acquaintances in common, and enjoyed a lively discussion of these unfortunate folks' peccadilloes. Once Philip had gone, carrying his penguin suit carefully over his arm, Louis was attentive and droll with Marie, who was soon under his spell. Eileen felt obscurely cut out of the action. Something was going on, though she could not have said what it was, and although it seemed to involve her, she sensed that it was out of her control.

'I'm going to change, Marie,' she said, standing up abruptly. 'Can I use the spare bedroom?'

'Of course, dear. I'll follow you in a moment.'

But when Eileen came down, now in her choral society get-up, Marie had not moved. She was laughing uproariously at something Louis had just said.

Louis looked up. He was grinning, his face flushed from the sun. 'I've been telling Marie about our friend Muriel,' he said.

Marie dabbed at her eyes. 'And singing your praises.'

'How embarrassing,' Eileen said. 'Shouldn't you get changed?'

'Yes, I'm just going.' A tiny frown creased Marie's brows at her friend's brusqueness, but she did not comment. When she had gone, Eileen busied herself clearing away the dirty dishes and stacking them in the kitchen. Louis watched her, twirling his half-empty glass between his fingers. 'Are you all right, Eileen?'

'Of course,' Eileen said coolly. 'Why shouldn't I be?'

The three of them walked down the Close and across the green, with groups of people ahead of them and following. Louis and Marie seemed in no hurry, and chatted and laughed all the way to the Abbey. The great west doors were open, and the huge venerable building was washed in unaccustomed light. Already the nave chairs were half-filled with people, while others milled about, greeting acquaintances. They left Louis looking for his seat and made for the crypt, where the choir was to line up before the performance. Eileen looked up the altar steps into the Quire, and remembered the last time she was here, two years ago, listening to evensong, on the day she had taken Michael to his family. The memory of Michael was a dull ache now, but this evening thinking of him caused a twinge of pain and a prickling of her eyes. *Enough.*

A little before seven-thirty the choir filed in, taking their places on the temporary staging in front of the altar. The orchestra, formally dressed, with music open and instruments to hand, was already in place between the front row of singers and the conductor's rostrum. The Abbey was packed with people, cheerful in summer colours, and the evening sun streamed in at the high windows. Stewards closed the doors and gradually the audience fell silent. Then there was clapping as the soloists emerged: first two elegant women, one tall and willowy in turquoise satin, the other short and rounded in a dress of crushed gold velvet, their shoulders bare, their jewellery catching the light. Following them came the tenor and the bass. Eileen leaned forward to see them better, and was surprised at the youth of the tenor, whose long hair was tied in a pony tail, and the thinness of the bass, who looked as if he had no room for the lung power he would need to sing the part of the prophet. But it was Philip, walking in behind the soloists, who was most transformed, in tail coat and white tie, his unruly hair smoothed down. He looked a little uncomfortable to be so on display, and Eileen realized that it was more usual for him to be hidden away, in the organ loft, or at the least swathed in a crimson cassock. But, true to form, when he raised his baton and looked over the choir with one sweeping glance, he was another being. Eileen's eyes sought out Marie, two rows down, and noted her friend's tiny, secret smile.

And then it began. In the expectant silence came four sonorous chords, then the bass's voice: "As God the Lord of Israel liveth, before whom I stand..." It was a voice of power, rich and controlled, utterly belied by the man's slender frame. Eileen was transfixed.

The orchestral overture gave her a few minutes to compose herself. The music was so close up, so immediate, that she was in danger of forgetting the part that she herself had to play; and that first huge choral chord, "Help, Lord!" was crucial, as openings must be. From the Israelites came a desperate pleading: there was no harvest, their children were hungry. Had God abandoned his people? Beneath the sweeping duet of soprano and contralto the people prayed for God to hear them in their distress. Then the young tenor, his diction sharp, his style operatic, took his place on the low dais, and for Eileen it was the first moment when her scalp prickled. "If with all your hearts ye truly seek me, ye shall ever surely find me."

But the Israelites were doubtful, believing that they were under God's curse, until the awe-struck moment when, in a moment of insight, they realize it is their own idolatry that has provoked God's anger. "For he, the Lord our God, he is a jealous God..."

The narrative then took over, with the angel sending Elijah eastwards to be taken care of by ravens at the brook Cherith, followed by his meeting with the poor widow, who helped the prophet with her last scraps of food, only to lose her only son. Elijah, with a mighty prayer, brought the lad back to life, and the widow sang God's praises.

The mood of joy and assurance darkened with the arrival of Ahab, that weak and wicked king spellbound by his pagan queen, and the contest between Elijah and the prophets of Baal. When Baal's followers failed to rouse their god, Elijah called the people tenderly to him. For a few minutes Eileen became an angel, inviting the people to "Cast thy burden upon the Lord...," a moment of quiet expectation and undiluted faith, expressed in a sweet four-part harmony. Jehovah answered his prophet's prayer, and fire roared down from heaven, consuming the sacrifice. God and his prophet were vindicated. Eileen, her eyes fixed on Philip, was concentrating wholly on singing, feeling herself a part of the Israelite throng astonished by the miracle of heavenly fire and rededicating itself to the service of the one true God. "The Lord is God! O Israel, hear! Our God is one Lord; and we will have no other gods before the Lord!" The oath of fealty was accompanied by massive sounds from the orchestra, with organ and percussion, and then, with a shudder, the false prophets were dragged off and killed.

Elijah's long, demanding solo followed, with frenzied strings, likening the word of God to a "hammer that breaketh the rock into pieces."

But the drought was still in force, and now there came solemn prayers, from Elijah and the people, to restore rain to the parched land. A little chorister, in his best school uniform, his shoes shiny and his hair combed, took his place next to the bass. Again and again Elijah sent the child to look for clouds, and every time, in a voice of piercing clarity, the boy reported nothing. Elijah's prayers became more and more fervent, until, against the iron earth and the brass heaven, there appeared a tiny cloud "like a man's hand." Immediately the skies were black with rain-clouds, whipped along by a howling wind, and the rain poured down, and the people rejoiced in God's power as the rushing waters lifted their voice in praise to the accompaniment of organ and brass thrusting through the fabric of the orchestral sound.

So the first part ended in joyful confidence and renewed trust in the one true God of Israel. As Eileen left the stage in file to enthusiastic applause, wishing it could just go on without a break, she reflected on the fickleness of mankind, knowing that twentieth century man was no less changeable than the ancient Israelites. How patient God was, both then and now.

Scanning the audience as she descended from the stage, she saw that Louis had found an acquaintance and was busy chatting. Not wanting to break the mood she slipped away, and after a visit to the ladies' went back into the crypt to await the second half.

Marie found her as they were lining up again. 'Where did you get to? You missed the interval refreshments.'

'Queuing for the loo. And after that feast you gave us I had no need of sustenance.'

'It's going well, I think,' Marie said.

'It's wonderful. Philip was right.'

Marie smiled. 'Where music is concerned, he usually is.' As her row began to move she turned to Eileen. 'I forgot to ask you: how did Christie's graduation ceremony go?'

'It was a great day. I'm afraid we got a little drunk.'

'We?'

'Christie and her friends, and one or two of their parents.'

'Disgraceful. Was David there?'

'He was, with Margaret. They stayed for the ceremony and long enough to congratulate Christie, then left. I think there was someone he had to see while he was in that neck of the woods, something to do with work.'

'Is he well?'

'Yes, he seemed in excellent form.'

'And did you wear a hat?'

'I did, one from the charity shop, and then later in the evening I threw it in the Exe.'

'Oh, dear.'

Part two began, its mood serious, darker. God, in the mouth of the soprano in full flight, asked his people why they were "afraid of man that shall die; and forgettest the Lord thy Maker..." Once again his generous love triumphed as he told them not to be afraid, for he would strengthen them, and the people responded in joyful relief: "Be not afraid, saith God the Lord." As she sang these confident words Eileen felt lifted, as if her feet had left the floor, and as if the very winds of heaven were rushing through her, filling her lungs with air.

But then it was time for Elijah to confront the sinful monarch and his evil queen. Ahab's idolatry had awakened the Lord's anger, and

Elijah told him that Israel would be shaken "as a reed is shaken in the water." Meanwhile Jezebel was rousing the people to fury. In a few short moments the people who had just been praising God turned against his prophet. Although Elijah had restored rain to Israel by his intercessions, the people had short memories. "Woe to him, he shall perish," they cried, "for he closed the heavens!"

Obadiah, secretly faithful, warned Elijah of Jezebel's determination to have him killed, and urged him to flee. Downcast by the people's faithlessness, to the sound of weary chords from the orchestra and a lone cello, Elijah trudged into the wilderness: a desert not only geographical but also spiritual; and there that great man of God fell into despair. All his life he had been "very jealous for the Lord God of Hosts", but the Israelites had "broken Thy covenant, and thrown down Thine altars, and slain all Thy prophets" so that only Elijah himself was left. "Now take away my life", he pleaded. "…let me die, for my days are but vanity!" It was a sad moment for such a valiant warrior of the Lord. How would God respond? As Elijah slept under the juniper tree, angels gathered round in a protective circle, and Eileen, with the other women, sang, telling Elijah, and us, to lift our eyes to the mountains and trust in the God who never sleeps, but rings the righteous round with angelic hosts.

An angel awakened Elijah, telling him to journey deeper into the wilderness. Once again, remembering what seemed to him his failure, the prophet poured forth his lament. "O Lord, I have laboured in vain; yea, I have spent my strength for nought." To her own astonishment Eileen felt tears come into her eyes, that such a hero should be so discouraged. Elijah pleaded with God to show his power. Harsh chords from the orchestra accompanied him as he sang "…make thy name known to Thine adversaries…" But then came the gentle voice of the angel: "O rest in the Lord…he shall give thee thy heart's desires." Recognizing the music, Eileen thought of Henry Hutton's funeral, and others she had attended, and wondered briefly what her own heart's desires were. Still, at almost fifty years old, she hardly knew.

God's response was, as usual, uncompromising. "He that shall endure to the end, shall be saved." But then there came what was almost an answer, as God, on the mountain top, bestowed on Elijah – in the mighty wind, the storm and the earthquake – overwhelming evidence of his power, and – in the still, small voice – an ineffably close sense of his presence. Would such an experience not stay with someone all their life? "I am in the innermost corners of your being," God seemed to say. As Eileen listened to the semi-chorus, and added her own voice to the answering affirmation, a vision of wonder struck her, making her dizzy, as if the glory of God, surrounded by the seraphim, had for a fleeting moment filled and flooded Osewick Abbey.

Assured that God has kept seven thousand people faithful, "...knees that have not bowed to Baal...," Elijah went on his way strengthened, ready to "suffer for Thy sake," knowing that "Thy kindness shall not depart from me." It came as a shock to Eileen that Elijah expected to be strengthened in order to endure further suffering. But God's response was, as it ever was, astonishing in its generosity, and she remembered something she had heard once, that God is no one's debtor. For now Elijah was whisked away to heaven in the fiery chariot and spared the pains of human death, to the accompaniment of a thundering organ, and Eileen felt herself lifted from one exalted plane to another as her lungs burned with singing and her heart was transported to the rolling of the drums. Then the tenor sang of how the righteous shall "shine forth as the sun in their heavenly Father's realm." Every believer that kept the faith would have Elijah's reward (though probably without the fiery chariot.) Eileen leaned forward in her seat to catch every note, and heard the tenor sing "...all sorrow and mourning shall flee away for ever." It was so easy to let the vision fade, among the petty woes of ordinary life, and she, with all humanity, was as fickle and forgetful as the ancient Israelites. As she contemplated the ending of sorrow a surprising memory came to her, of her mother, her life cut short.

And then, with the glorious quartet of soloists inviting everyone to "Come to the waters...and your souls shall live for ever," and the final chorus promising light to all and pouring out praise to God the creator, it was over. The idea of light breaking forth "as the light of the morning breaketh" made Eileen think of the dawn of Easter, the empty tomb, and the great revolution at the heart of creation. Louis had said, in his sermon on Easter day, that nothing would ever be the same because Jesus had risen; and Eileen felt that something irrevocable had changed within her as well. Singing "Elijah", for reasons she could not yet put into words, had utterly blown her away.

She stood with the rest of the chorus, hot and sticky, clasping her music to her chest, and received the applause as more and more people in the audience rose to their feet. Philip and the soloists went out and came back several times, taking their bows, and were given flowers and wine. Then the clapping died, people began to leave their seats, and the chorus trooped off the stage.

Eileen collected her jacket from the crypt and found Marie. 'You'll wait for Philip, of course,' she said. 'Congratulate him for me, won't you? He did a marvellous job. That was an amazing performance. I don't know how he holds it all together.'

Marie nodded. 'He works terribly hard.' She hugged her friend. 'See you soon, Eileen. I'll phone.'

Eileen made her way through the people still thronging the nave and found Louis leaning on a pillar. He raised his eyebrows enquiringly. 'Ready to go?'

She nodded. 'Let's see if we can beat the rush.'

They spoke little until they made it onto the main road and sped westwards through the half-darkness of the summer night.

'That was splendid,' Louis said. 'Very powerful. Did you enjoy it?'

'Too weak a word,' Eileen said. 'I missed the last couple of rehearsals, so I wasn't prepared for how it would be with orchestra and organ and soloists. It was...words fail me.'

'It must be a great thing to be able to sing,' Louis said.

'It is. Not that I am anything special. I'm sure singing is good for your health. Physical and spiritual.'

They were silent for several miles. Then Eileen said hesitantly, 'Louis, you know that bit, just before the end, where we sing about God raising one from the north – why the north? And God's spirit will rest on him, and it talks about wisdom and understanding and counsel and might. It sounds like that prophecy in Isaiah. Is it talking about Elijah or is it a reference to Jesus?'

'Both, I imagine,' Louis said. 'I was reading the programme notes, and it seems to me that the Bible verses were selected with hindsight, to emphasize the prophetic. Elijah is seen as a sort of Messianic forerunner.'

'There's that other bit, too, where we are invited to "come to the waters". That sounds like Jesus as well.'

'It does.' He glanced sideways at Eileen, and she saw him quell a smile.

As he pulled into Eileen's road Louis had clearly tuned in to her exalted mood. He parked at the kerb and turned off the engine. 'I'm glad this evening was meaningful for you,' he said. 'I think many people in the audience found it uplifting too. You all did an excellent job.'

'Thanks.'

'God doesn't give us many of those high-flying moments,' Louis mused, almost to himself. 'They are very precious, though we tend to forget them. If we can keep hold of them they keep us going, down in the dull valleys of life. But you know, that's where his work is done, in the dull valleys.'

'I suppose you're right. Regrettably. I guess we can't be on the mountain top all the time.'

'No. But such times make for great outpourings of praise. And that can't be a bad thing.'

'I must go. Thanks for taking me, Louis. See you tomorrow.'

'Not for a dull valley experience, I hope.'

'We'll aim for the foothills, shall we?'

Louis smiled as he started the car. 'Foothills, why not. Goodnight, Eileen.'

Eileen was too restless to sleep. She opened her Bible at 1 Kings and read the story of Elijah again. What did it mean, to be "jealous for the Lord?" She thought of Jesus causing uproar in the Temple, and his grieving over the blindness of the people, their idolatry, the broken covenant. That hadn't changed; people were still the same. If Jesus hadn't come to make things right, the world would still be helpless, unforgiven. She shuddered. To live this life, to go to death, without that hope, was unthinkable. Jesus was God, and though he was often downcast, he never despaired. Elijah, for all his heroic qualities, was a man, and he did despair. How did God respond? Lovingly, and yet with brisk instruction. *'Don't sit about moping – there's work to do.'* Eileen smiled to herself and closed the book. Elijah had kept faith, and been spectacularly rewarded. But for her there were more dull valleys to cross, more work to do. She sighed and stretched, suddenly weary. The clacking of the cat flap told her that Fletcher was in for the night. She switched off the lights and went to bed.

At three in the morning she woke with a start, her heart pounding, sweat pouring off her. She threw back the covers with a groan and went to the bathroom. Her dream came back to her in tattered fragments.

She was in a darkened cinema, alone, or so it seemed at first. The only light came from cracks around the doors, and from somewhere high up a torch beam flickered. She was wearing a very short skirt, and this embarrassed her. Although there was no one to see, she kept tugging it down. She knew that she shouldn't be in the cinema, but she was looking for a dog. Was it her dog, or someone else's? From time to time she caught sight of it, a small, white dog with curly fur and one black ear. But it kept disappearing down the rows of seats and popping out again where she least expected it. She pursued it for what seemed an eternity, without success, becoming more and more agitated, knowing that it would not be long before someone caught her, and then there would be trouble. But she could not leave without the dog. Eventually she came upon it suddenly, unexpectedly curled up asleep on one of the seats. She picked it up; but just as she turned to leave a tall, shadowed figure loomed over her and she cowered in terror. As she backed away from the menacing shape, there was a huge flash of light from the exit, and the double doors blew inwards with great force. Only then did she remember planting the bomb.

She fetched a glass of water from the kitchen and went back to bed. *What appalling junk there is in my brain. Pity I can't give that to the charity shop. Or throw it in the river, like an unwanted hat.*

Saturday 15 August 1998

The heat was overpowering. Sunlight poured in at the big window which dominated the far end of the ward. The few patients who remained indoors were dozing; several were outside in the garden, accompanied by Carol and Ollie. Josh was in his office, a desk fan threatening to consign his paperwork to an untidy heap on the floor, and Eileen was the only member of staff on the ward. It was just as well that there were fewer patients than usual in C Block; several staff members were on holiday. Eileen opened as many windows as she could reach, letting in a fresher breeze and the sleepy buzz of insects from the garden below. Even the birds were quiet.

She looked at her watch. It was almost six o'clock. She switched on the television in the communal area and was immediately aware that something terrible had happened. She looked up and saw Josh coming out of the bathroom.

'Josh, come and look at this.'

'What?' Josh came towards her, drying his hands on a paper towel.

'There's been a bomb in Northern Ireland. It looks bad.'

Josh muttered something she did not catch, and came to stand beside her. They watched in silence as the horrific images unrolled on the screen, with the BBC reporter talking over them, sombre and restrained. For six or seven minutes they listened to how a bomb had exploded in the market town of Omagh in County Tyrone on the last day of the annual carnival week, the town packed with shoppers taking advantage of the sales, so that many of the victims were women and children. They heard how a warning had been unclear and misconstrued, so that the police shepherded people to the very area where the bomb went off. The BBC's report dwelt on the rescue efforts, the nurses and doctors called in to help with the overwhelming numbers of injured, the bus commandeered for the walking wounded, other hospitals pitching in, the priests praying and comforting; but in the background, under a shroud of dust, was the shattering scene of buildings ripped apart, a body lying in the street, and the heart-stopping sounds of screams and moans. The reporter's voice droned on. Injured people were reaching the hospital, only to die while undergoing treatment; the number of injured was more than two hundred, the dead estimated at twenty and likely to rise. It was, he said, the worst atrocity in Ireland's long and bloody history.

Eileen glanced at Josh. He stood with his fists clenched at his sides, staring at the screen, an expression of utter horror on his face. Then Eileen heard voices from the corridor. 'Josh,' she said, touching his arm lightly. 'Some of the patients are coming back. Have you seen enough? Shall I switch to another channel?'

Josh nodded and strode away back in the direction of his office. Eileen heard the door bang. She switched the TV over to a vacuous comedy as three patients came down into the ward, chatting and laughing with Ollie.

'We left the others doing exercises with Carol,' Ollie said. 'I'm going to put the kettle on. You OK, Eileen?'

'Fine, Ollie. Pour one for me and Josh, will you? Just leave them in the kitchen.'

She knocked on Josh's door and went in. Josh was sitting at his desk, his head in his hands.

'Tea, Josh.'

'Thanks.' His voice was husky. He leaned back, took off his glasses and rubbed his eyes with the heel of his hand. He pulled his tea towards him. 'Dear God, Eileen. Bloody Ireland. It goes on and on. But this has got to be the worst.'

'That's what they're saying. This must take you back, Josh.'

'Yeah, it does,' Josh muttered. 'To a place I don't want to be. I don't want to remember all that stuff, but it hangs on. So many people gone. Not just Billy Painter. I told you about him, didn't I?' Eileen nodded. 'You know I was in Ireland quite a few times. You keep hoping they'll get it right, and you think maybe things are going to improve, and then something like this happens. It's on the news because of all the civilians hurt and killed, and I think of them too, but I can't help remembering the men I knew, men who left young kids behind, and the injured ones, men trying to find work when they've only got one hand or are blind. Why do we do this stuff to one another? Can you tell me that?'

Eileen shook her head. 'I don't understand it either. How people can risk innocent lives. Or how anyone can forgive when they've lost a friend or relative to blind violence.'

'Someone did, though,' Josh said, looking up, his face blotchy, his eyes full of anguish. 'Do you remember?'

Eileen frowned. 'Who are you talking about?'

'It was two years after I left the army,' Josh said. 'The bastards targeted the garrison but the bomb went off too early, and they got a bunch of townspeople at the cenotaph on Remembrance Day. Surely you remember? Enniskillen.'

Eileen nodded. 'Of course.'

'I had a mate whose brother was in that regiment, the Royal Inniskilling Fusiliers I think it was. The bomb was in an old schoolhouse. The whole building came down, and one wall collapsed on the people. That's how most of them were killed. The soldiers were lined up some way away, or they'd have copped it too. As it was they helped dig the people out. But it was too late for most of them. That young nurse was crushed to death, remember? It was her dad who said that on TV, about not holding a grudge. He said he prayed for the bombers every night. That was a brave man.'

'It's coming back to me now.'

Josh took a gulp of his tea. 'I can't remember his name for the moment, but I do remember he was a strong Christian chap, a Methodist like my old man. My dad used to go on about forgiveness a lot. Maybe it was because me and my brothers were always at loggerheads.' He smiled sadly. 'Could you do that, Eileen? Forgive someone who'd been responsible for the death of someone you loved? I'm not sure I could.'

'I don't know, Josh. I don't think anyone knows.'

Josh sighed. 'I'd have happily strung them up at the time, anyone who'd killed my mates, I was so angry. I feel a bit different now. Maybe that man had it right. Maybe it's the only way to get out of the cycle of hatred.'

'But it's so hard to do,' Eileen said. 'Sometimes I think it's easier to forgive someone who's offended me than when the hurt is done to someone else.' Eileen heard a tentative tapping and turned towards the door. 'I'd better go and see what they want.' She laid her hand on Josh's arm. 'Will you be all right?'

Unexpectedly he gripped her hand, nodding silently. She smiled, and he let her go.

Later, when the time came to go off duty, Eileen was delayed by Carol Macnamara wanting to chat. When she finally left the hospital, walking out into the summer evening, she saw Josh roar away on his motorbike. But when she got to where her car was parked she heard the bike's powerful engine again, and he came to a halt beside her. He pulled off his helmet.

'I was thinking,' he said, 'do you have a day off any time soon? It would be nice to get out of town again.'

Eileen thought. 'Friday's the next one. I'd have to check it on my calendar. But I'm pretty sure Friday's free.'

Josh smiled broadly. 'I'm free on Friday. Is it a date?'

'I'll pick you up early.'

Josh put his helmet back on and waved a gloved hand as his tail light disappeared into the deepening dusk.

Driving home in the gathering darkness Eileen's mental vision was crowded with shocking images of rubble and dust and broken bodies, and her imagination supplied still more. She thought of the people waiting outside the hospitals for news, their hope fading as the hours passed, and of the victims on stretchers in corridors, or undergoing emergency surgery, or simply dying where they lay. She thought of Josh and all the horrors he must have seen in his army career, and wondered that he was still so tender-hearted. She was sure there had been tears in his eyes: of grief or rage or simple bewilderment she could not tell. As she parked the car outside her block of flats and turned off the engine, she thought of the man who had lost his daughter and forgiven her killers, and reluctantly she approached that dark crevice of her mind where her own demon lurked. Like probing a throbbing tooth with her tongue she visited that tender and painful place where, in honesty, she asked herself whether she could forgive Maurice Bentley. Had he not lit the fuse that had blown Christopher's life apart?

She got out of the car, locked the door, and climbed the steps. Perhaps tomorrow she would talk to Louis.

She trudged up to her flat, made herself a drink and fed a vocal Fletcher.

Then the phone rang. It was Josh.

'I, um, just wanted to say thanks.'

'What for?'

'Oh, you know. Just listening to me.'

'It was a horrible thing, seeing those poor people suffer. And you've been there before.'

'Yes.' Josh paused. 'Did you check your calendar?'

'Not yet. I only just got in.' She glanced across to where the calendar hung on the wall. 'But I can see Friday is fine. The only minor blot is that I'm on night duty that night, so it would probably be a good idea not to have too long and tiring a day. I'll see you on Friday, Josh. Bright and early. Well, early, anyway.'

She heard the smile in his voice. 'OK. Goodnight, then, Eileen.'

She sat at the kitchen table trying to read her Bible, but her eyes were tired and the print blurred. *Tomorrow.* She got up with a sigh and stretched her aching back. The shrill jangle of the phone broke the silence. She frowned. Not many people rang her at ten-thirty.

'Mum? Sorry to ring you so late.' It was Natasha. 'You weren't asleep, were you?'

'No, I've not long got in from work.'

'Oh, that's why I couldn't get hold of you earlier.'

'Are you all right, Tash? Is something wrong?'

'No, Mum, I'm fine. I just thought I should tell you something I found out today. Have you heard from Christie?'

'I had a postcard from her last week. She seemed to be having fun.'

Natasha's voice lowered. 'She rang me today, Mum. She's having fun, all right. But she's not with Jenny any more. She's with John.'

'What? She's still in Italy, isn't she?'

'Oh, yes. Apparently John went over there to find her. He's split up with his wife. It's all broken wide open. Jenny got the hump and came home.'

'Tash, this is bad news. What are they going to do?'

'I don't know. Christie's on cloud nine and I couldn't get any sense out of her at all. I thought I'd better let you know.'

'Yes, thanks, dear. Oh, Tash. What a mess. Is there anything we can do?'

'Like what? Christie's made her mind up, it seems to me. The silly fool's madly in love and can't see beyond the bedpost. Nothing we can say, is there?'

'I guess not. Well, thanks for telling me, love. You're not about to do anything daft, are you?'

'Ha! I'm as big as a double-decker bus. Not much chance of anything.'

'Well, good. I'll ring you soon, Tash. Love to Sean.'

With her cat sprawled luxuriously across the foot of the bed, Eileen fell asleep almost at once. No dreams came to disturb her, or, if they did, they were insubstantial as mist and as threatening. But at two in the morning she snapped suddenly awake, her mind clear. An image was in her mind, already fading. She fought to hold on to it, somehow sensing its significance, though she could not have explained. It was not a dream in the normal sense, because it was so fleeting and so static; more a

172

picture, laden with meaning to which she could give no name. She saw a castle, strong and four-square on a low hill, with battlemented towers from which flew bright pennons, and surrounding all were thick, high walls. She was standing on the outside, holding a clipboard with a blank sheet of paper on it, and in her hand a pencil, hovering. Then she looked more closely at the castle and saw that, far from being well-maintained and impregnable, it was crumbling in several places, with piles of masonry in the courtyard. She understood that it was her job to make a survey and perhaps to repair the broken parts.

Fully awake, she wondered if the damage was due to the neglect of the years or to some enemy's malice. She shook her head and told herself not to be so fanciful. What did it mean, anyway? Probably nothing. But she could not get back to sleep. She tried to read, but could not concentrate. Her mind went back to the day, and she shivered, remembering the bomb and its victims. For some poor souls there would be no comfort that night; for some there would only be pain and life-shattering loss. She thought of Josh, and wondered if he, too, was lying awake, unable to repel tormenting memories. She had never seen him so rattled, and it made her feel alarmingly protective. Was that it, something so obvious? Was she that castle, seemingly so strong, whose defences were crumbling and in need of urgent repair? How could she be both castle and mason? Not for the first time, she reflected how foolish were the workings of her own unconscious mind.

But Josh remained, and would not go away. Something within her was insisting on honesty, uncomfortable as it was. Was she letting her friendship with Josh accelerate? Did she want it to? She couldn't answer for him; it was tough enough clarifying her own thoughts. She liked him, certainly; and if she allowed herself to she could easily imagine herself in situations with him that made her want to snigger and blush like a callow adolescent. But there were so many perils and pitfalls, and she had seen enough of the tender, hurting side of this tough Yorkshireman to want to avoid giving pain.

And then, there was Christie and John. What was she to make of that? Without talking to Christie herself she could come to no conclusions, and it was most unlikely that her daughter would want to talk to her any time soon. Eileen's anxiety was tempered by something altogether more fatalistic. Christie would do what she did, would succeed or fail, suffer or survive, and Eileen would be around if she was needed. But meanwhile she could hardly adopt a high moral pose, even if she felt so inclined, if she was embarking on some ill-thought affair with a man she hardly knew.

Lord, what a muddle, what a horrible mess. I'm thinking of those poor souls in Omagh. Merciful father, stand by them tonight. Comfort the dying and the bereaved. I don't know what to pray for them; it's beyond me. Forgive us, your flawed creations, for the wickedness we perpetrate on you and on each other. Please, Lord, be with my daughter. Don't let her come to grief. Help John's family too, in their hurt and bewilderment. And Lord, forgive me, for thinking about my own interests when others are suffering so terribly. The words of a hymn came into her mind then, as if from nowhere, something about neither father nor mother, brother nor sister, but herself being the one in need of prayer. *Yes, it's me. I think of that poor man, forgiving his daughter's murderers, and I am full of anger still towards a sick man who has not harmed me directly at all. Who am I, to be so hard and judgmental? Help me, Father, help me to change.*

Sunday 16 August 1998

Eileen hovered in the church porch after the morning service. 'Louis, are you in a hurry?'

Louis locked the door and turned to look at her, an enquiring half-smile on his face. 'I've been invited to lunch at the Dysons'. Otherwise I'm free as air, despite its being Sunday and the only day I am reputed to work.'

'There's something I need your thoughts on, that's all. But if it's inconvenient it can wait.'

Louis shook his head and started down the path to the Vicarage, with Eileen following. 'It's not inconvenient. You make better coffee than I do, anyway.'

'That might be because I wait for the water to be sufficiently hot. It helps.'

Louis slapped his forehead. 'What a fool I am! Life's simplest tasks are a mystery to me.' He opened the back door to his kitchen and ushered her inside. It was as chaotic as the last time she had seen it.

Eileen swallowed the comment that rose to her lips. 'I'll put the kettle on, then.'

'Please do. There might even be biscuits.'

'Oh? How old?'

Louis shrugged. 'A month or two. Or ten.'

'Perhaps not.'

Eileen made two cups of coffee while Louis half-heartedly cleared a space on the cluttered table.

'So, what's the latest?' he said as he sat down and picked up his cup.

'I need to talk to you about forgiveness.'

'Really? An open-and-shut case, I should have thought. No terrible theological tangles there. We have to do it. Or else.'

'Or else what?'

'Hold on.' Louis pushed his chair back and left the room. He returned a few moments later, Bible in hand. 'Here we are. Bottom line. Matthew 6 verse 14: "If you forgive others the wrongs they have done to you, your Father in heaven will also forgive you. But if you do not forgive others, your Father will not forgive the wrongs you have done."'

Eileen shuddered. 'Yes. That's the theory.'

'More than theory, I think,' Louis said, his dark eyes fixed on her with unnerving intentness. 'An absolute prerequisite. Just think of the parable of the unforgiving servant.' He waited, his head slightly on one side, his elbow resting on the table, his long fingers lightly tapping the side of his cup.

'I know you are right. Of course I do,' Eileen said at last. 'But how do you actually do it?'

'Let me read you something else,' Louis said. He flicked through the pages. 'Ephesians 4 verse 32: "...be kind and tender-hearted to one another, and forgive one another, as God has forgiven you in Christ." Well? Do you find that a problem?'

Eileen shook her head. She could think of nothing to say.

'We have to imitate God's attitude to us, all his graciousness, in our dealings with others. We pray it in the Lord's Prayer —"forgive us our sins, as we forgive those who sin against us." But surely you don't find this difficult, do you? I can't believe you are hard and unforgiving.'

Eileen shook her head again. Her throat felt choked, and to her shame she felt her eyes well with tears.

A small frown gathered between Louis' brows. 'Correct me if I am way off the mark. It's just one person you are angry with, isn't it? What's the man's name? Maurice Bentley. Did you ever meet him?'

Eileen blinked, and her voice, when it emerged, felt scratchy. 'No. And I know very little about him, only what Christopher told me. And he, Christopher I mean, always made excuses for Maurice. Which I don't seem able to do.'

'Even though his offence was against Christopher, not against you.'

Eileen's voice sunk to a whisper. 'Yes, I know. It's not something I am proud of. I guess I feel Maurice Bentley took something from me. But that's stupid. How can someone take something from you that you never really had in the first place?' She could not look at Louis; to her horror the tears began to overflow and run down her cheeks, and there was nothing she could do to stop them. Louis did not move or speak. After a moment or two of struggle she drew in a great heaving breath and wiped her face with her hands. 'I'm sorry. This is really silly. Just help me to know what to do with this, because I don't want to carry it around any more. Yesterday I watched TV and saw those poor people killed and maimed by the bomb in Ireland and I told myself to get a grip and not to be such a fool, to get things in proportion, to let the whole thing go. But it feels like bereavement.'

'It seems to me you've already begun,' Louis said gently. 'If you want to know what happens next, it's to ask for help. You've already asked me; now you have to ask God.'

'I will.'

'Do you want to start now? I could pray with you if you like.'

'I don't think I am very good at praying with other people.'

'Then you pray in the silence of your own mind, and I'll try and put together the right words. And the Holy Spirit will do the rest.'

Eileen nodded. 'All right.' She took a gulp of her coffee and began to feel revived.

Louis was quiet for a few minutes. Then he began to speak quite calmly, with long gaps full of thinking. 'Lord God, you have told us we must forgive each other as you have forgiven us, even though we are unworthy. Give us the will and desire to forgive each other when we are wronged, or when someone we love is hurt, even to seventy times seven, as you commanded us. And help Eileen to look on Maurice Bentley with mercy and compassion rather than anger and vengefulness, so that she might truly imitate your graciousness and in so doing lift this burden from her spirit. Lord, you are to us the model of sacrificial love; teach us to walk in your ways and truly forgive our brother from our heart. We ask these things in the name of him who nailed our fallen natures to his cross, our saviour Jesus Christ. Amen.'

'Yes. Amen.' Eileen finished her coffee and stood up. Her legs shook, and she gripped the back of the chair. 'Thank you, Louis. Now I must go home, and let you get ready for your lunch with the Dysons.'

Louis followed her to the door and pulled it open. 'Are you all right?'

Eileen sighed. 'Yes, of course.' She hesitated in the doorway. 'Louis, do you think that Maurice Bentley knew what he was doing to Christopher?'

Louis shrugged. 'You'll probably never know that. It's something you're going to have to live with, I think. But ask God to help you. If you ask with a real desire to learn, he will show you where you too need to be forgiven.'

Eileen nodded. 'Oh yes, I know I am far from blameless. I've thought about it over and over, and I see now, with hindsight, that I had alternatives, that perhaps I acted irresponsibly, arrogantly, following my own agenda. I contributed to Christopher's fate, I know that.'

Louis folded his arms and leaned against the doorpost. 'You also tried to help him, Eileen. You took him food and talked to him and showed him love. But you may have to accept that Maurice Bentley thought he too was showing Christopher love, even if we think it was a perverse and corrupting kind. Can you honestly say that you acted towards Christopher with pure and selfless motives? I don't think any human is capable of that.'

'I'm sure you're right. I'll go home now, Louis. Thank you for listening. I will pray about it when I'm on my own, quietly. Enjoy your lunch.'

Louis saluted her with a wave of his hand, and closed the door as she walked back down the churchyard path.

Eileen drove home through the thronged Sunday streets, feeling like an alien in an invisible spacecraft. People were in shorts and summer dresses and bare feet, ambling along pavements or sitting on their doorsteps with a can of beer and a cigarette, and in the local park as she passed there were scores of children and dogs and babies in prams. Eileen had wound down her window to let in a bit of cool air, and she could hear the children's shrieks and the sound of running water. But she was in a bubble, as if these evidences of normality were coming to her from an unimaginable distance. She parked the car round the corner from her block of flats and walked to her front door, dazed by the relentless sunshine and the tyranny of her thoughts.

Fletcher was asleep on the end of her bed and barely stirred to greet her. She made herself a sandwich and sat down at the table, chewing mechanically. She could have been eating brick dust and drinking sump oil. But gradually reality began to reassert itself, and the sense of being at several removes from life faded. She finished her sandwich and stood up abruptly. Thinking would have to wait. It was time for something positive, however trivial.

She blitzed the flat. For three hours she scrubbed and polished and cleaned, she leaned perilously out of windows to wash them, and even the oven got a going-over. By the time she ground to a halt the place was spotless and she was dirty and damp with sweat. She ran a bath, dropped her clothes into the laundry basket and wallowed in warm foam.

She was forced to climb out by the cooling of the water, and realized that she was ravenous. She dried and dressed and brushed her hair, her body relaxed and her mind agreeably blank. She found half a bottle of wine in the fridge; she poured herself a large glass, and took great gulps of it as she put a meal together. By the time she had eaten, the bottle was empty. The evening lay before her: she had no work, no chores, she expected no one to call, no one expected anything of her. She was free.

She put her dishes on the draining board, slumped into a chair and pulled her Bible towards her. She looked up every reference she could find to forgiveness and to mercy, and she reread the parable of the unforgiving servant, because Louis had mentioned it. To her discomfiture she felt tears spring again to her eyes. *What a weak and weepy fool I am becoming.* She read of God's great mercy and loving-kindness, and was ashamed. "... but God's mercy is so abundant," Paul wrote to the Ephesians in chapter 4, "and his love for us is so great, that while we were spiritually dead in our disobedience he brought us to life with Christ." *And I have been heedless and ungrateful.* "Come back to the Lord your God," wrote the prophet Joel. "He is kind and full of mercy; he is patient and keeps his promise; he is always ready to forgive and not punish." *But I have spent the last two years allowing contempt and blame to turn my soul rotten.* "Be merciful," said Luke, "just as your Father is merciful." And again, Matthew: "Happy are those who are merciful to others; God will be merciful to them." She closed her Bible. The conclusion was inescapable: she could not expect to be forgiven if she sat in prideful judgment on fellow-sinners.

She lay back in her chair and stretched her arms and legs. She tried to visualize Maurice Bentley, and realized that she knew almost nothing about him. Remembering what Christopher had told her she imagined a dapper middle-aged man in a pin-striped suit, with black wavy hair and sharp eyes, and a smooth, manipulating manner. *He's probably nothing like that at all.* To her surprise she could contemplate him without bitterness, and relief crept over her. She wondered what he was really like, where he was now, and where he had been all this time. Was someone sheltering him, and if so, who? Did he have family, friends? She would probably never know, so it was fruitless to speculate. But his spectre had inhabited the margins of her mind for a long time, and it was not easy simply to banish him. She closed her eyes.

Lord, please forgive me for my lack of compassion, my willingness to accuse. Perhaps I blamed Maurice Bentley to avoid blaming myself. I am sorry for my cowardice and my blindness. I have known your mercy but have failed to pass it on. Please help me to let the past go, not to let it lie on my heart so heavily. I need to attend to my present, to find how I can serve you in the here and now. She opened her eyes suddenly; the realization came to her that if she let Christopher slip away, she would come face-to-face with her own emptiness. But she knew also that she could not let this one thing, this one person, rule over the rest of her life. Christopher was dead; she was not. *Lord, you know I have other worries. There's Christie, burning bridges behind her, maybe setting herself up for grief and guilt. She's young and sillier than I'd hoped. Please help and guide her, and me, to know what to do when she finally gets in touch. And there's Penny. She's clearly avoiding me, ever since I told her about Karen. I don't know what to do. Please, Lord, take it out of my hands.*

Friday 21 August 1998

Josh was sitting on a low wall outside his block of flats when Eileen pulled up. He ambled over, opened the door and threw his backpack onto the back seat. 'I brought a hat,' he said, producing a shapeless khaki thing from his pocket and cramming it on his head.

'Very fetching,' Eileen said. She started the engine. 'So, where to?'

'Well, I was a bit stumped,' Josh said. 'We don't want to be out too long as you're on nights, but we want to get out of the smoke. Everywhere I thought of was going to be stiff with noisy kids. We were OK before, but now it's the school holidays.'

'I don't mind kids.'

'Nor do I, but you can have too much of a good thing. The little darlings are round my place all day, banging a ball about and yelling. Then I thought of Whiston Hill. It's only about ten miles away.'

'What's there? Apart from a hill.'

'It's many acres, I don't know how many, of an old estate that got broken up years ago. They've started to develop it over the last few years: there's an artificial lake and all sorts of stuff for kids to do, so it will be busy. But there's miles of walks where very few people will go. That part of it is still rough. So it'll weed out the toddlers and the mums with prams. They'll stay down by the lake. They can lie in the sun and eat chips and ice cream and play on the swings.'

'Such decadent pleasures.'

'Meanwhile we'll be striding out like the pioneers we are.' Josh looked at her sidelong and grinned.

'Maybe not. It's too hot for excessive energy. I fancy finding a quiet spot under a shady tree and nodding off.'

'A spot with a view.'

'Done.'

Eileen was silent for several miles. The traffic was heavy, with people trying to escape the city, cars and people-carriers full of children and dogs and frayed parents getting hotter by the minute.

'Take the next exit,' Josh said. 'It's signed Upper Whiston.'

After five miles and several turnings they were driving among fields and hedges. A mile further on, down what seemed to be a farm track, they came to a large car-park. A van selling hot-dogs and drinks was parked beside an ice-cream van. From both of them long queues trailed.

Eileen parked the car. There was no shade and the sun beat down. 'This reminds me of my childhood,' she said. 'Trips to the seaside.'

'Not for long,' Josh said. 'See that high ground? That's Whiston Hill. I thought we could climb to the top. It'll be cooler than here, because there's woods almost all the way.'

'OK, Sherpa. I'll follow you.'

By eleven o'clock they reached the summit. They admired the view northwards across more than one county boundary, and Josh pointed out the sights. Eileen sank to her knees at the top of a steeply-falling field whose grass was cropped short by rabbits. 'I could very easily polish off a can of ice-cold beer.' She stretched out on the ground.

'Sorry. I've got a compass, a map, and a waterproof in case it rains. No beer.'

'Shame.'

'It'll be all the more welcome when it finally slides down your parched throat.'

Eileen half-opened her eyes. 'Oh, so we are going to get some, then?'

'Well, I thought we'd scramble down the hill on this side and follow that little river. See it?'

'No, I've got my eyes shut. I'll take your word for it.'

'The river winds round the base of the hill and feeds into the lake,' Josh said. 'According to my map we pass the village of Lower Whiston. There must be a pub there.'

'I sure hope so,' Eileen mumbled.

'Sorry if I'm keeping you up.'

'You're not. I'm practically asleep.'

'Too many late nights out on the town?'

'Don't be daft.'

'So? Lots of worries, then.'

'What's this?' Eileen heaved herself up onto her elbows and brushed the dry grass off her hands. 'The Spanish Inquisition?'

Josh laughed. 'Unlike you, I am neither tired nor grumpy. I was hoping for a little conversation.'

'All right, you asked for it. I shall burden you with my family troubles.'

'Go ahead.'

Eileen frowned. 'Unfortunately, it really isn't very funny. My daughter is having an affair with a married man.'

'What, the younger one, that's just got her degree?'

'Yes.'

'You only went to the ceremony a few weeks ago.'

'Mm. There was no sign of it then. She was off to Italy with a friend. Maybe that's what she genuinely planned. But this guy's caught up with her, it seems. I don't even know where they are right now.'

'How old is she?'

'Twenty-one. He's in his forties, with a wife and two sons. I thought it was all over.'

'Oh, so you knew about it before?'

'Yes. It all blew up in March. But she said it was done with, and she was going to concentrate on her work. Which she did. I don't know any details; I got this news second-hand from my other daughter. Christie isn't talking to me right now.'

'Does she usually?'

'Yes. I wouldn't say she tells me everything; she's quite a private sort of girl. But she keeps in touch. I suppose at the moment she thinks I will be disapproving.'

Josh squinted in the sunlight, leaning on one elbow, trying to get her in focus. 'And will you?'

'Of course I will. She knows that. She's grown up, she must make her own decisions, but she's aware of the grief she's causing. I can't see anything but misery ahead, and I don't want her to be miserable.'

'I don't suppose she's miserable at this moment,' Josh said thoughtfully.

'No, but it's stolen happiness, isn't it?'

Josh was silent for a few moments. 'What about the bloke?' he said. 'Have you met him?'

Eileen nodded. 'Briefly. He seemed nice enough. But he's forty-something. Old enough to know better. And what about his family? For the sake of something quite ephemeral the two of them are busy wrecking several lives.'

Josh looked down at the peaceful view and sighed. 'That sort of love can be very powerful.'

'Yes, I know. And I don't want to sound harsh and judgmental. I'm not exactly a saint myself. But I'm worried. Whatever she does, she's still my child. I admit to being selfish too. There comes a point when you wish your kids would grow up and be happy and not worry you so much. Perhaps it's too soon for that. I love my girls dearly, but there are moments when parenthood seems like a life sentence.'

'Whereas I would like to be a bit more involved with my son's life,' Josh said. 'His mum has tried quite hard to cut me out of the action.'

Eileen turned to face him, shading her eyes with her hand. 'When will you see him next?'

'I've booked some leave in November,' Josh said. 'I'll go up to Yorkshire then, see my mum and my brothers and catch up with Martin.' He smiled wryly. 'Kath didn't totally succeed, happily.'

'How do you mean?'

'Martin and I always got on pretty well. We've survived her machinations.'

Eileen smiled. 'I'm glad to hear it. So what will you do in Yorkshire?'

'Oh, I don't know. Take my mum out to visit her pals. Go fishing with Martin. Hang out with my brothers, catch up with old buddies.'

'Revisit old haunts.'

'Maybe. The Dog and Duck, perhaps, or the Crown, or the King's Arms.'

'To name but a few.'

Josh smiled. 'There are some fine breweries in Yorkshire.'

'And you wouldn't want to miss an opportunity.'

'You're right. Speaking of beer, shall we move on? See what the local hostelries have on offer?'

Eileen groaned and scrambled to her feet. 'At least it's downhill this time. I think I am getting old.'

'Nonsense. You're just a girl.'

'A girl who'll be fifty this year.'

'No kidding!'

'No kidding.'

Eileen's attempt to get home early, avoiding the early evening traffic back into the city, was foiled by an accident on the main road which caused gridlock for almost an hour. A snaking tail of cars wound in front and behind, and nobody was moving except the occasional police car and ambulance thundering along the hard shoulder. People got out of their cars to give their dogs an airing or to take their desperate toddlers to the side of the road. Groups of young lads leaned on their cars, displaying bronzed torsos, shoving each other and laughing and smoking, to a background of thumping music. A chubby red-faced mother walked up and down the melting tarmac, soothing a fretful infant in a cotton sun hat. Grandparents passed bottles of lukewarm drinks to irritable children. And still the endless line of cars baked in the afternoon sun.

'At times like these I wish I had air-conditioning,' Eileen said. 'That cold beer seems a lifetime ago.'

Josh mopped his forehead with his crumpled hat. 'So how shall we pass the time? You've been very quiet. Still thinking about your errant daughter?'

'No, I was thinking about Karen Colley,' Eileen said. 'Do you know how she is?'

'Not really. She's at home at the moment. But I expect her to be back.'

Eileen sighed deeply. 'Poor Karen. She makes me feel helpless.'

'Well, if she comes back to us at least we know she's still in the fight. What worries me is if she tries to kill herself again and this time nobody finds her.'

'What an awful thought. Josh, speaking hypothetically, do you think she could really recover if her son was found?'

'You've asked me that before. I think she's very damaged. But getting him back is the only thing I can see that's ever going to give her a reason to live. And sadly that's not too likely.'

'So,' Eileen said after a pause, 'when are you next at work?'

'Monday early.'

'Oh, so am I.'

'You're doing a few shifts close together, aren't you?'

'Yes, but I've taken some time off lately – for Christie's graduation, for example. And I swap around. I try not to work too many Sunday mornings, so that I can play for services.'

'Right.' Josh leaned out of the open window. 'I thought I saw that lorry move, up ahead.'

'I don't believe it.'

But people were piling back into their cars, strapping in their children and starting their engines. There were a few cheers along the line, and finally the whole motionless jam began to move. Eileen let the car crawl forward, and felt the beginnings of a cooler breeze on her burning face. 'Praise the Lord,' she said feelingly.

By the time she arrived home it was past six. She ran up the stairs to her flat, keys dangling from her hand, thinking of all the things she had to do before she went to work. At the top of the stairs she stopped dead. Someone was sitting on the sill of the landing window, a small, rounded figure in a hooded jacket. The hood was pulled well down over the person's face but after a heartbeat recognition came.

'Maureen? It is you, isn't it? What are you doing here?' Before the words left her mouth, she knew, though Maureen had not spoken. Eileen took her unresisting hand. 'Come inside.'

She drew Maureen after her and shut the flat door behind them. Maureen's shoulders were bowed, her face still hidden in the hood. Gently Eileen pushed it back.

'Oh, Maureen. What has he done to you?'

Maureen's face was a mess of bruises and dried blood. There was blood caked on her upper lip, her left eye was swollen and closing, and a purple bruise was blooming on her cheekbone. As Eileen looked at her in horror Maureen's eyes filled up and tears trickled down her cheeks.

'You should be at A and E,' Eileen said. 'Let me drive you. How long have you been waiting? I'm so sorry, Maureen. If only I'd known.'

Maureen shook her head violently. Her voice, through puffed lips, was slurred. 'I'm not going to hospital,' she said. 'No one's going to see me like this. I don't think anything's broken. Believe me, it looks worse than it is. But I had to get away, Eileen. Before he did any more damage. He'd never forgive himself, once he was back in his right mind.'

'Well, let me clean you up and check that there are no broken bones.'

She took Maureen into the bathroom, sat her down on the toilet and ran a basinful of warm water. With a light touch she bathed and cleaned the ruined face, her stomach clenched with pity.

'Had you been waiting long? I got stuck in a traffic jam.'

'Since three-ish.'

'You poor thing. You must be parched. I'll get the kettle on in a minute.' She threw the bloodied cotton swabs in the bin. 'Can you move everything? Arms, shoulders, fingers? I think the damage is superficial, but you really should get it checked out. I'm no medic.'

'I won't go. Please don't try to make me. I just need a refuge for a while.'

'Of course. You can stay as long as you like. Did you bring anything?'

Maureen pulled up the shopping-bag she had been clutching. 'I stuffed a few things in here before I ran out of the house,' she whispered. 'Oh, Eileen, I was so frightened. I don't know where it all came from. He just seemed to go crazy. And I don't know where he is. He drove off in the car like a maniac. He could have an accident.'

'Let's not worry about him for the moment,' Eileen said. 'Let's concentrate on you. One thing at a time.'

She sat Maureen down in the kitchen and made her a sandwich and a mug of tea.

'You know I have to be at work tonight, don't you?' she said. 'I'll make up a bed for you in the spare room. If you need anything, whatever, just help yourself. I'll show you where things are. When I come home in the morning we can talk things over and you can think about what you want to do, OK?' Maureen nodded and sipped her tea. 'Do you think Des will guess where you've gone?'

Maureen shook her head. 'I shouldn't think so.'

'Maybe it would be better if you don't answer the phone,' Eileen said. 'If I ring I'll leave a message, and if you need me you can call the ward. Just lie low, all right?' She took her friend's hand and squeezed it. 'When did all this happen, Maureen?'

'At lunch time. He came in from buying a paper at the shop. I could tell he was in a bad mood because he hardly answered me when I spoke to him. And I don't know what it was I said that made him lose his temper.' Tears ran down her face again, and for a moment she was unable to go on. She brought herself under control with a visible effort. 'I was putting the plates on the table. He just turned on me. Food went everywhere, and I screamed. I couldn't help it. But it made him worse. I've never known him as bad as this, Eileen. Never.'

'So what then? He stormed out?'

'Yes. I heard the car roar away. I was shaking all over. I tried to clean the mess up, but I couldn't do it. I knew I had to get away before he came back. I was going to my sister's, but I was too ashamed. Then I thought of you.'

'I'm very glad you did. So how did you get here?'

'I called a taxi. And I put this jacket on and pulled the hood up so the driver couldn't see my face.'

'How did you get in the front door here?'

'I just rang the first bell I came to and a nice old lady let me in.'

'Good. At least you didn't have to sit on the outside steps. Now, what would you like to do? How about a warm bath?'

'That sounds lovely. But I don't want to be any trouble.'

'It's no trouble at all. I'll go and run it and while you're soaking I'll make up the bed. Then I'm afraid I'll have to get myself ready for work.'

'Of course you will. Thank you, Eileen. I'm very grateful.'

Eileen got up. She patted Maureen's shoulder. 'Don't you worry. We'll think of what to do when you've had a rest and a chance to think things through and recover from the shock.'

Eileen left the flat at eight-thirty, closing the door quietly behind her. Fletcher had been fed, and the cat flap was unlocked so that he could come and go. Eileen had showered and changed, had something to eat and switched on the answer phone. To her relief, Maureen was asleep.

For once the traffic was light for a Friday evening and Eileen found a parking space in the hospital car park without having to cruise round for ten minutes. She was on the ward and changed in time for the handover meeting. The ward was quiet; the patients had been given their bedtime drinks and night medication and were either sitting by their beds reading, watching television or already asleep. The meeting consisted of Christine the ward manager, Carol Macnamara, a young nurse called Michaela North, and Eileen herself.

'Not a lot to report from this afternoon,' Christine said. 'No incidents to speak of or anything arising out of the doctors' rounds this morning. Unusually we've got a number of empty beds. I don't know why, but my advice is just make the most of it while you can, because it's bound to change. It's a hot night and some of the patients will have trouble sleeping, but you girls know how to cope. Do the usual half-hourly checks of course, otherwise if anything crops up you can bleep the duty doctor. Any worries, anyone?' There was a general shaking of heads. Christine lowered her voice. 'Oh, one thing. It's not confirmed but we may be getting a new patient later this evening. It's late for someone to be admitted, I know, but there's been some problem with transport. He's coming from another area and as far as I know bringing his paperwork with him. I'm only telling you for information: you won't be involved in his care as he'll be going next door, into the secure unit. Much more than that I can't or shouldn't tell you. It may not actually happen tonight; you know what it's like round here, you get a phone call and start running round, then it all fizzles out. But I thought you'd better be aware. He'll have his own assigned nurse anyway so you can always get hold of him or her if you need to. But don't worry about it. Like I say, it's not going to be your problem.'

When she had gone Carol said, 'Time to get the kettle on, I think, Eileen. I don't know about you but I always need plenty of tea to get me through the night.'

Eileen followed her into the kitchen. 'What do you make of this new patient?'

Carol shrugged. 'We probably won't even see him,' she said. 'If they're in the secure unit they have a special care team. Last time there was anyone in there was that Chapman bloke, and we only saw him when they took him out to go to his trial. He wasn't there long. They never are.'

'I wonder why he's coming here.'

'No telling. That enough milk for you?' She handed Eileen a mug. 'Could be anything. Maybe he's got a history of upsetting the other patients. And you know it doesn't take much to get them fired up, some of them.'

'I hope it's not because he's violent.' Eileen thought of Maureen and shivered.

'Not necessarily, love. Anyway, he'll be locked up tight.'

'Supposing there's an emergency?'

'He'll have a pull-cord to get help. And his nurse will check on him regular. Don't you fret about him, Eileen. We've got enough to keep us occupied in here.'

The young nurse Michaela put her head round the door. 'Any tea going?'

'Course there is, love. I'll pour you one,' Carol said. 'Did I hear on the grapevine you're getting married? Come in, do. Don't hover in the doorway.'

Eileen finished her tea. 'I'll go and check on our charges,' she said. 'I think I can hear moaning.'

'That'll be Tony. He makes noises in his sleep. But he's all right.'

'See you in a minute,' Eileen said.

Just after ten the ward phone rang. Carol answered it. 'That was Christine,' she said. 'Wanted to know if everything was quiet. They're bringing that new patient up now.'

Ten minutes later Eileen heard the lift doors open and close, and there were footsteps and muffled voices in the corridor. Through the opaque glass of the ward doors she saw a number of indistinct figures. Then they passed out of sight.

'He came, then,' she said to Carol.

'That's probably the first and last we'll see of him,' Carol said. 'Oh, Eileen, Michaela's just been round, and she said that new lady in bay nine is crying fit to bust. D'you want to go and have a chat with her? You're good with the patients, and Michaela doesn't really know them as well as we do.'

'Sure. I'll just pop to the loo first in case she runs on.'

She spent the next twenty minutes holding the woman's hand and listening to her troubles. The woman, Janet, had never been in a psychiatric unit before, and she was terrified that she would never be let out. 'I miss my Bernie,' she said, wiping her face with a crumpled tissue. 'He looks after me. I dunno when I can see him. Will they let him come and see me? I can't get on without him. Not after all these years.'

'He can come in at visiting time,' Eileen said. 'You can see him every day. And of course you're going to go home. You're here to get better, not to be locked up.' She thought of the man in the unit next door. He was a prisoner of sorts: a prisoner of the system, or at the very least a prisoner of his illness. She turned back to the weepy woman. 'Do you and Bernie have children?' she asked.

'No,' Janet said. 'I can't hardly look after myself. Bernie looks after me. Now what will he do?'

'Well,' Eileen said, 'let's hope it's not for long. Would you like something to help you sleep? I can ask the nurse.'

Janet stretched out on the bed and sighed tearfully. 'Thanks, love. It might do me good, I suppose.'

When Janet was settled Eileen went back to the nurses' room. Michaela and Carol were already there, with Christine. 'There you are, Eileen,' Christine said. 'I'm off now. I've just been bringing these girls up to speed with our friend next door. Nothing to worry about: he's sedated and should be out for the count till the morning. Did your new lady settle down?'

'Yes, she's OK for now,' Eileen said. 'She's scared and disorientated and missing her husband.'

'What, already?' Carol said with a snort. 'He was only in here earlier this evening.'

'She's very dependent on him. Seems like he's been looking after her single-handed for most of their married life.'

'Poor sod.'

'If you're all right I'll disappear, then,' said Christine. 'You know where I am if you need me.' She smiled at them all brightly and left with a clacking of her three-inch heels.

'She's a rum one, that Christine,' Carol said, settling herself more comfortably. 'She dresses like someone from ten years ago. That big hair, and them heels. I don't know where she gets her clothes from.'

Michaela sniggered. 'Some crusty old catalogue from the eighties, I reckon.'

'Michaela was telling me about her wedding dress,' Carol said. 'That won't be coming from no catalogue.'

'No, it won't,' said Michaela. 'I'm getting it from that Brides shop in the Arcade. They're going to have to alter it though. It's tight in the bust.' She giggled.

'No wonder, love,' Carol said, giving the girl a friendly shove. 'With a chest like yours.'

'Did Christine tell you anything about the patient next door?' Eileen asked.

Carol leaned forward and lowered her voice. 'Funnily enough, we know him,' she said. 'He was here, right here in this unit, years ago. They brought him down from Leicester by ambulance today – don't ask me why Leicester. You won't remember him, love, because it was before your time.'

'So why have they brought him here?' Eileen asked.

'It's because this is where he came from in the first place, I suppose,' Carol said. 'No good asking me how they run things. I only work here.' She laughed throatily. 'Josh would remember him, though. Josh had more to do with him than I did. But I remember he wasn't like any other patient we'd ever had. He was so smart and well spoken, like.'

Despite the heat in the ward Eileen suddenly felt cold, and there was a singing in her ears. 'Do you remember his name?' she asked.

'You all right, Eileen? You look a bit washed out. Too much sun, maybe. Course I remember his name. Maurice Bentley, that's him.'

Eileen escaped to the washroom and laid her forehead on the cool white tiles. She wrapped her arms round herself as if to try to stop her heart beating so fiercely. Her head was pounding.

Lord, why are you doing this to me? What is this, some kind of test? I know I've been asking for help, but is this what you call help? Bringing this man, of all people, right here where I work? I know I probably won't see him, but that doesn't matter. I'll always know he's there, just beyond the wall, living and breathing, the man who wrecked Christopher's life and sent him to his death. Lord, are you asking me to put my money where my mouth is? It's too much. I can't do it. I can't do it alone.

Carol pushed open the door. 'You all right, Eileen?'

'Yes, thanks, Carol. You were probably right: I've had too much sun. Perhaps if I splash my face with some cold water it might help.'

'You got a headache? I've got some painkillers in my bag. You want to be more careful, love. We're at a dangerous age.'

Eileen smiled wanly. 'I'm afraid you're right.'

Saturday 22 August 1998

It was the longest night shift Eileen had known. Nothing of any note happened. The patients, for the most part, slept, peacefully or otherwise. Michaela browsed through a magazine, yawning incessantly, and Carol dozed, surfacing only to make another pot of tea. Eileen volunteered to do all the half-hourly checks, counting the patients, making sure no one was unwell or needing help. Although her headache had abated she felt both exhausted and restless, unable to block out the image of Maurice Bentley, in his drug-induced unconsciousness in the room beyond the wall. She became aware that Carol and Michaela were looking at her oddly. She made herself scarce in the linen room, folding sheets and towels. Still the night dragged on. Dawn came, and a grey light seeped in past the curtains that moved sluggishly in the early breeze. Some of the patients shifted and turned uneasily in their sleep, but no one woke, no one needed anything. She could not use practical activity as a defence against the battering of her thoughts.

Finally the slow-moving clock ground its reluctant way to morning, and then people were waking up and there was tea to make for the patients. At seven a staff nurse came up from another ward and dispensed drugs, assisted by a red-eyed Michaela. Then Ollie bounded in to start the early shift and after the briefest of handovers Eileen was free.

It was a fine summer morning, and as she made her way to her car Eileen thought of Maureen. Was she awake? What was she thinking? Eileen only hoped she had not changed her mind and called a taxi and gone back home to Des. Somewhere in her anxious brain Christina also hovered, and behind her, in the shadows, Karen Colley and Penny and Gus. But at the forefront, looming, vital, clamorous, was Maurice Bentley. No matter that she did not know him, that she had no idea even what he looked like; he was a threat that must be contained. It was only ten to eight in the morning, but she knew she had to see Josh.

She parked her car outside the flats and rang Josh's bell. He was some time in answering.

'Josh? It's Eileen. I'm sorry it's so early, but I need to talk to you.'

'Come on up.' The door-release buzzed.

Josh opened the door to her in his bathrobe. He was barefoot and his hair was damp: clearly he had just emerged from the shower.

He blinked. 'What's all this? You all right?'

Eileen stood in the hallway. She had a sense of something irresistibly powerful welling up inside her, and she clenched her fists. Her voice seemed reluctant to emerge, and when it did it sounded oddly cracked.

'Josh, I'm sorry. You must think I've gone mad. Were you going out?'

'Not this early,' Josh said. 'Come in and sit down. You look as if you've seen a ghost. Did something happen overnight?'

Eileen allowed herself to be led to the living-room. Josh swept a stack of books and a pile of laundry off the sofa and she sank onto it. He looked down at her, frowning.

'Yes, something happened,' Eileen said. 'It's not anything for you to worry about. But I think I'm going to have to tell you that story we were talking about.' She tried to smile, but to her horror she felt her eyes fill up and her throat close. She bent her head, hoping that Josh would not notice.

'I'd better put some clothes on,' Josh said. He patted her shoulder. 'I won't be long. Do you want a cup of tea?'

'No, thanks. I've had enough tea over the last few hours to sink a battleship.'

When he had gone Eileen stood up and walked over to the window. She watched the cars moving soundlessly up and down the street and felt calm return. Josh came in and stood beside her. He had put on a faded blue shirt and shapeless cotton trousers, and he was holding a steaming mug in his hand. 'Sure I can't get you anything?'

She shook her head and sat down again on the sofa. Josh took the chair opposite.

'I'm all ears,' he said.

'Are you certain I'm not messing up your day?' Eileen said.

'For goodness' sake, woman! Get on with it!'

'All right.' She hesitated. 'It was May two years ago. I met a young man in the woods. He was living there, hiding. At first I didn't know that. I soon knew he was in trouble, though. I tried to help him. But it all got a bit out of control. In the end I did find out what he was hiding from. But by then it was too late. I found that I couldn't help him after all. And then he died. He killed himself.' She gasped as a sob heaved up from her chest and her eyes overflowed. Head bent, she wrapped her arms round her knees and rocked and wept.

When she came back to herself a few minutes later Josh was sitting beside her on the sofa. Silently he handed her a box of tissues, and she mopped her face and blew her nose.

'Why don't you just start at the beginning,' Josh said quietly. 'Take it slow and don't leave anything out.'

Eileen took a deep breath. She told him about Christopher's illness, his family, his fears; about the voice that pursued him, and the angels. She told him about the trouble at the nightclub and how Christopher had witnessed the assault on Georgina Quilley; and how, finally, shamed and tortured, he had told her about the man he was running from. Her throat felt squeezed and choked as she told him how she had found Christopher dead in the rain-soaked woods. In the end her voice gave out. 'Can I have that tea now?' she croaked.

Josh said nothing. He shook his head and went out into the kitchen. A few minutes later he came back and handed her a large mug.

'Bloody hell, Eileen,' he said. 'No wonder you're in a state. But why now?'

Eileen took a sip of scalding tea. 'I told you about the man that preyed on Christopher, just when he was beginning to get his life back. That's why Christopher was living in the woods. He was running scared. Josh, I hated that man. I shouldn't hate anyone, and I sure don't hate anyone else. But I've blamed that man for Christopher's death for two years. Just recently I've been telling myself to get a grip, that it's time to let the past go. Seeing what happened in Omagh last week made me think I should get things in proportion. But then, last night, that man came into the hospital as a patient. Josh, that man is in our secure unit at this moment. And you know him. That's why I had to tell you now.'

'What? I know him? Who is he, then?'

'His name is Maurice Bentley.'

'Maurice? He dropped out a few years ago. I haven't seen him in a long while.'

'I know,' Eileen said. 'But Carol said you got to know him quite well when he was first admitted, and afterwards.'

'Well, I suppose that's true enough. I was newly qualified, and those days I had more time to chat to patients. I have to tell you that he was a lot more interesting than most. A lot more together. Except he wasn't, of course. He was a mess.'

Eileen nodded. 'That's what Christopher told me. He said he,

Maurice that is, was a very bright man, that he could fool most people into thinking he was OK.'

Josh took off his glasses and polished them on the tail of his shirt. 'So, what now? Is it going to be impossible for you to carry on working with this man you hate so close by?'

Eileen was shocked, though she had asked herself the same question in the privacy of her own mind. 'That would be wrong,' she said. 'It's my job; I should be able to cope with anything. But I need you to help me.'

'How, exactly?'

'I need you to tell me what you know about Maurice Bentley. Help me to forgive him, I suppose.'

Josh grinned and stood up, stretching out a hand to her. She took it and he heaved her up.

'You don't want much, do you?' he said. 'Well, if we're in for long stories I need some breakfast. Come into the kitchen and I'll make some toast.' Still holding her hand he pulled her after him and sat her down at the kitchen table.

He put two pieces of bread in the toaster and turned to face her, leaning against the kitchen counter with his arms folded across his chest. He seemed sunk in thought for several moments, staring at her unfocused. He took a deep breath. 'Maurice first came into the unit in, um, let's see, 1991,' he said. 'As I told you, I was a rookie then with everything to learn. I had a few long chats with Maurice. For some reason he liked talking to me. I think because I wasn't a gossipy type he trusted me. So I got to know his story, and believe me, I came to think that the poor devil was more sinned against.' The toast popped up. He put it on a plate and put two more slices in the toaster. Then he scratched around in a cupboard and found some marmalade, and took two plates from the draining board. He sat down opposite Eileen. 'Is this what you want to hear? The whole biography?'

Eileen nodded, her mouth full of toast. She found that she was ravenous.

'OK. So this is what I gathered. It's been a few years; I'll be pushed to remember chapter and verse.' He paused for a moment. 'Maurice was born during the war: 1941, I think he said. His mum was a typist in her early twenties, called Mavis. Dad was never on the scene. I guess he was a soldier or sailor on leave, and he probably never even knew that Maurice existed. According to Maurice his mother always said she suffered from "nerves." If she was my patient today I'd probably give a different diagnosis. But that's by the by, and we'll never know, because she died a while back. Apparently she used to claim that Maurice was the result of rape. Not sure if I believe that, but you can imagine how wanted it made him feel as a kid. Mavis, to cut a long story short, started drinking in a big way. She lurched from job to job and none of them lasted long. The pair of them, mother and son, were always broke. Maurice had to do his bit, paper-rounds and so on. Despite everything he was a bright little lad and worked hard. At eleven he got a scholarship to some posh school. He was a poor kid and they took the mickey out of him, but he stuck it and did well. Meanwhile Mavis met a bloke called, if I remember right, Dennis Adams. She met him in the pub: no surprise. By this time she was a full-blown alcoholic, and so was he. Anyway, Dennis had a nice house and a bit of money, and Mavis married him. Maurice wasn't bothered. He had his sights on passing his exams and getting a good job and leaving the two drunks to their own devices. But then Mavis got pregnant and produced another boy – Leonard.'

Eileen finished her toast. 'You've remembered all this amazingly well.'

'My memory can be rubbish,' Josh said. 'But I always seem to be able to remember patients. Maybe it's the result of all that paperwork, reading up their details and such. Where was I? Oh yes, poor little Len. Not surprisingly, neither Mavis nor Dennis were fit to be parents. When they were drunk they were uninhibited and irresponsible. Maurice told me they used to dance around the garden in their underwear, singing their heads off, in the small hours, while poor little Len screamed with hunger. Then, when they sobered up, they were morose and bad-tempered or slept the day away. So who looked after the baby? Big brother did. Somehow he kept that baby fed and clothed and whatever, as well as doing his school work, and he was only twelve years old himself. I think eventually he got Dennis, in a sober moment, to employ some woman to look after Len. There were a series of them; in the end they all packed it in, one after the other, because they weren't paid or Dennis and Mavis made life hell. It was one of these ladies who finally went to Social Services and told them what was going on. By this time little Len was seven and Maurice was nineteen and at college. The brothers were devoted to each other. Maurice was more like a parent to Len and Len looked up to him. But they took Len into care. They said Maurice wasn't old enough to take on a child despite the fact that he'd been doing just that all the boy's life. Maurice had never had much love from his mum, and now the person he loved best was taken away from him. They did let him see Len from time to time, so the brothers kept in touch to an extent. Maurice threw himself into work. He was determined to make something of his life, and he passed exams and got a good job, something in the Council, where he could work upwards. He did what he could for Len through the years. Len became an apprentice, got work, married young and moved up north somewhere. You still with me? Want some more toast?' Eileen shook her head. 'OK. You get the picture of a gifted man who is very sad and lonely. It may account for some of the things he did later. In his early thirties Maurice got married. I think he craved a bit of domestic stability, safety, affection, the things he'd never had. But he chose the wrong woman, by the sounds of things. She, his wife, Connie her name was, was older than him, forty or forty-one, a widow living on some measly pension. She saw in him a way to escape the menial jobs she was obliged to do. He was a bachelor with a nice house and good prospects, and he was as gullible as they come. He was clever, he'd read a lot of books, but when it came to people he was a child. Bear in mind I only had his side of things, so that's all I can tell you. Connie Bentley sounds to me like a cold fish, a calculating, manipulating snob. But she charmed and seduced Maurice and he went to the altar in a happy daze. Poor blighter. It didn't take her long to begin pressurizing him to work harder, earn more, move to a nicer district, have a posher house, so she could hold her head up in front of the neighbours. You get the idea. I think I need some more tea. How about you?'

'Please. But go on, Josh. I want to hear it all.'

Josh filled the kettle and switched it on. 'Well, poor old Maurice had made a pretty bad choice. Connie had him over a barrel. She could be nice when she wanted something, but she was deadly when he tried to stick up for himself. She used sex like a weapon and a whip, he said. He had to do as he was told. He wanted children; she held out on him, but things don't always go to plan and after a couple of years they had a child, a little girl called Tessa.'

Eileen made a strangled noise and Josh looked at her enquiringly. 'That mean something to you?'

'It's the name he gave to Christopher, when he had him all dressed up as a girl.'

'It figures. Shall I continue?' He put the steaming teapot on the table and got milk from the fridge.

'Please do.'

'Maurice adored that child. By all accounts she was a sweetheart, nothing like her mother, and she and her dad were close from the off. She gave purpose back to Maurice, and for quite a few years the poor bastard was happy. But it wasn't going to last, not with Connie around. Obviously there's a lot more to it, and a lot I don't know. But when

Tessa was ten or eleven, something happened between Maurice and Connie that Maurice would never talk about. And Connie got very vindictive, and accused Maurice of having an unhealthy love for the kid. Not in so many words, but she accused him of having incestuous leanings.'

'Do you think it was true?'

'Not really. There's no evidence that Maurice liked children in that way, but I suppose he was obsessed with Tessa. With hindsight, I think – and he thought too – that he was already beginning to experience some mental deterioration before all this blew up. Don't forget, his mum was none too stable. Anyway the upshot was that Connie, cruel bitch that she was, decided that Maurice loved Tessa just a bit too much. She left him and took the child with her, despite the little girl's protests. That would have been around 1987, I guess. He hung on in there as best he could, but losing his daughter was a terrible blow, and he really went downhill. And not long afterwards he came into the unit and I met him. By that time he'd lost his job and sold his big house. He sent money for Tessa to some address in Scotland that Connie had told him, though I doubt the child ever got it. And he put some away in investments for her for when she was older. He had enough sense for that. But the poor bloke was broken. He still made sense, he could be charming and articulate when he felt like it, but it was all paper over the cracks, and the cracks got wider and wider.'

'So what then?'

'Well, we must have taken good care of Maurice. He went up and down over the years, but he did begin to improve. He had a complicated diagnosis: there wasn't just one problem. They reckoned he had a borderline personality disorder, and there's not a lot anyone can do with those. But the obsessiveness and the paranoia and the depression we could help with. There came a time when Maurice was discharged and didn't come back. We heard he was doing better and taking his medication and more or less coping with life. The word was he'd been found a temporary place at a halfway house out of the county. I was pleased for him.'

'That was where he met Christopher,' Eileen said, 'at the house in Denbigh Street.'

'What, in your village?'

'No, in the next town, Caxford. Christopher was having trouble adjusting to a new drug regime and was out of it. I don't think he knew what was going on for a long time. He was very screwed up, poor lad.'

'What was his diagnosis?'

Eileen smiled. 'There speaks the professional. But he never said. Thinking back, knowing what I know now, little as it is, and comparing him with other patients, I'd say there was some kind of schizophrenia, but it was clouded, like with Maurice, and he had bouts of really bad depression as well. And it was complicated by his relationship with his family, especially his father, and his suspicion of religion, and his sexual guilt, and his self-hatred.'

'Well, you know,' Josh said, 'the shrinks go on about cases and diagnoses and theories, but every patient is different. Every one has a different life, different experiences, a different personality to start with. I wonder what happened to Maurice. Where has he been?'

Eileen sighed. A huge weight of weariness was settling on her like a stifling blanket. 'After Christopher's death, Maurice disappeared,' she said. 'The scandal of his part in Christopher's suicide came out at the inquest, but by that time he was long gone. It was a great embarrassment to all concerned. They didn't find him. But they didn't ask the right person, did they?'

'What?' Josh said, frowning.

'If they'd asked you, they might have figured out where he was. Who would he go to, if not his brother?'

'Of course.'

'Didn't you say Len had gone "up north" somewhere? Well, Maurice came to us from Leicester. You may not think that's very northerly, but it's north of here.'

'It makes sense.'

'The only thing we don't know is how he was discovered. And why have they decided to put him in a secure unit? He was sedated when he arrived, Christine said. It makes him sound like some dangerous wild animal.'

Josh got up and stretched. 'Maybe I'll find out this afternoon.' He looked down at her. 'Eileen, you look exhausted. Why don't you crash out on the sofa?'

'I should go home.'

'You've had a sleepless night. Plus the worry about your daughter. And now this, the shock of Maurice coming back, dredging up the past. You're not fit to drive.'

'And you're not insured to drive my car.'

'Besides which, I'd have to get home again to pick up my bike, and then I'd be late for work. I'd offer to take you home on the bike, but I think you'd fall off. No, Eileen, be sensible. I'll get you a pillow and a blanket.' He went towards the door.

Eileen pulled herself to her feet. A thought struck her. 'Oh, no. I've just remembered Maureen.'

Josh paused in the doorway. 'What about Maureen?'

'Do you remember I told you I was worried about her? Well, one shift I found her crying in the washroom. Eventually she came clean about Des and I said to her if it ever got too much she could always come and stay with me, as a refuge. And yesterday, when I got home, after I'd dropped you off, there she was, outside my flat. Josh, she looked terrible: her face was badly bruised, she had a swollen lip and a bloody nose.'

Josh swore under his breath.

'She refused to go to A and E,' Eileen said. 'So I cleaned her up as best I could and tried to make her comfortable. But then I had to go to work.'

'Where you were treated to yet another stressful thing,' Josh said. He crossed the room to where she stood, leaning wearily on the back of the kitchen chair, and put his arms round her. 'You poor little devil.'

The kindness in his gruff voice broke Eileen's frail defences, and she found she hardly cared that she was leaning on Josh's shoulder and weeping into his shirt.

'Come on,' he said, walking her into the living room and planting her back on the sofa. 'You are going to get some sleep.'

'What about Maureen?'

'Can't I ring her?'

'Then she'll know I'm here! I thought you were dead set on protecting your reputation.'

'And yours. OK, you ring her. The phone's right here. I'll get the blanket.'

Eileen dialled her own number and waited for the answer phone to cut in. 'Maureen? It's me, Eileen. Don't worry, everything's fine. I'm staying at a friend's place for an hour or two. I'll see you when I get back. Help yourself to anything you need, won't you? Oh, and Maureen? Could you feed Fletcher, please? See you later.'

She replaced the receiver and stretched out, and before Josh came back she was asleep.

She woke, hot and sticky, in the half-light. The sun was still strong, but Josh had closed the curtains. She threw off the blanket and put her bare feet on the floor. Her eyes felt scratchy and her head was heavy. She looked at her watch: it was after four. *I must get home. Maureen will think I've got lost.* Josh had left her a note on the coffee-table. "Gone to work. Have a shower if you want. Towels are in the airing cupboard. I'll ring you tomorrow. J." The pen he had used was still lying there, and Eileen wrote him a reply on the bottom of the scrap of paper. "Dear Josh, Thanks for everything. I am OK. Talk to you soon." She hesitated, then added an x. He probably wouldn't notice anyway. She retrieved her shoes and bag from where she had scattered them, closed the flat door behind her, and went to find her car. It was red hot after sitting in the sun all day. She opened both front windows and started for home.

'Maureen? I'm back. At last.' Only Fletcher came to greet her, winding his sleek body round her legs. The flat was quiet. Eileen felt a moment of pure panic. She looked in all the rooms, but they were empty, and there was no note anywhere. Had Maureen gone back to Des? Had he found out where she was and come and dragged her away? She told herself not to be so melodramatic, and then to her relief she heard a key in the lock and Maureen came in.

'Hello, Eileen! You're back.'

'Just. Sorry I was so long. I meant to come straight home, but I went to a friend's and fell asleep.'

'It's all right.' Maureen took off her hooded jacket. The swelling of her eye and mouth was beginning to go down, but her bruises were turning all sorts of alarming colours. 'I've just been out for a walk. It got so hot in here, and I needed some air. There's quite a nice little park.'

'How are you feeling?'

'Not too bad. A bit stiff and achy.'

'Have you thought about what you might do?'

'Yes, a bit. No real conclusions yet.'

'I need a shower. Then I'll get us something to eat.'

'Can I help?'

'You could do some salad if you like.' Eileen went to the fridge and pulled out lettuce, cucumber, tomatoes and peppers. 'I won't be long.'

They sat at the kitchen table over the remains of the meal. Eileen had found a bottle of wine at the back of the fridge and they had finished more than half of it.

'I expect you think Des is a monster,' Maureen said, 'but he really isn't.'

'You're more forgiving than me. But surely you can't be thinking of going back to him?'

'Oh, I'll go back,' Maureen said quietly. 'I promised to stick with him through thick and thin, and I will, God help me. I don't even *want* to leave Des, Eileen. Do you understand that? Yes, what he's done is terribly wrong, but he'd agree with that anyway. Des and I have been together for almost thirty years. What would I do if I wasn't with him? Apart from worry about him? Of course, there will be conditions. There will have to be. But I want him to stop this stupidity and sort himself out; I don't want to split up. We'd both be miserable.'

'Aren't you miserable now?'

Maureen nodded sadly. 'Of course. But I'm hoping we can work it out together. He needs to cool off and realize what the consequences could be if he doesn't change. Can I stay another night, Eileen? I'll mull it all over, and then I think I'll ring him tomorrow.'

'Of course you can stay, as long as you like.'

'Thank you, dear. I really do appreciate how kind you've been. And I know you won't go talking about it.'

'Not a word.'

'Let's do the washing up. Then I'll turn in, if you don't mind. I haven't done anything much, but I'm tired.' She pushed back her chair and started taking the dirty dishes to the sink. 'How was your shift?'

'Oh, you know,' Eileen said. 'Quiet.'

After Maureen had gone to bed Eileen watched a news programme on TV with the sound turned down. After ten minutes she switched it off. She tried to read, but could not concentrate. She paced around the living room. *I have to think. But it's difficult.*

She thought about Maureen, and sighed. Her loyalty did her credit, and Eileen wondered if she herself should have tried a little harder, persevered longer, with her own marriage. It was too late now, of course, and she asked herself why she was even bothering to think about it. *Because it is to do with the person I am, my peculiar blindnesses. I want to avoid repeating my mistakes.* She sat in an armchair, looking out of her open window as the sky turned slowly to deep dusky blue. Her Bible lay unopened on her lap.

She thought about Maureen and Des, and wondered that such an apparently ordinary man could so abuse the wife he undoubtedly loved. *How little, in the end, do we know our friends. It's hard enough knowing yourself.* Her thoughts went back to the hospital, and to Maurice Bentley, whom she had never met, and yet who had occupied her thoughts and stirred up her anger. She imagined him in his solitary ward, perhaps by now awake, and wondered whether Josh would be allowed to see him. There would have to be a care plan, whether or not she herself was party to it. How long would he be there? What treatment would he have? Would he be moved again? Would he be transferred into the open ward? She shivered at the thought, and got up to close the window. Her thoughts ranged to Josh, who would be on his way home by now. She remembered the morning, and crying like a fool in front of him, and his kindness, and wondered what he must think of her. All the while her emotions were disengaged, and she felt as if in limbo, suspended between one day and the next, like an actor in the shadowy wings, waiting for the curtain to rise on another act. But in her case the next act was not only unrehearsed but unknown. She opened the door that led onto the fire-escape. The night air flowed in, warm, with a faint scent of diesel.

'Fletcher? Are you coming in?' But it was too fine a night for a young cat to waste on sleep, and after a few moments she closed the door and turned the key. He would come back in his own inscrutable time.

She sat down again and opened her Bible at Psalms. "Zion, the mountain of God, is high and beautiful; the city of the great king brings joy to all the world," she read in Psalm 48. "We have heard what God has done, and now we have seen it in the city of our God, the Lord Almighty; he will keep the city safe for ever... People of God, walk round Zion and count the towers; take notice of the walls and examine the fortresses, so that you may tell the next generation: 'This God is our God for ever and ever; he will lead us for all time to come.'"

Amen to that. Please, Lord, forgive me for being such a poor witness, and teach me to do better. It may be that you have brought Maurice Bentley to my door so that I can no longer ignore him; but I am afraid. Thank you for what I have learned today, and thank you for Josh. Lead me, Lord, over the next few days. I am weak, but I am in your hands, and I know that if I fall you will be there to pick me up.

Sunday 23 August 1998

Eileen woke early, the sun slanting in through the thin curtains, across her bed and into her eyes. She got up, fed the cat, took a shower and ate some breakfast, all by nine o'clock. There was no sign of Maureen. Noting that the laundry basket was crammed to the brim she decided to take her washing to a launderette that was open seven days a week. It was in a parade of shops on her way to church, and if she spoke nicely to the attendant he would put her clean, wet washing in a dryer so that she could collect it after the service. She put the whole lot in a black sack and went down the stairs quietly, out into the summer morning.

The service was unremarkable; there were even fewer people in the congregation than usual, because one or two were on holiday, and Louis' sermon was brief, as if he was in a hurry. Afterwards, in the vestry, Eileen could see he was distracted.

'How are you, Eileen?' he said. 'Well, I hope. Busy, I imagine.'

'Yes to both, thank you. Are you all right?'

'Mm, fine. I am off to London in a moment, to see my sister. I am hoping to catch the twelve-ten train.'

'Ah.'

Louis looked up. 'It's not all pleasure, unfortunately. Rosemary, my stepmother, Frances' mother of course, is in hospital.'

'Oh, dear. Is it serious?'

'We don't know yet. But Frances felt in need of some support.'

'It's good that you have each other.'

'Yes. I must confess I haven't always been much of a brother, but as we get older I am finding that I am thankful to have Frances.'

Eileen drove home, collecting her washing on the way. As she lugged the black sack through the doorway she saw Maureen's bag in the hall. Maureen herself was sitting at the kitchen table, a cup of coffee in front of her. 'Oh, Eileen, there you are. I'm glad you're back. But of course I wouldn't have gone without seeing you.'

'Gone?'

'Shall I make you some coffee?'

'Yes, please.' Eileen slid into the opposite chair.

Maureen filled the kettle and turned to face Eileen. 'I rang Des, and he's coming to get me.' Eileen looked at her, but said nothing. 'We had a long talk on the phone this morning,' Maureen said. 'He was relieved to hear from me. I knew he would be worried.' She poured water into Eileen's mug and put it in front of her, together with a carton of milk. She sat down and leaned her elbows on the table. 'I've told him, Eileen. He has to get help, right away. And we're going to get ourselves sorted out and go to Canada, to be near Neil and his family. It's what I've wanted for a long time, but Des would never agree. Now he has. We'll put the house on the market, and I'll give in my notice. But first he's got to see someone about these rages of his. Otherwise things will be just the same, no matter where we are.' She leaned forward. 'He isn't a bad man, Eileen. He isn't cruel or arrogant. Just rather inadequate. He was never like this before he lost his job. I know it's no excuse, but his job was what gave him purpose and pride, and when he lost it he lost himself somehow. Well, I've had time to think it through, and I can't walk away when things are bad; that's not what I promised nearly thirty years ago. But he has to change, I know that. And so does he.'

'Supposing he won't? Or can't?'

'We talked about that. If he delays, or wavers, or if he refuses to talk to me, or if he shows any aggression towards me, then I will leave him. I'll go to Canada by myself. It will break my heart, but he knows I mean it, and he's agreed.'

Eileen sighed. 'You are a very remarkable lady, Maureen. I hope Des realizes how lucky he is.'

'In his own way he does, I think. He'll be here in a minute.' She got up and took the empty cups to the sink. 'Thank you, Eileen. You were there when I needed you. I'll never forget that.'

'Glad to help. I hope we'll keep in touch when you're in Canada.'

'Of course. You could even come on a visit.' She looked up. 'Was that a car horn? It could be him.' She went to the window and peered out into the street. 'It is. I must go.' Eileen followed her to the door, and Maureen turned and hugged her. Then she clapped her hand to her forehead. 'Oh, Eileen, I'm so sorry! With everything that's happened it went clean out of my head!'

'What are you talking about?'

'Yesterday afternoon, before you got home, there was a hammering on the door. I wasn't going to answer it, but then I heard Penny's voice, calling you, out in the hall. When I opened the door she was very startled to see me. She noticed my bashed-up face, of course. She said, "Maureen! What are you doing here? What happened to you?" I told her some cock-and-bull story, then I asked her what she wanted. But she wouldn't tell me. She said she could only talk to you. She looked very agitated, Eileen, and I'm sure she'd been crying. But she wouldn't stay: she'd left Gus downstairs. She rushed away with a great clatter.'

'I'll go and see her later.'

'I hope she's all right. There goes the car horn again – I'd better go. I'll see you soon, Eileen.' She picked up her bag and started down the stairs, pausing on the landing to give Eileen a wave. Eileen went back into the flat and looked out of the window. She saw Maureen get into a dark blue saloon. *I hope you know what you're doing, Maureen. Be safe.*

Still feeling oddly detached, unfocused, remote, thinking about nothing in particular, Eileen folded up her clean clothes and put them away. Then she made herself some lunch, and had just sat down to eat it when the phone rang.

It was Josh. Something about his voice brought her back to reality with a sense of shock. It was as if she had been floating in some alternative dimension, and only now had landed without warning in a turbulent tropical sea. With a mixture of horror and amusement at her own foolishness she found herself becoming uncomfortably warm, as if blushing all over. *Get a grip, for goodness' sake. You are almost fifty, not fifteen.* The memory came back to her, with uncomfortable vividness, of how it had felt to have Josh's arms round her while she sobbed into his shirt. She collected herself with an effort.

'I thought you'd like to know what I found out about our new patient,' Josh said. 'I've seen him, but I haven't spoken to him. I don't know if he remembers me, but he still seems pretty out of it. They must have dosed him to the eyeballs. He looks a wreck, poor bastard. Anyway, I collared his assigned nurse – that little blonde from A Block, Polly or some such name. Do you know her?'

'No.'

'I used my rough Northern charm on her, sat her down in my office and made her a cup of coffee.'

'No wonder she obliged with information.'

'Well, they're a tough lot on A Block by all accounts. She wasn't used to kind treatment.'

'Not like us lucky workers, then.'

'I'm glad you appreciate your good fortune. Anyway, you were right. Maurice did seek refuge with Len, and Len, being a loyal bloke who remembered everything his brother had done for him, gave Maurice shelter.'

'So what changed?'

'Len has three kids, two boys in their teens and an older daughter. He also has two tiny grandchildren. Over the time that Maurice was living there Len got most of his story out of him. It seems to have been Len's wife who put her foot down in the end. She'd gone along with it, reluctantly, but she couldn't abide the thought of someone who could be dodgy round children being in the same house as her daughter's little ones. I suppose you can't blame her. She'd put up with her husband's mad old half-brother for two years. So poor old Len told Maurice he'd have to leave. And Maurice lost it. I guess he panicked. Where could he go? He'd had a lot of rejection in his life, and now his last hope, his brother, was kicking him out. At this point Len rang someone – I don't know who, exactly, maybe Social Services. Meanwhile Maurice disappeared again. But this time they found him: on top of a multi-storey car park, threatening to jump. Someone must've talked him down. I imagine there were a few frantic phone calls, trying to decide where he belonged. In the end they sent him back here, on the basis that he was our patient originally. Nobody wanted this particular little problem. But he was very disturbed, so they sedated him. By the look of him they gave him enough to stun a horse.'

'Will you talk to him when he's fit?'

'Yes, I hope so. But that's as much as I know at the moment. Are you OK?'

'Yes, I'm fine.'

'What about Maureen?'

'Maureen has gone back home. Des came to get her. But she's laid down some very stringent conditions. I hope she's doing the right thing.'

'Well, it's down to her, not us.'

'Yes. Josh, I was thinking. About Maurice. You said yesterday you didn't think he was a paedophile, or even really incestuous. So what was he doing dressing Christopher up in pink frills and calling him by the name of his own daughter? Come to that, why did he choose Christopher in the first place? Christopher was, after all, a man. Does Maurice have homosexual tendencies as well?'

'Hm, good question, but I don't think it's as simple and cut-and-dried as that. Things rarely are, as you should know.'

'True enough.'

'Off the top of my head, I don't know. But my guess, for what it's worth, is that when Maurice stopped coming to the hospital he was nowhere near as well as he wanted us to believe. As you said, he was a very clever man, and probably a dab hand at pulling the wool over the eyes of psychiatrists. It seems to me that when he went to that half-way house he was probably a lot less stable than the powers-that-be thought. The only loving relationships Maurice had ever had were his brother and his daughter, and both of them had been taken away from him. The little I know about Maurice makes me think that he wouldn't have battened onto Christopher just because he was an easy target. I'd guess he genuinely liked him. He may even have persuaded himself that he loved him and was doing him good. Maurice was, and is, a very needy man under all that veneer of competence. It probably didn't matter much to Maurice whether Christopher was a bloke or a woman: he was a warm body that didn't complain, someone he could pretend with. That's all Maurice had: pretence. And having chosen Christopher for the role it was no big step to making him into a girl and calling him Tessa. I think he preferred women, and he certainly loved Tessa, so that was his way of putting all his needs into one pot. Including the need for sex, although I'd say it was more to do with the need for kindness and acceptance, to be honest.'

'Oh, Josh. What a mess. What are they going to do with him?'

'That I don't know. It's Sunday, so nothing will happen today. We'll keep an eye on him and let him come back to what senses he's still got and take it from there. He'll have to be properly assessed.'

'Yes, he will. A lot has happened since he was last in hospital.'

'What about you? Maurice may well be with us for a while. I doubt they'll keep him next door for long. Can you handle that?'

'I suppose I'll have to. But it's not really about me anyway, is it? And at least I'll have one person around who knows my connection with this man. But I don't want anyone else to know. It's got to be time to let the past die a natural death.'

'Good for you.'

'Well, thanks for filling me in, Josh. I'll see you in the morning.'

She put the phone down, feeling rather cross with herself. *Why am I thinking vaguely lustful thoughts, especially now, when things are so difficult, so complicated? I will have to think it through before much longer. I can't run the risk of giving Josh the wrong idea. He's too good a man. That's assuming he has any ideas, and that they're the wrong ones. I don't even know myself. And I wish I didn't have to think about it.*

By the time she had eaten her lunch and washed the dishes and done a few minor chores, it was well into the afternoon before she went downstairs and knocked on Penny's door. Penny was a long time answering, and when she did Eileen was shocked. Penny was normally neat and well-scrubbed, if not very fashionable: her skin glowed with health, her chestnut hair was glossy, her eyes sparkled. Now, as she stood in the doorway, she was unkempt, her hair lank, her eyes puffy and red-rimmed, her well-rounded body sagging, her face grey with fatigue.

'Come in, Eileen,' she said. Her voice was hoarse.

'Penny, what's the matter? Are you ill?'

'No, not ill,' Penny said. 'Come and sit down. I've got to tell you something.'

Eileen followed her into the living room. Gus was sitting on the carpet, surrounded by his toys.

'Hi, Gus,' Eileen said. She perched on the edge of the sofa. Gus scrambled to his feet and plonked a red wooden bus in her lap. 'For me? Thanks.' She looked up. 'Sorry I wasn't in yesterday, Penny. I was on my way back from work. What's up? You don't look right.'

To her astonishment and dismay Penny bent down and grabbed hold of Gus. The startled little boy wailed and wriggled, but Penny held him tightly. 'You were right,' said Penny, her voice catching. 'He isn't mine. I stole him.' Then she collapsed onto her knees on the carpet, still clutching Gus, and burst into racking sobs. Gus, bewildered, put his plump little arms round her neck and cried. Eileen knelt down beside them and put her arms round both of them. 'Penny, Penny, what are you saying? Hush, Gus, it's all right.'

Penny disentangled Gus's arms and thrust him at Eileen. 'Here, you take him,' she sobbed. 'Take him and give him back.'

Eileen picked Gus up and soothed him, patting his back and smoothing his hair. 'It's all right, sweetheart, Mummy's not feeling too well. We'll go and get you a drink, shall we? And you can show me that new puzzle.' She carried him into the kitchen, sat him on a chair and wiped his eyes. She poured him a beaker of juice and tickled him till he chuckled. Then she fetched the puzzle and put it on the table in front of him. 'Show me how clever you are, Gus,' she said, tipping the pieces out of the frame. 'See how quickly you can do it. I'll just go and talk to Mummy for a minute.'

She went back into the living room. 'Come on, Penny, let's try and be calm. It's no good having you and Gus both upset. Sit here, wipe your eyes, and I'll make us a cup of tea. Then you can start at the beginning and tell me what's on your mind.' Penny got up, sniffing and gulping. Eileen patted her shoulder and went back into the kitchen. She admired Gus's progress with his puzzle, made tea and took it back in to Penny.

'OK,' she said. 'Gus is fine for the moment. He's trying to put a square into a triangular hole.' Penny took her tea with a shaking hand. Tears were running down her cheeks.

Eileen sat down. 'What did you mean, you stole him, Penny?' she asked gently.

Penny took a sip of tea. 'I took him from his pram in that big shop, Tilman's,' she whispered, as if trying to keep Gus from hearing. 'He was just a little baby. He was asleep. It only took a minute. I put him in my pram and wheeled him away. Nobody saw me.'

'But why? Why did you?'

Penny's eyes filled up again. 'I think I was a little bit mad,' she said. 'Later on I saw the news on TV. It was a big story, how a baby had been taken and nobody knew what had happened. I felt clever for once, fooling everybody. And it was so lovely, having a little baby in my flat. I just pretended he was mine.'

'Weren't you scared someone would find out?'

Penny shook her head. 'No. Nobody would ever know. Nobody knows now, except you. And God. That's the trouble.' She cried again, a keening, desolate wail.

Eileen took her hand. 'Penny, start again. Louis said you were pregnant when you first came here, and when you first started going to church at St. Augustine's.'

Penny breathed deeply, trying to calm herself. 'Yes, I was. It was Dave's baby, like I told you. And I went to hospital, and I had a baby boy. Dave registered him, Augustine Frederick. Frederick is Louis' second name. Dave didn't like it, but I made him do it. And after a few days I brought baby Gus home. Dave was hanging round, pretending he wanted to be a proper dad, but I knew he only wanted to have sex with me, and when I told him you couldn't, not for ages after you've had a baby, he soon scarpered. Good riddance. I had all the stuff, you see, everything you need for a baby. A carry-cot, and a pram, and a baby bath, nappies and clothes and everything. I was very happy. Then it all went wrong.' She got up. 'I'm going to get some tissues.' Moments later she came back and sat down heavily. 'When little Gus was five days old, I got up in the morning and found he was cold and blue.' Penny's voice was tiny, and Eileen could hardly hear her.

'Are you saying your baby died, Penny? That's terrible.'

Penny sniffed. 'That's when I went a bit crazy, I think,' she said, her voice flat and sad. 'But mostly I was scared. I thought when that Health

Visitor woman came round she would think it was my fault. I knew they thought I wasn't fit to look after a baby. I didn't think I'd done anything wrong. But if I was a proper mum, why did he die? Do you know, Eileen?' She looked at Eileen with huge, wet eyes behind her owlish glasses, and Eileen's heart was squeezed with pity.

She shook her head. 'Tiny babies sometimes do die, Penny. It probably wasn't anything to do with you. Looking at how you've cared for Gus, I'd guess you looked after that baby as well as anyone. So what happened next?'

'Well, like I said, I was really scared, and I think I went off my head for a while. I waited to see if he would wake up, and when he didn't, I realized he was dead. I didn't feel anything at first, except scared. I couldn't understand what had happened, I suppose. I waited till it was dark. Really dark, after midnight. Then I put him in his pram and took him to the church. I went round the back where all the old graves are, where hardly anybody goes. I took a little spade with me, and dug a hole by one of the gravestones, and I wrapped him in his blue blanket and put him in a little wooden box I'd kept — it used to have Christmas decorations in it. I saved it from when my mum was alive. I didn't want the foxes getting him. Then I covered it all up with earth and smoothed it down and put the turf back so you couldn't tell. I said a prayer. I asked God to take my little one straight to heaven. Do you think he did, Eileen?'

'I'm sure he did, Penny.'

'Then I went home, and the same day I went out with my pram, and I took that other lady's baby. And no one ever knew what I'd done.'

'I see. You had your own baby, and all the things a baby needs. Nobody knew your own baby had died. So nobody would suspect you. You're right, Penny. You're a lot cleverer than people realize.'

'Yes. But I did a very bad thing,' Penny said hollowly. 'I knew that, of course. But I pretended I didn't. I couldn't bear not to have a baby. I pretended Gus was really mine, and I took care of him, and I tried not to think of his real mum.'

'Why are you telling me all this now, Penny?' Eileen asked, though she knew the answer.

Penny looked at her, and the raw misery on her round face was enough to soften stone. 'It was when you told me about that lady in your hospital,' she whispered. 'I started to think about her, and once she was in my head I couldn't get her out. I tried to tell myself she had other children, and I didn't have anyone, but it wasn't any good. I kept thinking about her having to go to hospital, and trying to kill herself, all because of what I'd done. And you told me her name, and that made me think of her, you know, as a real person. And I knew you suspected me. You did, didn't you? It was because of those baby clothes you found. They were my own baby's, and I couldn't bear to throw them away. And then you saw me in the churchyard. That day was the day I buried my baby – the anniversary. So I didn't know what to do. Then I remembered something Louis said in church once, about telling God all your troubles, and that's what I did. I knelt down by my bed and I asked him to help me so that I knew what was the right thing to do. I did that every night, while Gus was asleep. And then, last night, no, not last night, the night before, I was asking him to help me, and he answered.'

'Really?'

Penny nodded solemnly. 'I prayed to God a long time. Until my back ached. Then I went to bed. I had a dream. Some of those old men in the Bible had dreams, didn't they? And God spoke to them, and then they knew what to do. Well, God spoke to me.'

'What did he say?' Eileen said faintly.

'He said I had to tell you the whole truth. And then you would help me.'

Eileen felt sick. The weight of Penny's guilt, and her own responsibility, dropped on her with a crash as if the ceiling had suddenly collapsed in a cloud of dust and plaster.

'You will help me, won't you, Eileen?' Penny said.

'Of course I will. As far as I can. But Penny, you can't ask me to keep this a secret. That would be wrong.'

Penny nodded. 'I know. That's not what I meant. I know I've got to own up. And I will, I promise I will. I meant will you help me afterwards.'

'As much as I am allowed to, Penny. Of course. And so will Louis, I'm sure.'

'Will you tell him?'

'I think he should know, don't you? He is your friend too.'

'All right.'

There was a clatter from the kitchen as Gus clambered down clumsily from his chair. He came into the room beaming, the completed puzzle in his hands.

'Gus, you are a very clever lad,' Eileen said, taking it from him and admiring it. Gus climbed into Penny's lap and sucked his thumb. In the circumstances, it was the saddest sight Eileen had seen in a long time.

'It must be nearly time for Gus's tea,' Eileen said. Penny nodded, speechless, holding Gus close to her chest and rocking him. 'Let's get it ready together, shall we?'

Later, as she wiped food from Gus's face and hands, Penny said, 'Eileen, will I go to prison?'

Eileen turned to her from the sink where she was washing up. 'I don't know,' she said. 'But I guess it's possible.'

'Is it very horrible?' Penny said, her voice tremulous.

Eileen shook her head. 'I'm sorry, Penny. I just don't know.' She dried her hands. 'Shouldn't we be thinking about what to do next?'

Penny took a deep breath. 'Sometimes I think I would rather throw myself and Gus in the river rather than give him up,' she said, breaking into fresh sobs. 'I might as well be dead.'

Eileen put her arm round Penny's shoulders. 'You mustn't think that, Penny. Life is precious, even if it feels bad at this moment. And I know you would never do anything to hurt Gus.'

Penny shook her head. 'No, I wouldn't really,' she said, her voice slurred and thick with weeping. 'I remembered that story in the Bible about King Solomon and the two ladies, the ones who were quarrelling over a baby, and the real mum was going to give the baby away rather than let the king cut him in half. He was wise, wasn't he?'

'Yes. And so must we be. You have been very brave, telling me the truth like this, and you're going to have to be braver still. But please, Penny, promise me you won't do anything stupid. Even if it's the middle of the night, if you feel frightened or you think you're going crazy, just come upstairs and bang on my door. I won't mind.' Penny nodded. 'What do you want to do now?'

Penny thought. 'I'll play with Gus for a while, then I'll give him his bath and read him a story and put him to bed. Then I'll pray some more. I'll ask God to tell me what to do again. Then I'll sleep on it. My mum used to say that to me when I was a kid. "Don't rush into anything, Pen," she said. "Take your time. Sleep on it. And the answer will come to you." She didn't know about praying. But she was wise, too, like King Solomon.'

'That sounds like a good plan. Listen, Penny, I've got to go to work early tomorrow, and I won't be back till the afternoon. I'll try to get hold of Louis tonight, but he might not be back from London yet. I'll try to go and see him after work. All right?'

'Will he be angry with me?'

'No, of course not. He will want to help you. But once you have told someone – who are you going to ring? The police?'

Penny shuddered. 'I suppose so.'

'Well, they might not let us be with you much after that. I don't know how it works, but I'm sure someone will look after you.'

'What will happen to Gus?' Penny's voice trembled and cracked.

'I don't know. But he will be taken care of. They'll find someone nice.'

'Will they give him back to his real mum? Karen?'

'I hope so. Don't you?'

'Yes,' Penny said. 'Then she'll be happy. Perhaps she won't hate me too much. Will you tell her, Eileen? When you see her? Tell her I'm very sorry for what I did. Tell her I looked after her little boy.'

'I will, Penny. As soon as I can.'

'Thank you, Eileen. I'll be all right now. I'll start getting Gus ready for bed in a minute.'

Eileen got up. She put her hands on Penny's plump shoulders and looked into her round brown eyes. 'Don't forget, you promised me. Don't do anything silly. I'm just upstairs if you need me. And I'll be praying too.'

Back in her own flat, Eileen walked the floor, unable to settle, unable to range her chaotic thoughts in order. Was it possible, what Penny had said she had done? It was very plausible; so many enigmas were unravelled. But the story was so extraordinary. A peculiar thought struck her: was it even possible that Penny – stressed by Eileen's suspicion and the tragedy of Karen, or seeking notoriety or a significance she felt she lacked – had made it all up? Eileen shook her head. *No. I can't believe that. Penny has certainly proved to be cleverer than anyone gave her credit for. Driven by her own despair, she found a way – a foolproof way, till now – to fill her need. But she isn't devious. Penny is honest. What has she gained by her confession? Nothing, except the knowledge that she is trying to right a wrong. Other than that, she will lose everything: her freedom, her reputation, her child. What she has told me is true.*

She picked up the phone and dialled Louis' number. It rang several times and then the answer phone cut in. 'Louis, it's Eileen. I need to talk to you – it's quite urgent. I have to go to work tomorrow morning, but could I come and see you in the afternoon? I'll come home first so if it's not convenient could you leave me a message? Thanks.'

She made some toast and sat by the window, chewing mechanically. Outside, the sky was darkening. A bank of cloud was rolling in, obscuring the stars. Perhaps the long, hot days were over. She heaved a sigh. What would happen to Penny? Would she be treated as a criminal, or would there be some allowance made for her? Penny was such a mixture of innocence and shrewdness that sometimes it was difficult to argue that she had any mental deficiencies at all. But Penny was not like other people. Eileen shivered at the thought of what might lie ahead. *Lord, she will go to prison, I think. Please, stand by Penny. She needs you right now. She has trusted you, Lord. Help me, too. To know the right thing to say. To be a friend. If it comes to that, please give her a sympathetic judge. Thank you for Penny's honesty, her conscience. Thank you for the joy ahead for Karen. Please keep Karen safe till she gets her boy back. If that's what will happen. I am well out of my depth. How little I know. But then, maybe I don't need to know, to worry. Maybe I too should trust you, like Penny does, and put myself in your hands. Thank you for the opportunity to forgive the man I have thought of as my enemy. Please, forgive me for all my hateful thoughts. And, Lord, please look after Maureen. And Des, for that matter. Lord, I am so tired. My head aches. My brain is overloaded. Christina, Maureen, Penny, Karen, Maurice. I should sleep. But will I?*

She ran a bath and soaked for half an hour, her eyes closed. She heard the phone ring, but she ignored it. The familiar, automatic actions of drying herself and towelling her hair and cleaning her teeth were soothing. The cat flap clacked and Fletcher bounded in, his sleek tabby fur smelling of fresh air.

'Hello, stranger. I am honoured.' Eileen gathered him up and tucked him under her arm. His purrs were volcanic, like a pneumatic drill.

She picked up the phone and listened to the message. 'Hello, Eileen,' Louis said. 'By all means come round tomorrow afternoon. I'm not going anywhere.'

She gave Fletcher a saucer of milk, locked up, doused the lights and went to bed. For a while she sat up with her Bible, looking up references to the need for trust. "Trust in the Lord with all your heart," she read in Proverbs 3. "Never rely on what you think you know." *That one has to be for me.* And she found a verse for Penny, and scribbled it down on a scrap of paper as weariness overcame her. Isaiah 12, verse 2: "God is my saviour. I will trust him and not be afraid."

Monday 24 August 1998

Eileen woke to the sound of rain on her window and her curtain being sucked and released by a fresh breeze. Her headache had gone, but she felt heavy and lethargic, and groaned at the thought of getting up. She dragged herself out of bed and into the shower. At six-thirty she was on her way downstairs, pausing only to slip the verse from Isaiah through Penny's letterbox. She thought of the day ahead, and shivered.

Driving to work through the wet streets she wondered what, if anything, to tell Josh. He would have to know because of Karen. But she concluded that she would wait until she had spoken to Louis. Nothing was definite. Penny, as far as she knew, had yet to involve anyone official. Telling Josh would be premature.

She was already on the ward, in her uniform, when Josh arrived in a welter of dripping bike-leathers. He had his helmet under one arm, and his boots squelched on the ward floors.

'You'll be in trouble with the cleaners,' Eileen said, smiling. There was something in his return grin that made her stomach turn over, but she couldn't be sure whether it was alarm or something else altogether. She dismissed the thought; now was not the time.

Work took over. After the handover meeting and breakfast and morning medication, Maurice Bentley's assigned nurse appeared, and was closeted with Josh in his office for half an hour. Carol took them some coffee and emerged with eyebrows raised. 'Sounds heavy,' she commented enigmatically.

Eileen was busy with a patient when she saw Polly leave the ward and disappear up the corridor in the direction of the secure unit. A moment later Josh came out of his office, looked up and down the ward, and beckoned to Eileen. She finished with the patient and walked up the ward to his door.

'Come in, Eileen,' Josh said. 'Take a seat.' He sat behind his paper-strewn desk and leaned back in his chair. 'You all right?'

'Yes, fine.'

'How do you feel now you're here, with Maurice next door?'

'Reconciled.'
'Really?'
'Yes.'
'Good. Because I thought we would pay him a visit.' He was looking at her steadily, seriously, gauging her reaction.
'Aren't you being a bit too kind, Josh? Shouldn't you be expecting me to get on with it?'
He leaned forward. 'For anyone else, I would.'
She felt heat rise up her throat and into her face, and silently cursed her fair skin. She had nothing to say.
'I'll fill you in a bit,' Josh said. 'Polly's been keeping me up to date. She's a nice kid. Got a brain too. Maurice is a bit more sensible this morning; the drugs are wearing off, but that will mean he may be more volatile. I'm just warning you so you know what to expect. He's been reliving the last few years, and his memories are a bit suspect. He's still suffering from some confusion, and he talks about Tessa his daughter and Tessa meaning Christopher as if they were interchangeable. I don't know if he will get his intellectual capacity back. Basically he's a ruin right now. Polly thinks he's eaten up with grief and guilt. But he's not entirely with it. He doesn't seem to know why he is miserable and guilty, beyond a vague feeling. I need to go and talk to him this morning, because there's bound to be a planning meeting very soon, as soon as a psychiatrist has seen him, and I need to gather a bit of information on my own account. I thought you could come with me. You don't need to say anything. Maybe seeing him as he is now will help you lay the ghosts.'
'All right, Josh. I can't say I am keen, but I'll do it.'
'Let's go, then.'
'Now?'
'I think so.'
Josh led the way out of his office, out of the ward and up the corridor. Curious eyes followed them. Eileen felt a singing in her ears. Outside the door to the secure unit Josh took a bunch of keys from his belt, chose one and unlocked the door. He ushered Eileen in and locked the door behind them.
She saw an unremarkable room, with doors leading off: bathroom, cupboard, kitchen. There was a table and four upright chairs. An easy chair was set by the big window, which was barred. Maurice Bentley was sitting in one of the hard chairs, his arms leaning on the table, his head bowed. He did not react when they came in.
'Morning, Maurice,' Josh said. 'How are you?' He sat down opposite

Maurice, and Eileen hovered by the door to the kitchen. Maurice glanced up. He looked ill: he was unshaven, his eyes were sunken, and his skin had a yellow tinge. His clothes were stained and crumpled, and his feet were bare.

There was a long silence. 'They should have let me jump,' Maurice said. His voice was dull and flat. Eileen shuddered. She had heard this dullness before, from Christopher. 'I'm no use to anyone. Not even to myself. Why couldn't they let me get it over with?' Josh did not answer. Then Maurice frowned. 'Don't I know you?' he said. 'What is this place?'

'You're in Allerton Hospital, C Block,' Josh said. 'You were here a few times some years ago, but this is the secure unit, so you won't recognize it. I hope we can get you out of here soon. And you do know me. We used to have some interesting chats. Josh Randall.'

Maurice's eyes widened. 'Josh!' He jumped up with startling suddenness, and his chair fell backwards with a crash. 'I remember!' Then he saw Eileen. 'Who's this?' he muttered, looking Eileen's way with narrowed eyes.

'This is nursing assistant Eileen Harding,' Josh said calmly. 'You know we have to do everything in twos. She wasn't too busy, so I fetched her along.'

Maurice picked up the fallen chair and sat down. 'What are they going to do with me?'

'Well, you'll have to see Mr. Caton, I imagine,' Josh said. 'There'll be a meeting. You'll have to stay in hospital for a while. You've not been too well, I think. And trying to throw yourself off a roof will have them all buzzing like flies. You know that. But we'll try to help you, if you let us.'

Maurice closed his eyes. 'It's not a question of me letting anyone do anything,' he said. 'I can't stop you. I'm washed up. Dying, from the inside out. I just wish I could get my head clear. I keep thinking my Tess is dead.' He looked up, and there was pathetic pleading in his watery eyes. 'Is she dead, Josh? Did I kill her?'

Josh shook his head. 'No, Maurice. To the best of my knowledge, your daughter is alive and well. The young man you called Tess is dead. Christopher. But you didn't kill him. He killed himself, sadly.'

Maurice laid his head on his arms. His voice, when it came, was muffled, and Eileen realized he was crying. 'I remember. Christopher. He was a beautiful young man. Perhaps I didn't kill him. But I might as well have.'

Josh got up and went over to the slumped figure. He gripped Maurice's shoulder. 'Blaming yourself won't alter things, Maurice,' he

said gently. 'The fact is, you're still alive, and maybe we can make life a bit more bearable for you. Your nurse will be back soon. Polly. She'll let you know what's going on. We'll be off now.'
Maurice lifted his head. 'Will you be back?'
'Maybe. We'll have to see.'

Back in the corridor, Josh locked the door again. 'Are you all right?' he said.
Eileen shook her head. 'I don't know what I feel. Horror, revulsion, anger, pity. All of those. You'll have to give me time.'
'Fair enough.'
'Thank you for wanting to help.'
Josh smiled hesitantly. 'Got to keep the workers happy.'
She smiled back. 'You really are a very nice man, do you know that? Come on, we've been away long enough. Your reputation will be in shreds.'
He laughed, and they made their way back down the corridor. 'Maybe it needs shredding. I'm beginning to find I don't give a toss.'

Eileen could hardly wait for the shift to be over. She found jobs to do that didn't involve talking to colleagues: the linen cupboard proved a refuge, if only a temporary one. She didn't want to talk to Josh either, but because he was often immured with paperwork it wasn't difficult to keep out of his way. She wanted to be quiet, and brood. Talking to patients was less stressful, somehow. At lunchtime, once the patients were fed, she took her sandwich into the garden and sat on a bench in the shade of a tree, and resolutely closed her eyes and shut out the world. The rain had given way to thin clouds and fitful sun, but it was still warm. She thought of Maurice Bentley in his solitude upstairs and felt a pang of human sympathy which startled her. Was her hostility draining away? Could just seeing him do that? Perhaps the process was already under way; perhaps the pressing needs of two women and a child had eclipsed what was already done and could not be undone. To her surprise she found herself hoping that there would be some therapy for Maurice that would relieve his despair.

At the handover meeting she hung back at the margins, offering no comment. She caught Josh looking at her, a frown creasing his brows, but he would have to wait. As soon as she decently could she shed her uniform, picked up her things and left with a careless general goodbye. In five minutes she was on the ground floor and walking briskly through the car park. As she drove away she saw Josh come out of the main door. She gave him a casual wave and felt a twinge of remorse. But he would keep.

Having heard from Louis, there was no need to go home, and she drove straight to the Vicarage, pounding the dashboard impatiently when the traffic ground to a halt or the lights turned perversely red. She parked with a crunch of gravel and rang the doorbell.

Louis came to the door in his shirtsleeves, humming. 'Hello, Eileen. Come in. I've got the kettle on.'

Eileen followed him into the kitchen. 'You've tidied up, Louis.'

He looked sheepish. 'Actually it was Avril Dyson who did it,' he said. 'She volunteered.'

'Did she! What a trooper! It must have taken her several hours and a ton of elbow grease.'

'Probably.'

'How was your stepmother?'

'About the same, thank you.' He handed her a mug of tea and looked at her with eyebrows raised. 'Something urgent, you said. Perhaps we'd better go through to the sitting room.'

Eileen followed him down the passage. 'Has Avril been in here as well?'

'I'm afraid not. It still has all its antique dust.'

They sat down. Eileen took a deep breath. 'You're not going to like this one bit, I'm afraid.'

'Don't tell me you're emigrating as well!' Louis said, eyes wide with horror.

'No, I'm not. But Maureen may well be.' She told him about Maureen and Des, and he winced. 'I didn't know any of this. Perhaps I should have.'

'I don't see how. If Maureen was bruised she just kept away from church. But she couldn't do that at work, not too often anyway. And our hospital is an absolute hotbed of gossip. Otherwise I wouldn't know either. But it's not Maureen I want to talk about. It's Penny.'

'Go on.'

'Last night Penny confessed to me that Gus is not her own child. Louis, you must remember the case of the stolen baby, right here in Allerton, two years ago. I wasn't living here when it happened, but it must have been all over the papers and TV.'

'What are you saying?' Louis said sharply. 'That our Penny took that child? That she has been harbouring him ever since? I don't believe it. Penny doesn't have the wit or the guile.'

'That's what I thought too,' Eileen said, and a huge blanket of sadness seemed to envelop her in that moment. 'But we were all wrong. Louis, she told me how she did it, and it all hangs together.'

'But I met her when she first came to St. Augustine's. She was very pregnant then. Eileen, I baptized that baby.'

'I know. But the child you baptized wasn't Gus Schofield. It was Simon Colley.' She told Louis what Penny had told her: her own child's cot death, the secret burial, the taking of Simon.

Louis shook his head. 'Surely this is madness! I can't believe that no one has ever found out. Could she be making it up?'

'If Penny doesn't have the wit to carry something like this out, I don't think she'd be able to invent it,' Eileen said. 'Besides, whatever else Penny is, she is no liar.'

'If what she has told you is true, she's lived a lie for two years.' Louis got up and paced the room. He stood by the French doors and looked out into his garden, running his hand through his hair. 'I am finding this hard to credit, I have to say. So, tell me, why has she suddenly confessed? If it's all fact, she has everything to lose.'

'Do you remember the bag of baby clothes I found at the back of her wardrobe? They were her own baby's. And then there was the time I saw her round the back of the church, in the rain. I mentioned it to you. I found the flowers that Penny had left. Last night she told me that was the day she'd buried her baby, two years ago. The same day she went out with her pram and took Simon Colley. It was in a department store. Tilman's. There's no way she's making this up, Louis.'

Louis' expression was grim. 'I still don't know why she confessed.'

'That was my doing. I was worried and suspicious. I kept telling myself not to be ridiculous. Why should Gus be anyone other than he seemed? But, you see, the stolen baby's real mother is a patient in C Block. I know her. Louis, if you met her, she would break your heart too.'

Louis turned to her, his face like stone. 'So if you hadn't interfered, none of this would be happening.'

'What? What are you saying? That we should collude with crime? That, knowing the woman whose child was taken, and whose life is in ruins because of it, I should have kept quiet? I can't believe you can possibly mean that.'

'What did you do? Tell Penny about this other woman?'

'I mentioned it, in passing, to see what Penny's reaction would be.'

'And you didn't think that might encourage Penny to confess to something she hadn't done? Knowing how naïve and suggestible she is?'

'No, I certainly didn't! I thought, if Penny was innocent, she'd be

221

sorry for Karen and that would be the end of it. What on earth do you mean, Louis? Why would Penny say she'd done it if she hadn't? And why are you so angry?' Louis did not answer. He turned away from her, took a handkerchief from his pocket, and began to polish his glasses. Without them he looked tired and vulnerable. 'Look, Louis, I realize this is a very hard pill to swallow. But it's no use hiding from the truth. We have to deal with it.'

Louis put his glasses back on and folded his arms across his chest. 'You have stirred up this wasps' nest,' he said. 'Perhaps you should deal with it, as you say. I am inclined to think it's all hysteria.'

'Hysteria? On whose part? Penny's? Mine? Perhaps you can tell me what I stand to gain.' Louis did not answer; he simply glared at her. 'The fact is, you share the responsibility for what has happened, whether you like it or not. Penny has been worrying over this for weeks. Her conscience has been giving her hell. In the end she gave the problem to God, because of something you once said in a sermon. And she said she had a direct response, which was to tell me the truth – whatever the cost. Penny is a very brave girl, Louis. She knows that the outcome of this is likely to be disaster for her. You, on the other hand, don't seem able to face unpleasant truths.'

Louis' face paled. 'You may be right. But what do you know of the unpleasant truths I've had to face?'

'Nothing. But this is what's on our plates now. Penny trusts you. She thinks you are her friend. But if you won't help, I will have to do it alone. She hasn't got anybody else. And if she is telling the truth, you are bound to be involved sooner or later. If the real Gus Schofield is buried in the Chandler grave, the police will be digging up your churchyard.' She put her mug on the table and stood up. 'I'm going now. Last night I made Penny promise not to do anything stupid, but I haven't seen her since then and I don't want to leave her alone any longer.'

She left the room, closing the door quietly behind her. Outside, she got into her car and pulled out into the road. But her hands were shaking so much she had to park for a moment and collect herself. She was shocked and astonished at Louis' behaviour. As she gathered her thoughts, she had a moment of terrifying doubt. Was it possible that she had put the whole idea into Penny's mind? She shook her head. No: surely Penny could not have made up so detailed an account. She started the car again and joined the flow of traffic. She wondered what Louis was thinking. He had always been unpredictable, but she could never have foreseen his reaction. How could he have metamorphosed in a moment from kindly supporter into judge, jury and executioner? Why?

Was he, after all, just a fair-weather friend? Or was there some deeper cause?

The loss of Louis was driven from her mind when she turned into her own road. At the kerbside outside the flats was a police car. She parked behind it and ran up the steps. The front door was open. The old lady who lived across the hall from Penny, Mrs. Denman, was hovering anxiously in her own doorway. Eileen greeted her distractedly. Two uniformed officers, a man and a woman, were knocking on Penny's door.

'Can I help?' Eileen said.

The man faced her. 'And you are..?'

'Eileen Harding. I live on the floor above. Miss Schofield is a friend.'

'Would you know of her whereabouts, Mrs. Harding?'

'I'm afraid not. But I'm surprised she's not at home. May I ask why you are here?'

The policeman looked at Eileen as if trying to make up his mind. 'The station received a telephone call from Miss Schofield about an hour ago,' he said. 'As it was a matter of some gravity we decided to attend. Now, it seems, the lady has gone out.' He was clearly irritated, suspecting that his time had been wasted.

'If you want to have a look inside, I have a key to Miss Schofield's flat,' Eileen said.

'Yes, please. If you would.'

'Right. I'll just go up and get it.'

Eileen climbed the stairs to her own flat and let herself in. The light on the answer phone was flashing. She closed the door behind her and pressed the message button. After a pause she heard Penny's diffident voice. 'Hello, Eileen. I rang the police and told them. I think they're coming round. But then I thought maybe I wouldn't have much more time with Gus, so we've gone to the park. See you there.'

Relief flooded Eileen, and she felt her legs buckle. Visions of Maurice Bentley on top of a multi-storey car park alternated with thoughts of pulling Penny and Gus out of the river. She found the key and went back downstairs. The police officer unlocked the door.

The flat was silent, and as neat and clean as it always was. In the hallway was a large black rubbish sack, with a square of paper pinned to it. "Plese take to charaty shop," was written on it in Penny's laboured hand. Tears started to Eileen's eyes. Penny obviously had no hope of coming home.

'Better have a look around,' the policeman said to his colleague.

'Let me save you the bother,' Eileen said. 'There was a message from Miss Schofield on my machine. She's gone to the park.'

223

The policeman shook his head, clearly wondering at the eccentricities of the public. 'Right, we'll get down there. Perhaps you could show us where to go, Mrs. Harding.'

'Certainly. It's not far.'

They left the flat and the policeman locked up.

'I think I left my door open,' Eileen said. 'I'll just go up and shut it.' As she got to the first landing she could hear her phone shrilling. 'OK if I answer that? It could be Penny.'

The policeman nodded reluctantly. Eileen stepped into her hall, closed the door and picked up the receiver.

'Eileen?' It was Louis. 'I spoke like a fool earlier. A treacherous fool. Please forgive me.'

'Of course, Louis.' Her disappointment and anger drained away; he was himself, after all. 'I did rather dump it on you. I've had a bit more time to get used to the idea, but it still freaks me out. Look, I can't talk: the police are here. Penny rang them. But she's taken Gus to the park.'

'What would you like me to do?'

'Can you come down? I'm going in the police car to find Penny. You know the little park at the far end of my road? Meet us there. I think we're going to need you.'

It was a five-minute drive. In the car the police officers were polite, but inclined to be silent. As they approached the park Eileen knew she had to say something. 'Look, I expect you can't tell me anything because of confidentiality.' The WPC turned in her seat to look at Eileen, who was sitting in the back. 'But I know why you're here,' Eileen said. 'Penny – Miss Schofield – told me the whole story last night.'

'You didn't think to report it yourself?'

'No. She said she would sleep on it. I expected her to ring you today, and she did. Perhaps you should know that Penny isn't quite – I don't know how to put it. She's a bit slow. I hope you won't be too tough with her. The park's just down here.'

The policeman parked the car in the road a short way from the park entrance. 'Miss Schofield has reported a very serious crime.'

'Yes, I know,' Eileen said.

'One that has used considerable police resources.'

'I'm sure. But she knows she's done wrong. Now she's trying to put it right. If she hadn't rung you today, we'd all still be in the dark. An unsolved crime.'

The police officers, half-turned in their seats, looked at her as if she was slightly mad. 'Since you seem to be in Miss Schofield's confidence,

Mrs. Harding,' the policeman said with exaggerated courtesy, 'perhaps you can tell us why she confessed.'

'Yes,' Eileen said. 'In the end it was a matter of conscience. And the thought of the suffering of the real parents.' In the police car's wing mirror she caught sight of Louis, hurrying along the pavement towards them. 'Shall we go?'

All three of them got out of the car as Louis came alongside. 'Let me introduce Reverend Belmartin,' Eileen said. 'I'm afraid I don't know who you are.'

The police officers, in some embarrassment, produced their ID. 'What's your connection with Miss Schofield, please, sir?' the policeman said to Louis.

'I'm her vicar. And her friend. Her son's godfather.'

'And, if that isn't connection enough,' Eileen said, 'you might have to dig up his churchyard.'

The police officers looked at her in astonishment. 'All right, Mrs. Harding,' the man said. 'It seems to me we must tread carefully here. Seeing as you clearly know so much, you and the Reverend here will probably be needed as witnesses. Please say no more. Let's go and find Miss Schofield.'

Eileen and Louis followed the police officers.

'You got here very quickly,' Eileen said.

'Mm. I probably broke the speed of sound, let alone the speed limit.'

'Ssh. We're with the Law.'

'They've got far more serious things to think about than me dashing about in my rusty jalopy.' They fell behind, and Louis said, 'You're not too disgusted with me, I hope.'

'Of course not. Forget it. You're here, and I'm very glad you are.'

They entered the park. Few people were about: a jogger, an old man with a scruffy dog, and, at the lakeside, two familiar figures: a plump young woman in a floral skirt, and a dark-haired little boy, feeding the ducks.

'It's only by thinking of Karen that I can bear this,' Eileen said.

'And I don't have your advantage,' Louis said grimly.

They hung back as the two police officers walked up to Penny. The WPC touched her lightly on the shoulder, and spoke to her. Penny took Gus's hand and started away from the lakeside. She saw Eileen and Louis. Smiling, she let go of Gus and he ran towards them. Louis picked him up and held him over his head, and Gus squawked in delight. Then Penny came up to them and for a moment the three adults wrapped their arms round Gus and each other.

'Time to go to the station, Miss Schofield. You and Gus,' said the policeman. 'Perhaps you could follow behind, Mrs. Harding and Reverend Belmartin.'

The hours seemed interminable. All round them there was a buzz of discreet activity, a sense of tense excitement. People came and went, people in uniform, people with briefcases, people who stared at Eileen and Louis and looked away. Louis took off his dog-collar. 'If I must be thought to be a drunk or worse, it's better they don't connect me with the church,' he whispered. Eileen smiled feebly. He was trying to keep her spirits up, but it was an impossible task.

At first, after Penny had been led away by the WPC, Eileen and Louis had the care of Gus. Penny, always thinking ahead, had brought a bag of toys, and, apart from the occasional whimper, Gus was content. Then a large woman in a dark suit arrived, disappeared into an office, and emerged twenty minutes later. 'I'm Thelma Davies, the Duty Social Worker,' she said. 'We've managed to find someone for this young man. Come along, Gus. You have to come with me now.'

Gus howled and flung himself at Eileen, burying his face in her lap.

'Where are you taking him?' Eileen said, smoothing his spiky hair.

'Emergency foster placement,' the woman said. 'I'm sorry, laddie. We have to go in my car. We'll go and see a nice lady I know. She has two kittens you can play with.' She took Gus's hand and led him away, still sobbing.

'Louis, this is dreadful,' Eileen said. He nodded and looked out of the window.

More people came and went. Eileen recognized her own and Penny's GP, who nodded to her, his face a blank mask. Still Eileen and Louis sat in the waiting room.

At last the WPC appeared. 'Would you come with me, please,' she said. She led them to a small office with a desk, chairs, a filing cabinet and a phone. 'Sorry it's a bit cramped. Everywhere else is being used. This is only a small station, and because it's such a high-profile case there are a lot of people involved. Do sit down.' Eileen and Louis sat in plastic chairs, and the WPC perched on the edge of the desk. 'We should be able to let you go home soon,' she said. 'But we're waiting for the Chief Super to arrive. He'll want to talk to you. Meanwhile we thought you would have some questions, and we need to tell you certain things.'

'Where is Penny? Is she all right?' Eileen asked.

'Miss Schofield – Penny – is in an open cell,' the WPC said gently.

'My colleague is with her all the time. She is remarkably calm. She's had a cup of tea. There were a few tears when we had to part her from Gus, but to be honest with you she seems resigned.'

'What will happen to her? And who are all these people?'

'Well, her doctor is here to assess her, and a social worker from the Mental Health team, and a solicitor, and some one we call an "appropriate adult," who's there to facilitate communication between Penny and all the powers-that-be. There'll have to be a joint meeting. We — that is, the local police — will lose this case straight away. It'll be taken over by Thames Valley. They investigated it in the beginning, and as far as I know it's still wide open. Like I said, we're just waiting for the Chief Superintendent. It's lucky he's still around. It was his case when it broke. I bet he's a happy man tonight.'

'He's the only one who is,' Eileen said.

The WPC ignored this. 'As to what will happen to her, she'll stay in custody for now. But you two must be very careful what you say. You'll both be witnesses, I expect. Be very discreet. We don't want to prejudice the court case.'

There was a tap on the door. The WPC went out and spoke to someone. When she came back into the room there was a man with her, a tall, close-cropped man in his late forties, smartly dressed, with a jacket draped over one shoulder.

'Chief Superintendent Duell,' said the WPC. 'Mrs. Harding and Reverend Belmartin, sir. I'll leave you to it.'

'John Duell.' He shook hands. 'Just a few things, then I can let you go home. I've had a word with Miss Schofield, and it seems to me there's one thing we have to do right away. I need to confirm her story before I can charge her, so I propose to take a strong young PC with a shovel and see what, if anything, is buried in your churchyard.'

'Mrs. Harding has a better idea than I do where to look,' Louis said. 'Should we go now?'

Duell nodded. 'Soon. Before we lose the light. Then, assuming we find something, I'll have to tape it off and leave a guard. I've contacted Forensics and they'll be round first thing in the morning. We have to establish if a body has been unlawfully buried and if so whether it belongs to Miss Schofield's baby, as she claims. Until we confirm that young Gus is, in fact, Simon Colley, that's all we can charge her with. It'll be a few days before we get any joy from the DNA samples.'

'So what are you charging her with, exactly?' Louis asked.

'Burying a body without permission,' Duell said. 'We'll arrange for DNA to be taken from Miss Schofield herself, Gus, and the supposed real parents. If it turns out that Gus is really Simon, then we can charge her with kidnap.'

'Will she go to prison?' Eileen asked.

Duell turned to look at her. 'Oh, yes. There's no question. It's a very serious offence.'

'You do realize, don't you, that she's not altogether – '

'She's been assessed by qualified people,' Duell interrupted. 'Now, do you have any other questions?' Both Eileen and Louis shook their heads. 'Let's go and get this grisly business over, then.'

Dusk was falling as Eileen and Louis, in Louis' car, led Duell and a young constable, driving an unmarked police car, to St. Augustine's. They parked outside the Vicarage and went on foot into the churchyard. The constable carried a spade and Duell a powerful torch. 'Show us where to go, Mrs. Harding, if you will,' Duell said. The men followed Eileen across the grass, between the graves, to the rough area behind the church. 'Here,' she said, showing them the Chandler headstone. 'I think it was this corner where I saw Penny put her flowers. They're gone now, of course.'

'Right, lad,' Duell said to the constable. 'Get digging.'

It only took a few minutes. The PC was a burly young man, and the ground was soft from the recent rain. His spade struck something hard with a dull thud. He squatted down and scraped the earth away. 'A wooden box, sir. About eighteen inches square and maybe eight or nine inches deep.'

'All right,' Duell said. 'It looks like she's telling the truth, so far. Don't disturb anything more, lad. We don't want to spoil things for the Forensic people.' He turned to Eileen and Louis. 'There's no need for you to hang around now. We'll take it from here. I'll try to keep it as discreet as possible, but if anyone does notice the tape round the grave and the police presence, just say nothing, all right, sir? There'll be a Press conference tomorrow, but having reporters or nosy members of the public swarming all over the place won't help my investigation.'

'Right.'

'We'll be in touch. Thank you for your cooperation.'

Following Louis back to the Vicarage, Eileen could see his dejection in every movement of his feet. *Small wonder.* Why was it that doing the right thing was so often depressing?

'What do you want to do, Eileen?' Louis said.

'Go home. Would you mind driving me? My cat will be starving. And today has lasted quite long enough.'

'Of course.' He unlocked the car and Eileen got in. Neither said anything for the ten-minute journey.

'Thank you, Louis,' Eileen said as he parked. She opened the car door, and paused. 'Have you eaten?'

'Not since lunch.'

'Do you want to come up? I'll do something with eggs.'

'That would be good.'

The hallway seemed particularly dark, and Penny's door was a silent reproach. Eileen climbed the stairs, her legs feeling like stone pillars, and opened her door. At once Fletcher materialized, and howled until she fed him. Then, with an unmistakable glare, he stalked off to the bedroom.

'Sit down, Louis. This won't take long.'

She fed them both on toast and eggs and tea, and felt a little less like a ghost.

'I keep thinking of today as some kind of fiction,' she said. 'As if I've been watching a film, and any minute now the credits will roll and I'll walk out of the cinema and everything will be back to normal.'

'You're right. Everything has a sort of gloss of unreality to it. But I'm afraid what we have now is normality.'

'Poor Penny. I can hardly bear to think about her. And Gus. Will he be all right?'

'In the end, he'll probably be the most all right of anyone.'

Eileen stacked up the dirty plates and put them on the counter. 'I hate feeling helpless. We could pray for them, couldn't we?'

'If Penny is to be believed, it's prayer that got her where she is now. It's not for cowards.'

'God never spoke to me in that direct way,' Eileen said.

'Nor me. But perhaps we weren't listening.'

'Let's pray then. I'm feeling exhaustion creeping up on me.'

Louis rested his head in his hands for a few moments, breathing deeply. Then he said, his voice sombre, 'Father, we bear our sister Penny up before you, and pray that you will stand beside her over the next days and weeks. Let her be very aware of your presence, your strength, your compassion.'

'Thank you, Lord, for Penny's courage and honesty, even though it has cost her dear,' Eileen said. 'And please defend little Gus, and bring a good outcome for him.'

'Give all who deal with Penny kindness and a desire for truth.'

'And Lord, protect Karen and all her family. Even if Gus really is Simon, it won't be easy.'

They sat in silence for several minutes. Then Louis said, 'I'm going home now, Eileen. I'll leave you in peace.'

Eileen got up and followed him to the door. 'I saw Maurice Bentley today as well,' she said. 'In the hospital.'

'Did you? And then all this on top? I'm not surprised you're weary. What was it like, if I may ask, seeing him in the flesh?'

'He is a very sick, sad man.'

Louis nodded. 'We'll talk about all this soon. Have a good rest, Eileen. Keep me posted of any developments.'

'Yes. You do the same. Goodnight, Louis.'

Tuesday 25 August 1998

Eileen was awakened by the jangling of her phone. She groaned and buried her head under the bedclothes, but the ringing went on and on, and she remembered she had switched off the answer phone. She crawled out of bed, padded into the sitting room and picked up the receiver.

'Eileen, it's Louis.'

'Hell's teeth, can't you sleep?' Eileen said crossly.

'Oh, is it early?' Louis said.

Eileen squinted at the clock. 'It's almost nine,' she said with a resigned sigh. 'No, not very early. What is it, Louis?'

'I thought you would be interested to know that there has been a presence round the Chandler grave since first light.'

'A presence? What, an apparition?'

'No, a police presence. Though they do look a bit ghostly in their white suits.'

'So they're digging up the site?'

'I can't see exactly. I only have a view of that part of the churchyard from my spare bedroom window, and there's a huge yew tree in the way. But I guess that's what they're doing. Unless, of course, they aren't the police forensic team at all, and have actually landed from some distant galaxy.'

'They've heard about your sermons.'

'Very amusing. That's all I have to tell you.'

'Thank you. If I hear of any more apparitions, I'll be sure to let you know.'

'That would be appreciated. I imagine the next development, at least from the point of view of the ignorant public, including you and me, will be the story on the news in a day or two.'

'Do you think so?'

'It's what the Chief Superintendent was hinting, I thought,' Louis said.

'I hope someone prepares Karen for this. How dreadful if the first she hears of the possibility of her son being found is on the news!'

'Surely they'll send someone round.'

'I hope so.'

Eileen fed Fletcher, then went to the bathroom. Her thoughts were racing away. Automatically she showered and dressed, then went back to the kitchen, poured a bowl of cereal, and ate it without tasting it.

She put the bowl in the sink, picked up the phone and dialled Josh's number. A moment later she heard his recorded voice, inviting her to leave a message. 'Josh, there's something I need to tell you. Can you ring me when you get this?'

Ten minutes later he rang back. 'I've got to pick up a load of furniture for the charity,' he said. 'It'll probably take me a couple of hours, by the time I get it back to the warehouse and unloaded. What's the mystery?'

'I'll tell you when I see you. Can you come over when you've finished?'

'Yes, I suppose so. You'd better give me directions.'

Twenty minutes later the phone rang again. This time it was the police, asking if they could come and take a statement. She told them to come as soon as they liked.

Josh arrived in a battered van just as Eileen was switching on the one o'clock news. She buzzed him up, let him in and waved him to silence. But after half an hour of trouble in Ireland and the misdemeanours of American politicians she turned the TV off with a sigh.

Josh sprawled on the sofa, in grubby jeans and an old striped shirt. 'Are you going to tell me what all this is about?'

'I'm sorry, Josh,' Eileen said. 'I wanted to see if there would be any hint on the news. But it's far too soon.'

'Far too soon for what? For goodness' sake, woman, put me out of my misery!'

'I will. But let's have some lunch first. I'll make us a sandwich.'

They sat at the kitchen table. It was odd to have Josh in the flat, but it seemed also somehow natural. Eileen munched her sandwich for several minutes. Then she could stand Josh's glaring no longer.

'OK. You need to know this. There is a possibility that Karen Colley's baby has been found.'

'What! How do you mean, found? Remains?'

'No. A living two-year-old.'

'Are you serious?'

'I would hardly joke about something like that.'

'Well?'

'They're awaiting DNA confirmation,' Eileen said. 'That could take a few days, even if they rush things through. And I think they will, otherwise it will leak out and some garbled version will present itself as truth.'

'Could you please start again? I am confused.'

'Sorry. Would you like coffee?'

'Yes, I would. But talk while you're making it.'

Eileen filled the kettle. She leaned back on the sink and folded her arms, looking at Josh with a slight frown. 'Simon Colley was kidnapped, I believe, by my neighbour, the girl in the flat on the ground floor. I got worried and suspicious, because of little things she did that seemed odd. I tried to tell myself I was being silly. But because of Karen it wouldn't go away. Then Penny – that's my neighbour – actually confessed to taking Simon.'

'When was this?' Josh asked, his face a picture of incredulous consternation.

'Sunday evening,' Eileen said.

'You didn't say anything at work on Monday.'

'How could I? Nothing was certain. I didn't even know what Penny intended to do. Until she did something to make it public and official, I couldn't really say anything.'

'How certain is it now?'

'Well, the police are checking her story. So far everything is as Penny said it was. They've found where she buried her own baby. For me, I believe Penny. Now that she has decided to confess, she has nothing to gain from lying.'

'What's this about burying a baby?'

'Her own child died, a cot death. She buried him in St. Augustine's churchyard. St. Augustine's is the church I go to. That's how she got away with it.'

'Where is she now?'

'In police custody.'

'And the child?'

'With foster-parents, for the time being.'

Josh shook his head slowly. 'Eileen, this is incredible. What's your part in it all?'

'I'm afraid I broke patient confidentiality. I told Penny about Karen.'

'Why?'

'I couldn't think what else to do. When I came into work and saw the terrible state Karen was in, I had to do something. And it worked. It took almost two months, but in the end Penny's conscience got the better of her.'

'Hm. I understand, now. Those innocent hypothetical questions. Whether Karen would recover if by some miracle she got her son back.'

'You remembered.'

'Of course I did. I'm not completely gormless.'

'You're not gormless at all.' The phone rang. 'Excuse me for a moment.'

She picked up the phone. It was Louis.

'I've just been doorstepped by a reporter,' Louis said without preamble. 'I'm beginning to feel like a celebrity. And I've had the police round, asking me everything I know and writing it down. I only know what you told me, so it seems a bit pointless.'

'They've been here, too,' Eileen said, 'and I only know what Penny told me. Have the press noticed the police presence in the churchyard, do you think? They won't have had the press conference yet, will they? There was nothing on the one o'clock news.'

'Once the excellent Sergeant McManus had left, I spoke to the forensic people,' Louis said. 'They're hoping to have the DNA results by Thursday. Then they'll have the press conference. But the press have a nose for news, don't they? They might pre-empt the whole thing.'

'I really do hope not. So what did you say to the reporter, Louis?'

'I told him, rather grandly, in my best condescending Cambridge manner, that I was not at liberty to divulge anything, even supposing I had anything to divulge.'

Eileen sighed. 'I just keep thinking about Penny. I wonder how she is.'

'Yes. Penny's been on my mind too.'

When she rang off, Eileen found Josh staring at her narrow-eyed. 'Your friend the vicar, I suppose,' he said.

'Yes.' Eileen told him briefly what Louis had said. 'Why are you looking so furious?'

'I'm not. So, what now?'

'Well, I suppose we keep our eye on the news and see what happens.'

Josh sighed, and shifted into a more comfortable position on the sofa. 'It's an extraordinary story. And wonderful, if it pans out, for Karen. And the rest of her family.'

'Yes, but it's tragic too. If Penny's own child hadn't died, none of this would have happened. And now a twenty-year-old woman who's not, how shall I say, a hundred per cent, will spend quite a long time in prison. I can't imagine what that will be like for her. When I think about Penny I want to weep.'

'What? This Penny, she's not quite all there?' Josh said.

'Well, Penny's funny. In some ways she's capable and shrewd. And you couldn't criticize her as a parent. Gus — that's her name for him — is healthy and happy. But she's oddly innocent. It makes her vulnerable. She finds ordinary things difficult, like reading and writing and filling in forms. She's very straightforward and literal. She doesn't understand hints or innuendoes. Or even humour, not really. And she's afraid of things that shouldn't be threatening. When her baby died, she thought she'd be in trouble. That's why she did what she did, in some measure.'

'What a mess.'

'Yes.'

They were silent for a while. Then Josh said, 'Thursday, he said. Are you busy on Thursday evening?'

'Not specially. I'm at work Friday morning.'

'I promised to cook you a meal, didn't I? How about making it Thursday? You could come over early, and we could watch the six o'clock news.'

'Thank you. It would be nice to be cooked for.'

'Is there anything you hate?'

'No. I'm more or less an omnivore.'

Josh heaved himself off the sofa. 'Good. Now I must get this van back, or they'll think I've absconded. I'll see you on Thursday.'

In the end Eileen's restlessness drove her out of the flat. She took a bus, and drifted round the city centre shops, something she normally avoided. The sense of anonymity as she blended with the crowds was oddly comforting. On the way home the bus was slow, stopping frequently even when not held up by the rush-hour traffic. By the time she got home it was six o'clock, and her feet were aching. She switched on the news. But again there was nothing.

That night she lay sleepless. It was a fine night, speckled with stars, warm, with a barely-noticeable breeze. Someone on the other side of the road was having a barbecue; music and laughter floated over and in through her open window. She thought about Penny and Gus and Karen, and a frisson of anxiety chilled her; but there was nothing she could do, except pray. She felt a sense of unreality, as if time had been suspended. She sighed, turned over onto her back, and stared at the ceiling. Although she imagined the outcome a dozen times, and gave it to God and still came back to worry at it again, the situation was not in her hands, and never had been. And try as she might to avoid it, she had to face the uncomfortable fact that her concern about Thursday was more to do with Josh than with what might happen to Penny, or Karen's reaction.

Lord, I am in such a muddle. You see my heart and mind, I know. For me it's like a muddy pond; for you it's as clear as glass. What is Josh thinking? For that matter, what am I thinking? Lord, he is a lovely man, and it would be so easy just to fall into his arms. So easy. I could do it almost without thinking. It would be nice, for once, to give in, to shut my eyes, to go with the flow, to stop being so watchful. But what sort of trouble would I be stirring up? I seem all too capable of stirring up trouble, even when my intentions are good. Help me, Lord, to see what is right, and to do it. Help me not to hurt anyone, including myself. I don't admit it very often, not even to you; but there are times when I look into that gaping pit of loneliness and draw back from the edge, shivering. I know I shouldn't be motivated by my own neediness, but sometimes I think that if Josh were to touch me – I don't mean accidentally, in passing, but with conscious intention – I would be like a sudden fire, blazing up, crackling, destroying everything, disappearing in a shower of sparks. I'm being fanciful now, as my mother used to say. But the words you use don't change anything. Words can mask the facts, but the facts remain.

It was a hot, sultry night. She threw off the covers, and the sweat cooled on her bare skin. Every inch of her body seemed to be particularly sensitive. She found herself thinking about David, and the early years of their marriage, before the children, and her discomfort redoubled. She turned onto her stomach, groaning, and pummelled the pillow. How good it would be to slip into the oblivion of sleep.

It was dark: the middle of the night. She was floating around the deserted ward, alone, wearing a sea-green floor-length ball gown with a ragged hem. She carried, in one hand, a tray of medicine containers, and in the other a half-empty wine bottle. As she swayed and tottered on ridiculous high heels from one side of the ward to the other, the wine slopped and spilled. She stopped and looked at the red splashes, like blood, on the ward floor.

Then she heard the creaking of the fire-escape door, and saw a dim figure come stealthily in.

She cried out joyfully, 'Josh! There's plenty more in this bottle!' Then, without warning, she was lying on the floor. Her dress was wet, wine spread out from where the bottle had broken, and pills rolled everywhere. She was in pain; her leg was twisted up under her, tangled in the folds of the voluminous dress. She moaned.

A man was bending over her. 'Help me,' she said. But when she looked at him closely she saw that it was not Josh, as she had blithely, drunkenly supposed. It was Maurice Bentley.

She woke shivering in the first greying of dawn. The covers had slipped off onto the floor. She picked them up and wrapped them round herself. But the shivering was fright as much as cold. *Why should a dream about Maurice Bentley scare me? It seemed like he was the very incarnation of evil. But I know he is not. He is a sick, deluded, broken man.*

She got up, put on a bathrobe, went into the kitchen and made a cup of tea, then sat at the kitchen table. What were dreams, anyway? Were they random electrical flares in an over-active brain? The result of indigestible food, as her mother would have diagnosed? Meaningless nonsense made up of jumbled memories, some conscious, others buried deep? Or could some truth be read into them, even if that truth was personal, unique to the dreamer? She sipped her tea. She had told herself that she was relinquishing the past, banishing it to where it belonged: the dusty forgotten attic, where it would no longer have power over her. But was she fooling herself? Had it simply gone underground, its power all the greater because hidden? Could it ever really be over?

Thursday 27 August 1998

Eileen rang Josh's bell at five to six. He let her in, took her jacket and waved her into the lounge. She collapsed onto the sofa, out of breath, as Josh switched on the TV. 'The traffic was worse than usual. I forgot the road works.'
'The news will be on in a minute,' Josh said. 'I need to attend to my cooking. Call me if anything interesting happens. I hope you like fish.'
'Lovely.'
Josh disappeared into the kitchen.
Eileen sat upright. On the TV screen was a shot of Allerton city centre. 'Josh! It's on!'
Josh came in, leaned over the back of the sofa and handed her a glass of wine. The familiar face of the early evening newscaster was unusually solemn.
'There appears to have been a new development in the case of the mysterious disappearance of baby Simon Colley from an Allerton department store over two years ago.' He glanced down at his notes and cleared his throat. 'The case, known as "Operation Firefly," has continued to baffle the police. Despite intensive searches and wide-ranging interviews, the investigation foundered because of what seemed to be a total lack of leads. The case has, however, never been closed, and today the original officer in charge of the investigation, Chief Superintendent John Duell of Thames Valley Police, held a press conference.'
The camera showed Duell, sharply-dressed, laconic and calm as ever, fending off a cacophony of press questions. 'Our enquiries are ongoing,' he said, sounding almost bored. 'A local woman is in custody, and a child is in foster care. At the moment we are waiting for the results of DNA tests, so that's all I can tell you for now. A statement will be issued as soon as we have confirmation.'
From out of camera range a voice shouted over the din. 'Chief Superintendent, can you tell us if the Colley family know of this development?'

'They have been informed of the possibility. As I said, until we have the results of the tests, that's all it is – a possibility.'

Then the camera cut to a suburban street, and a modest house with a square of tidy lawn and a cherry tree. A shirt-sleeved reporter stood at the gate, microphone in hand. 'I am outside the house of Mrs. Karen Colley, the mother whose two-week-old baby son was snatched in June 1996. We have seen the original Police Liaison Officer arrive, but there's been no sign of Mrs. Colley herself, or of her partner, Mr. Duncan Weller.' Just on the edge of camera range Eileen saw swarms of reporters, cameramen, and sound people with huge microphones. Then there was a sudden palpable surge of excitement. The TV camera panned back to the front door, now open. Eileen saw the familiar face and bulky frame of Chopper, and behind him in the shadowed doorway a young woman in uniform. Chopper, grinning awkwardly, made his way to the gate where the pressmen thronged.

Chopper held up his meaty hand, and the noise abated.

'Mr. Weller, what have the police told you?' someone yelled from the back of the crowd.

Chopper coughed. 'We don't know much yet. But we're hopeful. Getting Simon back would be like…winning all the lotteries in the world,' he said triumphantly. 'Specially for Karen. His mum. It's been, like, hell for her. But we have to wait and see.' With that, smiling stiffly at the crowd, he turned and hurried back up the path and into the house. The uniformed woman closed the door behind him.

'Who's that?' Eileen asked, turning to Josh.

'Probably the Liaison Officer he mentioned,' Josh said. 'Maybe even the same one the family had in the beginning. The police assign them. The fact that she's there makes me think things look hopeful. The police have to be cautious. But they wouldn't have said anything if they weren't pretty sure.'

The TV cameras moved again, to another street, another front door. A woman in her early sixties stood in the doorway, frowning, a half-burnt cigarette in her hand. 'This is Mrs. Poulson,' said the reporter. 'The missing baby's grandmother. What would it mean to you, Mrs. Poulson, if this child did in fact turn out to be your grandson?'

The woman cleared her throat, narrowing her eyes against the smoke drifting up from her cigarette. 'It'd mean everything to all of us, especially Karen. Everything. I can't tell you what that poor girl has suffered, every single day since that wee mite was took. It cost her her marriage, for one thing. And her health.' She looked up, clearly scanning the pack of reporters prowling by her gate, and raised her voice. 'So I'm telling you, if this kiddie is our Simon, you leave my Karen alone. Let her be. She's had enough grief to last a lifetime.'

Another shot followed: another house, obviously filmed some hours before, showing a harassed-looking young blonde ushering Karen's two older children, in their school uniforms, out of Dean's four-by-four and into the house. Eileen recognized the young woman as Dean Colley's girlfriend, Mel. The reporter commented on the sad fact that the abduction of Simon and the stress on the family had led to Karen and Dean's divorce.

Then came a shot, vanishingly brief, which made Eileen exclaim softly. It showed, rather dimly, a great spreading tree, and under it several white-suited figures and a length of police tape. 'It's St. Augustine's churchyard!' Eileen said. 'How did they get hold of that?' Then the camera cut to the Vicarage drive, and a brief glimpse of Louis closing his front door. The reporter turned from Louis to the camera and said, in his rather unctuous, confiding way, 'The Reverend Belmartin was not available for comment today. Could it be that the unusual activity in this graveyard is somehow connected with the possible rediscovery, two years on, of baby Simon? We will have to wait and see. Over to you in the studio, James.'

The newscaster was talking about the probable effects of finding Simon, and how the child might be helped to reintegrate into his family. In the studio were an interviewer and an eminent child psychologist. 'You can turn it off as far as I'm concerned,' Eileen said. 'I don't think I can stomach pontificating pundits right now.' Josh switched off the set. For a moment Eileen sat stunned, trying to absorb all that she had seen. Josh refilled her glass. 'Time to eat,' he said gently.

Eileen sat obediently at the table, and Josh brought in several steaming, fragrant dishes. For a few moments they ate in silence, then Eileen laid her fork down. 'This is delicious, Josh,' she said. 'What's in it?'

'It's my own recipe, so better not enquire too closely,' Josh said with a smile.

'I'm relieved that they've told Karen something,' Eileen said. 'As long as it isn't a false hope.'

'I don't think so. Neither do you, do you?'

'No. Penny was telling it as it was.'

They finished eating, talking little. 'Thank you,' Eileen said. 'That really was very good, and most welcome.'

Josh leaned back in his chair. 'So that's your vicar friend, is it?'

'Mm. Do you suppose they'll be harassing him, once they find out that Penny was a member of his congregation? And a friend, and Gus's godfather.'

'Bound to. And they might be after you as well.'

'I don't look forward to that.'

'You know the press. If there's a good story they'll milk it for all it's worth. It might go quiet for a few days, but once they have the DNA results and proof that Gus is really Simon, there'll be more excitement, more interviews, more people getting in on the act. Then Penny will be charged, and there'll be more of the same. This one's really going to run. You'll have to be prepared for it.'

Eileen shivered. 'There are connections I hope no one will make.'

'Such as?'

'Where I work. Karen's mental state. I've had a horrible thought: will they let her have Gus – Simon – back if she's not considered capable? That would be insufferably cruel.'

Josh reached over for the wine bottle. 'It's probably best not to speculate too much. It can't do any good. Like everybody else, we have to wait. Would you like some ice cream? I found a rather exotic flavour in the corner shop.'

'What, armadillo and absinthe?'

'You guessed!'

'Thank you, I'd love some. And you're right. Let's put this out of our minds for the moment. Talk about something else.'

Josh went into the kitchen and came back with the ice cream. He waved the wine bottle at her enquiringly. 'No, thanks,' Eileen said. 'I've had quite enough. These glasses are enormous. One thing, though: some of the patients will be over-excited by this story, especially the ones that know Karen. I could be in for a volatile morning tomorrow.'

Josh nodded. 'So, what shall we talk about?'

Eileen hesitated. 'I had the oddest dream.' She told Josh about the ward and the broken bottle and Maurice Bentley. 'Why would I find him frightening? Or is it all random, without meaning?'

Josh shook his head. 'I don't know. Are you a dreamer normally?'

'Sometimes. Maybe, somewhere deep down, I am still afraid. No, not afraid exactly, untrusting. I don't trust him.'

'But that's rational. You know what he's capable of. You know as well as I do that with his illness he won't ever be completely cured. There are things he'll be prone to, for the rest of his life. How far can you trust anyone, anyway?'

'We have to trust some people, to some degree,' Eileen said, 'or we couldn't function. Unless we were all island-dwelling hermits, and then it wouldn't matter.'

'How do we know who to trust and who not to, then?'

'Experience. Instinct. The benefit of the doubt.'

'And you don't trust Maurice.'

'No. I'm trying to see things in perspective, to put myself in his shoes. That's not easy. I think I have forgiven him. If I'm wrong about that, I'll keep trying. But I don't blame his brother's wife for wanting him out of the way. What do you think? Is he dangerous?'

'I don't think he's a threat to children. The situation with Christopher was very specific. But all the time the thought of Tessa is eating away at Maurice I suppose there's a slim possibility that he might batten onto someone else, given the chance. But that's just what he won't have. Not any more.'

'Never?'

'Well, you can't watch someone twenty-four hours a day. But it'll be a long time before he leaves our care, I'd say. A lot of treatment, perhaps a different drug regime, and regular monitoring. But that's not really the point, is it?'

Eileen licked the last of the ice cream off her spoon. 'What do you mean?'

'The point is you've got him fixed in your mind as some kind of predator, even though you try to rationalize it away.'

'If that's true, am I curable?'

Josh smiled. 'Oh, I think so. With a bit of time. I have an idea about that.'

'Really?'

'Are you free on Sunday?'

'After the morning service, yes.'

'I thought we might go west. To where you used to live. Take a stroll in the woods. You could show me where you had your meetings with Christopher. Maybe, if you were up to it, you could take me to the place where you found his body. Exorcize some of the ghosts.'

Eileen looked at him, her eyes wide. 'Is this something you've just dreamed up?'

'No. I've been thinking about it for a while. Ever since I suspected there was something hanging over you.'

'Good heavens.' She fell silent, digesting what he had said, and the implications. 'All right. I'll do it. Sunday afternoon.' She pushed back her chair. 'I'll help you with the washing up.'

'You certainly won't.'

'Oh. Well, in that case, I think I must go home.' She stood up. 'I'm very tired suddenly. I've drunk more than I usually do. And I slept badly last night, what with all the dreaming.'

Josh handed her her jacket and followed her into the hall. He leaned over to open the door and she caught his faint scent of soap. She put her hand on the wall.

'You sure you're OK to drive?' Josh said.

'Yes. I'm just tired.' She paused. 'Thank you, Josh. For a lovely meal. And for being so kind.'

He was very close to her in the narrow confines of the hallway. To her surprise he brushed her cheek with the tips of his fingers, and she sucked in her breath. 'Why shouldn't I be?' he said.

'Why should you, more like.'

'Well,' he said quietly, 'I'm sure you know why.'

She felt sweat break out on her face. 'That's scary.'

'Why scary?'

'Oh, I don't know.' She looked down, away from his eyes. 'It's the old conflict, I suppose. The desire to be safe versus the fear of losing your freedom.'

'Most folks are afraid to have freedom, not to lose it.'

Eileen looked up. He was looking at her intently, and his face was grave. Perhaps he too was a little scared. 'Do you think so?'

'Anyway, it seems to me that both security and freedom, as human ideas, are illusions.'

Eileen frowned. 'That's a thought.'

'Besides which, don't you believe you are eternally safe and free in God's hands?'

Eileen's eyebrows shot up. 'I never thought to hear you say such things.'

Josh laughed. 'I'm not the son of a preacher for nothing. Even if I have gone astray.'

'Let me go home,' Eileen said. 'Or it will be me that goes astray.' She hesitated, then touched him lightly on the shoulder, for a brief moment feeling his warmth through the thin cotton shirt. He stood very still. 'Goodnight, Josh.'

Sunday 30 August 1998

Eileen drove through the city streets at midday, her windows down. It was still very hot, but the hard glare had gone, replaced by a heaviness in the air. She was mildly surprised by the quietness of the city centre until she remembered that it was the Sunday before a Bank Holiday. Many urban dwellers would already have left, for the country, the coast, or further still.

Josh was waiting for her outside the flats.

'You OK?' he said as he fastened his seat belt.

'Fine.'

'How was work on Friday?'

'Mm, bit of gossip, not much. Things were quietish.'

He nodded. 'Good. I assume you know the way.'

'I think so.'

He seemed disinclined to chat, and she was thankful. She was beginning to wish she hadn't agreed to this trip. What if it was all too much, and she fell apart – again? Did it matter? For some reason, probably not a very good one, she found that it did.

Caxford was somnolent too, but that was to be expected. As she turned on to the Holton road, once so familiar, she found apprehension building, a breathless feeling in her stomach. The fields were the same, though there were more houses now lining the road. At one development there was a pretentious brick wall and a builder's sign. "The Glades" it read. "Country living for the discerning homeowner." Eileen made a face. 'I wonder if there are new houses in Holton itself,' she said.

She slowed down as they entered the village, and was surprised by the number of parked cars.

'Maybe you were right,' Josh said. 'Can you see any new building?'

Eileen shook her head. 'No, it's the pub.' She found a space by the church and squeezed in. 'I can't believe how different it is. This used to be a quiet country pub, a bit spit-and-sawdust, with half-asleep locals propping up the bar. Now look at it.' The Ash Tree was alive with

244

people, sitting at picnic tables outside, spilling out of the doors carrying trays, thronging a paved patio with closely-packed plastic tables and chairs, while from the back garden floated the raised voices of children.

'Sounds like they've put a play area in as well,' Josh said. 'It's how it is these days with pubs. They have to do food, screen football matches and run quizzes to make a profit. Do you want a drink?'

'I could do with something, but I imagine there's a queue a mile long.'

'Let's see.'

They shoved through the crowds to the bar. It was slightly quieter inside. Eileen realized immediately that the place had changed hands. Not one of the people in the pub, neither clientele nor bar staff, was familiar to her.

She found a tiny table in a dark corner and Josh brought drinks.

He took a deep pull of his beer. 'That hit the spot. What do you want to do?'

Eileen thought. 'Let's cut through the churchyard to the woods. Then I'll see how the mood takes me.'

They finished their drinks and left, threading their way through the crowded tables. Eileen led the way along the front wall of the churchyard and in at the gate. The gravestones baked in the sun. 'At least this looks the same,' Eileen said. 'But who knows? If we were to go inside we'd probably find the pews all gone, and a drum kit in the corner.' She tried the door, but it was, as she expected, locked. She went on down the path, Josh following, and came to the gate that gave onto the footpath leading down into the woods. 'Nobody's been here for a while,' she said. 'Mind the nettles.'

They came to the back gate of Eileen's old house, and paused, looking up the garden. 'This feels mighty weird,' Eileen said. 'So familiar, and yet so strange. This was my place, but it looks very different now.' The cottage had been painted white. Cheerful checked curtains billowed from the open windows. The garden was neat and floral, and a small conservatory had been built out from the kitchen. 'Is this "discerning country living," do you suppose?'

'What would I know about that?' Josh said.

They turned down into the woods. Sunlight slanted through the trees, now in full foliage. Eileen realized that the paths had been cleared and widened; instead of an overgrown path tangled with assorted vegetation, they were on a broad, mown ride, the nettles and brambles slashed back at each side. Eileen followed her old route, and everywhere it was the same. Some smaller paths had been left to become, in time, impassable, and others were broad and easy, encouraging the casual walker to take the prescribed ways. Half-way up the path back in the direction of the church, Eileen hesitated. 'It should be here somewhere,' she said. 'Christopher's camp. I can't believe I would ever forget the way. But it's all so different. I'm not sure.' She looked around in growing dismay. Where was the tree stump where he had left his meagre belongings? Obviously in the clearance a number of trees had been cut down, leaving several stumps, and she could not tell.

A wave of sadness hit her, flooding up through her body and stopping at her eyes. Here, it was impossible to avoid thinking of all she had lost, things that belonged to this place and no other: her walks with Tillie, her girls at home, her chats with Marie, Michael flying in and out. It seemed to her then that it was all far more distant than two years, like another life lived by a different self.

She turned to Josh, who was standing quietly behind her. 'I don't know where it is any more. It's all changed. The agency who runs the reserve, Rural Heritage or some such name, must have finally decided to tidy up. They've made it accessible and public. It's lost its green magic.'

'Do you want to go back?'

'Let's do that.'

Again she led the way, up through the woods, along the path and into the churchyard by the back gate. As they passed the bulk of the church Eileen noticed someone kneeling by a grave, a trowel in his hand. 'It's Bill Mottram,' she said. 'I must go and say hello. I won't be a minute.' She made her way over the grass to where Bill was tidying his mother's grave.

'Bill, hello!' she called. He turned towards her, looking uncertain. Then he smiled, and clambered to his feet. He was as stout as ever.

'Well, well, what brings you here?' he said.

'Passing by, Bill. How are you?'

'Fair, thanks. Yourself? Where are you living now? How are those girls of yours?'

'We're all well. Christie has her degree, and Natasha is about to become a mother.'

'You a grandma, eh!'

'I know. Such a lot has happened. I live in Allerton now. Very different from here. But things have changed a lot in Holton, Bill, and down the Caxford road.'

Bill dusted his hands. 'That's a fact. Pub's changed hands, and the shop. Busier now.' He nodded in the direction of the street. ''Spect you noticed. Lots of folk from outside these days, specially at the weekends.'

'How is Mr. Jescott doing?'

'Oh, middlin', I'd say.'

'Are the Quilleys still here, Bill?'

'Aye. Young Georgina seems to be all right, far as I can tell. But old Arthur passed away. Did you hear?'

'No, I didn't. I'm sorry to hear it. Arthur was a dear man.'

Bill heaved a sigh. 'All that trouble they had, it was too much for an old chap like Arthur. It weren't long after the court case. They caught the feller responsible.'

'That's something, at least. Well, it's good to see you, Bill. Give my regards to Elsie.'

She went back to where Josh was studying an inscription. 'There's somewhere else I must see before I go,' she said. 'Is that OK?'

'Whatever you want.'

They left the churchyard, waving to Bill as they went. From the pub garden wafted a smell of grilling meat.

'Looks like the pub's doing a barbecue,' Josh said. 'Do you want something?'

'Yes, please. I realize I am starving.'

After something of a scrum, they managed to get hold of some sausages and bread, and munched them as they walked along the village street in the dusty heat, turning up towards Marie's old place and the further edge of the woods. The pathless road was lined with straggly mallow and yellowed grasses. Josh licked ketchup from his fingers and looked up at the sky. 'I wouldn't be at all surprised to have rain later, with those clouds,' he said.

'I don't want to be long.'

They passed Marie's garden, where two children were playing with a small white dog. Then the road turned into a track, and narrowed still further till it was no more than one person's width. Tall weeds hung over the path, unmoving in the windless afternoon. In a moment they were under the trees, in deep green shade.

'I don't think they've got to here with the clearance work,' Eileen said. 'That gives me a little hope.' As she said this she thought how strange it was to be talking about hope when it was the hope of finding Christopher's final resting-place intact. But it was the last memory she had of him. She led Josh in silence along the paths till they came to the tiny glade where she had found his body, that saturated June morning two years ago. She stopped and looked for a long moment, and felt stifled and choked. 'This is just the same,' she whispered.

'This is where you found him?'

'Yes. Just there.' She breathed deeply, fighting for calm, but the memory was keen as a cold wind, and she felt her eyes fill up. After a while she blinked the tears away and turned and looked at Josh. 'I guess it's only a matter of time before they get round to clearing this part of the woods as well,' she said. 'Then all traces of Christopher will be gone. But perhaps it doesn't matter: I won't be coming back to see it. I realize that I haven't left any part of me behind. I thought I had, but I was wrong. It's just a place I used to live, that's all.'

'It's a funny thing, going back somewhere,' Josh said. 'I have that feeling sometimes when I go up to Yorkshire. The places seem smaller, somehow, and less significant than you thought.'

Eileen nodded. She had a sense of the past falling away, and she knew she could not allow herself to fall with it. Silently, looking at the soft grass and leaf litter where Christopher had died, she thanked God for the blessing of a present and a future. She took a deep breath. 'Let's go home, Josh. I think you're right: it feels like rain.'

She drove home, pursued by ominous dark grey clouds. Then the rain started, heavy, fat drops falling onto the baking tarmac, bringing that peculiar smell of petrol, dust and hot cars. By the time they reached the outskirts of Allerton it was coming down hard and straight, washing away the dirt and heat. Eileen brought the car to a halt outside Josh's block of flats.

'Do you want to come in?' he said.

Eileen shook her head. 'I think I'll go home, thank you. I have some thinking to do. I'm best left alone for a while.'

'Are you all right?'

She turned to face him; he looked anxious. 'I'm sad, of course. Losing something, someone, whatever, is hard. Thinking about the past, trying to sort it out, is a bit frightening. I feel sometimes as if I'm the only person left on the planet. But I will be philosophical, I think, in the end. It's either that or go round the bend completely.'

'That's a technical psychiatric term, is it?' Josh said, smiling. '"Round the bend?"'

'Probably not.' She looked at the rain cascading down the windscreen. 'You're going to get very wet.'

'I dare say I'll survive.'

Josh was silent for a moment. He seemed reluctant to get out of the car. Then, in an unexpected gesture, he took her hand in his and raised it to his lips, kissing the back of her fingers. She looked down, feeling the blood rise to her cheeks.

He opened the car door, and the rain came gusting in. 'I'll see you at work,' he said.

Eileen lay on her sofa in the half-light, listening to the rain gurgling down the gutters. Her eyes were closed. In the silence of her thoughts she saluted Christopher's disappearing shade. *Go in peace.*

Later that evening she was ironing her work clothes ready for the morning when the phone rang.
'Mum, it's Christie.'
A frisson of shock made her scalp tingle. 'Oh, Christie! Where are you? Are you all right?'
'I'm fine, Mum. Honestly I am. I'm in a call-box at the airport, so I can't talk for long. We're back in England. Mum, I'm going to get a mobile phone. I'll let you know the number as soon as I've got it.'
'What are you going to do? Will we see you?'
'I haven't any clear plans yet, Mum. But of course you'll see me. I've got to go. I'll ring again soon, I promise.'

Lying in bed, half-asleep, Eileen thought of what she had said to Josh. Was it true? Was she learning to be philosophical? Until now, "accepting", "coming to terms," all the conventional wisdom, had seemed to her a caving in, a kind of moral cowardice. Now she was not so certain. She thought of Christina, speaking firmly of "we", and realized that John was a fixture, at least for now, for good or ill. And although she was still skirting cautiously round the edges of her own feelings, she had seen the look on Josh's face as he had taken her hand in his, and felt a little less inclined to blame.

Lord, it's all so complicated. I don't even want to cope with it any more. I give it to you, all of it: Christie, and Penny, and Karen, and Josh. And all the rest. I give you myself, too, for what it's worth. You've dealt with it all already, anyway. How could I forget? Dear Lord, I feel so ignorant and helpless. I have prayed this prayer before, and I probably will again: teach me to lean on you. What was it St. Paul said? Something about God's foolishness being wiser than human wisdom and God's weakness being stronger than human strength. That says it all.

Saturday 17 October 1998

When she got back from work she saw the red light flashing on her answering machine. She kicked off her shoes and padded across to the phone.

'Eileen, it's Sean.' His voice sounded tired, but then she heard a soft chuckle. 'While you've been slaving away at work your daughter's been working hard too. It's two o'clock now, and your grandson's been in the world half an hour. You'd better get over here.'

She looked out of the window. The maternity ward was four floors up, and from here there was a view across the western end of the city. Below, the streets were crawling with traffic: it was five-thirty and people were going home. Darkness was already creeping over the buildings, turning afternoon to evening, and most of the cars had their lights on. Eileen turned back to the brightly-lit room. Natasha was sitting up in the white bed, drinking tea. The baby was asleep in his hospital crib. Eileen had only relinquished him ten minutes before, and now he lay on his back, tiny fingers bunched into fists, long eyelashes making a dark smudge against his dusky skin. It was a long time since she had been so close to a newborn baby, and this one, her grandson, was absurdly beautiful, even allowing for bias. She bent over the crib, watching his chest rise and fall in regular rhythm.

'He's OK, you know, Mum,' Natasha said. 'You don't have to watch over him like a big mother hen.'

'I'm admiring him,' Eileen said. 'He's quite a stunner.'

'Sean's been ages,' Natasha said, frowning. 'It's not that far to his mum's. Perhaps she's taking her curlers out.'

'Miaow. I expect he's got caught up in the rush-hour traffic. Which is why I won't leave it too long before I go home.'

'Please, Mum, stay,' Natasha said. 'I don't think I can cope with her on my own.'

'Sean will be here,' Eileen said. 'It's about time you could handle your dear ma-in-law. Anyway, you'll probably be quite popular now you've produced this young man.'

'Hm. I doubt it. If she makes one stupid remark about him being light brown or something I might just forget my manners.' She put her tea cup down with a mutinous clatter, and the baby stirred in his sleep. 'Anyway, Mum, you never told me what happened with Penny, after all that hoo-ha on the telly. What did they do with her, you know, when she was arrested? And what's happened to the little boy? Gus – or is it Simon?'

Eileen sat on the edge of the bed, and sighed. 'He'll be Gus for ever now. The psychologist said he had been Gus for too long to change it. I don't think Karen minded too much. She was happy to have her boy back, no matter what. And as far as I know, he is fine. As soon as they had the DNA results and knew he was definitely Karen and Dean's child it seemed stupid to keep him in the foster-home any longer than they could help. Dean and Mel were obviously going to be able to give him a stable home, and they thought that having two older siblings around would help him to adjust. From what I hear he was a bit bewildered and asked after "Mummy" a few times at first. I'm glad I wasn't around to hear that. It's all too sad.'

'How do you know all this stuff?'

'From Carol Macnamara at work. A couple of weeks ago she ran into Karen in the shopping centre, and Karen had Gus with her. And one of our other ex-patients, a young girl with an eating disorder. I'm glad those two are still friends.'

'So his mum is allowed to have him, then?'

'Apparently. Once they'd done all the checks and paperwork and grilled everybody in sight, they said Karen and Chopper could have him on something called "supervised access." She has the other kids, after all, when she's well.'

Natasha looked thoughtful. 'Do you think she'll ever be a hundred per cent, though, Mum? After everything she's been through?'

'I really don't know, love. But I'm glad it wasn't me that met Karen in town.'

'How come?'

'I'd hate to think that seeing me might remind Gus of Penny,' Eileen said soberly.

'So what about Penny?' Natasha said. 'Have you got a date for the court case yet?'

'No, it's been postponed again. I don't get told much, but Penny is still in Holloway. They had to have psychiatric reports, and the whole thing seems to be going on and on.'

Natasha shivered. 'What will happen to her?'

'She'll go to prison. No idea which one, or whether it'll be near here or at the other end of the country, or how long for. Poor, dear Penny. What a lousy life.'

'Will you go and visit her there, do you think?'

'I hope to. When the dust has settled.'

'Oh, my. Look who the cat dragged in,' Natasha said, her grin wide. Eileen turned towards the door. Walking down the ward, her arms full of flowers and a teddy bear in an unlikely shade of blue, was Christina.

Eileen came to her feet. 'Christie,' she said, her voice faint.

Christina put everything down on the bed and hugged her mother. 'Hello, Mum,' she said. 'The prodigal returns.' Eileen held her tightly. She could say nothing.

'Well, little sis,' Christina said, disentangling herself. 'How are you?' She skirted round the end of the bed and bent to hug Natasha. 'Congratulations, clever-stick. So where's my nephew, then?'

'Asleep. And don't you go waking him up.' Natasha was beaming.

Christina hovered over the crib. 'Tash, he is wonderful. However did you manage it?'

'The usual way, I guess.'

'No, stupid, to have such a beautiful baby.'

'What are you saying?' Natasha said in mock offence. 'That I'm ugly, or something?'

'Of course. We all know that. Perhaps Sean's good looks made up for it.'

Natasha slapped her sister feebly. 'You're such a cow.'

'Can't I hold him?'

'When he wakes up. He'll be nice and noisy then. And if he's wet and smelly you can see to him, Auntie.'

Eileen found her voice, but it was ragged. 'How did you find out, Christie?' she said.

'Same way you did, I expect, Mum. A message on my mobile from a very proud dad.' She turned back to Natasha. 'So what are you going to call him?' she asked.

'Daniel. And Anthony, after Sean's dad. Oh heck, it's Sean back with his mother.'

'I'll go soon, Tash,' Eileen said. 'I'll come and see you when you get home.'

'Me, too,' Christina said. 'Look, these are for you.' She held up the flowers. 'Better get someone to put them in water.'

'But you only just got here!' Natasha wailed.

252

'You'll be home in a day or two. Then there'll be no keeping me away. Besides, there's something you and I have to talk about.' She glanced at her mother with a sly grin. 'A certain person's birthday.' She bent and kissed Natasha's cheek. 'Well done, kid. See you soon.'

Sean ushered his mother to the bedside. Eileen and Christina exchanged civil greetings with her and then, with a last grin at a moody Natasha, left the ward together. Struggling with chaotic feelings, Eileen was silent all the way down in the lift. Outside, in the car park, she turned to her watchful daughter. 'Christie, are you all right?'

'Yes, Mum. I'm fine. I've got a job, starting on Monday, working in a college library not too far from where we're living. The money's rubbish, but it pays the rent.'

'And John?'

'He's doing a bit of lecturing, at the same place. So we can have our sandwiches together. Very cosy.' She smiled a little sadly.

'You never told me what happened in Italy.'

Christie shrugged. 'There's not much to tell. I was on holiday with Jenny, fair and square. And John turned up. He'd already told Helen he was leaving. He thought it would be more honest that way, not to be hedging his bets. And according to him she wasn't even surprised. She must have realized something was wrong. If I'd turned him away, he'd have had no one. But I couldn't turn him away, Mum. He was such a wreck. The boys were the main problem. So much pain in the family.' Eileen was silent. She could not trust herself to say anything remotely helpful. 'I know what you're thinking,' Christie said. 'John had me over a barrel, he took advantage of my good nature, he's selfishly ruined my life. Please believe me when I tell you he is not like that. One day I hope you'll see it too. But I am happy, despite everything.'

Eileen looked at her, and saw that she looked well. She had even, she thought, put on a bit of weight. To her surprise, she found that her worry was giving way to anger. 'It's not your life he's ruined,' she said quietly. 'At least not yet. It's hers, and his boys'.'

Christina looked at her, her eyes full of tears. 'I don't want to feel split from you, Mum.'

'I'm sorry, love. I don't either. But it can't be helped. Everything you do has some kind of effect, on yourself and other people. And you have to live with it. I just wouldn't have chosen this for you, not in a million years.'

The tears were running freely down Christina's cheeks. 'Whatever happens, I'll be in touch. I'll see you at Tash's. We have Daniel now. We're all his family.'

'True.' Eileen sighed deeply. 'Are you going back to London straight away? Do you want a lift to the station?'

Christina shook her head. 'The walk will do me good.' She hesitated. 'I'll see you soon, Mum. Bye.' She put her arms round her mother's neck, and Eileen could feel the wetness of her cheeks.

'Bye, Christie.'

She watched her daughter's slight figure as she walked away. When she came to the corner of the hospital building Christina turned and waved, and the sadness on her face was like a corkscrew driven into Eileen's heart. Then Christina was gone, and only weariness remained.

Unable to sleep, unable to settle, Eileen sat at her kitchen table, her hands gripped tightly together as if trying to hold something in. *I let her go, just like that. How could I? Who am I to be so righteous? Didn't I nearly fall into a worse pit with Christopher? What if he hadn't died? Lord, help! I am such a hypocrite. What should I say to Christie? How can this thing come out right? Should I just act as if everything was normal? What do I know about John, what he's fleeing from, what he feels? Lord, it's such a muddle.*

Later, lying sleepless in bed, it came to her that she would talk to Marie. *She will understand. She must have had many bad moments, feeling helpless, with Stephanie.* She groaned and sat up, put on her glasses and took her Bible from the bedside table.

"Teach children how they should live, and they will remember it all their lives," she read in Proverbs 22. *What have I taught my children? Was it enough? Should I just trust them now? But, Lord, I am afraid. Please look out for Christie. Whatever the outcome, don't let her be swallowed up in disaster.*

She remembered Christie as a small girl, tiny but determined, bright and full of fun and hope. *She isn't lost. This is a chapter in her story, no more. And I, yet again, must teach myself to trust.*

Saturday 14 November 1998

'You share a birthday with Royalty, I see,' Louis said, bringing the drink that Sean had just poured for him and sitting down opposite Eileen in the tiny living room.

'We are both fifty today,' Eileen said. 'But I believe he is a few hours older. Not to mention a good deal richer.'

Louis shook his head. 'He couldn't be richer in love, judging by the number of people crammed into this little house.'

'Well, if he has friends half as good as mine he should count himself blessed.'

'Have you had a lot of people come and go already?'

Eileen nodded. 'Work colleagues, one or two neighbours. At the moment Ollie is here, with his wife, Sarah, and their three children. I hadn't met his family before, but you can't miss Ollie: he has an unmistakable laugh.' As if on cue, Ollie's infectious chuckle came from the direction of the kitchen.

Keeping their plotting secret, or so they believed, Christina, Natasha and Sean had arranged a birthday party for Eileen that they thought she would hate least, inviting her friends to come and go as they pleased throughout the afternoon and evening. Natasha and Sean's house was chosen because of the baby, and the drop-in arrangement suited the smallness of their house, as well as giving Eileen the chance to talk to everybody. She had been permitted to do nothing. Sean was plying the guests with drinks, and food kept coming from the kitchen to replace what had been eaten. The two girls, helped by Carol Macnamara, had invited everybody they could think of.

Natasha emerged from the kitchen carrying two laden plates which she deposited on the dining room table. 'How's it going, Mum?'

'I never thought I would say this, but I'm having a whale of a time. You clever kids have done great things.'

'We thought this would be the nicest way for you to celebrate.'

'You were right. How's that good-looking boy?'

'Sean or Daniel?'

255

'Daniel, of course. I can see for myself how Sean is.'

'He's asleep, but I wouldn't be surprised if he wakes up soon. Beats me how he can kip through all this row.' Ollie's children, two girls and a small boy, were chasing each other and shrieking. A moment later their mother, a tall, stately woman swathed in a long, bright print dress with matching headgear, swept in and rounded them up. 'We must go,' she said. She bent and kissed Eileen's cheek. 'Thank you for inviting us. I hope these horrors haven't been too noisy. Enjoy the rest of your day.'

The doorbell rang, and a moment later Marie and Philip came in. After the greetings and congratulations and drinks they were soon laughing at some witticism of Louis' and Eileen's mind began to wander.

Several people from work had come together: Christine the ward manager, in her trademark high heels, with her accountant husband, and Carol and John Macnamara.

'Any more news of Karen and Gus?' Eileen asked Carol while the others were collecting food.

'Not that I know of, love. But they seemed OK when I saw them. Karen looked better, still a bit paranoid, though, never took her eyes off Gus for a second.'

'Not surprising. It must cost quite an effort of will to take him out in public at all.'

'Well, from what I gathered, the psychologist that's dealing with the family said she wasn't to wrap Gus in cotton wool. She's got to work towards giving the little lad a normal life. The hardest thing, Karen said, was when Mel and Dean have got him. You can imagine she worries herself sick. That's why she had Alice with her that day, for moral support, I suppose.'

'I hope that worry will fade as the years go on,' Eileen said. 'She's had enough mental torment. How was Alice?'

'Not exactly fat, but on a reasonably even keel,' Carol said. 'Got herself a part-time job in the local shop. She said she was hoping to get her own flat with a friend as soon as she had some money saved. It would probably be a blessing to get away from her mother. 'Course, Dawn's tried her best in her own way.' She looked around the room. 'There's Maureen and Des.' She waved, smiling. 'Looks as if they're just going.'

'I had a chat with Maureen earlier,' Eileen said. 'They're hoping to go to Canada soon. It's all going through. I don't know how long these things take, do you?'

Carol shook her head. 'No idea. Is Des behaving?'

'I think so. Well, he must be, or she wouldn't be with him.'

'What I mean is, is he sticking with the counselling?'

'So Maureen says.'

Carol narrowed her eyes. 'He'd better be.'

The others came back with loaded plates.

'Don't you want anything to eat, Carol?' Eileen said.

'In a minute. I'll pop outside for a fag first. I might not eat so much then. I need to lose some weight.'

John sat down heavily beside her, balancing his plate. 'Good job I like my women chunky,' he said with a smirk.

'What do you mean, "women"? How many you got?' Carol heaved herself to her feet. 'No, don't answer that. I don't want to know.' She scanned the room. 'Pity Josh couldn't make it.' She looked at Eileen enquiringly, her head on one side.

'It's a long way to come from Yorkshire,' Eileen said. She felt the heat rise unbidden up her throat. 'He's had this leave booked for months.'

'Oh. Right. Well, I'm going to brave the weather and have my smoke. See you in a minute.'

Marie was saying something.

'What? Sorry, dear, I was woolgathering.'

Marie smiled. 'You were miles away. I was wondering how things are with Christie.'

Eileen sighed. 'After I chatted to you on the phone, it made me think that I was getting everything wrong. Christie's never been much trouble, has she? Stephanie gave you far more grief, for far longer, and you've hung in there faithfully.'

'I didn't feel there was much choice,' Marie said. 'So have you spoken to Christie?'

'Yes. We were over here a couple of weeks after Daniel was born. We took him for a walk round the block in his pram, just the two of us, to let Tash and Sean have a rest. He'd been keeping them up at night. Anyway Christie and I had a long talk and sorted things out, as far as we could. I've had to accept what's happening, whether I like it or not. I don't think I could bear to fall out with her and never see her. Now, I guess the next hurdle is seeing her with John in tow.'

'It's all you can do,' Marie said. 'She knows what you think. She's made her choice, at least for the time being. But she's still young. No telling what will come of it.' She looked up. 'Hello, some new arrivals.'

Eileen stood up and greeted Sean's mother, Joan, and her friend, Alan Draycott. Behind them came Sean's sister, Caroline, with her husband Graham and their two girls. Eileen introduced everybody. Joan went in search of her son, and Caroline leaned over and spoke quietly to Eileen, a sly smile on her sharp-featured face. 'I've given Mother a bit of a talking-to,' she said. 'Things should improve. Keep me posted, OK?'

'Thank you, Caroline. I'm glad you're an ally, rather than otherwise.'

Caroline laughed. 'I told her straight, Eileen. "Your son's a happy man," I said. "What more do you want, you ungrateful old bat?" You should have seen her face.'

'No one but you would dare.'

'True enough,' Caroline said. 'Perhaps it's time she put poor old Alan out of his misery. Then she'd have a bit more to think about. Anyway, Eileen, I'm going to find my brother and some liquid refreshment. I'll talk to you later.'

Gradually Natasha and Sean's house began to empty, leaving a wake of discarded glasses, screwed-up napkins and crumbs. The kitchen was in disarray, and Natasha, bringing Daniel downstairs after feeding him, looked weary. She handed the baby to Eileen. 'Hold him upright, Mum,' she said. 'Here, have this towel in case he's sick over your nice new party dress.' Eileen took her grandson and held him close to her shoulder, supporting his wobbly head with her hand. He was frowning sleepily and making gurgling noises. Feeling the solid weight of his tiny body brought back the infancy of her own children in a vivid rush.

'You look happy,' said Louis from somewhere behind her.

She turned carefully. 'Do I? Well, I know grandparents are supposed to be adoring, but I've surprised myself. I'd have to be a poet, which I'm most definitely not, to tell you what it's like to see your own grandchild in this world and to hold him in your arms.'

'That's poetry enough, for my money. Eileen, I should go. Your loyal family have been working flat out and are in need of a rest.'

'I'll give this fellow to his dad and see you out,' Eileen said. 'Here you are, Sean.'

She followed Louis into the hallway. 'I suppose we'll soon be thinking about Christmas,' she said.

Louis paused, one arm thrust into his coat. 'Well, no, I don't think so,' he said slowly.

She raised her eyebrows. 'What? Is it cancelled?'

Louis looked at her, his dark eyes serious. 'For St. Augustine's, yes,' he said. 'I'm sorry, Eileen, I was going to tell you this very soon, and I wouldn't have said anything today, but since you've mentioned it, I suppose I must.'

'What are you saying, Louis?'

'You remember those meetings I had with the Bishop? I couldn't say anything before, because nothing was finalized. But now it is. I'm moving on, Eileen. The Bishop has asked me to take over a big parish in London, and I've agreed. There'll be a curate to help me, and a smaller, modern house. And I'll have a congregation!'

Eileen shook her head, her eyes wide. For a moment she could find nothing to say. She took a deep breath. 'I always felt you should have more of an outlet for your talents,' she said at last. 'I'm very pleased for you, Louis. You deserve it. But what were you saying about St. Augustine's?'

Louis sighed. 'You know as well as I do how things have been going over the last few years. The congregation is an aging one, and inevitably people die.' He shrugged. 'I've tried to get a children's ministry going, but it's been an uphill slog. The dear old place just isn't viable any more. There are too few worshippers to justify paying a full-time priest. The idea is to amalgamate the congregation with St. Martin's. It's not far. And the chap there, Rob Portman, seems to be doing better than I ever did in getting – what's the vulgar phrase? – "bums on seats." So there you have it. There won't be Christmas at St. Augustine's. I know it seems short notice, but there was a vacancy in the London church that needed filling. And it may be, too, that the Bishop decided to move things along, after all the media interest in us lately. Don't say anything about this, will you? Not until it's announced officially.'

'No, of course not. What will happen to the church building?'

'Ah, yes. That will take longer. The C. of E., in its wisdom, must go through the correct procedures. But eventually the site will probably be sold.'

'You will be greatly missed, Louis.'

He smiled. 'Thank you. Perhaps. But only by a very few people.'

'Well, "bums on seats" may be a consideration, but I think it's a question of who and how good, not just how many. But I can see the attraction of a big, vibrant parish, Louis. And you'll be nearer to your sister.'

'That had occurred to me. She's the only family I have.'

'Hm. Everything has a plus side, I suppose. I can quietly give up my feeble attempts at organ playing.'

'You have been a great help to me, and I shall always be grateful.'

'Just don't tell me they need an organist at St. Martin's.'

Louis grinned. 'To the best of my knowledge, Rob has a music group of sorts.'

'Fine. I can sing along to anything.'

'I must go.' Louis buttoned his coat. 'I'll see you tomorrow, I hope,' he said. 'Your career as an organist is not quite over yet.'

Eileen wandered back into the now-empty living room and began to collect plates and glasses. Natasha came in and flopped onto the sofa with a groan. 'I am knackered,' she said. 'How are you doing, Mum?'

'I've just heard from Louis that he is leaving,' Eileen said. 'Quite soon, too. They're going to close the church. I'll have to find somewhere else.'

'That's a shame. You'll miss Louis, won't you? Now that I've chatted to him a bit I can see he's quite a funny guy. Like a vicar, but not.'

'I know what you mean. Tash, it's getting late. I think I'll go home. You look all in.'

'I could do with some sleep, if his lordship will let me.' Natasha yawned.

'Today's been great. I appreciate all your efforts, especially when you've got a young baby to look after.' She bent and kissed Natasha's cheek. 'Thank you.'

'You're welcome, Mum. I'm glad you've had a good time.'

'I'll just go and say goodbye to Christie and Sean.'

'They're in the kitchen, washing up.'

'I can tell that from all the splashing and shrieks. Those two are like five-year-olds.'

'Aren't they just.'

Eileen dropped Christina off at the station on her way home. 'Thanks for organizing everything, love,' she said. 'I've had a memorable birthday.'

'I'm glad, Mum.' She paused, leaning in at the car's open window. 'I'll see you very soon. Perhaps,' she hesitated, 'next time it'll be with John.'

'You'd better go and catch your train,' Eileen said. 'You've spent quite long enough away from him, working yourself to a frazzle for your old mother. Bye, Christie. Take care of yourself.'

She drove home through streets that were beginning to look wintry. Trees swayed in the chill wind and leaves rattled in the gutters. She parked the car and looked up at her flat. Everything was in darkness. She climbed the steps, feeling suddenly weary, and let herself in. Mrs. Denman from the ground floor flat opened her door as Eileen entered the hall, and stood in a sudden rush of light from her living room. Penny's flat was still empty.

'There you are, dear,' the old lady said. 'Had a good day?'

'Very good, thank you.'

'I fed the cat at six o'clock,' Mrs. Denman said. 'I haven't seen him since, though.'

'Not to worry,' Eileen said. 'He'll turn up when he feels like it. Thanks for your help, Mrs. Denman. That was kind.'

'Not at all, dear. Oh, hang on a moment.' She disappeared indoors and came back a minute later with an armful of flowers in crinkly paper. 'These came for you this afternoon.'

'Oh. Thanks. I should have birthdays more often. On second thoughts, perhaps not.'

The old lady smiled. 'I don't want them too often, not at my age. Goodnight, dear.'

Eileen let herself into her flat and switched on the light. She kicked off her shoes. It was ten-fifteen by the kitchen clock. She put the flowers on the table, went into the bedroom, stripped off her party finery and put on pyjamas and slippers. Then she padded back into the kitchen and put the kettle on. There was a small white envelope stapled to the wrapper round the flowers. She tore it off and opened it.

"Dear Eileen," she read. "Happy birthday. Love from Josh." She chuckled at the brevity of the message, but it was no surprise. She noticed the red light was flashing on her answering machine. She made a cup of tea, then pressed the button. There were three messages from people who couldn't be at the party, then Josh's familiar growl. 'Hello, Eileen. Hope you've had a good day. I am bored with sitting in the pub, and looking forward to getting home. I've come to the conclusion that it's too late in the year and too cold to be doing long journeys on a motorbike, especially for an old man like me. And Eileen, keep Wednesday evening free. You have a date. I might even put on a collar and tie. I hope you realize what an honour that is. I'll pick you up at eight. Don't worry, I'll leave the bike at home and come by taxi. Till then. Goodnight.' Eileen pressed her hand hard against her stomach, trying to still the agitation within. Why was it that pleasure and terror felt so much the same?

Twenty minutes later she surveyed her handiwork. She possessed only two vases and the rest of the flowers were arranged tastefully in an assortment of jam jars. There were so many of them that the kitchen looked like a florist's.

She smiled to herself and went to bed. Fletcher arrived with a clatter of the cat flap and an enquiring miaow, bounded onto the bed and curled up on her feet.

Lord, I am fifty years old today. As, of course, you know. More than half my life is over, unless I live to be a centenarian. Which I am not sure I'd want. Still, all that is in your hands. Thank you for today, for my wonderful children, including Sean, of course. And for Daniel. Thank you for those dear people who came to wish me well. You have blessed me very much, Lord, and I am thankful. For the first time in a longish while I am feeling moderately hopeful, and I am grateful for that too. But I still need guidance, and I guess I always will, while I am in this body and in this life. Teach me to know and do what you want. And Lord, please watch over Louis in his new job, and give him the joy of knowing he is serving you.

Louis was right. Things are better when I am in touch with you.

Sunday 22 November 1998

Louis climbed the pulpit steps. He took off his glasses and cleaned them on the hem of his surplice. Eileen, sliding off the organ seat and taking her place in the empty choir stall, noticed that the surplice was not its usual limp, off-white self, but clean and crisp. *Avril Dyson again, perhaps?*

Louis put his glasses back on and smiled at his congregation. There were more of them than usual; word of his departure had spread.

'Most of you will know,' Louis said after the opening prayer, 'that very soon I am moving to London to take up work in a large parish there. You will also know that this church will close during the next few months. If you are interested in the reasoning behind this decision, there is an information sheet at the back of the church for you to take away and read. Many of you will, I hope, be planning to attend St. Martin's, and next Sunday the vicar there, Rob Portman, and I will be changing places. You might say that it's an appropriate date: next Sunday, November 29th, is the first Sunday in Advent, a day for new beginnings and the hope that is born with Jesus' incarnation. Rob will be here at the ten-thirty service so that you can start to get to know each other. The people at St. Martin's are less fortunate. They've got me.' He smiled, then grew serious again. 'Because very soon I will not be with you any longer, I want to share with you today some of the thoughts I have had over the years about the destiny of the church. I don't mean this church, this physical building, St. Augustine's. There will be a time when this building will not exist as a place of worship, or, indeed, at all. I am talking about the universal church, the fraternity of believers. That, I believe, will always exist, until the sky is rolled up like a scroll. No one can destroy what God has made and daily sustains, and we, embattled as we often feel in this world, should take strength from that thought.

'What better place to start than the words of our Lord himself? In Luke chapter 12 verse 49 Jesus says, "I came to set the earth on fire, and how I wish it were already kindled!" Again, in Matthew 10 verse 34, he says that he "did not come to bring peace, but a sword." We, as his disciples, should not expect an easy ride. Where the truth shines brightest, there also the opposition will be fiercest.

'In his first letter to the Corinthians, chapter one, verse 23, Paul says, "As for us, we proclaim the crucified Christ, a message that is offensive to the Jews and nonsense to the Gentiles..." You know, the mindsets exhibited by these "Jews" and "Greeks" are still prevalent today. We have all heard them in one form or another. Modern-day "Jews" think that a universal brotherhood, living in peace, can be achieved by our piety and moral uprightness. Together with other great religious traditions, we, the human race, can create a heavenly kingdom on earth. The "Greeks" among us go even further. For them, the enquiring mind, unaided by God, will ultimately answer all questions, control nature and create a new world order. For them both, the very idea of the cross is shameful, incomprehensible, repugnant. But we must not be deceived. Jesus himself, then and now, points to the cross as the only route to glory. We should be very wary of our natural tendency, as sinful humans, to glorify ourselves. Isaiah says, in chapter two, verse 11, "A day is coming when human pride will be ended and human arrogance destroyed. Then the Lord alone will be exalted." I, for one, very much look forward to that day.' Louis paused, seeming to gather his thoughts. Then he looked up again. 'Let's think for a moment about some of the ways in which modern thinking has departed from God's way. How do many people, if they think about it at all, think about the nature of humanity and its place in the universe? Doesn't it go something like this? Human beings are intelligent apes. Caring for each other, and our planet, is the highest good. Each of us has a right to his or her own mental furniture, provided that no one puts any bad thoughts into practice (as if that could be possible.) Doesn't that sound familiar?

'So what, then, is God's view? And, of course, the church's and every Christian's? Here, mankind is the high point of God's creative act. We belong to him, but we are in a state of rebellion. We have fallen from grace and are far from his presence; our vaunted "independence" is sinful. The only way back is through the sacrifice of Jesus, through faith and, as a corollary, the works that spring from faith in obedience. This view, not surprisingly, is repellent to worldly thinking, with its emphasis on individual freedoms, relative values, the right to decide for yourself, the demand for proofs and reasons, the assumption that we can, and should, understand all things. But, you know, this view is an illusion. More, it is a deception of the Enemy. To follow Jesus, through the cross, is to reclaim what makes us truly human in the sight of God, and to rediscover the purpose he has for us. This, in the fullest sense, is why we are alive, and is a theme throughout Scripture.

'So, how does this translate itself into our daily walk? What should we be doing? I think we all know the answer, or answers, to these questions. We should be using the gifts that God has given us in the service of his church and his world. We should be shepherds to his sheep, for love of the Good Shepherd. We should be living, as St. Paul tells us further on in 1 Corinthians, as if there is not much time left; even valuable things should be worn lightly. These things are, of course, easier to say than to do. But if we are discouraged, remember that others before us have felt the same, and God gave them assurance. I have often felt inclined to echo Elijah, when he complained in 1 Kings 19 that he was the only prophet left faithful to God, to which God briskly replied that he had kept for himself seven thousand men in Israel who had not bowed the knee to the false god Baal. And again, we all know the story in Judges where God told Gideon to send most of his army home and defeated the mighty Midianites with a mere three hundred men.'

Louis paused, his head bowed, and there was silence in the church. Then he looked up again, and his face radiated a confidence that was almost defiant. 'In Acts 20 Paul says, "But I reckon my own life to be worth nothing to me; I only want to complete my mission and finish the work that the Lord Jesus gave me to do, which is to declare the Good News about the grace of God." That, of course, is the work of the church also, and of each one of us within it. Jesus spoke time and again about how God had sent him into the world for a purpose, and in turn he sends us out into that very world, and with a similar purpose. "Go, then," says Jesus at the end of Matthew's gospel, "to all peoples everywhere and make them my disciples: baptize them in the name of the Father, the Son and the Holy Spirit, and teach them to obey everything I have commanded you." This is terrifying to most of us, I know. But Jesus does not end there. Instead, he ends with that wonderful assurance, "And I will be with you always, to the end of the age."

'Let me conclude with a word of encouragement. I do not believe that God can ever wholly disown that which he has loved into existence. Scripture abounds with examples of his patience and loving-kindness. He does not want us to perish, and this longing culminates in Jesus' atoning work on the cross. "I am the Lord, and I do not change," says God through the prophet Malachi. "And so you, the descendants of Jacob, are not yet completely lost." Paul again, speaking of the unleashed power of the Gospel, says to Timothy, "... the word of God is not in chains..." Because, in the end, the dream is God's, it cannot die.

Because the story is God's, it will have the happiest of endings. This is our hope, and the ground of our joy.'

Again Louis fell silent, and when he spoke again he was smiling. 'Finally, let me read to you some glorious verses from Psalm 60.' He looked up and out over his congregation, every member of which was staring at him. '"From his sanctuary God has said, 'In triumph I will divide Shechem and distribute the Valley of Sukkoth to my people. Gilead is mine, and Manasseh too; Ephraim is my helmet and Judah my royal sceptre. But I will use Moab as my washbasin and I will throw my sandals on Edom, as a sign that I own it. Did the Philistines think they would shout in triumph over me?"

'God will have his way,' Louis said, lowering his voice. 'His enemies, the Moabites and Edomites and Philistines of every age, will bow the knee. We, his people, are his helmet and his sceptre. Two thousand years ago, men crucified Jesus – but God raised him. Men opposed the apostles, and many were martyred – but God established his church. People oppose the church today, ridiculing, marginalizing, persecuting and martyring – but God will continue to build it. What God wills will happen, and we have been given the extraordinary privilege of having a part in his victory. May we, whatever life throws at us, count ourselves blessed.'

Eileen battled through a short Bach prelude which she could just play, and then, in a spirit of recklessness, embarked on the far more complex fugue. After a dozen bars she regretted it, but now there was no turning back. She knew why she had done it: very soon she would not be playing any more, and while in most ways it was a relief, she was also sorry. And there was the sense, with Louis going, of something ending, and she felt an obscure need to mark it. She hobbled on to the end, lurching in fits and starts. *So dies a perfectly good piece of Bach.* She switched off the organ and gathered up her music. The church was already empty. She heard Louis say goodbye to someone, and then close the door against the battering wind. She walked slowly to the vestry, holding her music in her arms.

'Louis, that was some sermon. What do they call it? A *tour de force*. Were you up all night working on it?'

Louis smiled. 'No, but I've been thinking of the themes for some while. About seven years, as it happens.'

'We'll miss you. When I think about how much you know, how much you understand, of the important things, I realize how much *I* will miss you. Who will help me when I'm in a muddle?'

'You must read your Bible. And invest in some commentaries.'

'But they won't be speaking to me, will they? Not just to me.'

Louis was hanging up his surplice and had his back to her. When he spoke, his voice was strange. 'So, why don't you come with me to London?'

'What?' Eileen grinned, trying to think of some piece of retaliatory wit. Then Louis turned round, and she saw his face. To her dismay she understood that he was serious, and in the space of a few silent seconds the implications of what he had said came rushing in. She had no time to untangle them, but instinct lent her wings. She knew she must answer him as if both of them understood the joke. She quailed at the thought of his humiliation if she could not carry it off.

'Well, you know I cannot possibly leave Allerton,' she said. 'Not now that I have a new man in my life to keep me here.'

A look of horror came into Louis' eyes. 'A new – ?' Seeing Eileen's broad grin, understanding began to dawn. 'Ah. You are referring to young Daniel, of course. Foolish of me to suppose I could tear a doting grandma away.' She could almost see him retreating, back behind his peculiar defences, and she felt a pang of sadness. *Dear Louis. If only I were the person who could join you in your lonely tower.* On an impulse she stepped towards him, put her arms round him, and briefly hugged him; and in that short moment, before he could control himself, she felt him flinch.

She backed away. 'I will see you before you go, I hope.'

He sat at the table, and picked up his pen. 'Of course. I haven't gone yet. And even when I have, we will meet again. Eventually the slow wheels of the law will turn, and we will be summoned to Penny's trial.'

'Yes. I had almost forgotten. Not Penny, I don't mean that. The whole legal process. It's been months. I wonder how she is.'

Louis sighed. 'All we can do for her now is pray. Later, we can visit her in prison. Maybe I will see you there. But I think Penny is stronger than we realized. What she did, confessing to you and to the police, knowing that she would lose everything that mattered, was very brave.'

'She learned a lot from you, Louis. She said as much herself.'

Louis smiled sadly. 'I never felt I was able to help her as much as I should have. But after the trial, once she is somewhere permanent, maybe I can contact the prison chaplain and ask him or her to keep an eye on Penny.'

'Yes. That would be good.'

Louis turned away from her, back to his writing, and she understood that his defences were in place. 'I must go home,' she said. 'Goodbye, Louis.'

He looked at her sideways, and the light from the vestry window glinted on the rim of his glasses. He waved a hand in her direction, and she walked away.

For a few moments she sat in her car, parked in the road outside the church. She closed her eyes, and let her racing thoughts wind down. *Lord, how arbitrary our life seems sometimes. I know your hand is on the tiller, but your direction is a mystery. But then, everything about you is mysterious, and so it must be.* She found herself grinning idiotically at the inanities of her life, and quelled herself with a frown. *Lord, I am not mocking Louis. I love the man dearly. But how little we know each other, in the end. Please take care of him. I hope you know what a fine servant you have there. Well, of course you do. Thank you for this opportunity for him to serve you in a wider sphere and for more people to benefit from his great learning and wisdom. But, Lord, I pray for something smaller and more human for Louis as well: for healing of that inner hurt about which I know nothing, and yet which I sense is there at the centre of his being, crippling and binding; and for the warmth of some present, human love, to shield and defend him from life's chilling disappointments. I am grateful for the hope I have in you, which of course he shares, but also for the human hopes you have kindled in me; and I want him to taste a little of that too. Whatever you do will be good, and for our good.*

The foolish chuckles that she had kept at bay came bubbling uncontrollably up, breaking out in snorts and howls of eye-watering laughter. She leaned her forehead on the steering wheel, her chest aching. Then she wiped her eyes, took a deep breath, and headed for home.